The Divided Child

by
Ekaterine Nikas

Avid Press, LLC   Brighton Michigan   USA

Published by
Avid Press, LLC
5470 Red Fox Drive
Brighton MI 48114-9079 USA
http://www.avidpress.com
1-888-AVIDBKS

The Divided Child
ISBN 1-929613-75-X

Cover photo of Corfu by Ekaterine Nikas

To Dani,
the sister I never had

and

To Don and Elizabeth,
who fill my life with love

And the king said,
Divide the living child in two, and give half to
the one, and half to the other.

— 1 Kings 3:25

ONE

It's hard to remember a place you've never been.

But when the turquoise sea darkened, and the oncoming storm filled the sky with clouds—obscuring the brilliant sunlight for which Greece is famous—I stared down from the wall of Corfu's Old Fortress at a scene suddenly familiar.

A curving bay of steel-blue water. Cream-colored buildings rising gracefully above a grey stone escarpment. A verdant swath of trees draped around the town like a necklace, and a veil of grey clouds darkening toward the horizon to match the sea. All that was missing was the frame.

As a girl, I'd often gazed up at the small watercolor hanging above my bed, dreaming of adventure and faraway lands. Some days I'd wander the twisting streets searching for pirates. Other days I'd dive into the cool water of the bay and emerge from the surf with arms full of treasure. And sometimes, when I was feeling especially brave, I'd board one of the brightly painted ships anchored in the harbor and sail off in search of my father, a wanderer lost on his journey home.

The memory made my throat ache.

I contemplated the view. It had changed remarkably little in twenty-eight years. My parents had been to Greece only once—on their honeymoon. I was born nine months later, and my grandfather considered it an established fact and a point of great honor that I'd been conceived on Greek soil. Perhaps that's why the picture had been hung in my room, though I can't say for sure. Mother never talked about it. I was fifteen before I knew it had been painted by my father.

My reminiscences were interrupted by a sudden spate of

German. Two tourists, a blond man and a blonder young woman, walked hand-in-hand past where I sat on the crumbling wall. He offered me a brief nod, she a cursory smile, before their attention snapped back to each other. I watched them climb out of sight, their feet scrunching on the loose gravel, and felt—with relief—the past recede.

I stood up and dusted off my pants, reminding myself this was a vacation, not a wake. A cold gust of wind whipped by, causing me to shiver. The clouds overhead had grown darker. It was time to leave, before this unexpected May rainstorm did more than just threaten. I hesitated, then turned to go.

Fate is a strange thing. The ancient Greeks believed a person's destiny was a thread to be spun, measured, and cut at whim by the gods. Yet we don't live in isolation; our fates are woven together. And sometimes a single act—a small tug on a delicate line—can pull the weave apart. If I'd just gone back to my hotel that morning and forgotten my father's painting come to life, things would have turned out differently. But I, like Orpheus, could not resist temptation. I looked back, anxious for one last glimpse of that scene from my childhood, and inadvertently I started the whole bloody pattern unraveling.

I don't remember how the letter got into my hands. I must have disinterred it from its resting place in my wallet, but I did so mechanically, without conscious thought. One minute I was staring at the view, the next my eyes were fixed on a single blue sheet, worn and creased from countless readings.

Christine,

    I don't know how to make this clear without just coming out and saying it. I don't want to see you again. Difficult as it may be for you to accept, you're no longer a part of my life. You're a grown woman now. It's high time you forget the past and get on with creating a life of your own.

Angus

I stared down at the signature. Angus. Strange how he'd never wanted us to call him anything else, almost as if by refusing the title of father he could avoid its reality. Yet names don't matter to children; when he'd gone, the hurt had been the same. I crumpled the letter, angry that reading it had somehow made me feel a child again. Against my will, I began to cry in small, hiccuping bursts.

A gull keened loudly overhead, mocking me. I sent the tightly wadded letter sailing over the wall and out of sight, and for a moment felt a profound sense of relief. Then depression returned, hastened no doubt by the darkening sky. I turned away and for the second time prepared to leave.

"Excuse me—"

I spun around. The voice had seemed to come from directly behind me, but behind me was only the wall and empty air. I looked left and right. Nobody. My heart began to beat faster.

"Down here."

The voice was high and sweet. I felt rather sheepish as I moved toward the wall and looked down. A young boy, perhaps nine or ten, stood looking up at me from moss-covered steps some fifteen feet below. He had brown hair and pale skin and green eyes which curved down at the outside corners. His expression was solemn for a boy his age, like a grave little owl.

"Sorry. Did I frighten you?" His proper British enunciation added to his strange grown-up air.

"It's all right," I said. "I'll recover."

He regarded me closely. "Care to have my handkerchief?"

"That obvious, eh?" I pulled a Kleenex from my purse and blotted my eyes.

He shook his head. "I heard you crying."

"I was remembering something sad, that's all," I murmured, embarrassed this young stranger had been a witness to my weeping.

He looked up at me with sympathetic eyes. Something in the look made my lip tremble dangerously. Time to change the subject.

"How did you get down there, anyway?" I demanded in a firmer tone. I peered to the right where the stone steps rose up and disappeared behind a curve in the wall. He didn't answer, so I circled around and found the archway where the steps began. It was barred with a locked metal gate, and there was a sign warning in Greek:

ΚΙΝΥΝΟΣ! ΜΥΝ ΕΛΑΤΕ
DANGER! DO NOT ENTER!

Craning to see around a large, ferny plant, I could see the reason for the sign. Descending steeply about fifty feet, the steps led down to a flat balcony of rock. Beyond that, there was no railing or parapet, only a cliff which dropped several hundred feet to the sea.

I ran back to warn him, but when I leaned over the wall, he was gone. The mossy step he'd been standing on was empty. I retreated backwards, trying to think of a rational explanation, but frightening mental images of the boy tumbling into the sea kept pushing rationality aside.

The tap on my arm made me jump. I whirled around to find him looking up at me, his green eyes quite innocent.

"How—"

He smiled and for a moment was transformed from sad owl to mischievous elf. "There's a secret passage. Care to see it?"

"I think so. It's about to rain."

As heavy drops began to pelt our faces, he took my hand and led me across the gravel to a cobblestone road which led downward toward the castle's base. His secret passage—a narrow tunnel from the interior of the fortress out to the battlements—proved an excellent shelter from what turned out to be a very brief downpour. When we emerged out onto the flat balcony of rock I'd seen before, it was puddled with water, but the rain had diminished to a mere drizzle.

"Lucky I met up with you," I remarked.

"Happy to be of service." He flashed a grin that sent his eyebrows adorably askew. "Oh, that reminds me!" He dug his hand into his pocket and pulled out something blue and crumpled. "The reason I called up to you. You dropped this."

He held it out to me. It was the discarded letter. I snatched it from his hand, shoving it quickly back into my purse.

His grin began to fade. "I saw the writing," he said. "I thought it might be important."

"No." My sharp tone caused what was left of his smile to disappear. "Look, I've got to get going," I said. "Goodbye."

"Goodbye," he echoed softly.

I started to leave. He made no move to follow. "You will be careful out here, won't you?" I asked, suddenly anxious at the thought of leaving him there alone. He nodded, but halfway through the tunnel I realized I couldn't just walk away. He'd probably be fine, but I had to be sure. I turned and went back. "It's none of my business, but does your family know you're here?"

For a moment he looked defiant, then slowly he shook his head. That did it. Now I was stuck. "What hotel are they at?" I asked reluctantly.

"We're not staying at a hotel. We have a house north of town." He flashed me a worried look. "You're not going to tell them I was here, are you?"

"No," I admitted, "not if you don't want me to. But I can't in good conscience leave you to wander around here by yourself, either. It's not safe. Perhaps I should put you in a taxi home."

"But I can't leave yet!" he exclaimed, his voice high with chagrin. "I'll be careful, I promise!"

I frowned. It wasn't really my place to tell the poor kid what to do, but I felt a nagging sense of disquiet at leaving him on his own. The mental image of him tumbling over that cliff had been a little too vivid.

"Please, I just want to stay another hour or so." His voice had turned coaxing. "An hour won't hurt anything, will it?"

"An hour, eh?" I glanced at my watch. It was only a little after nine. "Sounds okay to me. Now that the rain's over, maybe I'll tag along."

He hesitated for a moment, then gave a small shrug. "Suit yourself."

I sighed. So much for reverse psychology. "Great. My name's Christine, by the way. Christine Stewart." I held out my hand.

After another moment's hesitation he took it. "I'm Michael Redfield."

"Well, Michael, what would you like to do now?"

He didn't answer.

"How about taking me on a tour of this place? You seem to know quite a bit about it."

He seemed to accept the suggestion. I motioned for him to

take the lead, and as we abandoned our balcony of rock for the more solid ground of the tunnel I felt a strong sense of relief. Trotting along in an attempt to keep up with his boyish pace, I also realized that my black mood had vanished. Perhaps I wasn't the one doing the good deed after all.

We started at the bottom of the citadel, at the bridge called the Contrafossa, and worked our way up along the northern side of the castle. Michael knew the place inside out. Every wall, every parapet, every crumbling piece of stone seemed familiar to him. He showed me the lighthouse, the clock tower, the cannons, the turrets. I felt myself slipping back in time, imagining soldiers in colorful uniforms shouting away in Greek and Italian.

"Are you sure you don't do this for a living?" I teased him, as we stopped on the south side of the fortress, at a building which looked like a classical temple, but which, Michael informed me, had actually been the Anglican Chapel of St. George. We crossed to a bench behind the now abandoned church and sat down.

"No, but I wish I did," Michael replied, his tone suddenly tense. "Then I'd have some money of my own to spend."

I looked at his clothes, his shoes, the cut of his hair; all bespoke wealth. "If I may say so, you don't exactly look hard up. What do you need money for?"

He regarded me for a long moment, then turned away and muttered in a fierce young voice: "For a detective."

It was such a surprising answer, I almost laughed. But one look at his face warned me not to. I sat in silence, and tried to marshal the seriousness to speak. I didn't want to hurt his feelings. Finally I told him, "It's almost ten."

His head snapped up in surprise, and he lifted his arm to check the boyish but obviously expensive watch strapped around his thin wrist.

"May I stay here a few minutes by myself," he asked, "if I promise to go home directly afterwards?"

I felt surprisingly hurt by the dismissal, but hid my feelings. "Giving me my walking papers? Well, that's fair. If you promise to head home, I'll leave you in peace. Thanks for the tour, Michael; I enjoyed it."

He began to say something in reply, but I never got to hear it.

To this day, I'm not sure what made me look up. Perhaps there was some sound, though I don't remember any. There was a flicker of shadow, but it only registered afterwards, after I gazed skyward and saw part of the grey stone wall some hundred feet above us begin to sway—and then fall.

I lunged at Michael, dragging him off the bench. We hit the ground rolling, and almost at the same time there was a horrible, heart-stopping crash.

When I finally remembered to breathe again, I almost choked on grit and dust. Then I opened my eyes. The bench we'd been sitting on a moment earlier was now a splintered wreck, wood and broken stone forming a jagged heap. I rolled onto my side, releasing Michael who was pinned under me.

"Are you all right?" I gasped.

He nodded, wide-eyed.

I checked him all over. His lip was bleeding, one arm was scraped, but nothing seemed broken. I lightly touched his chest and stomach, but nothing seemed seriously amiss. I struggled shakily to my feet, beginning to become aware of some damage to my own anatomy. "Can you get up?" I asked.

"I think so," he said.

I reached down to help him. He winced when I took his left hand. "Let me see that. Can you move your fingers properly?" I felt along the wrist, but nothing seemed broken. With luck it was only a sprain.

Michael looked up at me, his face white, his hand trembling in mine. I put my arms around him. "It's all right," I assured him. "There's no danger now. We're safe."

He shook his head and reached up to lightly touch my right cheek. My own hand went up, and I felt something warm and sticky on my fingers. When I looked down at them, they were covered with blood.

It didn't occur to me until much later to wonder what the taxi driver must have thought of his two passengers during that twelve-mile ride to Michael's home. We were dirty, blood-stained, scraped and scratched. My blouse was torn, Michael's lip was swollen, and the long cut on my cheek still bled sporadically.

The scenery on the drive north was lovely, but I couldn't enjoy it. I kept a watchful eye on Michael, anxious to make sure he was all right. I wasn't looking forward to handing him back to his parents looking as if he'd just lost a prizefight.

Which is why I felt a mixture of relief and trepidation when Michael pointed to a large stone gate bearing the legend "Villa Ithaki," and the taxi turned down a gravel driveway lined with cypress trees. At first, all I could see was a large grove of pines. Then the driveway veered to the left, bringing the house into view. The elegant mansion that loomed ahead was not quite what I'd envisioned when Michael had casually mentioned his family's summer house.

The car came to a scrunching halt on the gravel. "This is the place you wish?" the driver asked in Greek. Even in another language his skepticism was evident.

"*Malista*," Michael replied, answering for both of us. I fumbled in my purse for money to pay the fare. My fingers felt clumsy as I counted out hundred drachma notes and handed the wad of bills to the driver. I climbed creakily out of the car, and Michael reached out to steady me.

"Thanks," I said, as we stood there watching the taxi disappear back up the drive. Strangely, Michael seemed as reluctant to enter the house as I did.

"Something wrong?" I asked.

"I didn't tell them where I was going. And I rode into town with the gardener. I don't want to get him into trouble."

"Don't worry. All your family's going to care about is getting you back in one piece." I held out my hand and he took it. We approached the massive front door together.

I knocked, but for what seemed an eternity nothing happened. Unsteadily, I knocked again. I was beginning to feel an almost desperate need to sit down. Finally, the door opened. A man stood framed in the doorway. For a moment his dark brown eyes widened in surprise, then his expression became coldly neutral.

"So, you have returned," he said, addressing Michael in English that bore only the lightest traces of a Greek accent. "What have you been doing? You do not look in the best of shape." His gaze shifted to me. "And who is this?"

In a subdued voice, Michael said, "Miss Stewart, this is my Uncle Spiro. Uncle Spiro, this is—"

"Christine Stewart," I snapped. "And in case you haven't noticed, we've had an accident. I don't think Michael's badly hurt, but he's had a nasty scare, and I suspect his wrist is sprained. The sooner a doctor looks at him, the better."

"I see. Come in." He motioned for us to enter. "Perhaps you are in need of a doctor as well?" he asked as I brushed past him into the hallway.

"It can wait."

He gazed at me skeptically, and then turned to lead the way. "My sister will be relieved to hear of the boy's return. She has been worrying since he disappeared this morning." There was a questioning note in his voice which I purposely ignored. "Indeed, I have just returned from searching for him in town."

"Spiro, who is it?"

The voice was sharp and spoke in Greek. Before he could answer, a woman emerged from a room at the end of the hall. She was petite in stature, but moved with commanding grace, and the elegant black dress she wore was stylish and expensive. She had large, dark, almond-shaped eyes and shiny black hair drawn back in a chignon. Her mouth was small and delicately shaped. At sight of Michael, it opened and then snapped shut.

Her brother said quickly, "There has been an accident, Demetra. Michael does not appear badly injured." He added with an odd emphasis, "I do not know about the young lady."

"I told you," I said weakly, "I'm fine."

He ignored me. Instead, he called to a middle-aged woman who had slipped into the room. "Maria, telephone Dr. Aristides and tell him we have two patients for him."

His sister's attention was on me now. "Who is she, Spiro? How is she involved in all this?"

"Her name is Christine Stewart, she is here because she brought the boy back to us, and as to how she comes to be with him in the first place ... well, I suggest we wait to consider such questions until after the doctor has seen them both."

Michael stood silently between them. I tried to smile encouragement at him, but my lips felt heavy and difficult to move. The room was hot, the air still. I tried to shift my gaze from Michael to his mother and uncle, but though I could make out their faces, I couldn't bring them into focus. They swayed and shimmered, as did the furniture, the walls, the ceiling. Suddenly my head seemed far away and my body unable to keep its balance.

I heard someone swear, saw a dark flash of motion, and through a fog realized I was falling.

"Will she be all right?"

"I think so. The cut's not too serious. She's lost some blood and may have a slight concussion, but there's no obvious fracture to the skull."

The voices, speaking rapidly in Greek, seemed quite close, but it was too much effort to open my eyes. I listened lazily.

"Should she be moved to the hospital?"

"I don't think it will be necessary. I suspect all she needs is rest, but I'll check back later to see how she is doing."

"Thank you, Doctor. We appreciate your coming at such short notice."

"*Brey*! What am I, a banker?"

Someone laughed.

I heard receding footsteps and a door open and close. I still couldn't seem to open my eyes and drifted back to sleep. I woke sometime later, and found myself lying in a large mahogany bed between cool linen sheets. A scarlet and gold coverlet was pulled up under my arms, and I was wearing a satin negligee in a beautiful shade of rose. My cheek ached horribly. I touched it and realized it was bandaged.

"Does it hurt?" a low voice asked softly in Greek.

I started. I'd thought I was alone in the room. I turned my head slowly, trying not to jar my sore neck or make the throbbing in my cheek any worse than it already was. A man was sitting in a blue armchair at the far end of the room. He stood up, and crossed to stand by the foot of the bed. He was tall and fair, with tousled blond hair and green eyes of a familiar shade.

"I believe I overheard something about the doctor putting in stitches," he continued. He stepped closer and gazed down at me. For a moment, concern flickered in his eyes. Then his expression hardened and he remarked coolly, "Aristides is an able old quack. With luck you won't be left with a scar."

"You really know how to cheer a girl up, don't you?"

His attractive mouth tightened. "Your Greek is very fluent for an American."

"My mother is Greek. Look, can you please tell me what happened? The last thing I remember, I was feeling dizzy—"

"You fainted." Suddenly he spoke in English, and I realized he was British, like Michael.

"Fainted?"

"Dead away. A textbook swoon. When I arrived on the scene, you were draped quite decoratively in Skouras's arms."

I decided Skouras must be Michael's Greek uncle, Spiro. "And where am I now? Whose room is this?"

"Skouras's, I should imagine."

"You mean I'm in his bed?"

"Yes, Goldilocks, I suppose you are." His tone was biting, and he flashed me a mocking smile that sent his rather devastating eyebrows all crooked. Suddenly, despite the hostility of his expression, he was the spitting image of Michael.

"Are you Michael's father?" I asked.

The mocking smile vanished. His expression grew grim. In precise and carefully controlled syllables he said, "Michael's father is dead. I'm Michael's uncle, Geoffrey Redfield."

I remembered Michael's solemn face, and felt a sharp pang of sympathy. I knew firsthand how hard it was to grow up without a father. "I'm sorry," I said.

Geoffrey Redfield said nothing. I tried changing the subject. "How is Michael? What did the doctor say?"

His expression relaxed a little. "He has a sprained wrist and a few cuts and bruises, but Aristides thinks he'll be fine."

"I'm glad," I said, relieved. I sank back into the cool pillows, and for a while neither of us spoke. Then he seemed to grow impatient with the silence. He drew closer to the bed and bent over me.

"I haven't yet thanked you, you know."

"Thanked me for what?"

"For such a good morning's work, of course. For what you did for my nephew." His eyes were the same cat green as Michael's, but there was an odd gleam in them that was doing strange things to my stomach.

"You don't need to thank me for that," I said faintly.

"Why not?" he demanded. There was an edge to his voice I didn't understand. "Didn't you rescue him from the very jaws of death?"

"I didn't rescue anyone! The stone began to fall and—" I broke off. Glancing up, I was distracted by the nearness of his face to mine and the faint scent of his cologne.

"Yes?" he prompted, pressing a hand into the pillow next to my head.

I blinked. "And I just jumped out of the way. That's all."

"Taking Michael with you."

"Yes, taking Michael with me."

"Why so reluctant to play the heroine, Miss Stewart?" he asked softly, the warm flutter of his breath sending tingles down my neck.

I felt like a mouse pinned by a much too enticing cat. I slid sideways, setting off some painful fireworks in my right shoulder. "Perhaps I'm not right for the role."

"Perhaps not," he agreed, straightening. "Though no one could accuse you of not looking the part." His eyes went to my bandaged cheek.

"Do I look a pitiful sight?" I asked lightly, trying to make it a joke.

He stared down at me assessingly, and I felt my face grow hot. I could almost hear the mental tabulation: disheveled brown hair, a bandaged cheek, passable blue eyes, but a nose too classic to be cute coupled with a chin both pointed and prominent (stubborn, an old boyfriend had called it). His gaze drifted briefly south, where the negligee I was wearing, obviously belonging to a smaller woman, revealed a lot more than it hid.

"A pitiful sight? No, not really," he said, looking away.

I pulled the sheet up. "Do you know where my clothes are?"

He turned and moved off toward the French windows. "I haven't the foggiest. Perhaps Maria's made off with them. She has a tendency to wash clothes that don't really need washing."

"Maria?"

"The housekeeper."

"Oh."

We lapsed into silence. Feeling tired, I closed my eyes, but he was obviously not done with the conversation. "The bench you and Michael were sitting on when all this happened," he said. "I believe Michael said it was the one by St. George's?"

Reluctantly I opened my eyes. "St. George's is the church that looks like a temple?"

He gave a short, impatient nod.

"Then, yes," I said.

"How did you and Michael come to be sitting there?"

"Michael had just given me a tour of the fort. We were finishing up, and we sat down on the bench to rest. At least, I wanted to rest. Michael was just keeping me company. It was purely by chance."

The planes of his face seemed to harden. "Michael's only been on the island for a few weeks now. How did you two become acquainted?"

"We just met today."

"But you've known Demetra for some time, I suppose?"

I gazed at him blankly.

"My sister-in-law, Demetra Redfield," he elaborated.

"Michael's mother? I've never seen her before in my life."

"Then Skouras? Perhaps he's the old friend?"

I shook my head, setting off more fireworks in my neck. "How would I know him? I told you, I only met Michael today. Look, why are you asking me all these questions?"

He leaned close again, so close I could see the gold streaks along the tips of his eyelashes. "You truly expect me to believe your meeting Michael today was mere coincidence?"

"I don't care what you believe," I snapped, "it's the truth. Why on earth should I lie about it?"

"I think we both know why, but let's put that aside for the moment. Instead, why don't you tell me what caused you to look up at the precise moment that stone began to fall?"

"I don't know," I admitted.

"Another coincidence?"

"Look, I don't know what you're getting at, but I'm tired, and my cheek hurts, and I don't want to talk to you anymore."

"Who paid you to follow Michael?" he demanded.

I stared at him in disbelief. "You're crazy! Nobody paid me to do anything. Why would anyone have a little boy followed?"

"Dammit, you know why!" he said, seizing me by the shoulders. "How did they know I was meeting him?"

"You're hurting me!" I cried. He let go abruptly. "I think it's time I was going," I said, trying to sound calmer than I felt.

"We're not finished yet."

I didn't answer. Instead, I struggled to sit up, stiffly swinging my legs out of the bed and dangling them toward the floor. Unfortunately, the bed was an expensive antique and ridiculously high off the ground. Hoping to get a more solid footing, I launched myself forward, but my knees buckled and I started to fall. There was a muffled crash. Then I found myself on the floor cradled in Geoffrey Redfield's warm, strong arms.

"Do you make a habit of collapsing onto every man you meet?" he inquired acidly.

"No one asked you to catch me," I snapped back, tears of pain welling up in my eyes. His arms dropped away.

"Are you all right?" he asked through clenched teeth.

My cheek was burning, my neck ached, and I found myself shaking so hard it hurt. "I'm fine," I whispered, turning my head away so he wouldn't see the tears starting to spill. He turned my face back towards him and swore.

Taking out a handkerchief from his pocket, he wiped the tears away with surprising gentleness. Then he picked me up and placed me carefully back on the bed. For a moment, his arms lingered around me, then the nearby murmur of voices seemed to snap him from his reverie. He straightened abruptly.

"Look, I've no more time for games," he declared in an urgent undertone. "I need answers, and I need them now. Can't you understand how important this is?"

"Can't you understand," I retorted, "that I haven't the vaguest idea what you're talking about?"

For the first time, uncertainty flickered in his green eyes.

"You truly don't know?"

"No!"

He raised a finger to his lips.

"No," I repeated more softly.

"But you speak such fluent Greek—"

"So? Since when is that a crime?"

"You didn't ring my hotel? You didn't leave a message saying Michael was in hospital?"

I stared at him, flabbergasted. "Of course not! Why would I do such a thing?" Suddenly outside the room I could hear the approaching click-clack of high heels.

"Perhaps I've leapt to some hasty conclusions."

"I'll say!"

He held up his hand. "If I have, I apologize. If not, at least we both know where we stand." He backed away toward the French windows, his eyes on me, his attention fixed on the approaching footsteps. "But if it's true you simply stumbled into this … well, then someone ought to warn you."

"Warn me? Warn me about what?"

The footsteps had stopped, and I heard the door open. I turned to see who it was. Michael's mother glided in, followed by her brother.

"Ah, Miss Stewart, you are awake," she said, casting a significant look back at her companion. "I told my brother it was so, but he would not believe me. You see, Spiro. Did I not tell you I heard voices coming from this room?"

Her brother flashed me a quick appraising look, then gazed past me. "And to whom, dear sister, would Miss Stewart have been talking? The room is empty. There is no one else here."

Startled, I looked back toward the French windows. Spiro Skouras was right. Geoffrey Redfield was nowhere to be seen.

Two

Demetra Redfield seemed as startled by Geoffrey's absence as I was. "But it was his voice I heard!" she insisted, as she scanned the room. "I tell you, he was here!"

I was about to speak up and tell her she was right, when Spiro replied in Greek, "Why would he risk breaking in here to speak to a stranger?"

His sister turned and regarded me through narrowed eyes. "I doubt she is a stranger to *him*. He probably came to instruct her what lies to tell us."

"Nonsense. You heard the boy describe how they met. It was pure chance. Geoffrey could not have been behind it."

She made a dismissive sound. "I don't believe—"

"It doesn't matter what you believe," Spiro interrupted. "Remember, we are not alone." Switching back to English, he added pointedly, "We have not yet introduced ourselves to our guest."

She shot him a resentful look and said stiffly, "Of course." She paused and turned to address me. "Miss Stewart, I am Demetra Redfield. This is my brother, Spiro Skouras."

"Pleased to meet you," I murmured.

She gave a small, noncommittal shrug. "There. We have done what is polite. Now may I ask her what Geoffrey was doing in my house?"

I was no longer in a communicative mood. "Who?"

"Geoffrey Redfield, the brother of my dead husband. I heard him in this room. Do you deny he was here?"

"Demetra!" her brother exclaimed sharply. "We owe the young lady our gratitude, not an interrogation. Please excuse my sister, Miss Stewart. Michael's close escape has upset her."

Her small mouth tightened and she murmured in Greek, "I am not a fool, Spiro. Don't treat me like one."

He ignored her. To me he said, "I trust you are feeling better?"

"Yes," I replied, "though my cheek hurts like the devil."

He looked perplexed for a moment, then said, "Ah, you are in pain. The doctor left some pills. Demetra, you will bring them? They are in the study."

"Fetch them yourself," she snapped in Greek.

Spiro cast a wary look from her to me before heading out the door. His sister waited for him to leave, then declared, "My brother can think what he likes, but I know Geoffrey was here with you."

Unsure what to say, I said nothing.

She continued, "I suppose it was you who helped Michael sneak off to town today? No, don't bother answering. I'm in no mood for more lies. What I cannot understand, however, is how you managed to slip the boy the note."

I stared at her in bewilderment. Was everyone in Michael's family crazy? "Note?" I said. "What note?"

Her dark eyes smoldered. "Even in Greece we have laws, Miss Stewart. Laws against stealing other people's children."

I suddenly felt cold, but before I could ask her just what it was she was accusing me of, her brother reentered the room. He set down the tray he was carrying, and gazed from his sister to me with a frown. "I hope you have been telling Miss Stewart how grateful we are, Demetra."

"*Grateful?*" his sister echoed in Greek. "For what?"

"For saving the boy, of course!" he snapped in the same language. He added carefully in English, "After all, we are deeply in her debt. If it had not been for her quick action, Michael might have been seriously hurt, even killed."

Demetra flashed him a strange look. "Yes, how can we ever properly express our gratitude to her for that?"

My cheek was throbbing and I was tired of being spoken of in the third person. "You might begin by giving me one of those pills," I said.

Spiro brought me the small bottle and a glass of water. After

I'd taken two of the painkillers, he said to his sister, "Demetra, Dr. Aristides left some tablets for you as well—to help you sleep. I think perhaps you should go take one now and lie down in your room."

His tone of voice made it less a suggestion than an order, but to my surprise she did not protest. Instead, she jerked her chin in my direction and said softly in Greek, "What will you do about her?"

"Nothing," he replied in the same language, "except apologize for your less than hospitable behavior."

She made a derisive sound, but before she could say anything more, he took her arm and led her to the door. When she had gone, he crossed to the bed and looked down at me with an earnest expression. "Miss Stewart—Christine," he began, switching once more to English, "please excuse my sister. Her husband died suddenly two months ago, and I believe she has not yet recovered from the shock. Michael's disappearance this morning and then his return in such a state has only added to the strain, I fear."

"But Mr. Skouras—"

"Please! Call me Spiro." His dark brown eyes were warm and friendly.

"Spiro, then. I'm afraid I don't understand. I'm sorry about your sister's loss, but I don't see why that should make her so suspicious of me. While you were gone, she practically accused me of kidnapping Michael."

His expression grew troubled. "Christine, I am sorry. She has had these irrational spells since her husband died. I apologize for her behavior. She mistrusts you because she believes you are involved with her brother-in-law."

"But I'm not!"

He nodded. "But Redfield is trying to take custody of the boy from her, and she believes him responsible for Michael's disappearance today. Your arrival so unexpectedly with the boy has caused her to suspect that you, too, might be involved."

So that was it. I'd landed smack-dab in the middle of a nasty custody battle. "I see," I said heavily.

"Please, do not let my sister's suspicions trouble you. I will soon make her see that your involvement in all this is purely accidental." He reached out and placed his hand on mine. "Now, you are tired. I will leave you to rest."

"I *am* tired," I agreed. "Could you find out what happened to my clothes? I'd like to get dressed and head back to my hotel."

"Your hotel?" he exclaimed. "But you are most welcome to remain here!"

"Oh, no. I wouldn't want to impose—"

"Impose? Nonsense! We are in your debt. Besides, the doctor recommended that you have rest."

"I've got a perfectly good hotel room to do that in," I assured him.

"A hotel is no place to rest! Here you can sleep, eat, swim— we have a beautiful beach, and it is completely private."

"It sounds lovely, but really—I don't think your sister would appreciate me as a houseguest. Now, about my clothes...."

"I assure you, Christine, after I have spoken with Demetra, she will be most happy to have you here. And it will please the boy as well. He has developed quite an attachment to you."

"I like him, too. But I still want to go back to my hotel."

Spiro gave a reluctant shrug. "Very well. In that case, I will escort you there."

The Hotel Kerkyra was small and quaint and tucked away on a short, winding street in Corfu's old town. As I climbed the three flights of stairs to my floor, I was grateful for the strong arm spotting my back, and glad that Spiro had insisted on seeing me up to my room.

Once there, however, I wanted to be alone. The pills the doctor had prescribed were making me groggy, but hadn't yet blunted the pain, and the tight dress I wore only added to my discomfort. Demetra Redfield had loaned the dress to me, because Maria had taken my clothes away to be washed, but I had no illusions she was being kind. I suspected she would have given me the clothes off her back to get me out of her house.

"You are certain you are well enough to be alone?" Spiro asked, as I sank into an armchair by the bed and closed my eyes.

"I'll be fine after I get some sleep."

"Very well, then," he said. "I will leave you to rest."

I forced my eyes open and smiled—despite the tight, painful tug it cost my cheek. "Thanks for the escort, Spiro."

"Christine—"

"Yes?"

"Do not judge my sister too harshly. Since her husband died, she has not been herself, and this battle over the boy has made things worse."

"Just out of curiosity, why is she so worried about Geoffrey challenging her for custody? She's Michael's mother, after all. How can a mere uncle compete with that?"

He gazed at me in surprise. "Demetra is not Michael's mother, Christine. She is his—how do you call it?—*mitryiá*. Stepmother. Michael's real mother was William Redfield's first wife. They divorced when the boy was two."

"But if that's the case," I said, "why isn't Michael with his real mother now that his father is dead?"

Spiro made a gesture with his hands. "She is dead also. She was killed several years ago in an airplane crash."

"Oh, no! Poor Michael."

Spiro shook his head. "To the contrary, the boy is very, very rich. William Redfield was an extremely wealthy man."

"I meant it's sad that both Michael's parents are dead."

He shrugged. "There are worse things."

I bit my lip. "Spiro, I'm tired. I'd like to be alone now."

"Of course." He flashed me a smile, his large white teeth bared in a blinding grin. "I am going." He raised my hand and kissed it, his lips lingering on my fingers. "*Kalispera*, Christine." He crossed to the door and opened it, but with one hand on the knob, he turned. "About Geoffrey—"

"Yes?" I replied warily.

"I think Demetra may be correct in one thing. He may try to use you and the accident today to assist his cause."

"Why does he want custody?" I asked.

"The money, of course. When William Redfield died, he left most of his fortune to his son to be held in trust until the boy's eighteenth birthday."

"But if the money's held in trust, what good does it do

Geoffrey?"

"To be the guardian of such a wealthy boy can provide one with a very comfortable living."

"But not *that* comfortable, surely!"

Spiro's mouth quirked. "Comfortable enough. My brother-in-law's estate is valued at over thirty million pounds."

My breath caught at the size of the fortune. Poor Michael.

Spiro said, "You probably will not feel like going to a restaurant this evening?"

Distractedly I said, "No, I don't think so."

"Then I will bring dinner here."

"That's very thoughtful of you, but—" I paused, my tired brain fumbling for an excuse.

Spiro shook his head, dismissing my hesitation with a chiding grin. "I cannot let you starve," he said as he disappeared out the door. With a sigh, I pulled off Demetra's tight dress and decided I'd worry about her brother's return later. I was too tired to think. I threw on a T-shirt and shorts and crawled into bed. I think I was asleep before my head hit the pillow.

The room had grown dark from the dwindling sunlight. Sad, pale shadows flickered across the floor, and it seemed as if the ceiling had retreated higher.

I found myself staring up at the ceiling. It wasn't a particularly interesting ceiling, as ceilings go, but it had one highly unusual feature. It was swaying. Back and forth, back and forth. The swaying became more violent, and soon the ceiling was creaking, buckling from the strain. Any moment, I realized, it would break free and crash down on me.

I tried to move, to get off the bed and escape, but my frozen limbs refused to budge. The ceiling split away, broke open, and began to fall. As it smashed into me, I screamed....

I woke, trembling, and it took me a moment to differentiate the pounding at the door from the pounding of my heart. I slid weakly off the bed and crossed to open it. When I turned the key, I had to jump out of the way as the door burst open and Geoffrey Redfield rushed into the room. He came to a halt and spun around, his gaze settling on me grimly. "Are you all right?"

"I almost had my nose flattened by the door," I replied, "but other than that I'm fine."

"What made you cry out like that? I thought you were being murdered."

"I had a bad dream, that's all." I turned my back on him and retreated to the armchair. I needed to sit down.

"A bad dream?" he exclaimed. "You expect me to believe that?"

"I don't expect you to believe anything. What are you doing here, anyway? I don't recall inviting you."

I was gratified to see him look uncomfortable. "I came to apologize," he said stiffly.

"Apologize?"

"For my behavior this morning. I may have jumped to some hasty conclusions."

"I'd say so."

"I had my reasons," he insisted.

"Really?"

His gaze met mine straight on. "I'd like to explain them to you, if you'd care to listen."

"All right," I said faintly. The look in those intent emerald eyes was having a now familiar effect on my stomach. I motioned toward a chair by the window. "Take a seat."

He closed the door. Instead of sitting down, however, he crossed to where I was sitting and removed something from the pocket of his crisp white Oxford shirt. "Here," he said in a low voice that sounded oddly abashed. I looked down at what he was holding out to me. It was a crumpled piece of blue paper carefully smoothed out and folded closed. Realizing what it was, I grabbed it from him.

"I took it from your purse," he said in tight, clipped syllables. "I was looking for the key to your hotel—to know where to find you—and I saw that. I thought it might be important but didn't have time to read it before you woke."

"But I suppose you've read it now."

"Yes." He paused. "I'm sorry."

I was too embarrassed to speak. I smoothed the paper with my hand, staring at it on my lap.

"Perhaps you'd like me to leave?" he asked.

I looked up. "No," I said, my mood grim. "You promised me an explanation, and I still want it." I gestured to the chair by the window again, and this time he went to it and sat down.

"Where would you like me to begin?"

I stared at his face: the straight nose, the well-shaped mouth, the grave, green eyes so like Michael's. It was a strong face, an attractive face. Too bad it belonged to a man who saw his nephew as nothing but a meal ticket.

"Why do you want custody of Michael?" I asked.

The question seemed to catch him by surprise. The taut arc of his jaw tightened to fierce angles. "Does it matter?"

"I think it does. Michael is a very wealthy boy."

His green eyes darkened. "You think I'm after his money?"

"I don't know."

"Affording me the benefit of the doubt?"

"Trying to decide how low you'd stoop," I corrected.

His mouth tightened to a white-lipped line, then his gaze went to the letter on my lap and his anger seemed to drain away. "I suppose I deserve that," he said. I waited for him to say more, to protest his innocence, to tell me he wanted custody of Michael because he cared for the boy and wanted to make sure he was happy and loved. I waited, but in vain. He turned and looked out the window. "How much have you told Demetra?"

"About your little visit? Nothing."

He turned back and flashed me a searching look. "Thank you."

I shook my head. "No need to thank me. Your sister-in-law's just as suspicious of me as you are. I didn't want to get caught in the middle any more than I already was, that's all."

"I see."

Silence stretched uncomfortably between us. Finally I asked, "Why did you think someone had paid me to follow Michael?"

He hesitated for a moment, then said, "Challenging Demetra's custody is extremely difficult while Michael is here in Greece. If he were in England, it would be a different matter."

"So that's why Michael went off without a word," I said. "He went to the Old Fort to meet you."

He nodded. "I wanted an opportunity to speak with him, to

make sure he was being treated decently. At the villa, I'm never allowed to see him alone."

"With good reason, it sounds like."

"No, you're wrong. I simply wanted to speak with him. As it turned out, I never got the chance." He looked down at his hands, which were steepled together in his lap. Unwillingly, I found my gaze following his.

He had nice hands, with long, tapering fingers and well-shaped wrists. The cuffs of his shirt were folded back. His tanned forearms were covered with golden hairs that curled down to the band of his watch. Fighting a sudden desire to brush my fingers along those silky hairs, I focused on the watch instead. It was a simple but expensive-looking timepiece, and it suddenly reminded me of Michael's boyish one. "Of course!" I exclaimed. "Ten o'clock! That's why he wanted to get rid of me. That's when you were supposed to meet him, wasn't it?"

He was watching me now—intently. "You really didn't know, did you?" he said, a smile beginning to play at the edges of his lips. "Yes."

It irked me that just when I thought I'd come up with some-thing to put him on the defensive, he acted as if I were the one who had passed some test. "So why didn't you show up?" I demanded.

"I was late. I arrived just in time to see you and Michael climbing into a taxi together. The taxi pulled away as I ran up, and by the time I'd managed to hail another, you'd disappeared. I thought it likely you'd head back to the villa, so I followed you there. The rest you know."

"Hardly. Why were you late?"

His expression turned somber. "As I was leaving my hotel, a woman rang up saying Michael had been in an accident and was in hospital. I was too shaken to think clearly and didn't stop to wonder how someone could have known to contact me. I think I assumed Michael had given them my name and hotel. However, when I arrived at the hospital no one knew anything about Michael or the message, and I began to suspect a trick. I rushed to the Old Fort, only to find Michael driving away with you."

"You didn't recognize the woman's voice?"

"No, she spoke rapidly in Greek and I was only listening with half an ear until Michael was mentioned."

"So when you found out I spoke Greek, you thought I was the one who had called with the phony message."

He nodded. "It was all too pat; you showing up by chance right after I'd been tricked into not arriving. I was sure you had to be involved."

"I can see how it might have seemed that way," I conceded. "What made you change your mind?"

He grinned ruefully. "You did. At first I couldn't believe you were as innocent as you kept claiming to be, but after a while I began to wonder." He stood up. "Look, can I move this chair closer? I feel a bit of a fool talking across the room at you."

I told him I couldn't care less what he did with the chair, so he set it down right in front of me. "There, that's more like it. Now I can see your face properly."

"The better to tell if I'm lying?" I snapped, disconcerted by his closeness.

"No. The better to see those pretty blue eyes of yours," he replied softly.

I looked away in surprise, only to have my gaze caught by the rather too attractive view of throat and chest revealed by his open shirt. "Don't you think it strange someone would go to such lengths to keep you from meeting Michael?"

"No. My dear sister-in-law is determined to keep me away from him, which is why she brought him to Greece." He paused and continued in a gentler tone, "Look, I'm sorry I was so hard on you at our first meeting, but Michael's accident gave me a bad scare, and when Skouras threw me out, I was determined to confront you and get the truth."

I grimaced. "It's almost comic in a way: you convinced I must be working for your sister-in-law; your sister-in-law convinced I must be working for you."

He ran a hand through his hair. "You must think us all quite mad."

"Yes, but I'm willing to accept that I might be wrong."

"Are you?" he asked with a sudden smile. "Well, that's progress."

I returned the smile. I couldn't help it. For a few moments

we sat in amicable silence. Then I said, "Look, about Michael—I know it's none of my business—"

I was interrupted by a knock at the door, which was probably just as well. My words had driven all friendliness from Geoffrey's expression. I started to get up. "No, let me," he snapped, crossing to the door and opening it.

It was Spiro. He was holding a delicately balanced tower of dishes with an ease that would have put a waiter to shame, but the tower almost collapsed when he saw who had opened the door. "Redfield!" he exclaimed, sounding anything but pleased.

"Skouras," acknowledged Geoffrey, in an equally unfriendly tone. The two men eyed each other like dogs ready to circle.

"May I enter?" Spiro inquired. "I have brought Miss Stewart her clothes and some dinner." Geoffrey reluctantly moved out of the way, and Spiro crossed to the table, setting the dishes down and laying my laundered clothes to one side. "I did not realize, Redfield, that you and Christine were acquainted."

"We're not," Geoffrey replied in clipped tones. "I simply dropped by to thank her for saving Michael's life."

"Very proper. Though I wonder how you knew where to find her."

"Mmmm," I interrupted. "That food smells wonderful."

"Yes, I think you will enjoy it," Spiro replied without shifting his attention from Geoffrey. "Demetra cooked several of the dishes herself, and she is an excellent cook."

"Well then, we shouldn't let it get cold, should we?" I said, struggling to my feet. "There are only the two chairs, but I can sit on the bed."

"No," Geoffrey said sharply, "there's no need; I won't be staying. I've taken up too much of your time as it is." He took my hand in his, and the warmth of his fingers contrasted sharply with the coolness of his voice as he said goodbye. As he strode out the door, I wondered if I would ever see him again.

After Geoffrey had gone, Spiro said little. He busied himself getting everything ready for us to eat. It wasn't until we were well into the second course, delicately seasoned chicken with creamy *pastitsio*, that he finally brought up the subject of Geoffrey's visit.

"I hope he did not bother you?" he asked. "I wish I had been here when he first arrived."

"It was okay. We just talked a little."

"What did he want?"

I hesitated, unable to come up with a ready answer. "I don't really know."

Spiro flashed me a skeptical look, but said nothing. For a few minutes we ate in silence, then he asked, "Did Redfield speak of the morning's events?"

"He mentioned them," I replied reluctantly.

"What did he say?"

"Spiro, do you mind if we don't talk about him or what happened this morning anymore?"

His dark brown eyes regarded me searchingly for a moment, then he said, "Of course. I understand. You have had a frightening experience, and now you wish to forget."

I wasn't sure which he considered the frightening experience: my near brush with death or my encounter with Geoffrey, but I was grateful he seemed willing to drop both subjects.

"You need something to take your mind from these things," he said, opening the door that led out to the balcony. "The night is beautiful. Come, breathe some of the fresh air." He took my hand and led me outside.

It was dark and the air was cool. The moon, large and full, spilled light onto the tile roofs of the town and into the fuzzy darkness of the trees. A light breeze carried the tang of wild rosemary. I leaned against the railing, enjoying the feel of the cold metal against my skin. "It's a lovely view," I said.

"Yes," he agreed, "the light from the moon makes many things beautiful." He smiled and ran a hand up my arm. "A beautiful night...." The hand slipped back and stroked my hair. ". . . a beautiful woman." His voice was low, seductive, oddly mesmerizing. He leaned forward to kiss me.

He kissed well, he kissed very well. He was, indeed, an expert. Which is perhaps why it took him by surprise when I pulled away after it was over.

"Christine?"

"Spiro, I think we should call it a night."

"You are tired?"

He'd been kind to me and I didn't want to insult him. "Yes."

Again he regarded me with those dark, unfathomable eyes. "It is understandable. You have done a great deal today."

For some reason, his words left me unsettled. We moved back into the light of the room and he began quickly gathering up plates. When he was ready to leave, I thanked him for the dinner.

"It was my pleasure," he replied. "I hope tomorrow you will feel better."

"Me, too," I said, holding out my hand.

He took it and held it. "Do not dwell too much on what has happened. It is best to forget and continue with your holiday. When you are better, I will take you around the island and show you the things the tourists do not usually see."

"Do you think we couldtake Michael with us?"

His expression grew wary. "I do not know. I would need to discuss it with Demetra, and unfortunately…." He threw up his hands and shrugged.

"I know. She trusts me about as far as she can throw me."

"I beg your pardon?"

"It's an expression. It means your sister doesn't trust me at all."

"Yes, I'm afraid that is true."

"Why is she so anxious to keep custody of Michael? If he's not really her son—"

Spiro's handsome face suddenly lost its charming amiability. "Goodnight, Christine," he said, starting for the door.

"Wait, Spiro, I didn't mean—"

He paused and turned back. "Demetra clings to the boy, because he is all that is left of her dead husband. William Redfield gave her no child of her own, you see."

I bit my lip in chagrin. "I'm sorry."

"I, too, am sorry. Now I should leave you to your sleep."

"Goodnight, Spiro."

"*Kalinykta*, Christine." He stepped closer. "May I offer you some advice?"

"What?"

"Do not believe everything Redfield tells you. He is different from his late brother in many ways, but in one respect he is the same. When he wants a thing, he will do anything to get it." He reached up and touched the bandage on my cheek. "And I do mean anything, Christine."

THREE

I woke the next morning to find the room filled with sunshine. The brightness of the light and the wispy memory of the pleasant dream I'd been having filled me with a sense of well-being.

Unfortunately, the feeling quickly vanished as I remembered the events of the previous day and started to feel my aches and pains. I had never been so stiff and sore. I lay there for some time trying to summon the will to move. I had just begun inching one leg toward the edge of the bed when someone knocked softly at my door. Then a key rattled in the lock and the door opened.

"*Kalimera!*" cried Kyria Andriatsis, the grandmother and matriarch of the family that owned the hotel. As she pushed the door open with her hip, I could see she carried a large tray loaded with food.

"*Kalimera*, Kyria," I said, sliding out of bed, "and thank you, but I didn't order breakfast."

"Why, you speak Greek!" she exclaimed. "My son didn't tell me." She carried the tray over to the small table and set it down. "I am glad, because my English is not so good."

The food looked and smelled heavenly, but I was certain it was meant for someone else. "Kyria, I'm afraid there must be some mistake—"

"No mistake. Your young man thought you could use a good breakfast, and I have cooked you a very good breakfast."

"My young man?"

She nodded, then eyed me up and down, her dark eyes reminding me of the raisin eyes of gingerbread men. "I have just the lotion for those scrapes."

"But Kyria—"

She smiled and shook her head. "Enough talk, you must eat. While the food is hot. *Ella*," she said, reaching out a brown hand to guide me. "Come, sit down."

I did as I was told. She arranged the chair at the small table so I faced the sliding glass door that opened out on the balcony. Then she drew back the curtains and slid open the door, revealing a view that was remarkably different in the daylight. The tile roofs, which had appeared a cold beige in the moonlight, now glowed a warm red in the sun. The trees, no longer nebulous pools of darkness, unfurled like green flags against the turquoise sky. Suddenly, the air was filled with the peal of church bells.

"Saint Spiridon's," she said in answer to my questioning look.

I nodded. I had visited the church honoring the island's patron saint my first day on Corfu.

"Now eat, before it gets cold!" she chided, heading for the door. "I'll come back for the dishes later."

It was a delicious omelette, filled with feta cheese and sweet onions. The eggs tasted hen-fresh, and the bread was still warm from the oven. There was sugar for the coffee, and even—miracle of miracles—cream, and a bowl of delicious goat's milk yogurt topped with dark honey.

When I'd finished eating, I sat back in my chair, patted my full but happy stomach, and looked out at the beautiful day. My mood was definitely improving, and my sore arms, stiff neck, and aching cheek receded to the background. Even the finicky shower seemed to cooperate to keep my spirits high. The hot water was actually hot, and the pressure remained strong, helping to massage out the nastier kinks in my neck and shoulders.

The only check to my improved spirits was the shock of removing the wet bandage from my cheek and staring at the ragged wound and small black stitches in the mirror. It looked terrible, but I resolutely told myself that it would soon look better.

I had thought Kyria Andriatsis might come to pick up the breakfast dishes while I was in the shower, but they were still sitting on the table when I got out. I was not surprised, then, when I heard a knock at the door. I dropped my towel on the bed, pulled on my robe, and went to open it for her.

"Oh, it's you!" I exclaimed foolishly, as I saw who was standing there. My robe started slipping open, and I clutched it closed. "I was expecting—"

"I can imagine who you were expecting," Geoffrey interrupted coolly, "dressed like that. Didn't he stay to breakfast?"

Irritated now, I asked, "Did you have some reason for coming by, or were you just in the mood to be rude to someone?"

He didn't answer, but stood there staring at my face. I'd forgotten the bandage was gone. "Your cheek!" he exclaimed.

I clapped my hand over it and turned away. "Sorry. I wasn't expecting visitors. I haven't had time to bandage it up again yet."

He circled around me and gently pulled my hand down from my face. "I hadn't realized how badly you were hurt, that's all."

"Why are you here?" I demanded, unnerved by his touch.

He let go of my hand and stepped back. "I was hoping I might take you sightseeing. There's something important I think you ought to see."

"Thank you, but I don't feel like playing tourist today."

He started to say something, then seemed to change his mind. Finally he said incongruously, "I suppose you plan to see Spiro Skouras again?"

The sudden switch of subject caught me off balance. "I—I don't know. What business is it of yours, anyway?"

"Skouras can be—" he stopped, frowned, and began again. "Some women find him attractive—"

"Most women, I would think."

His mouth tightened. "I thought you intelligent enough not to judge solely by outward appearances."

I had no real interest in Spiro, but I wasn't about to admit that to him. "Oh, he's not just a pretty face. He's also charming, and has treated me with courtesy and consideration, which is more than I can say for you."

"I understand you have a thoroughly low opinion of me," he snapped. "You've made that abundantly clear. However, I feel an obligation to warn you of the danger you're in."

"Danger?" I exclaimed. "What are you talking about?"

His gaze fixed on my cheek. "Your accident yesterday was no accident."

I stared at him. "That's crazy."

"Is it?"

"Yes!"

"Then why did that stone block fall when it did?" he asked.

"Who knows? The whole place is crumbling to pieces. Probably the thing's been ready to fall for years and it just happened to go at the wrong time."

He shook his head. "No, it was the right time—for someone. If you hadn't looked up when you did...." He allowed the implication to sink in.

"That's crazy," I repeated, but this time I felt a shiver of doubt.

"Come with me, and I'll show you it's not."

"I think I'd rather stay here."

He regarded me intently. "Very well, but promise me you'll steer clear of Skouras—and Michael."

A sudden suspicion filled me. "Is that what this is all about: my keeping away from your nephew? What are you afraid of? That I might somehow get in the way of your lovely custody battle?"

"What I'm afraid of," he retorted angrily, "is that in your stubborn ignorance you may plunge into a situation you don't understand and get yourself hurt or even killed."

I turned my back on him. Pulling my robe more tightly about me, I retreated toward the window and the reassuringly picturesque view of Corfu Town. "I can take care of myself."

He followed me and swung me around to face him. "Can you?" he demanded. "This time it was only a cut cheek. What if you're not so lucky next time?"

"If I'm in some kind of danger, why should I trust you?"

"Perhaps the safest thing would be for you not to trust any of us, to leave Corfu and this whole business behind you."

I thought about it. He was right. If there was any risk, the sensible thing to do was to stay out of the whole thing, go on with my life as if nothing had happened, pretend I'd never met these people, and forget them as soon as I could.

The only problem was: some of them I didn't want to forget.

"I'm probably going to regret this," I said, "but all right, you've piqued my interest. I'll look at what you have to show me."

"Good," he said. But his expression was unreadable, and I couldn't tell if he was pleased with my decision or disappointed.

I warned Geoffrey that it would take me some time to get dressed. He told me he'd be back in an hour.

It took me almost the entire time to ease my sore body into clothes, rebandage my cheek with some gauze I'd been foresighted enough to include in my makeshift first-aid kit, and comb and dry my unruly hair. I surveyed the results of my labors in the long, narrow mirror on the wall with mixed feelings.

I had decided to wear a sky blue halter dress I'd bought in Athens, partially because the color cheered me, but mostly because it was the only dress I had that I could wear without a bra (sore as I was, maneuvering on a bra was impossible.) As I looked in the mirror, I was pleased with how the dress looked on me, but neither the dress nor my hair, which for once was cooperating and drying in symmetric waves around my face, could make the large white bandage on my cheek look less obvious. I thought about the scar I might have and contemplated a career as a lady pirate. Perhaps it was time to go shopping for a parrot.

Such musings were interrupted by a knock at the door. I went to answer it half-expecting, after my recent experiences, to find some new and unexpected visitor on my doorstep, but it was only Geoffrey. Perhaps he was expecting someone else, too, for he stared at me with such a look of surprise that I nervously looked down. "What is it?" I said. "Is something wrong with my dress?"

"Quite the contrary," he said, and for a moment the gleam was back in his eyes. Then he looked away. "Shall we be going?"

I grabbed my purse and key. "I don't suppose you want to tell me where we're going?"

"I thought you might already have guessed."

"The Old Fort?"

He nodded. "As I said, there's something there I think you ought to see."

"That's what I thought yesterday," I quipped, closing the door, "and look where it got me."

Geoffrey was in a pensive mood during the taxi ride over. He spoke only a few words of instruction to the driver and to me not at all. He paid the driver silently, but apparently tipped him well, for as Geoffrey helped me out of the car, the driver wished us happiness and many sons.

Geoffrey flushed and strode quickly away. I struggled to catch up, and reluctantly he slowed his long stride to match mine as we crossed the Contrafossa and wound our way up the hill. We climbed to the lighthouse and the remnants of the old castle that had been converted to a school for Greek army officers during World War II. It was empty now, abandoned to tourists. We passed through deteriorating rooms with mustard-colored walls built upon ruins seven hundred years old. We turned down a hallway decorated with murals depicting the martial virtues, and then the mustard colored walls gave way to a damp stone tunnel.

"Where are we going?" I asked my silent companion.

"I told you I had something to show you—watch your head!"

I ducked to avoid an overhang of porous rock. A large, cold drop of water splashed down the back of my neck. "But Michael and I didn't come this way yesterday," I said.

"I suspected you hadn't." We reached a point where the tunnel became quite dark, and he took my hand. "Careful, we'll be rounding a corner—here." He guided me to the left. Suddenly there was more light, and in the distance I could see a small rectangle of sky.

"You certainly know your way around this place," I said. It wasn't a fact that made me altogether easy.

"My family used to summer on Corfu when I was a boy. My brother was older, and preferred not to have me follow him about, so whenever I could get away, I came here and explored. It's changed a little over the years, but not much."

"And Michael?"

"I used to tell him stories about the place when I visited him at school. Then my brother decided to reinstate the tradition last year and summer here with his family. William was still too busy to be bothered with little boys, so Michael spent a great deal of the summer here, by himself, exploring."

"Well," I said, "he certainly knows it inside out. He gave me quite a history lesson yesterday, though we didn't come this far." I looked up, noticing a series of large, irregular holes in the stone overhead. "What on earth are those for?"

Geoffrey grinned and shook his head. "You won't like it."

"What's that supposed to mean?"

"Just that I think you'd be happier not knowing."

His amused tone set my hackles up. "You certainly enjoy making snap judgments about people," I said, pulling my arm free of his. "And deciding what is and is not good for them. No wonder you want custody of Michael. A lonely little boy you can boss around. Perfect. Just ignore that a messy custody battle will probably be pure hell for him."

"You're quite right," Geoffrey said with steely politeness, "it's not my place to decide what you should and should not know. Those holes were part of the defenses of the fort. If invaders managed to scale the walls and storm the castle, the fort's defenders would pour boiling oil and pitch through those holes onto the intruders, burning them quite hideously."

I looked up and shivered. I felt deflated after my tirade and suddenly wished I hadn't demanded to know.

"Regarding your other point," he continued icily, "whether I choose to sue Demetra for custody of Michael or not is none of your bloody business, and I would appreciate it if, in future, you kept your views on the matter to yourself."

I could think of nothing sufficiently withering to reply, so I plunged forward, scraping my arm on the sponge-like black rock that formed the walls of the tunnel. Continuing on with more caution, I made my way out to the open air.

I emerged on a high rampart. I crossed to the northern wall of it and stared out across the water at the town, which looked bleached and unfamiliar in the brilliant sunlight. Not unfamiliar enough, however. Déjà vu sent a shiver through me. I turned my back on the town and looked out toward the stretch of sea that separates Corfu from the Greek mainland. Out of the corner of my eye, I saw Geoffrey emerge from the tunnel, but I ignored him.

Instead, I concentrated on a pair of birds soaring and swooping over the water in an intricately choreographed dance. Suddenly they separated, flying up and away from each other before turning and hurtling at each other with single-minded abandon. They locked in a mating embrace and began tumbling toward the sea. I ran toward the southern wall to see if they would part in time.

Then someone was running after me. My arm was seized, and I struggled to break free. "I'm not trying to hurt you!" Geoffrey yelled as I turned and kicked him in the shins. I tried to twist away, but only managed to move a few steps backward. The rough stone of the wall pressed into my back, and I leaned against it, hoping to gain enough leverage to push him away with my feet.

He shouted something and grabbed me around the waist. There was a horrible grating sound, then the stone behind me slid away with a sickening lurch. I screamed, and Geoffrey pulled me toward him. From somewhere below came a loud crash. I turned in the safe circle of his arms and looked back at the wall. Two large blocks were missing. "Are they all loose?" I demanded hoarsely.

"No," he replied, his voice ragged. "Just the two."

"The two?" I repeated, at a loss. My head felt clogged, as if all my thoughts had tangled together in a single mass, like a knotted ball of string.

"The two over the bench." His arms fell away and he took a step back. "They were loosened beforehand—with a tire iron, I think."

I stared down at where he was pointing, and ran a hand across the newly exposed stone. There it was: a long, thin groove running down the center. I ran my fingertips across the place where the second block had stood and found a twin groove there. I moved to the left, past the gap, and tested the wall. It felt solid. Carefully, I leaned over to take a look, and I didn't struggle when Geoffrey reached out to brace me.

Several hundred feet below us was the Chapel of St. George. To its left, and directly beneath the gap in the wall, was an area temporarily roped off from visitors. In the center of the roped off area was a splintered bench covered with broken stone.

"I'm sorry," I murmured as I stepped back. "I guess I owe you an apology—and a thank-you for saving my life."

"No need," he said, bending over and gingerly rubbing his leg. "I was partially to blame. I should have warned you that the block was loose." He grimaced as he straightened up.

"Why *didn't* you warn me?" I demanded.

His gaze locked with mine. "I had to find out how much you knew."

"Oh, I see. If I fell over the wall and was killed, then you would know you could trust me?"

"I didn't let you fall over, did I?" he exclaimed. "Despite, I might add, being pummeled and kicked by the closest thing to a she-donkey I ever hope to meet." He pointedly massaged his left arm where I'd punched him.

"It was your own fault," I said "If you hadn't jumped on me like some kind of maniac—"

"Well, if *you* hadn't hurled yourself at that wall like a crazy fool—"

We glared at each other for about ten seconds. Then the edge of my mouth began to quiver. I thought I saw his lower lip give an answering tremor, but he quickly tightened his mouth to cover it. I tried to do the same, but the ridiculous image of myself as a donkey kicking wildly in all directions while Geoffrey jumped nimbly back and forth across my back filled my mind and sabotaged my best efforts to stay angry.

Giggles rushed up my throat like bubbling champagne, but it wasn't my laughter that suddenly erupted like a geyser near my ear. Startled, I looked up at Geoffrey's grinning face and all the tension of the last twenty-four hours seemed to drain away. Without thought I stepped into his arms. Just as naturally, he drew me close and rocked me to the rhythm of our shared laughter.

Then, just as quickly as it had come, the laughter subsided, and I realized I was standing there with my eyes closed and my cheek pressed against his chest. I thought I felt his lips brush against my hair, but I must have imagined it, for when I finally found the courage to look up, he was gazing pensively into the distance. He looked like a man waiting patiently to be released. Mortified to realize how tightly I was clinging to him, I jerked backwards and turned away so I wouldn't have to meet his gaze.

"Perhaps we should start back down," he said quietly behind me.

"Sure," I agreed, hoping my voice didn't sound as shaken as I felt.

As we descended, I noticed we were taking a different route than we had taken up. So I wasn't all that surprised when we turned a bend and came out onto a rather overgrown portico overlooking St. George's. As we climbed down some mossy steps and rounded the church, I hesitated. I wasn't sure I wanted to see this. Geoffrey took my hand and led me up to the ropes. Then all I could do was stare.

The second block had fallen slightly to the right of what remained of the broken bench. It hadn't split apart into as many pieces as the first one had, but instead had embedded itself into the hard earth almost six inches deep.

"I don't understand," I murmured. "Why?"

Geoffrey was silent.

My mind rebelled against the implications. "I don't suppose it could have been a mistake, or the result of some stupid prank?"

"A rather deadly lark, wouldn't you say?"

"You're right. Someone would have to be crazy—" I looked up in sudden hope. "Wait, that could be it! Some nutcase—"

"What? Was wandering about the place with a tire iron ready to hand just in case he came upon an opportunity for mischief?"

"All right," I said. "What's your explanation?"

"I think the blocks were loosened ahead of time, perhaps after dark. There's a Sound and Light show held here in the evenings. He could have come the night before—"

"Or she," I added.

"I doubt a woman could have done it," he said.

"Why not? Granted, she'd have to be strong, but not that strong. That mortar crumbles to the touch. She could have loosened the blocks beforehand, left the crowbar hidden somewhere nearby, and then—when the time was right—used it to lever the block from the wall."

"You paint a very clear picture of how it was done," he said.

"Of how it might have been done. You don't have to look at me that way. In case you've forgotten, I was the target of that rather heavy gift from the sky!"

"I hadn't forgotten," he assured me quietly.

I frowned. "The thing that still doesn't make sense to me is how anyone, man or woman, could have known that Michael and I were going to be sitting on that bench yesterday morning."

Geoffrey stared up at the rampart high above us. "I don't know how anyone could have known you were going to be there, but at least two people knew Michael would be."

"But that's impossible! It was pure chance Michael and I sat down there."

"No, it wasn't."

"Yes, it was!" I exclaimed. Then I remembered. Michael leading us to the bench, suggesting it would be a good place to rest. Michael looking startled when I mentioned the time. Michael asking to be left alone. I said slowly, "That was where you planned to meet him."

"Yes."

"And the person who phoned and told you he was in the hospital—"

Geoffrey nodded grimly. "Expected Michael to be sitting on that bench at ten o'clock. Alone."

Four

There was a note from Lieutenant Mavros of the Corfu Police waiting for me when I returned to my hotel. Kyria Andriatsis looked both curious and concerned as she handed it to me, but my emotion upon receiving it was a sort of spiteful satisfaction. You see, Geoffrey had just warned me off.

Now I'm not a particularly reckless person. My imagination is too vivid and my confidence in fate too tenuous to be an enthusiastic risk-taker. But this situation was different. Geoffrey had convinced me that someone had tried to kill me. No one could expect me to walk away from that.

No one, that is, except Geoffrey.

"What do you mean, I'm to stay out of it?" I'd demanded during our taxi ride back to the Hotel Kerkyra. "First, you go out of your way to prove to me that someone tried to murder me. Then you turn around and advise me not to bother my little head about it."

"You weren't the intended victim," Geoffrey said, his voice thick with exasperation. "You were simply incidental—someone in the wrong place at the wrong time."

"Why, thank you. That makes me feel so much better."

A muscle in his cheek twitched. "What I'm trying to explain to you is that if you keep out of the way, you'll be safe. Whoever did this has no quarrel with you—"

"And what makes you so certain Michael was the target? Perhaps someone is after me, and Michael was the one in the wrong place at the wrong time."

His eyebrows flew up in disbelief. "I suppose you're going to tell me you're being chased by a jealous lover?"

"It's possible," I said airily, irritated by his tone. "Maybe I should ask Spiro if I can hide out in that villa of his."

As I knew it would, the mention of Spiro sent Geoffrey's temper flaring. "Ithaki belongs to Michael," he snapped. "And if after all I've shown you today, you could be such a fool as to—"

"My point is," I interrupted, "regardless of whether I was attacked on purpose or just as an afterthought, I'm not about to ignore the fact. I think we should go to the police."

"I've already been," he said heavily. "I went first thing this morning, and was directed to a Lieutenant Mavros. He listened very politely to my story, then dismissed me, saying that while he thought I possessed an excellent imagination, he would prefer it if, in future, I kept the exercise of it to myself."

"In that case, what are we going to do?" I demanded.

"*We* are not going to do anything. *You* are going to finish up your holiday and then go home and forget any of this ever happened."

I didn't reply. There was nothing to say. I wasn't about to forget being nearly squashed by a large piece of Byzantine rock, but arguing with him was getting me nowhere. If the police weren't going to help, then I had to do some serious thinking about what to do next.

When we arrived at the Hotel Kerkyra, Geoffrey walked around to open my door. "So you'll stay out of it, Christine?" he asked as he took my arm and helped me out of the car. His hand slid down to grip my own. "You'll stay away from Ithaki and all its occupants?"

"If you were so anxious for me to bow out and disappear, why did you drag me back to the Old Fort in the first place? I believed what happened was an accident. I wasn't planning to make waves."

"I had my reasons."

"Which were?"

He hesitated for a moment and then said quietly, "You seemed interested in Spiro. I thought you ought to know how dangerous that interest might be."

I stared at him. "You think *Spiro* is the one who attacked us?"

"I believe it's a distinct possibility."

"I know you don't like the man, but attempted murder? And of a boy in his sister's care? What proof do you have?"

He shook his head grimly. "No proof. Just a gut feeling. Which is why I have my hands full making sure Michael remains safe. I can't be worrying about you as well."

He squeezed my hand for emphasis, but apparently the gesture was an unconscious one. When I made a small sound of protest, he looked down in surprise, as if he'd forgotten that he held it. "Did I hurt you?" he murmured, lifting my hand to his mouth and brushing his lips apologetically across my fingers.

Mutely, I shook my head.

He turned my hand over and gazed at my palm. Slowly he began to run his thumb over it in small, caressing circles that sent ripples of pleasure tingling up my arm. "Christine," he said softly, withdrawing his thumb and pressing a kiss there, "please, promise me you'll forget about all this and go home."

"I can't forget—even if I wanted to."

He drew back at that. Without another word he climbed into the taxi and told the driver to go. I watched the grey Mercedes disappear down the narrow street. Then, pressing my palm to my cheek, I went inside the hotel.

The note from Lieutenant Mavros was brief and to the point. He was most anxious to speak to me about a certain unfortunate incident, and could I please come by to see him as soon as possible? He greatly appreciated my assistance, and hoped that he was not inconveniencing me.

This last made me smile. I didn't plan to tell the lieutenant just how very convenient his invitation was, but I felt a wave of relief. The police were going to investigate after all. I was off the hook. For all my brave words to Geoffrey, I had no idea how to safely go about ferreting out an attempted murderer, and I was quite happy to leave the job to the police.

Five minutes into my interview with Lieutenant Mavros I realized my relief had been premature.

I'd arrived at the police station without mishap and had

informed the gruff officer at the front desk who I was and why I was there. Mention of Lieutenant Mavros's name had galvanized the man into action, and I was quickly passed from one policeman to another like a file urgently needed yesterday. Soon I stood outside the lieutenant's office, waiting as the sergeant who had escorted me the last leg of the relay went in and announced me.

The door to the office opened. Lieutenant Mavros motioned me in with a bow of his head and a wave of his hand. He was younger than I expected, somewhere in his mid-thirties. His features were blunt and plain, but his blue eyes were intelligent and his manner was both polite and intimidating.

I sat down in a green leather chair. The room was sparsely furnished, but didn't share the institutional ugliness of the other rooms I'd passed through. The floor was bare, but it was hardwood, not linoleum, and the antique rosewood desk the lieutenant returned to was delicately carved and beautiful.

"Thank you for coming, Miss Stewart. I apologize for the interruption to your vacation, but I felt it necessary to speak with you in person about this unfortunate incident. I will be grateful for any help you can give to us in our investigation."

"I'll be happy to help in any way I can," I assured him.

He nodded. "Thank you. Now when Spiro Skouras telephoned me yesterday afternoon—"

"Mr. Skouras called you?" I exclaimed. "Yesterday?"

"Yes. You seem surprised." He spoke casually, but his eyes were alert and curious.

"He just never mentioned it to me. About going to the police, I mean."

"I doubt he considered calling me as 'going to the police,'" the lieutenant explained drily. "Spiro and I have known each other since we were children. He merely called to tell me of the accident so someone could be sent to the *Paleon Frourion* to rope off the area and insure no one else would be harmed."

"I see," I said, dismayed to learn he and Spiro were such old friends. "If Mr. Skouras's contact with you was so casual, what made you decide you needed to see me?"

Something flickered across the policeman's face. "This morning I received a visit from Geoffrey Redfield."

I nodded in relief. "Yes, he mentioned he'd been to see you."

"When was this?" he asked, watching me closely.

"This morning," I said. "Sometime after he saw you. He came by my hotel. He wanted to show me evidence that our accident yesterday might not have been an accident after all."

The policeman's mouth twitched derisively. "The loose stone, the groove in the mortar?"

"Yes. You don't find them convincing?"

He closed his eyes and shook his head, as if dismissing the answer of a backward student. "As evidence, they are suggestive, perhaps. Nothing more."

"But isn't it your responsibility to investigate all possibilities, even the ones you consider unlikely?"

He steepled his fingers together and pressed them against his lips. "Yes, Miss Stewart. That is why you are here."

I swallowed the rebuke and said quietly, "What do you want to know?"

"Let us begin at the beginning. Tell me your version of yesterday's events."

I told him everything. He listened without interruption, and when I'd finished, his only question was, "Did you not wonder why young Redfield was so determined to remain at the *Paleon Frourion* until ten o'clock?"

"No, it didn't occur to me to wonder about it." I tried to keep my voice casual, but I was shaken to realize Geoffrey hadn't told the policeman of his plans to meet Michael.

"Really, Miss Stewart? You surprise me. You seem a very astute woman. Don't you find it curious now?"

"Perhaps."

He leaned back in his chair. "Was anyone aware that you were going to the *Paleon Frourion* yesterday morning?"

Reluctantly I said, "No."

"So it is unlikely anyone wishing to harm you could have known that you would be sitting on that bench?"

"I suppose that's true."

"But, of course, you were not sitting there alone, were you?"

"No."

"You were in the company of young Redfield."

"Yes."

"So if there truly was an attack, and if the attack was not aimed at you...." His voice trailed off, and he gazed at me expectantly.

"Then it was probably aimed at Michael," I finished.

He nodded, as if acknowledging that this was a possibility to be considered, instead of the conclusion he'd been pushing me toward all along. "So we must look to see who knew the boy would be sitting on that bench at that hour."

Here it comes, I thought.

"Would it surprise you to learn that the boy went to the *Paleon Frourion* to meet with someone in secret, and that this meeting was supposed to take place at ten o'clock?" The expression in his blue eyes had suddenly grown hard.

I hesitated for a moment. "Whom was he going to meet?"

"I hoped you might be able to tell me."

I hesitated again and then said, "I'm sorry. I can't help you."

"Cannot, or will not?"

"Have you asked Michael about it?"

"Yes, and the boy refuses to answer. The meeting was not, by any chance, with you?"

"No," I answered. "Michael is adorable, but I'm a bit old for him. His rendezvous must have been with someone else."

The policeman was not amused. "As of this moment, Miss Stewart, I still classify the events of yesterday as an accident. If I change my mind, however," he said, looking me straight in the eye, "I will insist on serious answers to my questions." He stood up. "Do you understand?"

"Yes, Lieutenant. I understand perfectly."

"Good, then you may consider this interview over." He crossed to my chair to escort me out.

I remained seated. "May I ask a question before I go?"

His expression hovered between irritation and curiosity. "What?"

"If Michael isn't talking, how did you find out about the meeting?"

He gave me a long look and then said, "Spiro's sister also visited me this morning. It seems the maid who looks after the boy found a note hidden in his room listing the time and place of the rendezvous. She gave the note to Mrs. Redfield, and Mrs.

Redfield gave it to me."

"And when did the maid find the note?" I asked.

"What does that matter?"

"You surprise me, Lieutenant. You seem a very astute police-man. If the note was found yesterday morning, then two people besides the person Michael went to the Old Fort to meet knew he was going to be on that bench at ten o'clock: the maid and Mrs. Redfield."

He regarded me gravely for a moment and then shrugged. "I suppose that is true. And now, Miss Stewart, I am afraid I have another appointment. You will excuse me?" He crossed to the door and opened it. I stood up to leave.

"Lieutenant, I hope it's occurred to you that if what hap-pened yesterday wasn't an accident, Michael Redfield may still be in danger."

His plain face looked troubled. "I am quite aware of that possibility," he said. "Good day."

The door closed behind me, filling me with a profound sense of frustration. So much for the police taking over.

I gazed up and down the deserted hallway. In vain I tried to remember which way I'd come in. I was beginning to contem-plate the irritating prospect of having to ask Lieutenant Mavros for directions, when a tall man with blond hair, a beautifully tai-lored suit, and an air of quiet authority turned the corner and came walking down the hall toward me. Something in his man-ner tempted me to pour out all my woes to him, but in the end I settled for asking him directions.

"*Parakalo, kyrie*—" I began.

"*Den ... mylao ... Ellinika*," he replied, with an apologetic shake of his head. "I'm afraid I don't speak Greek," he repeated in English.

"Oh, sorry," I apologized, switching to English myself. "I was just wondering if you could give me directions out of here."

He had an aristocratic face and the meticulous grooming of a diplomat, but his hazel eyes were friendly and the grin he flashed me put me immediately at ease. "It is a bit of a maze, isn't it? I don't know about directions, but I think I might be able to lead you out the way I came in. Will that do?"

I assured him it would. "I hope I'm not taking you away

from anything important," I said, as we wound our way back through the labyrinthine corridors.

"Not to worry. The matter's not urgent as far as I can tell, only odd." We walked some way before he added, more to himself than to me, "Yes, decidedly odd. Still, accidents do happen."

"Accidents?" I said sharply.

He flashed me a curious look, then explained, "A client of mine, the son of an old friend, had a mishap yesterday. I was on my way to speak to the constable in charge of the matter when I met you."

We emerged out into the lobby. "This client of yours," I said, "he doesn't happen to be a boy of nine or ten?"

I suddenly had his full attention. "He's a lad of nine."

"And his name is Michael Redfield?"

"It is," he replied, "though I'm at a loss to explain how you come to know that, Miss—"

"Stewart. Christine Stewart."

His eyes widened. "What a coincidence."

"Not as much as you might think, Mr.—"

"I'm Robert Humphreys," he said, holding out his hand to me. I took it, enjoying the cool firmness of his clasp.

"Who is the policeman you were on your way to see?" I asked.

He pulled out a thin leather portfolio from the inside pocket of his coat and opened it. "Hmmm. A Lieutenant Mavros." He looked up and nodded. "Ah, I see. I suppose you had just finished with him?"

"I don't know if I'd finished with him," I said with a grimace. "But, yes, he had definitely finished with me."

He gave me a considering look. "Miss Stewart, do you think we could go somewhere and talk? I found Mrs. Redfield's narrative a bit difficult to follow, and I'd appreciate hearing a clearer account of what occurred yesterday before I speak with the lieutenant myself."

We stopped for coffee at a nearby café, or rather, I had coffee and he had tea. Greeks make good coffee and lousy tea, but Robert Humphreys expressed neither surprise nor disappointment when he poured the weak brown liquid from a small, stainless steel teapot. He must have noticed my questioning look, because he shrugged ruefully and explained, "I've grown accustomed to what passes for tea here."

"Have you been on Corfu long?" I asked.

He shook his head. "I arrived today. But I've visited before, and as a boy I spent several summers here with the Redfields at Ithaki."

"I suppose you flew in after you heard about the accident?"

"No," he said, with a slight frown, "actually I came because there were some papers I needed signed by Michael's stepmother. I only learned about his close call after I arrived at Ithaki. I asked to see Michael and was told he didn't feel up to a visit. That's when Demetra Redfield told me what happened yesterday."

I pressed my hands flat against the cool metal of the table. "I can imagine what she said about my part in it all."

He smiled reassuringly. "Don't worry. I'm quite aware of her tendency toward the dramatic. Believe me, I take everything she says with a rather large pinch of salt. Which reminds me—" he raised his hand to flag down a waiter, "I've changed my mind about the tea. It tastes as if it's been brewed in sea water."

The waiter arrived, and Robert ordered us baklava and two more coffees. Then he settled himself to listen and said, "Now, if you wouldn't mind, I'd like to hear your version of events."

I told him everything I'd told Lieutenant Mavros. When I'd finished, his expression was somber. "It seems Michael is quite lucky you happened along."

"That's what worries me."

"I beg your pardon?" he said.

"Have you spoken to Michael's uncle?"

"Geoffrey?" he exclaimed, sounding puzzled. "No, not yet."

"Well I think you ought to, and soon. You see, he doesn't believe that what happened yesterday was an accident."

He swore softly under his breath. "Not again!"

The waiter picked that moment to appear with our coffee and baklava, so I had to wait until the waiter had gone to ask him what he meant.

Reluctantly, he explained, "Geoffrey's brother was killed in a car crash two months ago. William was driving in a thick fog and went over a cliff. A passing bicyclist saw the accident and reported it, but by the time they retrieved the car, William was dead."

Robert sighed. "Geoffrey did not handle the news well. I think the senselessness of it all was hard for him to bear. He refused to accept the inquest's verdict of accidental death and instead insisted foul play was involved.

"He kept after the police, and he even engaged a private detective, but neither found any evidence to substantiate his suspicions. Eventually, he shifted his attention from William's death to Michael's future. I took that as a hopeful sign. But now...." His voice trailed off.

I'd lost my appetite for the baklava, which was just as well; I'd nervously shredded it to honey-clumped bits listening to him describe Geoffrey's reaction to his brother's death.

"Christine, is there any evidence that your mishap yesterday wasn't an accident?" Robert asked, a frown of concern on his face. "Did you see or hear anything that supports the idea of foul play?"

I admitted I hadn't, but told him about Geoffrey finding the loose block and grooves in the mortar.

"What did the lieutenant have to say about that?"

"He didn't find it convincing," I admitted. "He said it was 'suggestive, nothing more.'"

He frowned. "I'm afraid I'm inclined to agree with him," he said, "especially since I can't see what possible motive there could have been for a deliberate attack. You don't seem a woman likely to generate enemies."

"Geoffrey thinks whoever did this was after Michael."

His hazel eyes looked troubled. "I see."

"I know, I find it hard to believe, too," I said. "Still, let's just say for the sake of argument that someone is trying to kill Michael. Well then, there has to be a reason. Perhaps if we could figure out what the motive is—"

"But that's just it. There isn't any motive—at least, not for anyone who counts."

"What about the money Michael inherited from his father?" I asked. "If Michael dies, does it revert back to his father's estate?"

His sandy eyebrows fluttered upwards. "You mean does Demetra Redfield suddenly become a multi-millionaire?"

I nodded slowly. "Thirty million pounds could be a pretty strong motive for murder."

"It could," he agreed quietly, "but I'm afraid you have it wrong. Michael's money wouldn't revert to his father's estate. Though in trust, it belongs to Michael and in the event of his death would pass to his heir."

A cool breeze fluttered against my skin and caused me to shiver. "Go on."

"Michael is a minor—the legal term is infant—and cannot make a will. Therefore, if he dies before reaching his majority, he would die intestate, and the entire fortune he received from his father would go to his closest living blood relative."

"But isn't that—"

He nodded. "Yes, Geoffrey. So you see, the one person who might have had a reason for staging yesterday's accident is the very same person trying to convince everyone it wasn't an accident."

I shook my head. "It doesn't make sense."

"Yes, that's what worries me," he said.

I pensively pushed clumps of baklava back and forth with my fork. "I suppose Geoffrey and his brother were quite close?"

Slowly, Robert shook his head. "No, not really. There was too great a difference in their ages, and, more importantly, in their temperaments. But I think William's death was a great blow to Geoffrey. Greater, I think, than he is willing to admit."

"You sound as if you knew them both well."

He flashed a rueful smile. "I ought to. We grew up together. Their family and mine lived on adjoining estates. We used to play together as boys, and William and I were at Eton and then Oxford together. Later, I was his solicitor."

"And you don't think there's reason to believe his death was anything but an accident?"

He paused for a long moment and then shook his head. "I'm afraid not, Christine. No more than there is to believe your mishap yesterday was."

Perhaps he was right. Perhaps Geoffrey's obsession with his brother's death had carried over to later events, causing him to mistake the crumbling state of an old wall with evidence of foul play. This explanation grew more compelling as I walked back alone to my hotel. Surrounded by the sights and sounds of the bustling city, I found it impossible not to feel drawn back to sane reality. The experiences of the last two days seemed to recede like a dream, like a nightmare that in the light of day doesn't make sense. By the time I reached the Hotel Kerkyra, I was firmly convinced that the stone block had fallen entirely by itself.

FIVE

As if to reinforce my new conviction, I had no more visitors that day. I slept through the afternoon heat in my room, and woke from my siesta to find a cool breeze fluttering in through the half-open windows. It carried the smell of the sea.

I decided it was time to get back to being a tourist.

I dressed quickly, slipping on a mint green silk dress and cream-colored pumps. I skipped putting on hose and enjoyed the feel of the cool leather against my bare feet. My grandmother's pearls felt similarly cool and pleasant around my neck.

In the lobby of the hotel, Panayiotis, one of Kyria Andriatsis's many sons-in-law, was behind the desk. I asked him if he could recommend a good restaurant for dinner. With typical Greek tact, he asked if I was eating alone. His eyebrows rose in flattering disbelief when I said that I was.

"Then you must go someplace that has music and many people. There is a place in Kinopiastes—every night there is dancing. Many tourists go there, but the food is not bad. It's a little expensive, but...." He shrugged his shoulders as if to say "What does money matter?"

"Is Kinopiastes far?" I asked.

"On an island, nothing is far," he said with a grin. "And don't worry, the taxi drivers know the place."

When I stepped out of the hotel, I found that the light had dimmed from bright white to a cooler blue. A breeze slipped past and nipped at my bare arms. It was only a little before six, early yet for dinner by Greek standards. I decided to walk for a bit and enjoy the town bustling back to life after its afternoon sleep. People began to fill the empty streets. Shops selling everything from kitchen sponges to gold jewelry reopened their doors, and the sound of voices—talking, laughing, yelling, cajoling—rose through the air like a swelling chorus.

I hadn't planned to walk long, but the energy of the awakening town was infectious, and I found myself wandering up and down streets I didn't know, exploring this shop and that boutique. I found an English language bookstore where I browsed for an age, and when I emerged I had four new books tucked under my arm.

The bells of St. Spiridon Church chimed eight, reminding me of dinner. Surely it was late enough to eat now? After a bit of hunting, I found an empty taxi. The driver knew both Kinopiastes and the restaurant and needed no further direction, so with a pleased sigh I settled back in my seat to enjoy the ride.

We traveled south, winding our way inland through rolling hills. As we drove, the sun sank behind the trees in a crimson blaze. As we arrived in Kinopiastes the blaze softened into a violet glow that cast a gauzy veil over everything. Enchanted with the sight, I had the driver drop me on the outskirts of the small town so I could enjoy the view in solitude.

Sometime later I made my way to the restaurant. It wasn't difficult to find, and I could see that it was as popular as Panayiotis had claimed; large groups of people were clustered outside waiting to get in. With a sinking feeling in my rather empty stomach, I wondered how long it would take to get a table, but when I spoke to the headwaiter he astonished me by saying my table was already waiting.

He moved off to lead the way before I could tell him he'd made a mistake. I decided to wait and see what he offered before I refused it. We threaded our way past crowded tables and a small area of bare floor where a dance line was beginning to form. A man and woman in traditional dress moved out to lead it, encouraging the restaurant's diners to join in.

"Here you are, *Thespinis*," the headwaiter said, motioning to a small table set in a relatively quiet corner of the room. "I hope you will enjoy your dinner." Before I could reply, he'd bustled away, leaving me alone with my prospective dinner partner, whose elegant dinner jacket and black tie made me sorely conscious of my wrinkled dress and bare legs.

"What are you doing here?" I exclaimed, embarrassment mixing with pleased surprise.

Geoffrey Redfield stood up and pulled out a chair for me. "I thought it was my turn to offer you dinner."

I sat down. The dance line was beginning to sway to the music like a drunken snake. "But how in the world did you know where I'd be?"

"I stopped by your hotel." He circled around the table and sat down opposite me. "They said you might be coming here."

"The operative word was 'might,'" I said. "I could easily have gone somewhere else."

"True." He picked a menu up off the red tablecloth and handed it to me. "I thought it worth the chance. Hungry?"

I nodded. It was almost nine, late by my stomach's internal clock, which hadn't yet accustomed itself to the Greek schedule for meals. A waiter passed by carrying a tray laden with food. The mouth-watering aroma in his wake hit like a wave and my stomach gurgled in protest. From the expression on Geoffrey's face, I surmised his stomach was complaining, too. "How long have you been waiting here?"

"About an hour-and-a-half," he replied with a grimace. "Have you decided what you'd like?"

I took the hint and quickly scanned the menu. Though I'd been brought up on Greek cooking, many of the Corfiote dishes were unfamiliar to me. In the end, I settled on a selection of appetizers that appeared to be a sort of tourists' greatest hits, and Geoffrey ordered the same, whether to show solidarity or because I'd chosen well, I couldn't tell. He also ordered a bottle of wine whose expense impressed the waiter tremendously. He left beaming at Geoffrey as if he were a long-lost son.

The waiter's bustling departure left an uncomfortable vacuum at our table. I didn't want to be the first to speak, and neither, apparently, did Geoffrey, so we sat in uneasy silence and turned our attention to the dance floor. The *syrto* was reaching its climax. The dancers, their arms tightly linked to keep the whirling circle from spinning apart, sped their steps to match the tempo of the *bouzoukia*. The circle's leader twirled and twisted from the handkerchief linking him to the rest of the chain. Then he leapt into the air, slapping the side of his boot and coming to a perfectly poised stop just as the last chord was struck. The room erupted in applause. I turned back to face Geoffrey, and found myself staring into a pair of disquieting emerald eyes.

I'm not sure which of us looked away first. Feeling a little breathless, I stared down at the tablecloth, fiddled with my fork, and tried to recover my equilibrium. When I finally looked up again, he was staring off into space, his expression unreadable.

"Why did you really come here tonight?" I asked.

The question seemed to surprise him. "I thought my reason rather obvious," he said. "Why do you suppose?" He regarded me intently, his neatly brushed hair glowing golden in the candlelight.

I hesitated, then said, "I suspect you want to know how my interview with Lieutenant Mavros went."

His expression changed. "I wasn't even aware you'd been to see him."

"You expect me to believe that?"

"Obviously, you don't. But it's true, nonetheless."

"You could have saved yourself a lot of trouble, you know, and just called me. I'd have been happy to make my report over the phone."

"And what precisely is that supposed to mean?"

"It means I don't think you went to this much trouble simply to have dinner with me. This morning you told me to forget everything and stay out of your way. Now you're sitting there looking at me as if—"

His green eyes darkened. "As if?"

I drew a ragged breath. "It doesn't matter. Why don't I just tell you what you want to know so you can go?"

"I'll leave now, if that's what you want." He rose from the table. "Forgive me for intruding on your dinner." He opened his wallet and laid a stack of thousand-drachma notes on the table. "That should cover the bill."

"Don't you want to hear what the lieutenant said?"

"No." He turned and left.

For some moments I just sat there, immobilized by surprise and a rather potent sense of regret. Then the paralysis wore off. I grabbed my purse and books and ran after him, hitting my shin twice on people's chairs in my haste to catch up.

Outside, the sky was dark and moonlight provided the only illumination, but I could see he was already halfway down the street. "Geoffrey, wait!" I called. He stopped and turned, but made no move to come back. I realized the mountain had no intention of coming to Mohammed, so, ignoring the painful throb of my bruised shin, I started down the street.

"What's wrong with your leg?" he demanded. I ignored the question and continued hobbling toward him. With a sound of irritation, he strode forward. "All right, I'm here. Why did you call after me?"

"I didn't want you to leave like that."

The moonlit planes of his face softened a fraction. "Really? I thought that was precisely what you did want."

I shook my head. "I'm sorry. I know I was rude. It's just—well, I never seem to know whether I'm coming or going with you."

"The feeling's entirely mutual, I assure you." His lips relaxed into something almost approaching a smile. "What now?"

"Perhaps we can start the evening over again?" I suggested.

"I'm willing, if you are," he said. "Shall we go back in?"

I shook my head. "I'd rather not."

He frowned, and I quickly explained, "I was in such a hurry to catch up with you that I ran into a few chairs, and unfortunately some of them still had people in them at the time."

His mouth twitched. "So that's what happened to your leg. Well, I see how the place might hold painful memories for you—"

"Very funny."

"— so perhaps we should return to town. We could have dinner at my hotel."

"All right," I agreed. "It will serve you right to pay for two meals. But how do we get there?" I gazed up and down the quiet street. "I suppose there must be a taxi somewhere...."

"No need, I've hired a car." He pointed to a black Mercedes coupe parked across the street, then slid an arm around me to take some weight off my sore leg. "Step this way, my accident-prone miss."

The Corfu Palace was a large, sprawling hotel located slightly south of the Esplanade overlooking Garitsa Bay. It had obviously seen better days, but it was still impressive, with an air that was more than a little romantic. As the Mercedes slid into the last empty parking space in the Palace's small lot, I gazed up at the hotel's imposing façade and tried to ignore this last fact. Even if Geoffrey's protestations were true, and he wasn't after information, he still had plenty to gain just by being friendly, by assuring I was on his side, especially if there was any chance Lieutenant Mavros might begin an investigation.

So I studiously tried to ignore the atmosphere. What did it matter if lights fountained up around the hotel's entrance? If the soothing sound of lapping water blended with the trill of cicadas? If the tangy smell of pine wafted in through the coupe's rolled-down windows? If Geoffrey's nearness in the dark and silent car was as unnerving as a touch?

I swung open the door and got out. "Thanks for the ride into town, but you don't really have to treat me to another dinner, you know. I can catch a taxi back to my hotel—"

He came round the car, took my arm, and turned me towards him. "Is that what you'd prefer?"

What was it about him that made it so hard to lie? "No," I admitted. "I just thought it might be best."

"You still doubt my motives."

I nodded.

He reached up and brushed a loose strand of hair back off my bandaged cheek. "And if I told you that I want to have dinner with you very much, what would you say then?"

"That it's hardly surprising," I replied, trying to keep my voice light. "After all, you must be starving by now."

He frowned, shook his head, and then laughed. "You are the most unpredictable woman!"

"You're not exactly like clockwork yourself."

He seemed surprised. "No, I suppose I haven't been lately." For a moment our eyes met, and I was startled by the anguish— or was it anger?—I saw there. Then he looked away. "Odd part of it is, I fancy if you asked friends back home, they'd tell you I used to be quite a predictable fellow."

"Sometimes it feels good to shake free of people's expectations."

His mouth curved bitterly. "And sometimes one hasn't any choice."

I thought of my own life, of the disastrous encounter with my father that had driven me to Greece. "I know," I said softly.

For a moment he stared down at my face. Then his arms slid round me and he pulled me so close I could feel his heart beating. "Do you?" he whispered against my hair.

"Yes." The word came out a sigh. I tilted my head up and breathed in the scent of his skin, all rational thought lost in the anticipation of his kiss.

"Geoffrey?" a voice called out behind us.

I opened my eyes to find Geoffrey's lips only a hairsbreadth from my own. He cast one long, lingering look at my mouth, then straightened reluctantly and turned to face the man who had hailed him. To my surprise and chagrin, it was Robert Humphreys.

"So sorry to interrupt, Geoffrey," he apologized, "but I've been looking for you all over and—" He stopped abruptly as he recognized me. The look of startled speculation on his face vanished almost immediately, replaced by a lawyer's veneer of imperturbability, but I could well imagine what he was thinking.

"Robert!" Geoffrey exclaimed with a sudden smile. "I didn't know you were on Corfu. When did you arrive?"

"Just this morning. I had some papers to deliver to Demetra." As Robert turned his hazel-eyed gaze toward me, I felt like an embarassed schoolgirl, but to my relief his tone was friendly, even faintly teasing, as he said, "Why, Miss Stewart, we meet again. What a pleasure."

Geoffrey's arm tightened around me. "You two have met?"

"Yes," Robert replied lightly, "I had the pleasure of making Christine's acquaintance this afternoon—at the constabulary." His expression sobered. "Which brings me to the reason for my untimely interruption. Geoffrey, you and I need to discuss yesterday's events without delay."

"Surely it can wait until tomorrow? Christine and I were

about to have dinner."

I realized my mouth had dropped open. I snapped it shut.

Robert shook his head. "I'm scheduled for an early flight tomorrow, and I don't want to leave the island until I've talked things over with you. Christine, I'm sorry for stealing your dinner partner, but you understand the necessity?"

Reluctantly, I nodded.

Geoffrey, however, was not so amenable. "We can talk after Christine and I have eaten."

Robert shrugged. "Very well. Shall I meet you in the hotel bar at eleven?"

"Eleven-thirty," Geoffrey countered. "It's nearly ten now."

"Eleven-thirty, then," Robert agreed with a grimace. He turned to me. "I always said he was the one who should have been a lawyer; his bull-headedness would have made for some extremely interesting litigation."

"Feel free to hurry along," Geoffrey urged.

"Very well. I take the hint. Until later. Christine, it's been a pleasure." And with that, he strode up the marble steps and disappeared into the lobby.

I turned back from watching him go, to find Geoffrey eyeing me warily. "You two seem to have become well acquainted this afternoon."

"Not really," I said.

"What did the two of you talk about?"

"Do we have to discuss it now? I thought we were just about to go in and have a delicious meal."

Geoffrey cocked an eyebrow at me and said in a low voice, "What we were about to do had nothing whatsoever to do with food."

"That may be," I replied with feigned lightness, "but if I don't get something to eat soon, I may slump unconscious at your feet."

His eyes gleamed mischievously. "Don't tempt me."

I made a face at him.

"All right, all right," he grumbled. "Shall we go in?"

Six

The hotel restaurant wasn't crowded, and it was easy for us to get a table off by ourselves. "Is it always this empty?" I asked.

Geoffrey shook his head. "I fancy it's late."

"I thought people liked to eat late here."

"The natives, yes. But we tourists are a soft-stomached lot." He grinned at me. "We go quite weak in the knees if we aren't fed on time."

"The natives usually eat a very large and very filling lunch," I retorted. "I missed lunch altogether today."

"Excuses, excuses," he murmured, his eyes twinkling.

"Are we going to spend the rest of the evening discussing my stomach?"

"No. Actually, I was planning to ask you about your holiday. Where else in Greece have you visited?"

At first I assumed he'd picked the topic because it was safe and easy and had nothing to do with Michael or the accident at the Old Fort, but after a while I began to realize he was genuinely interested. He asked me countless questions. Had I been to Delphi? Mycenae? Knossos? What other islands had I traveled to? Had I visited the excavations at Akrotiri? Had I seen the Acropolis by moonlight?

I answered his questions and listened to his comments about the beauty of this temple and the wonder of that site, and time seemed to pass without either of us noticing. The food arrived and we ate it. Between mouthfuls we argued about the unique quality of Greek light.

"But surely all countries along the Mediterranean have the same glittering sunshine?" I said.

He shook his head adamantly. "No, it's not the same. I can't describe the difference or put a name to it, but the light here in Greece is different from anywhere else in the world."

"I guess I'll have to take your word for it," I said. "I've never been anywhere else besides home."

"You mean to say this is your first visit to Greece?" He sounded disbelieving. "Why did you wait so long?"

"You make it sound like some sort of pilgrimage."

"Well, isn't it? Most Greeks I've met, no matter where born, seem to gravitate back to Greece like homing pigeons."

"I'm only half Greek," I said.

"I doubt that matters. What's the other half?"

"Scots."

"Your father?"

I nodded reluctantly, disliking the direction of the conversation. "I suppose you're through and through English?"

He smiled crookedly. "Not actually, no. My grandmother was an American. She was wildly mischievous and great fun to be with and helped me through some difficult times when I was a boy." He stared off into space for a few moments, lost in thought. Then his attention returned to me. "And what do you do when you're not playing tourist or saving young boys from large falling objects?"

"I put together custom computer systems for artists."

His eyebrows flew up in surprise. "Do you mean the type that allow one to paint on a computer?"

"Paint, animate, do special effects. Especially special effects. That's our hottest area right now. We've been putting together systems for lots of small production companies who are trying to get into movie work."

He nodded. "It's amazing how sophisticated it's all gotten. A colleague of mine purchased a system he uses to compose mural-sized paintings. It's an interesting process, and the results are impressive. I've been toying with the idea of purchasing a similar set-up myself."

I stared at him in dismay. "You're a painter?"

"The galleries that sell my work say so," he replied dryly, "though there are one or two critics who might dispute the point. I also do some illustration work—books for children, mostly. Is something wrong?"

"No," I said.

"Then why are you looking at me like that?"

"My … uh, father illustrates children's books."

"Why do I suspect that's not a point in my favor? What's his name? Perhaps I've heard of him?"

"Angus Stewart," I murmured unwillingly.

His eyes widened. "*The* Angus Stewart? The one who's won three Caldecott awards and had twelve books on the Times' best-seller list?"

I stabbed my fork into a stuffed tomato on my plate. "Yes."

He whistled softly. "I've never met him, but he has quite a reputation."

Rice began spilling everywhere as I sliced the tomato to pieces. "Does that reputation include the fact that when his first book became a success, he abandoned his wife and two daughters and moved to New York?"

Geoffrey frowned. "No."

"Unfortunately, his next few books were flops, so of course there wasn't any money for alimony or child support. My mother had to work two jobs to make ends meet, and my grandparents used their savings to send me and my sister to college. Eventually, his books started doing well again, but by then he'd remarried and didn't have much use for old family ties."

Geoffrey reached across the table and caught my hand. "Christine, I'm sorry."

I shook my head, embarrassed by my outburst. "No, I'm the one who should be apologizing. I didn't mean to let loose with all that. It's just … well, he's a bit of a sore subject at the moment." I paused, and then added, "A couple of weeks ago I was on a sales trip. My father was on the prospect list, and I got the brilliant idea to use that as an excuse to go see him."

"It didn't go well?"

Feeling the betraying prick of tears at the back of my eyes I kept my response to a minimum. "No."

"Is that why you came to Greece?" he asked.

Startled by his insight, I nodded. " I just couldn't settle back into my normal life. After a while, I gave up. I called my boss, told him I was taking all my saved-up vacation time, and caught a cab for the airport. I bought a ticket on the first flight out to Greece."

"And here you are," Geoffrey said in a low voice.

"Here I am," I agreed softly, suddenly more aware of the intoxicating warmth tingling up my arm from his touch than the hurt that just a moment ago had seemed so raw. "But right now I think I may have had too much to drink."

He shook his head. "You know it's not the wine."

I gazed at him helplessly but was saved from having to reply by the headwaiter, who sidled up to the table to inform us the dining room was about to close. Geoffrey reached out for the bill. I stopped him. "Let me get it."

"But I invited you," he protested.

I shook my head. "It wouldn't be fair for you to pay for both dinners, and it's my fault our other one went to waste."

"I recall a certain comment about it 'serving me right' to pay for both meals," he reminded me.

"Please, Geoffrey, I've changed my mind."

His teasing grin faded. "I'll have to watch out. When you look at me like that, it's difficult to refuse you anything. Very well. I'll let you pay—on one condition: you promise to dine with me again before you leave Corfu."

"All right, I promise," I said with exaggerated reluctance.

As we got up to leave, he slid a possessive arm around my waist. We were halfway to the door when his grip tightened. "Angus!" he exclaimed.

"What?"

"The letter in your purse," he said, "it was signed 'Angus.' It was from your father, wasn't it?"

"Yes," I admitted tensely.

He started to smile, then caught himself and stopped.

"I'm glad you find the idea amusing."

"Not amusing, Christine, merely a relief. I thought 'Angus' was some ex-lover you were pining over."

"Hmmm," I murmured, my anger mollified. "And if he had been?"

His mouth twisted crookedly. "I would have considered it my duty to help you forget him, of course." His tone was light and teasing, but the expression in his eyes could have lit any number of small fires.

We walked out toward the lobby, and he offered to drive me back to my hotel, but I reminded him he was already late for his meeting with Robert.

He turned to face me. "You haven't yet told me what the two of you discussed this afternoon."

Suddenly uncomfortable, I shrugged. "I told him about yesterday. He seemed a bit startled when I said you didn't believe it was an accident."

"Startled?" Geoffrey said. "Or disbelieving? No, don't bother to answer. I think I can guess. I suppose he told you about my brother?"

I nodded. "Why didn't you tell me?"

"And if I had?" he said grimly. "What would you have thought of my credibility then?" His gaze locked with mine. "What do you think of it now?"

"Geoffrey, I know it must be hard to accept your brother's death, but if the police can't find any reason to believe—"

His mouth tightened into a hard line. "There's a cab rank down the hill. You should be able to find a cab there to take you back to your hotel." He reached into his wallet and pulled out a folded thousand-drachma note. "Here. For the fare." When I hesitated, he pressed it into my hand. "Take it. Dinner cost you nearly your last penny, and I know you've no money to pay the fare yourself."

"I can walk."

"Don't be a fool. It's nearly midnight."

"All right," I reluctantly agreed. "Thank you."

I waited for him to turn and go, but instead he stood there looking down at me. "Christine—"

"Yes?"

For a moment I thought he was going to finish the kiss he'd started earlier, but instead he just shook his head.

"Nothing. Goodnight."

"Goodnight," I replied, disappointed. I turned and walked out of the lobby.

I was sitting on a mountain waiting for my lover. A baby in a basket floated by on a river, but I knew I couldn't save it because if I tried to, I'd be swept down to the sea. Church bells began to ring in the valley below....

I woke with a start. Not church bells. The phone. Groggily I reached out to grab the receiver. The room was dark, though a few pink rays of light were slipping through gaps in the curtains.

"Hello," I rasped.

"Miss Stewart?" whispered a familiar voice.

"Michael! What on earth!" I fumbled for my watch and tried to get my eyes to focus. It was only ten after five.

"I woke you, didn't I? Sorry."

"That's all right," I said with a sigh. "What are you doing up so early, and why are you whispering?"

"I didn't want to wake anyone. They're all sleeping."

Lucky them, I thought. "Is something wrong?"

"N-no," he said unconvincingly. "I was just wondering if you might stop by sometime? I mean, before your holiday's finished?"

"Would you like me to?"

"Yes!" he exclaimed. "I mean, if you've time, of course."

"Unfortunately, time's not the problem. I don't think your stepmother wants me to see you again."

There was a pause. "Was she very rude to you?" he asked.

I tried to be tactful. "She feels I'm somewhat responsible for your accident, so understandably she doesn't want me around."

"But what happened was my fault, not yours."

"No, it wasn't," I said.

"You don't know—" he began.

"Yes, I do," I interrupted gently. "I know why you went to the Old Fort, and why you wanted to stay, and why we ended up sitting where we did. But none of that matters."

There was an even longer pause. "You're not angry with me?"

"With the guy who saved me from a drenching? Of course not. If it weren't for you, I might be lying here with a pink nose and double pneumonia."

He gave a soft chuckle of relief, and the sound left me smiling wistfully at the receiver. "Now when do you think you'll be accepting callers today?" I asked.

"You mean you'll come?" he exclaimed in surprise. "What about Stepmama?"

"Don't worry, I'll figure something out." He sighed, and the sound made my throat ache. "Michael?"

"Yes?"

"Everything's going to be okay," I said. "I promise."

"I'd best put the phone down now," he whispered. He sounded reluctant. "I think someone's coming."

"Goodbye then," I said.

There was only a click in reply, and the line went dead.

I didn't try to go back to sleep. I knew the whirling in my head would make it impossible. Instead I got up and opened the curtains. The sky glowed pink. I pulled a chair over and watched as the sun rose over the rooftops and the light brightened from pink to orange to white. I sat and gazed and thought, and by the time the sky had turned turquoise, I had made up my mind what to do.

Having come to a decision, it was difficult to wait to put it into action. I showered, dressed, and took a walk, but when I returned to my room it was still only eight. I used up some more time packing. Then I sat down and wrote postcards home and tried not to feel nervous about what I was planning to do.

Around nine there was a soft knock at the door. It was Kyria Andriatsis bringing me breakfast again. Since meals weren't included in the price of the room, I tried to pay her for it, but she only smiled, shook her head, and insisted I owed her nothing. I followed her to the door and tried to slip some money into the pocket of her apron. She batted my hand away.

"No! Your young man has paid for everything."

"My young man? What young man? I don't know what you're talking about."

She clucked impatiently. "Yesterday he comes and asks to me to cook breakfast for you, since you are not well. He gives me money, too much money, and I tell him I cannot accept so much. He smiles and tells me he is sure my cooking is worth every *leptá*." She chuckled at the memory. "He has a honey tongue, that one."

"Who does?" I demanded in exasperation. "Kyria, will you please tell me who it is you're talking about."

Her eyes widened in surprise. "Why, Kyrios Redfield, of course! For so much money, however, I cannot make only one breakfast, so I bring you today, and also tomorrow."

"Thank you, but I won't be here tomorrow."

For the first time she noticed my packed bags. "You are leaving? But I thought you were to remain one more week?"

"I'm going to stay at the home of a friend."

Her expression grew solemn. "Make sure you get one of these first." She tapped the gold band on her finger. "No man—not even such a one as your Kyrios Redfield—can be completely trusted."

"But I'm not—"

She held up a silencing hand. "I am not your mother, *koritsi.* You don't have to explain to me. But if things are not good, if you are not happy, come back here. There will be a room for you." She patted my arm and then picked up her tray and left. I gazed at the closed door with a frown.

After I'd eaten, I went out to look at the town one last time from the balcony. Gazing out over the red tile rooftops, I was suddenly overwhelmed by a reluctance to leave my safe haven.

Of course, it was possible nothing was wrong, that Michael was in no danger, that I was jumping into a situation I had no business being in for reasons that existed only in my imagination.

It was possible, but I didn't think it likely.

Because while I'd sat watching the sun rise and pondering Michael's phone call, I'd remembered something about the morning at the Old Fort that gave all my worries a solid grounding in reality. When I'd asked Michael why such an obviously wealthy boy needed money, he'd replied with three simple but ominous words.

"For a detective."

SEVEN

It felt strange to knock on that door again and wait for it to open. As before, I was feeling a strong need to sit down, but this time it was from nervousness, not loss of blood. I'd decided against calling first, knowing from experience it's harder to turn someone down in person than over the phone. So I was standing uninvited on the doorstep surrounded by luggage.

I heard the approach of footsteps and braced myself.

The door opened. I was about to launch into my carefully prepared speech, when I realized it was only the housekeeper, Maria.

"Thespinis Stewart!" she exclaimed with a smile. "*Embrós*! Come in!"

I shook my head and pointed to my luggage. "I'd better wait here. Is Mr. Skouras in? I'd like to speak with him."

She nodded, eyeing my luggage with a puzzled air. "I will bring."

She went off in search of him, leaving the front door open. Unfortunately, while she was gone, Demetra Redfield crossed the hallway and noticed the open door. She moved forward, squinting into the bright sunlight. "Miss Stewart?" she exclaimed sharply as she saw me. "What are you doing here?"

I flashed my most placating smile. "Your brother invited me to stay for a few days, and I've decided to accept his invitation."

I saw her color rise as she noted the suitcases at my feet. "The house does not belong to him."

"True. I understand it belongs to your stepson."

Her hand tightened on the door as she prepared to slam it in my face. "I suppose Geoffrey sent you here to insult me in this way?"

I'd been hoping Spiro would make a timely appearance to save the situation, but time had run out. I had to take a gamble and hope it worked. "Actually, Geoffrey Redfield *is* the reason I've changed my mind about accepting your brother's invitation."

The swing of the door was arrested. Demetra stared at me, wariness vying with curiosity. "So you admit—"

"That he won't stop bothering me? Yes. He keeps coming by my hotel, pestering me with his ridiculous theories. You see, he doesn't believe what happened at the Old Fort was an accident. In fact, he keeps trying to convince me that you and your brother are somehow responsible for what happened."

I had to give her credit. Only the slight tightness around her mouth and the fluttering pulse in her throat betrayed how much my words upset her. "It is a lie, of course," she said tensely.

"Of course," I replied. "I didn't say that I believed him, only that he was proving very persistent."

"I don't understand. Even if what you say is true, how will it change anything for you to come here?"

"At Ithaki," I explained, "Geoffrey can't just come and go as he pleases. I'll have some peace. More importantly, if I'm your guest, he'll realize it's no use trying to convince me to side against you, and he'll leave me alone."

"It makes an odd sort of sense," said a deep, masculine voice behind me. I spun around to find Spiro eyeing me with curiosity. "Maria said you wished to see me?"

"I wanted to know—"

He gazed down at my luggage. "If my invitation to visit remains good?"

I looked him in the eye. "Yes."

"And it is because of Geoffrey you have changed your mind?" Was it my imagination, or was there skepticism in his tone?

"In a manner of speaking."

"Well, then," he said, "I will have to thank him the next time I see him for providing us with such charming company." He flashed me a dazzling smile and bent to pick up my two suitcases. His sister started to say something, but he cut her off with a single word spoken forcefully in Greek: "*Argotera*." Later.

He led the way to a small but attractive room decorated in a silvery shade of green that reminded me of olive trees. "I hope you will be comfortable here," he said, setting down my suitcases and crossing to the French windows. He opened them out onto a large patio. "This room, like mine, faces the sea. There is a path leading down to the beach." He turned, and came back in. "The bathroom is here." He opened a door on my right. "It connects to my room, but there are locks on both doors, so you can assure yourself of privacy." A look of amusement suddenly flickered across his face. "It is to your satisfaction?"

I gazed about me. "It's wonderful, thank you."

He nodded. "And the location pleases you?"

"The location?" I repeated, puzzled.

"It was a clever story you told my sister, Christine, but I find it difficult to believe you are here only because you wish to escape Geoffrey's company." He lifted one eyebrow in inquiry, and there was a look in his brown eyes that made me uneasy. "Perhaps there is another reason you have come?"

My mouth suddenly felt dry. "What would that be?"

For a moment his gaze swept over me with an assessing intensity that set my heart pounding. Then his mouth relaxed into a smile. "Perhaps you are here not to avoid a man's company but to seek it?"

My lurching pulse slowed. "You've found me out," I murmured.

His dark eyebrows rose in wry agreement. "Yes."

"You understand why I told your sister what I did?"

"It is none of her affair," he said. He took a step closer. Before I realized what was coming, he had me enfolded in his arms.

Luckily, Maria chose that moment to bustle into the room with fresh sheets and towels. Spiro—with an adroitness born, I suspect, of much practice—swiftly let me go and slipped from my side without even seeming to do so.

"And now," he said casually, "I fear I have business in town and must leave you. Maria, please see that our guest has everything she needs and inform my sister that Miss Stewart and I will be dining out tonight." The housekeeper acknowledged the request with a silent nod.

"But Spiro—" I began.

He shook his head, flashed me a blinding smile, and was gone. Maria set down the linen and began making the bed.

In the mood I was in, it would have felt good to join her— to fling, tug, and chop the sheets into position. But Maria silently refused my offer of help, and I ended up sitting demurely in the corner while she made up the bed by herself.

When she had finished smoothing out the bedspread to her satisfaction, she picked up the stack of green towels and disappeared into the bathroom. Relieved of her inhibiting presence, I crossed to my suitcases and opened them up.

I'd hung up my dresses and was starting on my blouses, when Maria emerged from the bathroom and said disapprovingly. "No, this is not good. I help you." With quick, deft movements she proceeded to unpack, refold, and reorganize every article of clothing I possessed, separating out with a practiced eye anything I'd worn to be washed. When my suitcases were empty, she picked them up, and stowed them inside the large mahogany wardrobe where my dresses hung limp and wrinkled.

The sight was too much for her. She yanked the dresses out, saying she would iron them and bring them back later. "You go make swim now," she said, sounding like a mother telling a child to go play. She gathered up the clothes, and motioned with her head at the bathing suit she'd left lying on the bed. "You go to beach. When you come back, all is ready." She turned to leave.

"Wait! Please, before you go—can you tell me where Michael is?"

She stared at me in surprise, and then slowly her expression softened. "The young master? He is—how you say—*ston kypo*."

"In the garden?"

She nodded. "Yes, in the garden, with Paul."

If I hadn't been in such a hurry, it might have occurred to me to ask her where the garden was and how best to get there, but as it was, I was impatient to find Michael and didn't want to waste time on unimportant details. After all, it couldn't be that hard to find a simple garden, could it?

It could.

Part of the problem was the mental picture which had sprung up full-blown in my head when I'd heard the word 'garden.' As I stood on the patio outside my room, I scanned the grounds for an area of bright color, a profusion of blooming flowers devotedly tended, no doubt, by some aged gardener with gnarled hands.

So much for imagination. What I actually saw when I looked out from the patio was a picturesque but rather wild landscape of pine and chaparral sloping down to a pebble beach far below. Not sure what else to do, I descended the patio's stone steps and started down the path, which appeared to curve away from the villa towards the sea. But I hadn't gone far when the path split.

Mentally flipping a coin, I veered to the left, climbing a small incline towards a large thicket of pine. The path through the trees was liberally covered with dried needles, which rasped under my feet as I walked along. There was the twitter of birds and the thin trilling of insects, but I heard no voices, and when I sniffed the air for the scent of flowers, all I smelled was the tang of wild rosemary blending with the pine. Suddenly I heard the rustle of needles behind me.

"Hello?" I called out, turning. There was nobody there. *Just the wind,* I told myself, though the air was still and warm. *No reason to be frightened.*

I continued on. I'd walked another twenty yards or so when I heard the rustling again. This time the sound was nearer and more clear: unmistakably a foot crunching down on brittle needles. I spun around and called out, but there was no answer and—though my gaze flicked nervously from point to point all around me—no sign of the person who was following me.

The only direction I dared go was forward. I began walking more quickly. The footsteps behind me crackled and grew louder as my pursuer increased his or her stride to match mine. This time I didn't stop to turn. Heart pounding, I began to run.

I burst out of the thicket and kept running. Then suddenly

the ground beneath my feet seemed to slip away. Too late I realized the path ended abruptly at the edge of a small cliff. Waving my arms wildly in the air, I fought to reverse my momentum, but it was too late. A desperate prayer burst to my lips.

And was miraculously answered.

A steely grip seized my arms and yanked me back to solid ground. "What in hell do you think you are doing?" a voice demanded roughly in Greek.

I turned to see my rescuer. He was tall for a Greek, and slimly built, but the rolled-up sleeves of his white shirt revealed well-muscled arms, and his olive skin was tanned dark from the sun.

"Well, can't you speak?" he snapped. "Are you dumb as well as crazy?" The strong grip, which moments earlier had saved me, was now painful.

"Hey, that hurts!" I exclaimed in Greek. "Let me go!"

He released me, but didn't bother to apologize. "Ah, so you do talk. Good. Then perhaps you can tell me why you were about to throw yourself off this cliff?"

"Don't be ridiculous! I wasn't trying to throw myself off. I was running away from you, and I didn't realize that the path ended at a cliff. It ought to be marked. It's dangerous!"

His deep-set blue eyes fixed on my face. "Running away—from me?" His incredulous tone was exasperating.

"Well, what did you expect when you kept hiding every time I turned around! I didn't know what you were up to. You scared me!"

"You really are crazy. I first set eyes on you when you burst from the trees headed straight for this cliff. You're lucky I was so close, or else—" He shrugged his shoulders and motioned with his chin toward the pebbled beach beneath us.

I felt a sudden wave of uncertainty and fear. "Then you weren't the one behind me?" He flashed me a look that indicated his doubts about my sanity were growing. I hesitated a moment and then said, "But someone was following me"—I jerked my head toward the trees— "in there."

"Who?"

"I don't know."

"What did he look like?"

"I don't know."

His mouth curled. "You don't know much, do you?"

"Look, I didn't see the person! I just heard his or her footsteps."

"Footsteps?" he repeated with raised brows.

I said tightly, "The pine needles are dry and make a sound when someone steps on them."

"So the crackling of a few dead needles was enough to send you running as if the Furies themselves were after you?"

"Someone was following me, I tell you!"

He shrugged. "It doesn't matter. You shouldn't be here in the first place. This is private property. You're trespassing."

"I'm sorry," I said curtly. "I was just following the path. I didn't realize I'd wandered off Redfield property."

He stared at me in surprise. "You haven't. This is all Redfield land. I don't understand. You're a guest at the Villa?"

"Yes, I arrived today. My name is Christine Stewart."

Something flickered in his eyes, as if he recognized the name. "I am Paul."

"Well, Paul, I guess I should thank you for rescuing me."

He gave me an odd look. "There is no need. Now, you will excuse me? I should be getting back." He turned and started walking toward the pines.

"Wait!" I called out. "I think I'd better go with you."

"If you like. But it is impossible to become lost. The path leads directly to the house."

"Actually, I don't want the house. I'm trying to find the garden. You wouldn't happen to know where it is, would you?"

His mouth twitched into the ghost of a smile. "I might be able to find it," he said drily.

"Have I said something funny?"

"Yes, a little. You see, I am the gardener."

I smiled weakly. So much for the faithful old retainer with gnarled hands.

It turned out the garden was located in a small field to the south of the villa, and that if I'd taken the path branching to the right instead of the left, I'd have found it easily enough. Not that it was anything like what I'd imagined. There weren't any flowers at all, except for a few bright blossoms on the zucchini vines. There were tomatoes and cucumbers, squash, eggplant, and green beans, and a patch full of herbs. There were fig trees, and grape vines laden with fragrant purple fruit, and in one corner, some round watermelons ripening in the sun.

Paul watched me as I took it all in. "You are disappointed?"

I was, but not because flowers are prettier than vegetables. Aside from us, the garden was empty. "Maria said I'd find Michael here."

His expression grew guarded. "He comes each morning to help, but today it's hot, so we stopped early." He glanced at the sun, which was high in the sky and beating down fiercely. "It's cool in the house. You'll probably find him there or at the beach."

"Yes, well, I guess I'll be getting back then."

He nodded, and reached down to pull a large clump of grapes off the vine. "Here," he said, tossing it to me, "they taste best hot from the sun."

"Thank you," I said in surprise, cupping the warm grapes in my hand. He didn't bother to answer, but turned his back on me and began picking figs and dropping them into a basket.

As I climbed up the patio steps and crossed to my room, I pinched off a few grapes and popped them in my mouth. I was astonished at the sweet lusciousness of their flavor.

"Miss Stewart!"

Distracted by the fruit, I'd entered the room without noticing the small figure hunched in the green armchair in the corner. Now as I looked up, he wriggled out of the chair and came running. I thought he was going to land on me in a sort of flying tackle, but at the last moment he slowed and came to a tottering and breathless stop just short of where I stood.

"You came!"

"Didn't you think I would?" I said with a smile.

He was too tactful to answer. Instead he asked, a trace of awe in his voice, "However did you get Stepmama to invite you to stay?"

"Well, to be truthful," I admitted, "I sort of invited myself, though your Uncle Spiro originally extended the invitation a couple of days ago. I'm not sure what he or your stepmother really think of my being here, but as long as I behave myself, I don't think they'll kick me out."

"How long will you stay?" His voice was wistful.

"How long would you like me to stay? I have about a week of vacation left. If you like, I can spend the whole thing here."

"That'd be smashing! Only, I wouldn't want to spoil your holiday.…"

"What do you mean 'spoil'? It'll be nice to have some company. Now, why don't you sit down while I look for something to put these grapes in."

I ended up putting them in a ceramic bowl that had been holding a dozen bars of elegantly wrapped soap. After rinsing the grapes, I returned to the room, wiping the dripping bottom of the bowl with one of the luxuriously-thick towels Maria had set out for me. "Michael, there's something I want to ask you."

He gazed up at me expectantly.

I held out the fruit to him and he pinched off a handful of grapes and popped them into his mouth with a grin. "The other day," I began hesitantly, "you said something to me at the Old Fort which I've just remembered and I'm kind of curious about."

The grin disappeared. I forced myself to continue. "It was just before the stone fell and everything got crazy."

His gaze dropped to fix on his lap.

"Michael, why did you want money for a detective?"

Slowly, he shook his head.

"You don't remember?" I asked.

"I'd rather not talk about it, please."

"But, it's important!"

His cheeks grew flushed, and he shook his head again, this time more violently.

"All right, all right. I won't press you. Just tell me this: is there something you're afraid of? Because if there is—"

There was a sharp rap on the door. It swung open and a woman entered. At first I didn't recognize her, then I remembered. Her name was Helen, and I'd met her two days before in Michael's room when I'd stopped by to say goodbye. Spiro had introduced her as a maid, but I'd gotten the distinct impression her role was more that of watchdog.

"Excuse me," she said stiffly, "but I have come for the boy." As her dark eyes fixed on Michael, tight angry lines gathered round her mouth like shattered glass. She strode across the room and grabbed his arm. "Are you a *kleftis* to slip away like that?" she demanded, giving him a shake.

"Stop that!" I exclaimed.

Her grip loosened, but she didn't let go. "I am responsible for his safety. I feared he had run away again and was lost."

Michael pulled his arm free. "You can see I'm not lost! I just wanted to say hello to Miss Stewart."

"The lady is the guest of your uncle, not of you," she snapped. "Now we must go. It is lunch time." She put one hand on his back and gave him a small push toward the door. "I apologize for the intrusion," she said to me.

"Michael's visit was no intrusion," I replied, trying to keep my anger under control. "I expect I'll see him at lunch?"

"Today he eats in his room—alone."

"But he's done nothing wrong!"

She shook her head. Michael rebelliously twisted out of her reach long enough to bid me goodbye as she tried to herd him out.

I was in no mood to eat when Maria arrived a few minutes later to lead me to the dining room, but for Michael's sake I had to try to get on a better footing with his stepmother, and I decided standing her up for lunch probably wouldn't serve that end.

The meal was served by a pretty young woman named Aphrodite. With quick, graceful movements she poured dark red wine into our glasses and heaped our plates with salad, roast lamb, and *tyropitas*, cheese pies made with flaky filo pastry. Demetra did not bother to speak to me. She merely signaled the meal was to begin by spearing a piece of cucumber with her fork and slicing it into small bits with a glitteringly sharp knife. Watching her, I took a deep swig of wine, for I had the unnerving feeling she was imagining the piece of cucumber was me.

We ate for some minutes in silence. Every once in a while she would cast a dark glance my way, and I would smile back at her, determined to work my way into her good graces. But her expression remained icy. I complimented her on the food.

She inclined her head stiffly. "Maria is an excellent cook."

"You're not bad yourself."

Her voice was frigid, "I have a small talent for it, yes."

"The dinner your brother brought me the other night was delicious. Thank you for cooking all that wonderful food for me."

"It was not for you that I cooked. I often work in the kitchen when I am troubled. It is soothing to the nerves. That night I was very upset and I cooked much food. Spiro took some for a friend. He often does this, you see? He has many friends—many women—he likes to impress with his sister's cooking."

She waited for my reaction. I flashed her a bright smile and said warmly, "I'm not surprised to hear he's got women swarming all over him. He's a very attractive man, isn't he?"

Her perfectly shaped eyebrows rose in surprise. She looked as if she were about to say something, but just then Maria entered with our dessert: thick slices of cold, juicy watermelon.

"This looks wonderful," I commented, slicing myself off a piece. "I suppose it comes straight from your garden?"

Demetra gazed at me oddly. "You know of our garden?"

"Yes, I ran into Paul this morning, and he showed it to me. It's quite impressive. He's done a good job with it."

She nodded faintly. "It was Maria's garden originally. My brother hired Paul when Michael and I arrived from England, so Maria would have more time to cook and take proper care of the house. But you are right. He is a good gardener, and useful in other ways as well."

So Paul was a relatively new member of Ithaki's household. I pondered our initial encounter and his amazing timing in catching me at the cliff. Had it been simple good fortune, or had he been the one following me all the time?

Demetra Redfield rose from the table. "Miss Stewart, you will excuse me?"

"Of course. Thank you for the wonderful lunch."

She inclined her head and started toward the door.

"Oh, by the way," I said, calling after her, "I thought I'd spend the afternoon enjoying your lovely beach. You don't mind if Michael joins me for a swim, do you?"

She turned around to face me, and her mouth twisted into a faint smile. "No, I do not mind."

"I'm glad."

She swept an imaginary speck of dust off her dress. "However, I fear the boy will be unable to make a swim with you this afternoon, because he comes with me to town."

"Perhaps when you get back—"

"I do not think we will return before evening. I have many errands and several friends to visit."

"Perhaps tomorrow?" I persevered.

She regarded me with those dark, unreadable eyes. "We shall see, Miss Stewart. We shall see."

EIGHT

After lunch, I walked down to the beach and vented my frustrations in a long swim. When I returned to my room, the bed was turned down and the drapes drawn to leave everything cool and dark. It was an invitation to siesta I was inclined to accept; I was tired, and I had nothing better to do now that Michael was off limits for the rest of the day. I wondered whether Helen had any other duties besides watching him and, if not, how I was going to get another chance to speak with him alone.

Stripping off my wet swimsuit, I took a brief shower and then slipped between the cool sheets. I felt the tension seep out of my body. The pillow, soft and round, felt cooler even than the sheets, and I pressed my face into it, savoring the scent of the clean linen. Before I knew it, I was asleep.

I must have slept deeply, because for a moment when I woke I had no idea where I was. Then I realized I wasn't alone. "Well, Sleeping Beauty," a voice said coldly, "it's about time."

I started to sit up, then remembered I was wearing nothing but the sheet. "Has anyone ever told you that you have an irritating habit of popping up where you're least expected?"

Geoffrey Redfield's green eyes glinted. "Funny thing, that. One could say the same of you." He was sitting in the chair Michael had sat in earlier, but his expression was as hostile as Michael's had been welcoming. "Now would you care to tell me what you're doing here?"

"Why should I? I don't need to explain my actions to you."

"True, I'd say they were reasonably self-explanatory. I may be a fool, but even I have my limits."

I frowned. "How did you find out I was here? I meant to call you later."

"Did you? Excuse me if I find that hard to credit."

"Why?"

"Can you really ask?" he demanded. "Two days ago you said there was no connection between you and Skouras or his sister, yet today I find you settled in cozily in the room adjoining his."

"There's a simple enough explanation—"

"Oh, I'm certain you've quite a convincing one prepared," he interrupted, "though I wonder why you bother. Mavros refuses to investigate, and my opinion doesn't count for much."

"I'm here because of Michael."

"Of course!" he exclaimed mockingly. "Skouras, out of the kindness of his heart, decided the boy needed a companion, and you volunteered for the post. Of course, if I were you, I'd be careful where you plan your next excursion, lest dear old Spiro decide to have another go at killing two birds with one stone."

That was it. I'd had it. Grabbing the sheet and clutching it tightly around me, I scrambled up and started toward him, but my foot got caught in a fold and I stumbled and went sprawling.

He reached up to steady me, but to my dismay I ended up sprawled on him instead of the floor. At first I was too mortified to move, then mortification gave way to awareness, as I became acutely conscious of every point of contact between his body and mine. For a long moment I remained fixed and still, then it occurred to me he was probably impatient to have me off of him. My face was pressed against the side of his neck; I breathed in the scent of his skin, then began to pull away.

But he wouldn't let me go. His arms tightened around me and he turned his head and pressed his mouth lightly against my ear. The warm tickle of his breath and teasing touch of his lips sent a shiver through me, but the words he whispered quickly transmuted desire back into anger.

"I was serious about the danger, Christine. Whatever may exist between you and Skouras, you're a fool if you think it will protect you in the long run."

This time there was nothing reluctant about the way I pulled away from him. As I jerked to my feet, he followed in one graceful, fluid motion. He took one end of the sheet that was threatening to slip away and draped it carefully over my shoulder, then said in a deep undertone that tingled its way up my spine, "Since your boyfriend's not about, perhaps you'd best put some clothes on, else I might be tempted to start something we both would regret."

"If you really care about your nephew," I snapped, as I gathered up the traitorous yardage and flung it over one arm, "you'll spend a little less time worrying about my love life"—I crossed to the armoire and snatched up some clothes—"and a little more time wondering why Michael phoned me, a relative stranger, in the middle of the night wanting to talk." I disappeared into the bathroom and slammed the door shut behind me.

When I emerged dressed, five minutes later, he was standing where I'd left him. "Why are you still here?" I demanded.

"Michael rang you up?"

I gave a short, tight nod.

"In the middle of the night?" His eyes sought mine, but I looked away.

"Actually, early in the morning. A little after five."

"What was the matter?" he asked. "Why did he call?"

Hearing the worry in his voice, I reluctantly met his gaze. "He didn't actually say anything was wrong. He just wanted to know if I was coming to see him again. I told him I would."

Geoffrey crossed to where I was standing. "You said there was a simple explanation for your being here. I'd like to hear it."

As always, his nearness affected me. Trying to remain cool, I countered, "And I'd like to hear why you didn't tell Lieutenant Mavros that Michael went to the Old Fort to meet you."

"And what do you fancy the good Lieutenant would do if he knew I was the one who arranged for Michael to be on that bench at the time he was attacked?"

"You could have told him about the call decoying you away to the hospital," I insisted stubbornly. "That might have convinced him Michael is in danger."

"Do you really think he'd believe in a mysterious phone call that provides me with my only alibi?" Geoffrey demanded.

"He might have then. He certainly won't now," I snapped.

"Now he knows Michael went to the Old Fort to meet someone, because he has the note setting it up. He asked me if I knew who it was from."

Geoffrey regarded me grimly. "And you told him?"

"No," I said. "He's an old friend of Spiro's. If I told him the note was from you after you failed to tell him anything about the meeting—well, I suspect he wouldn't bother investigating anyone or anything else, he'd just assume you were responsible."

He tilted my face up to his. "Thank you."

"I didn't do it for you," I insisted. "I did it for Michael. He has too few people watching out for him as it is; it wouldn't help him any to have Lieutenant Mavros throw you in jail."

The hand under my chin was withdrawn. "And here I thought you'd acted on my behalf. Beggars can't be choosers, I suppose." He retreated a step. "I'm grateful for your reticence. I trust it won't get you into trouble with Skouras?"

"Are we back to that again?"

"You were going to explain how you come to be here," he reminded me.

Sensing his willingness to listen, I relaxed a little. "Actually, Spiro invited me to stay that first day, but it was obvious how Demetra felt about me, so I turned him down. I didn't think there was anything to be gained by staying here, or at least, I didn't until Michael phoned this morning. Then I began to wonder if I shouldn't accept Spiro's invitation after all."

"Michael's phone call caused you to change your mind?"

"I got to thinking someone should be here to keep an eye on him. Knowing how your sister-in-law feels about you, I decided I was the likeliest candidate, so I exercised my feminine prerogative to change my mind, and here I am."

"As easy as that?" he said. "Demetra didn't protest?"

"Oh, she wasn't crazy about the idea, but I managed to convince her my being here was the lesser of two evils. I told her you'd been pestering me endlessly to convert me to your cause."

"And Skouras? What was his reaction to your change of heart?"

"He doesn't believe the explanation I gave his sister."

He grimaced. "That I was making such a bloody nuisance of myself you had to get away?"

"He thinks I'm here because I've changed my mind about his manly charms."

The already taut line of Geoffrey's mouth tightened further. "Oh, he does, does he?"

"Yes, he thinks I'm using you as an excuse to stay here and be near him. I guess that's why he put me in this room."

Geoffrey ran an angry hand through his hair. "That door," he demanded tensely, "it used to lock on this side. Does it still?"

"Yes."

"Make sure you keep it locked at night."

I had, of course, intended to do just that, but there was no way to say so now without having him think I was taking orders. "Afraid Spiro might pay me a late-night visit?"

"Dammit, Christine! Be serious. Don't you realize the danger you're in?"

"What danger?" I demanded archly. "According to you, I should be perfectly safe. After all, I'm working for Spiro and his sister, aren't I?"

He flashed me an exasperated look.

Lowering my voice, I said, "Look, much as I'd love to spend the rest of the afternoon arguing with you, I don't think your being here is a good idea. If Demetra or Spiro get wind of it, I'll be out on my ear." Suddenly, as if on cue, there was a knock at the door. "*Hide!*" I hissed.

He shook his head. "If anyone asks, I'll say you invited me."

"But they'll throw me out!"

"Exactly."

I glared at him and crossed to the door. "Who is it?"

"It is Maria, Thespinis. I come to bring your laundry."

I let out a breath, and opened the door a crack. She stood there with a stack of neatly folded clothes. She looked past me, but I blocked Geoffrey from view with my body. "I was just about to get in the shower. Could you come back later?"

I was afraid the words sounded ungrateful and rude, but Maria simply nodded and left. After she'd gone, I closed the door and turned angrily on Geoffrey. "What was that all about?"

He looked away. "Your being here is an unnecessary risk."

"All I plan to do is keep my eyes open and provide Michael

with a little company if I get the chance."

"Have you forgotten? Someone tried to kill him and they may try again."

"But if I'm here keeping an eye on things," I protested, "I may provide some degree of protection for him."

He seized my hands and brought them up to press against his chest. "And if Spiro and his sister are responsible for the attempt on Michael's life?" he asked. I could feel the tense rise and fall of his chest through the fine linen of his shirt.

"Then I'll be a whole lot safer if you're discreet about your visit."

He sucked in his breath. "Very well," he said reluctantly.

"Does that mean you accept my help?"

"It means," he said, "that though I'm sorely tempted to act the caveman and drag you out of here by your chestnut hair, I suspect it would do no good and perhaps considerable harm. In any case, you may be right. It's possible your being here will provide Michael with some degree of protection."

I smiled triumphantly.

He released my hands and slid his arms around me, jerking my body tightly against his own. "Don't get cocky," he whispered in my ear. "I'm only agreeing to this on the condition you promise not to do anything to put yourself at risk. Listen and watch, but don't play detective."

His breath on my neck sent delicate tremors radiating down my throat. "Don't worry. I'm the world's biggest coward."

His lips slid from my ear to press a light kiss above my bandaged cheek. "Somehow, I doubt that."

"You'd better get going," I said, pushing against his chest with unsteady hands. "You've been here much too long already."

He let me go and stepped back. "Yes," he agreed reluctantly, "I suppose it would be unwise to seduce you in the enemy camp. Very well, when can we meet again? If we're to tackle this together, there's a great deal we need to discuss."

"I'd say tonight, but Spiro's planning to take me out to dinner. How about tomorrow—late, after everyone's asleep?"

"Where? Here?" he asked.

"No, someone might hear us. How about down on the beach? Say around midnight?"

His mouth curved into the ghost of a smile. "At midnight then, Cinderella, and don't forget the glass slipper."

An hour later, as I wandered through the quiet and seemingly deserted villa, I found myself wishing I hadn't been so quick to send Geoffrey on his way. It was the middle of siesta, and the melancholy afternoon sunlight slipping in through the shuttered windows left me feeling lonely and slightly depressed.

Feeling a need to escape the strange, artificial twilight of the house, I slipped outside. The heat of the day hit me like a slap, and my mood cleared. What I needed was to move, to act. I decided to explore the grounds of the villa.

I started toward the garden. From there, the path curved down to Ithaki's private beach, but I'd already been that way when I'd gone swimming, so I left the path and continued to the right, up a winding hill, past a thicket of pines, and toward a wall of cypress trees that towered overhead. Passing through the verdant wall, I found myself halfway up Ithaki's long drive.

Surprised to realize I'd come so far, I was about to turn back when I heard the scrunch of footsteps on gravel further up the drive. Curious, I followed the sound, confining my own steps to a narrow border of dirt I could tread noiselessly. Unfortunately, the dirt verge was covered with the same thistle-like weeds which seem to grow along every Greek road, and I was soon debating whether a quiet approach was worth all the pricks and scratches I was accumulating on my sandal-clad feet and bare ankles.

Turning a curve in the drive, I decided it was, for suddenly I could see whom I was following: Helen, dragon of the playroom. There was something furtive in her manner; she kept looking behind her, as if to make sure no one was following. As her glance swept toward me, I slipped behind a cypress tree, trying to disappear behind the narrow oblong of foliage. I was sure I must be sticking out a mile, and began to imagine the difficulty I'd have explaining this strange game of hide and seek to Spiro or—heaven forbid—his sister Demetra.

I was so immersed in this uncomfortable vision, I didn't notice the footsteps continuing up the drive. Peeking out from behind my makeshift blind, I realized my quarry had disappeared. Ignoring Geoffrey's admonition not to play detective, I sprang to the chase. There had to be something suspicious about Helen sneaking off this way. Where was she going? What was she up to?

I reached the stone pillars marking the entrance to the drive without seeing any sign of her, so I turned out onto the road. Off in the distance, I saw a small, receding figure and I stared after it in amazement. You had to give the woman credit. She might have the personality of a warthog, but she could set a mean pace. Sucking in a deep breath, I set after her at a jog.

We continued at this gasping pace for several miles, until we finally approached the outskirts of a town. Helen slowed, no longer, it seemed, in any hurry. I followed her at an almost sedate pace as the road curved around the hillside, and the olive groves above and below gave way to graceful, whitewashed buildings with heavy wooden doors and iron-railed balconies.

Koussaki, as I later learned it was called, was a pretty town, sleepy and small, with few of the excesses to be found in the resorts to the south. Since it was siesta, the streets were almost empty of cars, and the warm quiet was disturbed only occasionally by the growl of an unmuffled moped roaring past.

Helen turned down a narrow street and I followed, stretching the distance between us as far as I could and still keep her in sight. Luckily, as we walked the town began to wake. Doors opened, window shutters were thrown wide, and the narrow street began to fill with people. Finding safety in numbers, I worked my way closer to Helen, which was a good thing, for she made a sudden turn down a small alley, and if I had been any further back I would have lost her.

As she continued to weave her way through the back streets of the town, however, I began to have misgivings. Had she seen me? Was she leading me on a wild goose chase, or did she have something more sinister in mind? As we took more twists and turns, I began to feel like Theseus without Ariadne's thread; if there was something nasty at the center of this labyrinth, how was I ever going to find my way out? I was mulling over these uncomfortable thoughts when Helen suddenly disappeared.

I don't mean to say she vanished into thin air, though in the mood I was in that might not have surprised me. No, what actually happened was that she made another quick turn down yet another street, and this time when I followed her I found the street came to a dead end. And she was nowhere to be seen.

The street was really just a short alley. It ended abruptly at the wall of a building which formed an "L" around the right side of the cul-de-sac. The backs of two smaller buildings closed the "L" into an inescapable "U." Only two doors—one in the farther of the two buildings, the other in the long end of the "L"—could have provided a possible exit for her. I tried the door on the left.

Would I find the lady or the tiger?

Neither, as it turned out. The door was locked. The rusty knob turned so far and no farther. I crossed the street to the other door and tried again. This time the door swung open with well-oiled ease, and I peered into the darkness, trying to make out what was inside. My eyes were too accustomed to the still-bright afternoon light. I couldn't make out a thing. Swallowing hard, I decided I'd have to chance it. I walked into the darkened room and closed the door behind me.

I stood still for a minute, waiting for my eyes to adjust. As they did, I began to notice slivers of light along the floor to my left. As my eyes adjusted further, I realized that the light was coming from under several doors.

I felt along the nearest one for a knob to turn, but the surface of the door was smooth and it swung back under the pressure of my hand. I held it open a few inches and gazed out into a large chamber dimly-lit by candlelight and sunlight filtered through stained glass. The walls were hung with icons and lined with wooden seats; the main door was flanked by a large candlestand and an icon framed in silver and gold. In disbelief, I pushed the door open further to illuminate the room I was standing in. I stared at the cloth-draped altar in dismay; I was trespassing on the church's sanctuary.

My first instinct, as a well-raised Orthodox girl, was to leave immediately. But as I glanced out into the nave to make sure no one had noticed my intrusion, I saw Helen. She stood near the candle-stand with her back to me, and she was talking to a tall man hidden behind one of the two columns which framed the doorway. In the dim light of the church, all I could see was the back of his head which was illuminated by the flickering candlelight. The golden sheen of his hair seemed somehow familiar, as did the shape of his head. My breath caught. Geoffrey? What was he doing meeting with Helen?

I would have given a great deal to hear what they were saying to each other, but I was too far away to hear a thing. I considered trying to sneak up on them, but the nave of the church offered few places to hide. I was about to push the iconostasis door open further, to see if there was anywhere closer to stand, when suddenly I heard someone cough. I let the door go, and spun around in a panic.

I was still alone in the sanctuary. Belatedly I realized the sound had come from out in the church. Slow, shuffling footsteps crossed calmly from one side of the nave to the other. I eased the door back open slightly to see who was there.

She was small and swathed in black, and apparently she was there to clean the church, for though she was old, with worn brown hands and great cloud of white hair, she set a heavy bucket of soapy water down with ease and settled spryly onto her hands and knees to begin scrubbing the floor.

Satisfied that her attention was occupied by her cleaning, I opened the door wider. I looked toward the candle-stand. Helen and Geoffrey were gone. No doubt they had slipped out of the church when the cleaning woman had entered. I realized it would do no good to question her. She wouldn't have paid attention to two worshippers leaving the church, especially if they had walked out casually.

Well, if they could do it, so could I.

I opened the door quietly, and stepped out in front of the iconostasis, minding my footing so as not to knock over the red glass jars in which candles burned before the icon of the church's patron saint. For a moment I gazed up at the painted face which wore a patient and long-suffering smile. Sorry for the intrusion, I apologized silently. I think it's in a good cause.

As if in reply, the cleaning woman turned around, her dark eyes regarding me strangely. "May the Lord send his angels to watch over you," she said in the formal Greek of the Liturgy, "and protect you from the evil one." Her thumb and two fingers pressed together and swept out the figure of the cross in my direction, then she turned back to her scrubbing. Startled, I stared at her bent back, then turned and walked quietly out of the church.

Its courtyard opened onto a small town square containing a fountain, trees, and scattered groups of red wooden tables belonging to several outdoor cafes. Strands of colored lights were draped through the trees, and local men sat drinking coffee and arguing, while a group of boys, with a young girl toddling excitedly after them, played soccer.

There were few outsiders to be seen. A couple in brightly-colored swimsuits sat sipping beer at one of the cafes, and a tall man with blond hair disappeared into a small souvenir shop just off the square.

Walking quickly, I started toward the shop, but suddenly a hand tapped me on the shoulder. Startled, I whipped around.

"*Per favore, Signorina*—" said a beautifully bronzed and amazingly hairless young man in Italian. He was wearing a skimpy fuchsia Speedo that left little of his anatomy to the imagination.

"You startled me," I complained, not distracted enough by his appearance to forget my mission or forgive his interruption of it.

"Pardon me," he said, switching to English and flashing me a smile bright enough to melt ice. "But please, you take photo my girl and me?" He held up a camera in one hand and motioned back at his companion, a lithe young woman in a green one-piece who was straddling a bright red moped. The pose was a bit reminiscent of a Playboy cover; with those colors, perhaps a Christmas issue.

"I'm sorry," I said, starting to move away, "I'm in a hurry."

He put a restraining hand on my arm. "It will not take long—one minute." He held up a finger to emphasize the point. "Please, miss! A photo for souvenir."

"Sorry! I don't have time."

"It will take one minute only," he repeated stubbornly. His hold on my arm was loose, but intractable. I could break away, but it would mean making a scene.

"Oh, all right," I said, exasperated. I snatched the camera from his hand, relishing the look of irritation that passed over his face. "Go on, get over there." I held the camera up, framing the shot around his girlfriend. As I'd hoped, he released his hold on me and rushed to her side. I clicked the button and then tossed the camera to him still whirring from the automatic advance of the film. Without waiting to see if he'd catch it, I turned and headed for the shop, but as I drew close, I realized it was too late.

The shop was empty save for the owner. Geoffrey was nowhere to be seen.

NINE

When Maria stopped by my room again that evening with my clothes, I asked her if Michael and Mrs. Redfield had returned. She shook her head and told me the two would be dining in town. "And Mr. Skouras?" I asked. "Will he be having dinner here?"

"He will not," Spiro replied from the doorway. "Have you forgotten? I am going to take you out this evening."

Maria slammed the door of the large armoire shut. "There, Thespinis, your dresses now are ready."

"Thank you, Maria."

"*Parakaló*," she murmured.

"That will be all," Spiro said, dismissing her.

But the housekeeper didn't seem quite ready to go. She asked in Greek, "What should I tell the mistress when she returns?"

"About what?"

"About where you and the young lady have gone."

"That is no business of yours—or my sister's," he snapped.

She shrugged. "She will ask. I only wish to know what I am to say."

"Tell her—" he bit off the words and drew a deep, angry breath. He began again in a calmer tone. "Tell her I am taking Miss Stewart to dinner and then we are going to the Achilleon. We may be late, I have a key, and no one need wait up. Now, I think that is all you need to know, so please leave us."

She bobbed her head and left. Spiro watched her retreating back, then turned to me. For the first time he seemed to notice my dusty and disheveled appearance. He frowned.

"Can you be ready by nine o'clock?" he asked. As it was only half-past seven, the doubt in his voice was hardly flattering. "The dress at the Achilleon—it is formal. You have something appropriate?"

I crossed to the armoire and quickly scanned my dresses. I pulled out my green silk. Thanks to Maria, it was spotlessly clean and perfectly pressed and looked one hundred-percent better than when I'd worn it the night before to dine with Geoffrey.

Spiro was less than enthusiastic. "I will find something of Demetra's and some jewelry as well, and perhaps Aphrodite can do something with your hair."

I bit down hard on my lip, suppressing a retort. If I was going to be of use to Michael, I had to develop a thicker skin. "That will be fine," I said.

"Good," replied Spiro, sounding unsure. He surveyed me once more, gave a faint shrug, and turned and left the room. As his footsteps receded down the hall, I sat down on the bed, feeling a bit like a melon that had been squeezed and found wanting.

Aphrodite did do wonders with my hair. She plaited my unruly locks into an elegant French braid which she threaded with gold ribbons that glittered in the light. The ribbons were to match the elegant dress Spiro had extracted from his sister's closet for me to wear. The shimmering gold gown was beautiful, and I felt an almost atavistic thrill as Aphrodite slipped it over my shoulders, though the thrill was tempered by dismay at the thought of squeezing my bountiful curves into a dress belonging to a woman of much more fashionable and moderate lines.

Yet in the end, I had to give Spiro credit. He obviously knew women's bodies, and he had guessed correctly in thinking I just might fit into this particular dress of his sister's. For though the lovely beaded sheath clung to my torso like a second skin, and the satin folds of the bodice dipped into a deeper and more expansive décolletage than I had ever worn, and though the flaring tulle skirt rode higher up my thigh than I suspect it was ever intended to do by its designer, when I turned to gaze at my reflection in the mirror, I felt magically transformed.

I slipped on the exorbitantly expensive but highly fashionable gold sandals I'd been foresighted enough to fall in love with in an Athens boutique, and Aphrodite put the finishing touches on my coiffure. She curled the hard-to-manage hair at my temples into loose ringlets and secured them in place with two gold combs encrusted with emeralds (another unwitting loan from Demetra Redfield courtesy of her brother.) Aphrodite then draped the matching necklace around my throat. When she was done, she scanned me up and down, then kissed the tips of her fingers in satisfaction.

Spiro knocked on the door a few minutes later. When Aphrodite stepped out of the way, his eyebrows flew up in pleased surprise, but his only words were, "You are ready?"

"I guess so," I said, reaching for my purse.

He shook his head, and held out a gold satin clutch purse.

"Spiro," I protested, "I don't want to use any more of your sister's things."

He crossed to me and put the purse in my hands. "It looks much better with this," he said impatiently, his hand briefly touching his sister's necklace. It did seem silly to accept the loan of a dress and such expensive jewelry and then demur at a purse, so I reluctantly accepted the clutch and scooped the contents of my own bag into it.

As Spiro took my arm and escorted me from the room, I sensed how keyed up he was, but I had little time to wonder at the reason before I was distracted by a figure standing in the shadow of the hallway, watching us. With a start of recognition, I realized it was Helen. She stood still and motionless as we walked by, but her gaze bore into me with an intensity that unnerved me. For a moment, I was tempted to emulate my grandmother and make the sign against the evil eye. Instead, I drew closer to Spiro.

He was too caught up in his own thoughts to notice my disquiet, but as the solid oak front door closed soundly behind us, I felt better. Spiro led the way to the garage where his red Lamborghini was parked. It was an impressive-looking car with sleek lines that screamed money. As he opened the door and helped me in with practiced gallantry, I settled into the handcrafted leather seat and wondered just what my host did for a living.

The Lamborghini climbed slowly up the gravel drive, but when it turned out Ithaki's gate onto the paved highway it gathered speed and hurtled south. The road, winding narrowly above high cliffs, had seemed wonderfully scenic that morning in the taxi, but now it was dark save for the sweep of our headlights and the distant light from the rising moon. After three consecutive hairpin turns where the road seemed to fall away into nothingness just ahead of us, I decided to risk creasing Demetra's borrowed dress and slipped on my seat belt.

Spiro, finally seeming to relax now that we were moving, grinned. "You do not trust my driving?"

"Let's just say this road makes me a little nervous."

"Don't worry. I could drive this stretch—how do you say it?—with closed eyes."

"I'd rather you didn't."

He laughed. "Only a fool would close his eyes when there is a beautiful woman sitting next to him."

Spiro was a skillful driver, and he seemed to know the road well, so I forced myself to relax and enjoy the drive and the glimpses of scenery visible in the moonlight. I also, from time to time, stole glances at him. With his hands set loosely yet commandingly on the wheel and a small line of concentration visible between his brows, he looked quite prepared to tackle anything that got in his way. *Even a little boy?* I wondered.

We sped through Corfu Town, continuing south past the airport. The highway curved around a large bay and then back down to the sea, and we drove some distance with the sea shimmering like silver cloth to our left. Then Spiro swung the Lamborghini sharply to the right, and we turned up a narrow winding road that seemed to climb straight up. We drove some minutes in wooded darkness before coming round a curve to face a well-lit white building of cascading curves. The car turned down a beautifully paved driveway and pulled to a stop before marble steps and wide crystal doors that glistened in the darkness.

It wasn't a restaurant, but a private club, and the dining room Spiro and I were led to was ornate but almost empty. A

He shook his head in disgust. "I see Geoffrey has been busy with his lies."

"What do you mean?"

"I suppose he claims my sister murdered her husband?"

I shook my head, startled by Spiro's directness. "He told me he doesn't believe his brother's death was an accident, but he never accused your sister."

"Except to the police."

"*What?*"

"The English have little love for foreigners, and the police were quite ready to believe Redfield's accusations. Fortunately, they could find no evidence that the automobile had been tampered with."

"If there's no evidence," I said, "why do you think he's so reluctant to accept that his brother's death was an accident?"

"Besides wishing to make trouble for my sister?" Spiro shrugged. "Perhaps he cannot accept his brother's death because of the guilt he, himself, feels."

I tensed. "Guilt? What do you mean? What does Geoffrey have to feel guilty about?"

Spiro watched my reaction closely, and I suddenly worried that he saw all too much. "What does he have to feel guilty about?" he echoed in a voice that held more than a trace of mockery. "Why only that he hated his brother so much that he once tried to kill him, that's all."

young waiter appeared. His greeting to Spiro was formal but enthusiastic. They murmured briefly together, and then the waiter led us to a table overlooking a large picture window. Spiro ordered for both of us, and then the waiter strode off, leaving us to face each other over a white linen-clad table. Perhaps it was my imagination, but it seemed to me that Spiro averted his eyes whenever his gaze wandered to the bandaged side of my face.

"So, how did your business go today?" I asked, anxious to shift his attention.

He started, and glanced at me sharply. "What?"

"Your business," I repeated. "The business that took you into town today. How did it go?"

"Ah, that." He shrugged. "It went as I expected." His mouth compressed into a tight line. "And you? Did you enjoy your day at Ithaki? I hope you did not find it too dull?"

I wanted to laugh, but instead just shook my head. I gave him a brief and heavily expurgated description of my day, leaving out entirely my visit from Geoffrey, Helen's rendezvous, and the details of my run-in with Paul.

The food soon arrived, and we kept up a patter of small talk while we ate, but neither of us seemed to have our hearts in it. Spiro once again grew distracted, and from time to time would stare out the large window. I looked to see what had him so fascinated, but the only thing visible was leafy darkness.

I decided it was time to start digging for information. Fiddling with my fork, I said casually, "Spiro, I've been thinking about what happened Tuesday. Don't you think it a bit odd that Michael should have such a close call only two months after his father was killed in a car crash?"

Spiro's attention snapped back to me like an over-stretched rubber band. "It is a coincidence," he declared, "nothing more."

"Hmmm, perhaps. But I can't help wondering if maybe Geoffrey's right. Maybe someone is trying to hurt Michael."

Spiro's dark eyes suddenly flashed with anger. "Who, Christine?" he demanded. "Me? My sister?"

"Of course not," I said quickly. "But what if some stranger is behind all this? What about Michael's father? Is your sister sure that his death was an accident?"

TEN

It had been built as a refuge from the Hapsburg court by a grieving Empress Elizabeth of Austria and had become a summer palace for Kaiser Wilhelm II. Now it was neither refuge nor palace, but a casino, and as Spiro and I walked up the Achilleon's red-carpeted marble staircase, I was glad for my borrowed finery. The glittering crowd surging up around us seemed to have come straight from Monte Carlo.

At the top of the stairs was a mural-sized painting depicting Achilles's triumph over Hector. The surging crowd spilled past us as I stopped to gaze at it, and Spiro tugged at my arm to remind me to keep moving. He led the way out to the terrace and one of several roulette tables, and managed to get both of us seated despite the crush. Once more I sensed in him a pent-up tension and I wondered if he was an addicted gambler, but he placed relatively small, conservative bets and seemed more intent on explaining the rules and showing me how to play the odds than on succumbing to gambling fever. Eventually, I decided his excitement must have another source. I thought the source might have arrived, when a soft, caressing voice called out his name.

She was short and generously curved and dressed in a silver gown cut tightly from breasts to hips and then flowing in a foam of ruffles and tulle to the floor. "Aspasia," Spiro murmured, rising to his feet. To my surprise, he did not sound pleased.

"Spiro, my sweet!" she exclaimed softly in Greek. "What luck meeting you here." Her tone was casual, but the look in her dark eyes was not. She slid a beautifully manicured hand along the lapel of his jacket. "Come, darling, buy me a drink. It's been much too long since I saw you last." Spiro looked anything but enthusiastic about her proposal, but she didn't seem to notice.

She was, I estimated, in her mid-thirties, with honey-blond hair cut short and full around a small, sharp-featured face. Her olive skin was deeply tanned, and large diamonds sparkled at her bare throat and wrist and right ring finger–the finger Greek brides wear their wedding rings on. This last diamond flashed as her hand slipped through his arm to lead him away.

"I'm not alone," he remonstrated, resisting the gentle tug. Switching to English he added, "Allow me to introduce you to a friend. Aspasia, this is Miss Christine Stewart. Miss Stewart is staying at the villa for a few days."

Her glance swiveled from Spiro to me. She inclined her head politely and echoed my name, but there was a note in her voice like the far-off warning of a teapot ready to boil.

"Christine," Spiro said, "this is *Mrs.* Aspasia Sminiotiou." The slight emphasis he put on the word "Mrs." caused her small lips to tighten. "Aspasia is an old, old friend." The lips tightened still more, leaving creases in her pink-frosted lipstick. "Her husband happens to be one of the most influential men on the island: president of the Bank of Kerkyra, and an old school mate of mine." He flashed her a dazzling smile. "Where is Panos, by the way, my dear? Didn't he accompany you here this evening?"

Two thin and carefully shaped eyebrows lowered angrily. "Of course," she snapped in Greek, "does he ever not?"

"Ah, yes, I see him now. Over at the baccarat table. I must go and say hello. Christine, you will excuse me?"

"Of course."

"Aspasia?" He held out his arm to her in a gesture that held more challenge than gallantry; she declined it with an outraged toss of her head. Spiro shrugged as she swept away like a regal tornado. Then he, too, left.

Their exchange had been the focus of much attention, and I was chagrined to realize I, too, figured in the amused speculation that now rippled round the roulette table. My first instinct was to leave, but pride kept me in my chair. I focused on the bouncing silver ball and placed bets I didn't care whether I won.

Yet strangely enough, I did. My small stack of counters grew to a fairly large pile, and the curious glances and soft whispers were soon replaced by cheers of encouragement and speculation at how long my run would last. I began to feel reckless and excited, and setting aside enough counters to repay Spiro, I slid the remaining stack onto a single number and settled nervously back in my chair to await the outcome.

It seemed that everyone clustered round the table wanted in on the game, and minutes ticked by as the bets were laid. Impatiently glancing around the terrace, I suddenly saw something that made me forget all about my reckless bet: in one of the doorways leading out to the terrace, Geoffrey Redfield was chatting amiably with Aspasia Sminiotiou. As I watched, the two seemed to turn in unison and look over in my direction.

"*Deka-eksi*!" called out the croupier, and a murmur of excitement circled the table.

"You have won, you have won!" exclaimed an elderly woman on my left. She slapped my back in congratulations and almost knocked me over onto the green baize table. In stunned disbelief I watched the croupier slide an enormous pile of chips my way.

"What next will you bet?" demanded an avid young man on my right.

I shook my head. "That's enough for me. I've already pushed my luck too far." I opened my borrowed purse and swept the pile of counters into it until it bulged. The young man looked at me reprovingly, but the elderly lady gave me a quick nod and a wink.

"Smart girl," she murmured.

I smiled at her and rose, glancing briefly toward the doorway, but Geoffrey and Aspasia were gone. Spiro and Aspasia's husband had also disappeared from the baccarat table, so I wandered down the terrace steps toward the gardens. Leaning against a balustrade, I gazed out at the view. Empress Elizabeth had chosen the site well; from here one could see all the way to the moonlit sea.

"Do you think it altogether wise wandering down here alone in the dark? Especially dressed like that," said a deep voice directly behind me. "Where's Prince Charming?"

I didn't turn to look at him. "As far as I know, Spiro's talking with an old friend of his. Didn't the friend's wife mention that, or were the two of you too busy discussing me?"

"Wife?" Geoffrey repeated, sounding curious. "Don't tell me Skouras is off chatting with Panos Sminiotiou?"

"Why so surprised? As I said, they're old friends."

"*Were* old friends," Geoffrey corrected. "Panos is notoriously jealous, and he's quite aware of his wife's interest in Skouras. From what I've heard, he and Spiro have scarcely exchanged a dozen words in three years. I wonder what the devil they can be talking about now?"

I shrugged. "I don't know, and I don't particularly care."

"Hmmm." His voice grew soft and low. "Have I mentioned how utterly delectable you look this evening?" I didn't answer, and he moved closer, sliding his arms around me and pressing a kiss onto my bare shoulder. "We weren't really talking about you," he murmured, trailing kisses up the side of my neck, "at least, not in the way you think." I shivered. "Are you cold? Here." He draped his jacket over my shoulders. "I looked over at you, and Aspasia followed my glance and asked me what I knew about Spiro's new girlfriend. I asked her which one, and that irritated her enough she forgot the catty remark she'd been about to make."

I still wouldn't look at him. With an impatient sigh, he turned me around. "Don't you believe me?"

"That's not why … I'm upset," I said, slipping off his jacket and stepping out of the warm circle of his arms.

"Then what?" His face was swathed in shadow, but his voice betrayed exasperation.

"Is it true," I demanded in a low voice, "that you hated your brother? Hated him so much you actually tried to kill him?"

Geoffrey went absolutely still for a moment, then he let out a long breath and leaned against the balustrade next to me. "Skouras has a nasty little mouth on him, doesn't he?"

"Is it true?"

"In a way." Geoffrey turned to stare out at the darkness.

"What happened?"

"Nothing much really. My brother and I simply fell in love with the same woman."

I stared at his darkened profile. "Michael's mother?"

He nodded. "Her name was Elizabeth. I met her at University, and when I graduated and obtained my first position, I asked her to be my wife. She said yes, and I took her home to meet my family. My father and William adored her. My mother was less enthusiastic, but for my sake hid it well. We set a date to be married.

"Then I received a commission which took me out of the country for six weeks. When I returned, Elizabeth had changed her mind. The wedding was canceled. I buried myself in my work and consoled myself with the thought that she was simply suffering from cold feet, and that—given time—she would reconsider.

"But several months passed and I heard nothing from her. Then one day I had a surprise visit from my brother. He announced Elizabeth was going to marry him. He said he hoped I'd accept the matter gracefully and pointed out that he had much more to offer a wife, especially a wife like Elizabeth, who deserved only the best. I told him to go to hell."

Geoffrey's voice was flat, emotionless, and yet somehow the whole scene seemed to rise up hauntingly before my eyes. I reached out and gripped his hand, and he turned his head to look at me. My eyes had adjusted to the darkness, and I saw his expression change, soften. "Do you always go about dispensing your sympathy so freely?" he asked.

I withdrew my hand and turned away.

In a voice devoid of all the tender nuance it had possessed a moment earlier, he continued, "They were married three months later. I avoided the wedding, and spent much of the day getting thoroughly drunk. I arrived at the reception just as the happy couple were setting off for the honeymoon, and my brother and I got into a shattering row. Our argument soon turned physical, and without realizing it we fought our way toward the main staircase. Landing me a particularly humiliating blow, William barked at me that it was obvious Elizabeth had picked the better man, so why didn't I just crawl home and sleep it off?"

Geoffrey paused and turned, meeting my gaze squarely. "Needless to say, I didn't take kindly to the words. In what I can only describe as a blind rage, I lunged at him, almost sending us both crashing down the stairs. Fortunately, he was more sober than I was and grabbed at the banister at the last minute. He managed to stop our fall, but hit his head in the process. As it turned out, it was only a glancing blow, but William considered, perhaps rightly, that I'd almost killed him."

I moved closer, reaching down to slip my hand in his once more. "Did the two of you ever make it up?"

Geoffrey gave my hand a squeeze and then shook his head. "After Elizabeth left William, he and I reached a sort of wary truce, but no, things were never the same between us."

"That must have made it harder when he died."

"When he was killed," Geoffrey corrected harshly. "And yes, it did make it harder. Much harder."

I understood now why Robert wondered at his objectivity. I asked gently, "It was two months ago?"

He gave a small, stiff nod. "March 15th, to be precise."

I murmured uncomfortably, "The Ides of March."

Geoffrey grimaced. "Yes. William was a bit like Caesar in the financial world. Empires fell before him."

"He must have made a lot of enemies," I said.

"Perhaps. But he also kept a phalanx of servants and employees about him to fend them off."

"Then how could somebody have tampered with his car—if they did?" I asked.

"That particular day William gave all his servants the day off. He was alone in the house, and the garage was deserted. It would have been an easy enough thing to manage."

"Did your brother do that often?"

"What?"

"Give all the servants the day off."

"No," Geoffrey replied tensely. "As far as I know it was the first time he'd ever done it."

"That's interesting."

"He didn't send them off because he was thinking of doing away with himself, if that's what you're thinking."

"Is that the police theory?"

"One of them." His tone was bitter.

I shook my head. "If he was planning to drive himself off a

cliff, I don't see that there'd be much point in getting rid of the servants. He was going to be miles away anyway. On the other hand, I don't see how anyone else could have known he was going to give his staff a holiday, unless—" I bit my lip. "You said your brother was alone in the house. Where was Demetra?"

"In London. Shopping."

"So she has an alibi, of sorts."

"Of sorts," he agreed. "Though I would hardly call it iron-clad. Unfortunately, Skouras's is a bit more solid. He didn't arrive in the country until the following morning."

"Spiro was in England?" I exclaimed in surprise.

Geoffrey nodded. "He made a habit of visiting my brother and Demetra from time to time—usually when he needed money."

"Was that the reason this time?" I asked.

"Unfortunately, I haven't been able to find out one way or the other."

"Hmmm. He doesn't give the appearance of being short of cash. But wait! I've just thought of something. Remember what you were saying about how odd it was that Spiro was talking to Panos Sminiotiou?"

"Yes. So?"

"Well, isn't Sminiotiou a banker?" I said.

Geoffrey stared at me and then said slowly, "He is indeed."

When I returned to the terrace, Panos Sminiotiou was back at the baccarat table and Aspasia was holding court at the bar, but Spiro was nowhere to be seen. I searched for him for a long time, then gave up and went to cash in my chips. I finally discovered him a good while later, standing near a row of stone nymphs, scanning the tables for me. His expression was grim, and I wondered if the meeting with his banker friend had gone badly. When he saw me approach, the tense planes of his face smoothed into a look of neutral inquiry. "You tired of the roulette?"

I gave a small laugh. "On the contrary, I was afraid it might tire of me."

"I don't understand."

"I had a streak of luck and decided I'd better stop while I was ahead. I won quite a bit. See?" I opened his sister's purse and showed him a formidable stack of ten thousand drachma notes.

His eyebrows rose. "So, at least one of us has had a profitable evening. Good. You will not mind if we leave early?"

The drive home was fast, and, for the most part, silent. Spiro vented his frustrations on the road, and the Lamborghini slalomed back down toward the sea at a speed that caused me to press both hands against the dashboard. Obviously, whatever Spiro had gone to the casino for, he had come away empty-handed.

When we reached Ithaki, the villa looked dark, but as we rattled noisily down the gravel drive, lights began springing on, and as we swung past the house toward the garage, the front door opened and Maria peered anxiously out into the dark. Spiro turned off the ignition with an angry twist, and came round to help me from the car. As he took my arm to guide me out of the darkened garage, I struggled to undo the clasp of his sister's necklace.

"Do not bother with it," he said impatiently. "It can wait until morning."

"I don't want your sister to think her jewelry's been stolen."

"She will not—"

"Help me, will you?" I interrupted, turning my back to him.

"Very well," he snapped, pulling aside the hair that obscured the fastening. "If that is what you wish." With one deft movement he unclasped it, then holding both ends of the necklace to prevent it from slipping off, he bent down and kissed my neck.

Somewhere behind us someone discreetly cleared her throat. My first instinct was to spin around, but Spiro held me rigidly in place while he gathered up the necklace, deposited a second kiss next to my ear, and murmured, "We shall continue this later." Releasing his hold on me, he slipped his sister's necklace into his pocket and turned around. Chagrined, I followed suit.

Maria stood at the entrance of the garage watching us. "Forgive the interruption, *kyrie*," she said, addressing Spiro in Greek, "but your sister has telephoned from town. There has been another accident, and she is anxious to speak with you."

At the word "accident," my knees went weak. I placed a steadying hand on the car and exclaimed tensely, "Is it Michael? Is he all right?"

Maria nodded and crossed herself. "Yes, he is fine, thanks be to God! Poor *poulaki*, he has a few more cuts and bruises, but he is a boy, he will heal."

Spiro was staring at me oddly. Too late I realized my entire exchange with Maria had taken place in Greek. I pulled the borrowed combs from my hair and held them out to Spiro. "Hadn't you better go talk to your sister?"

He accepted the combs, but retained my hand when I tried to pull it away. "Actually, at this moment I would rather speak with you. But you are right, I must go." He raised my hand to his lips, while his dark eyes fixed on my face. "Do you know, I begin to wonder if I have judged my sister too harshly."

"How so?" I asked faintly.

"Until this evening, I thought her fears to be irrational and unjustified."

"And now?"

Spiro eyed me with a calculating look. "Now?" he repeated, abruptly releasing my hand. "Now I wonder if my sister has been right all along."

Eleven

Friday dawned hot and still.

After a restless night, I woke late and ate breakfast alone. Maria informed me Demetra was in bed with a headache and Spiro had left early for town. No mention was made of Michael. After breakfast I looked for him in the garden, but neither he nor the gardener, Paul, was there. I went by his room, but the door was opened by Helen. When I asked her where Michael was, she simply shook her head and closed the door in my face.

Needing some outlet for my growing restlessness, I went for a swim, but even the beauty of the Ionian Sea was insufficient to quiet the thoughts racing through my head. Try as I might, I could not stop thinking about Michael's second "accident."

I had gleaned the basic facts from Aphrodite at breakfast. Sometime around eleven-thirty the previous evening, Michael and Demetra had been standing outside a house in Benitses, a suburb south of Corfu, saying goodbye to the friends who had invited them to dinner. Demetra had been standing near the hosts' front gate, and Michael had been standing a little further out in the street keeping a lookout for Paul, who was late picking them up.

Suddenly a car without lights had come roaring up the narrow road. One of the friends had called out a warning, and Michael—who was directly in the car's path—had dived over a low stone wall and down a small embankment to safety. The car had hurtled heedlessly on, but another of Demetra's friends had seen enough of it to give the police a description. The car had later been found abandoned near the Achilleon, which was less than a mile up the road. The car had been stolen from the

Achilleon's own parking lot, and the police theory was that it had been taken by joy riders and abandoned after the incident with Michael.

I might have found the theory plausible, had it not been Michael's second near-fatal accident in three days.

I kicked the azure blue water. I had come to Ithaki believing Michael might be in some vague, hypothetical danger. Now the threat seemed all too real, and I was afraid.

After my swim, I went back to the house, but lunch was another solitary meal. After lunch I read in my room for a while, but my attention kept straying from the pages. One of the times my gaze wandered, I noticed Demetra Redfield's purse on the blue chair, where I'd tossed it the night before. Maria had already discreetly taken Demetra's dress off to be cleaned, but had left the purse, perhaps not realizing it belonged to her mistress.

I emptied it out and took it next door to Spiro's room, glad of an excuse to ask him where he'd been the night before when I'd looked for him on the terrace. But there was no answer to my knock. Presumably he was still in town. I returned to my own room and propped the purse up on the bureau so I'd remember to give it to him later.

As I was putting the stuff I'd dumped out of Demetra's purse back into my own, I came across something that didn't belong: an appointment card that had obviously been purse for some time. The corners were bent and the expensive ivory card stock was smudged.

Curious, I read the name printed in neat black type: *THE WHITCOMB GROUP*, and underneath, *Specialists in Infertility.* The address was in London, and at the bottom of the card was a date and time written in careful script: *15 March, 11:00 a.m.*

Embarrassed to have intruded on something so personal, I was about to put the card back, when the significance of the handwritten date stopped me in my tracks. *March 15.* The day Geoffrey's brother had had his accident.

It might just be a coincidence, but I was getting tired of those, so I found a piece of paper and copied the information. Then I put the card back into Demetra's purse and slipped the paper into my wallet behind my driver's license.

I returned to my book, but it was harder than ever to concentrate. After rereading a single page three times, I gave up and decided to go for another swim. An hour later, I was tramping soggily back up the path to the villa, when I heard the sound of two men arguing up ahead, their lowered voices carrying clearly in the still, warm air.

"I'm only asking for thirty-thousand!" exclaimed a voice I recognized as Spiro's. "And I will pay back the money by the end of the year."

"Sorry, I just can't do it," replied Robert Humphreys stiffly. "A trust is a trust, and I can't go breaking it—"

"But the boy is worth millions!"

"True, but he shan't be for long if I go parceling off his inheritance bit by bit. Surely you can get the money elsewhere?"

"Do you think I would demean myself to borrow from a child if I had any other choice?"

"Your sister?" Robert asked.

"You know very well her situation! Redfield left her some property, but her money is tied up almost as tightly as the boy's. That husband of hers was a miser himself, and he expected her to live as one also. If it were not for—"

Belatedly, I realized the voices were growing louder and that the two men were headed my way. Turning, I ran back down the path toward the beach. Unfurling my beach mat as I went, I threw it down under the trees, tossed my towel on top of it, and slid as quietly as I could into the water. I began paddling softly about, my eyes fixed on the place where the path turned out onto the beach.

For some minutes, no one appeared. I strained my ears for the sound of voices, but all I could hear was my own thumping heart. When at last a single figure made its way out onto the pebbled strand, I was surprised to see it was Robert who approached, not Spiro, as I'd expected.

"Hello, Christine," he called to me. "Enjoying your swim?"

I nodded and began wading toward him. I stepped gingerly over the large and somewhat algae-covered stones at the water's edge, but my left foot slipped slightly, and I jammed my toe into a jagged rock. I hopped out of the water, cursing.

"You've hurt yourself," Robert commented unnecessarily as

he put an arm around my waist to steady me. Together—me limping, he having his fine linen suit dripped upon—we made our way to where my beach mat lay sprawled beneath the pines. He helped me down onto it, and then he unfurled his handkerchief, a magnificent square of snowy white linen, over the grey stones of the shingle, and sat down next to me.

"Well, Christine, slippery rocks aside, what do you think of Ithaki?"

I hugged my legs and gazed out at the azure sea. "It's a nice house, and a beautiful stretch of beach."

He smiled faintly. "And what of the residents? How have they been treating you?"

"All right, I suppose, considering that I'm intruding on their hospitality. Mrs. Redfield's none too pleased to have me here, but Spiro seems willing to put up with me. "

"I must admit," he said, "I was rather surprised to learn you were here." He flashed me an inquiring look. "Demetra claims Geoffrey's been pestering you?"

I hesitated for a moment, then decided it would be best to tell him the truth. "Actually, I just said that to convince her and her brother to let me stay."

He nodded. "I thought it might be something like that. I suppose you're here to keep an eye on Michael?"

I shrugged. "I hoped my being here might give the kid some kind of protection." I picked up a smooth grey stone and flung it angrily into the water. "But it hasn't done much good so far."

His expression turned grave. "Yes, I heard what happened last night."

"I suppose you think it's just another unhappy coincidence?"

He hesitated, and then said, "To be honest, Christine, I don't know what to think. Drivers in this country are a reckless lot, and it is plausible that a would-be thief would be more reckless still."

"But this is the second close call Michael's had this week!"

"I know." Robert's tone was somber. "And I confess, I'm worried. That's why I've come back. I find the whole situation very troubling."

I felt a rush of impatience. "It's a damn sight more than that! Next time Michael might not be so lucky. The killer might succeed."

"If there is a killer," he countered quietly. "Despite the events of the last few days, I'm still not convinced there is."

"I know," I snapped, "there's no motive."

"Unless you think it was Geoffrey behind that wheel."

"Of course I don't!"

"You needn't scowl at me like that. It's precisely because I think him incapable of hurting Michael that I find it so difficult to believe these mishaps are anything but the accidents they appear." He reached out and touched my hand. "Still, I appreciate your concern for the boy."

"I can't help it. He's a sweetie."

His hazel eyes twinkled. "And so like his uncle."

I studiously ignored this last comment. "I also know how tough it is to lose one's father at this age."

Robert's expression sobered. "Yes, the poor lad has had a difficult time of it. Still, I'm not sure you're doing him a favor by remaining here. Demetra seems determined not to let him out of her sight while you're on the premises."

"Then I'll just have to convince her I can be trusted," I said. "In the meantime—"

One sandy eyebrow fluttered upwards. "Yes?"

"Perhaps you could speak to her as well?"

He flashed me a wry smile. "I'll do my best."

Robert stayed to dinner. And whether it was his influence or simply that Demetra decided there was safety in numbers, Michael was granted leave from his room and joined us at the table.

He looked so pale and withdrawn when he entered the room, I felt a pang of concern, but he became more animated as the evening progressed, especially when Robert invited Demetra for a walk on the beach and suggested Michael be allowed to stay behind and join me in a game of chess—under Helen's watchful eye, of course.

I've never been better than an average chess player, but Michael was quite good, and it took little pretending to turn our game into a genuine contest. I was mourning a lost bishop and considering my next move when Michael leaned across the board and inquired in a loud whisper, "I say, Miss Stewart. Is it true? Did you really break the bank at the casino?"

"Where in the world did you hear that?" I asked.

He grinned. "Uncle Spiro told me this morning."

"I'm afraid he was exaggerating a bit."

"He was?" he said in disappointment. "Oh, well. I suppose I should have known. Uncle Spiro tends to rally one a bit. He once told me his grandfather was Lord Byron's illegitimate son. I believed it until I did my sums and realized his grandfather would have had to have been nearly a hundred-and-thirty-five when Uncle Spiro was born."

"That does undermine the story's credibility somewhat," I said dryly. "What did he say when you pointed that out to him?"

"He shrugged and said his father and grandfather both married late in life."

We looked at each other and began to laugh. Soon Helen was inquiring testily from across the room what the joke was, but though we tried to stop, we kept breaking into giggles every time our eyes met. Finally, she marched over and announced frostily that it was time for Michael to go to bed. Instantly we sobered, but seeing my expression, Michael darted one of his mischievous elf looks at me and said it was just as well, because in three more moves he would have checkmated me. I felt better until he wished me goodnight, and I noticed the drooping curve of his shoulders as he followed Helen from the room.

Fighting the urge to kick something, I gritted my teeth and put the chess pieces away, then went outside on the patio and began pacing up and down, gulping the cool night air in the hopes it would cool my anger.

Suddenly someone appeared out of the shadows in front of me. "Something has upset you?"

Startled, I gasped.

Spiro raised one dark eyebrow mockingly. "I frightened you?"

"It's just you weren't at dinner. I thought you were in town."

He shook his head, but offered no explanation. "You have

not answered my question. Has something upset you?"

"No, not really. I'm just restless."

He smiled grimly. "I, too. Come, let us take a drive. It is a warm night and the fresh air will do us good."

"I don't know, it's getting late...."

"Nonsense," Spiro said, taking my arm. "The evening has just begun. You cannot wish to go to bed so early. Even the chickens are still awake."

I tried to hang back. "I don't know. I'm awfully tired."

He frowned. "Yet a moment ago you said you were restless. I hope you are not avoiding my company."

Our eyes met. "Of course not," I murmured. "All right. I suppose a short drive won't kill me."

He smiled—baring all those brilliant white teeth—as if my choice of words amused him. "Shall we?" He led me down the steps and around the house toward the garage.

"Shouldn't we let someone know we're going?" I asked.

His grip on my arm tightened. "There's no need. Come."

For a moment, I felt a rush of panic. I wondered if I should make a scene, yell, even run away, though I knew if I did it would mean the end of my stay at the villa. Then I saw someone watching us from the shadows.

Geoffrey. No doubt he'd arrived early for our meeting on the beach and had overheard my conversation with Spiro. I relaxed against Spiro's grip, and allowed him to lead the way.

We reached the garage. Suddenly the faint footsteps I'd been straining to hear grew louder. Spiro turned, as did I. A man's dark form stood silhouetted in the doorway. He stepped forward into the light of the garage, and my heart sank.

The man standing there smiling at us was not Geoffrey, but Paul. "A nice evening for a drive," he commented in Greek.

Spiro relaxed. "Yes. What brings you out here at such an hour?"

"I was wondering if I could borrow the Fiat. There's this girl in Kassiopi—"

"Go ahead," Spiro said impatiently, "take it. Just see to it you're back by morning."

Paul shrugged and flashed a grin. "I will try."

As we drove south to Ypsos, Spiro's mood was difficult to

gauge, but we sped the ten kilometer distance in less time than I care to remember. As we descended the dark, curving road into the brightly lit main drag of the resort town, the road began to fill with people and the air to vibrate with music.

"Do you wish to stop for a drink?" Spiro asked as he swerved the car into a tiny parking space at the side of the road. I presumed he meant it as a rhetorical question, so I didn't bother to answer as we got out to walk.

We entered a bar decorated in pink neon. It was crowded, and full of cigarette smoke, but at least its sound system was muted, and one didn't have to yell to be heard over the music.

To my chagrin, Spiro ordered ouzo for us both. Perhaps my chagrin was evident to the waiter, or perhaps he took pity on my weak female constitution, for when he brought us our glasses and the tall, thin bottle of ouzo, he also brought me a small pitcher of ice water. I beamed him a grateful smile, and dashed some water into my glass before Spiro could fill the thing entirely with the clear liquor. With the addition of water, the drink turned milky—a transformation Spiro observed with a grimace.

"You spoil the beauty of it," he reproached, before pouring himself a full glass and tossing it off. He poured himself another, and made as if to add some more ouzo to my glass, but I covered the top of the glass with my hand.

"I'm fine, thanks."

He shrugged and set the bottle down. Then he picked up his glass and stared at it moodily. "Tell me. In those American schools of yours, did they ever teach you of the goddess Nemesis?"

"A little," I said, curious at his choice of topic. "She's the goddess of retribution, isn't she? The one who punished Polycrates, even though he threw his ring into the sea?"

He nodded grimly. "It came back to him, you know, in a fish. Poor devil, try though he might, he could not escape his fate."

"Well, from what I remember of the story, it was no great loss. He didn't exactly sound like a great guy."

Spiro's fingers tightened on the glass until his knuckles turned white. "Who are you to judge? You cannot know why he did what he did!"

I was startled by his vehemence. "I'm sorry. You're right. I'm in no position to judge. I don't even know if this Polycrates was a real person."

Spiro glowered at me, and then suddenly he relaxed back into his chair and shrugged. "It doesn't matter whether he was or not." He lifted his glass as if making a toast. "The truth is, Christine, men make their own fates." He downed the contents of his glass in one long gulp.

The determination in his voice made me shiver. I took a sip of ouzo and tried to come up with another topic of conversation. Spiro, however, was no longer in a talkative mood, and as the level of liquor in the bottle went steadily down, I began worrying about how I was going to get back to Ithaki. I certainly wasn't going to let Spiro drive me anywhere with that much ouzo in his system.

I emerged from these worrying reflections to find him gazing at me with an expression that made me realize wrestling him for the keys might not be my biggest problem.

"Spiro," I said a little desperately, as he poured the last drops from the bottle into his glass and seemed about to order another one, "it's getting late. Shouldn't we head back soon?"

He flashed me a decidedly wolfish grin. "An excellent idea," he said, gesturing somewhat unsteadily for the waiter. The waiter ignored him. Spiro signaled again. Again, the waiter pretended not to see. I glanced at my watch and silently swore. It was almost twelve. Geoffrey might already be waiting.

I was contemplating going after the bill myself, when Spiro rose carefully to his feet, crossed to the waiter, lifted him several feet off the ground, and in rather colorful language asked the man if he'd been struck deaf, dumb, and blind, because if not, he wanted the *logariasmós*—now!

I was so relieved to be going, I had little pity to spare for the waiter, and didn't even protest when Spiro slid an arm around me as we walked up the stairs to the street. Truth be told, I thought it would at least steady him and help me to get him back more quickly to the car.

However, as we staggered down the main street (by this time, he was holding me so tightly I felt welded to his side),

Spiro suddenly changed course and started for the beach, and no amount of reasoning or coaxing on my part could turn him back toward the car. We were almost to the lapping sea when he abruptly stopped of his own volition; I was so unprepared for the sudden halt I almost fell on my face, but drunk though he was, Spiro caught me and swung me around to face him.

"Have you ever made a swim naked in the sea, Christine?" he asked, a wicked grin plastered across his face. "With the moonlight shining on the water?"

I shook my head, remembering with sudden empathy the waiter squawking in mid-air.

He bent down slowly, swaying a bit, and touched his fingers to the incoming surf. "The water is warm," he invited.

"No, thank you. I'd rather not."

He straightened up and gave his shoulders an uneven shrug. "A pity," he murmured. "I would have liked to see you rise like Aphrodite from the foam." Then leaning precariously forward, he planted an amazingly accurate kiss on my mouth. Before I could remember to protest, he began sliding to the ground, completely passed-out.

I stared at his neatly collapsed form in despair. "How am I ever going to get you back to the car now?"

A voice called out behind us. "'Scuse us, miss, but you in some sort of trouble?"

I turned around to find a trio of young Englishmen, dressed in shorts and T-shirts. The closest one, the one who'd spoken, was regarding me with a mixture of curiosity and concern. His two friends were merely curious.

"As a matter of fact," I said, "I am, rather. And I think you three are just the help I need."

Even with four of us, it was an awkward job to haul Spiro all the way back to the car, but eventually we had him strapped into the passenger seat of the Lamborghini. Keys in hand, I turned to thank my rescuers, but they merely nodded and the first who'd spoken assured me they were pleased to be able to help.

"Don't s'pose you need someone to drive this beauty for you?" asked one of his comrades, wistfully.

Smiling, I shook my head. "No, I think I can handle it."

"Well, g'night then," they called out. "And good luck!"

Though at first I was intimidated by the Lamborghini's power, I was soon enjoying the drive, and I managed to get us and the car back to the villa in one piece. To my dismay, however, it was almost one o'clock by the time we got there, and I still somehow had to get Spiro into the house before I could head down to the beach for my rendezvous with Geoffrey.

I drove the car into the garage. For a moment my breath caught as a figure detached itself from the shadows and came round to my door. Then I realized it was just Paul. He opened the door and helped me out.

"Date end early?" I snapped irritably.

He nodded nonchalantly. "And yours?" He gazed in amusement at my unconscious companion.

"Stop smirking and help me get him to his room."

Paul clicked his heels together, saluted, and then crossed to the passenger side of the car and heaved Spiro out, tossing him over his shoulder like a bag of potatoes. I scurried ahead, fumbling through Spiro's keys in search of the one to the front door lock. Breathing hard, Paul merely pounded on the door; it was soon opened by Maria, looking remarkably awake considering the hour. Paul pushed past her and made a beeline toward Spiro's room. I ran ahead, opening the door for him, and he dropped Spiro onto the bed with a gasp.

"*Evharistó*," I thanked him.

"*Parakaló*," he replied. "Do you need help with anything else?" His expression was bland, but his mouth seemed to twitch suspiciously as he looked from me to the man sprawled on the bed.

"No, thank you," I said tartly.

He shrugged and left, and I quickly followed. I decided it would be safer to slip down to the beach through my own room.

It was dark, and I had to fumble around a bit searching for the light switch. When I finally found it, I pressed the curved toggle, and for a moment the light flickered. Then it flared full force, illuminating … everything.

I gasped for breath, feeling as if I'd just been punched in the stomach.

Both of my suitcases were slung open on the bed, and

clothes had been strewn all over the floor. Three dresses that Maria had just washed and pressed had been torn to shreds and splattered with a deep red liquid that turned out, to the relief of my pounding heart, to be only nail polish. Two of the books I'd bought in Corfu had been flung against the wall, and a third had been ripped up completely, the torn pages tossed about the room like so much confetti. I found my purse in the corner. It had been turned inside out and sliced to pieces.

My passport had survived unharmed. I found it carefully propped up on the bureau, underneath a single Greek word that had been scrawled on the mirror in pink lipstick.

"*Fighasete!*" it read.

"Get out!"

TWELVE

I stood there staring at the angry message for several minutes, before my numbed mind remembered Geoffrey waiting down on the beach. Stumbling toward the French windows, I pushed them open and started running.

I didn't really expect him to still be there. I burst from the pines and went skittering along the shingle fully expecting to find myself alone.

"So, you finally decided to come," said a voice in the dark. Like a compass needle homing north, I spun towards the sound of it. "I trust you and Skouras had a good time." A familiar silhouette stepped out into the bright moonlight, and without thinking I launched myself toward it.

"Geoffrey!" I cried, barreling into him.

He uttered a startled exclamation as his arms swung up and enfolded me. Then he pushed me back so he could look into my face. "Christine," he said sharply, "what's wrong?"

I stared up at him and suddenly wondered what to say. If I told him about the attack on my room, he might insist on my leaving the villa. I listened to the soft lapping of the water on the rocks and tried to think of a safe answer.

"Christine, answer me! What's happened? Are you all right?"

The night had grown colder. "I-I'm f-fine," I assured him through chattering teeth.

"Like hell you are!" he growled, pulling me close and wrapping his arms around me a second time. "You're shaking like a leaf!" The comforting warmth of his skin radiated through the thin cloth of his shirt, and succumbing to temptation, I buried my face against his chest.

His hand reached up and stroked my hair. "It's all right," he murmured. "You're safe now. You're home and dry."

The strong beat of his heart and the steady rise and fall of his breathing soothed me. "Strange thing to say to a girl from California standing on a damp Greek beach," I muttered into his shirt. He laughed, and his embrace tightened.

"You'll have to excuse me. It isn't every night I have you fly into my arms like this."

I looked up at that, searching his face for any trace of mockery. But there was no amusement in his eyes, only a look that fixed me motionless. He reached up and brushed his fingers softly across my lips. The gentle touch seemed to ripple through me—like waves across an all-too-still pond. Without thought, my hands slid up to curl around his neck, and I reached up on tiptoe to press my mouth to his.

His lips were cool, but his breath was warm and smelled faintly of mint. For a moment his mouth was still against my own, and I felt like a rider on a roller coaster who has just climbed to the top of a precipice only to hang uncertainly over a drop she cannot see. Then his lips began to caress me, his tongue to explore me, his mouth to claim me with a ferocity that chased all fear away and hurtled me safely down a blissful trail of sensation.

I have no idea how long the kiss lasted; I only remember the sensation of being dropped much too abruptly back to earth when he tore his mouth away and whispered huskily in my ear, "Fond as I am of this beach, my dear, do you think we could find someplace a tad drier and a bit more comfortable to continue this very pleasant demonstration of your affection?"

His tone was teasing, but his words were like a slap.

With a feeling almost akin to panic, I realized I was doing it again. Acting on impulse, betraying my feelings, exposing my heart like a naive idiot so that, when the inevitable rejection came, it would all the more easily be ripped in two. With a shudder, I pulled away.

"Christine?"

Mutely, I retreated another step.

"What's wrong?" He tried to draw me closer.

I resisted. "Please. Let me go."

He complied so quickly I stumbled. With the withdrawal of his touch, apprehension gave way to regret, but it was too late to admit that, even to myself.

"I did not fly into your arms," I insisted with the intensity one reserves for statements one knows are false.

His eyes glinted angrily in the moonlight. "No? And how would you describe it?"

"I'd had a shock, that's all."

"A shock?" he said sharply. "What type of shock?"

I bit my lip. "Not a shock, really. Just an unpleasant surprise. I overreacted."

"Overreacted to what?"

"Does it matter?"

"Christine!"

"Oh, all right. While I was gone tonight, someone went in my room and tore things up a bit."

He stood there a moment, his expression frozen. Then without a word he swept past me and started up the path to the house.

"Where are you going?" I called out. He didn't answer. I ran to catch up with him, lowering my voice to a frantic whisper. "Wait! Geoffrey, please! Someone may hear you!"

My pleas had no effect. Except, perhaps, that he stepped a little more lightly as he mounted the stairs to the porch two steps at a time. I pulled off my shoes and ran after him.

The French windows still stood open. I followed him inside and heard him swear as he caught his first glimpse of the havoc. He began circling the room, picking up my cut-up purse, a torn-up book, my red-splattered dresses. As he picked up these last, I saw the color drain from his face. "It's only nail polish," I assured him.

"And next time?" he demanded.

I pointed to the mirror and my passport propped neatly underneath. "I'm sure it was just meant to scare me. To chase me away. I doubt whoever did this means me any real harm."

"I'm not about to put it to the test."

"Meaning?"

His voice rose impatiently. "You're leaving here tonight. Now. With me."

"Keep your voice down!" I exclaimed in a whisper. Shutting the French doors behind me, I crossed to the bathroom door and closed it tight, too. "Have you forgotten? Spiro's room is right next door!"

He grimaced. "I don't care whether he hears me or not. After you've gone—"

"Geoffrey, I'm not going anywhere."

"Yes, you are." The expression in his green eyes was determined.

"No, I'm not. I'm not about to cut and run after the first little scare. Do you think I want to give the person who did this—" I looked around at my wrecked belongings and felt the first stirrings of anger. "Do you think I want to give that person the satisfaction of frightening me away?"

"This isn't a game, Christine."

"Don't you think I know that? I may be stubborn; I'm not stupid. I know the danger is real. But don't you see? Someone is awfully anxious to chase me away. Well, then, there has to be a reason. Perhaps my being here is gumming up the works; perhaps it's even protecting Michael in some small way. If that's the case, what's going to happen if I just up and leave?"

His mouth twisted in surprise, and he ran a distracted hand through his hair. "You've hardly even seen him."

"True," I admitted. "But that might change. Besides, it's possible just my being here is enough to make our attacker think twice. I'm an outsider, a witness, and I'm keeping my eyes and ears open to find out anything I can."

"That's what worries me."

"Look," I said. "We both know the only way to stop whoever's after Michael is to figure out why someone wants to kill him. Since you're the one who gets his money if he dies, money can't be the motive, unless...."

His voice was flat and void of inflection, "Unless what, Christine?"

"I'm sorry, but I have to ask: where did you go last night after you left me in the Achilleon gardens?"

"Well, let's see. I nipped round to the car park, stole a car, and tried to run Michael down. Then I hurried back to my hotel for a nightcap with Demetra."

"Geoffrey, please! Be fair! You're the only one with an obvious motive, and you were right there at the Achilleon about the time the car was stolen."

"So was Skouras! Have you asked him where he was?"

"No," I said. "I thought that might not be such a smart thing to do. I figured you'd have a perfectly innocent answer; I wasn't sure he would."

He flashed me a rueful look. "I'm sorry. You're right, it's a reasonable enough question. If you must know the awkward truth, I spent the time in question lurking in the shrubbery—keeping an eye on you. I wanted to make sure Skouras behaved himself."

I felt an odd pang at the thought, and forced a smile. "I wish I'd seen you. It must have made quite a picture."

"Shall we change the subject?"

"Sure." I was just as glad to think of other things. I looked around the room, almost grateful it was such a distracting sight. "Well," I said, "at least now the police will have to take this thing seriously. Even Lieutenant Mavros can't claim this mess happened by accident."

"Was anyone with you when you found the room like this?"

"No."

"Not even Skouras?"

I shook my head. "When I took my leave of Spiro, he was sprawled on his bed, dead to the world."

A muscle twitched in Geoffrey's cheek. "I see."

I said in exasperation, "He was passed-out drunk."

"That explains everything, of course."

"It should," I said impatiently. "Anyway, why does it matter if there was someone with me or not?"

"It would be helpful if there was someone to back up your story."

"Why does it need backing up? Don't you believe me?"

"What I believe is irrelevant. All that matters is what the lieutenant believes, and without someone to corroborate your story, he may choose to believe you faked this all yourself."

"Why would I trash my own room, destroy my own things?"

"So you could point an accusing finger at Demetra and her household?" Seeing my expression, he reached out and touched my hand. "I'm just speculating as to what Mavros may think or my dear sister-in-law may claim."

I realized he was right. I could just picture Lieutenant Mavros gazing around the room with skepticism and suspicion. Suddenly, I felt very tired. I walked over to the bed, pushed one of the suitcases aside, and sat down. "So what am I supposed to do?" I asked.

"Leave," he said.

"I told you, I'm not going anywhere."

"Christine, please! If you're right, if your presence here is hampering our would-be murderer, he or she may try more direct methods next time to remove you from the scene."

"It's possible," I admitted, staring down at my hands. "But if I run away and something happens to Michael, I don't think I'll sleep very well at night."

He tilted up my chin so I was forced to look into his eyes. "And how well do you think I'll sleep if something happens to you?"

I bit my lip and said nothing.

He muttered something under his breath, pushed the other suitcase aside, and sat down next to me. "Very well, if you're determined to stay, we'd better decide on a course of action. What do you plan to do about all this?" He gestured to the chaos in front of us.

"I don't know. If it won't do any good to go to the police, I guess I'll just clean it up."

He nodded, looking thoughtful. "That might not be a bad strategy. This was meant to frighten you away. If, come morning, you're still here and acting as if nothing happened, Demetra may get rattled and reveal herself in some way."

"Demetra? You think she did this?"

"It had to be somebody in the house. Somebody who knew you would be away from Ithaki for the requisite amount of time. Somebody who could persuade Skouras to keep you safely occupied."

"But Spiro didn't tell his sister we were going out."

"He probably didn't have to," Geoffrey said. "She was probably the one who suggested it in the first place."

"All right, let's say she was the one who did this to my room.

What about the attempts on Michael? She was right there when that car almost ran him down. She couldn't have been driving it."

"True. But her brother could have. You yourself know he was gone long enough from the Achilleon to have done it."

I nodded. "But I still don't see why he should. What motive does he have for hurting Michael?"

Geoffrey frowned. "Robert's made the same point. I keep thinking it must have something to do with my brother's death. But Spiro wasn't even in England when he died."

"Maybe Demetra did something to your brother's car," I suggested, "and Michael knows something about it."

"It certainly would supply a motive," he agreed. "The only problem is that Michael couldn't know anything. He was at school—forty miles away—the day my brother died."

I sighed. "It's so frustrating. Every time I think we're getting somewhere there's a new piece that doesn't fit."

"I know," he said, "but my money's still on Skouras. I don't suppose you've learned anything more about his financial state?"

"As a matter of fact, I have. It turns out he does need money—fast. Thirty thousand pounds to be exact."

Geoffrey's eyes opened wide and he let out a low whistle. "All right, Sherlock! Would you care to explain how you found that out?"

I grinned. "Elementary, my dear Watson. I eavesdropped on Spiro asking Robert for a loan."

"You *what*?"

"You don't have to huff like that. I know it wasn't the most ethical thing to do, but—"

"Ethical be damned! It was dimwitted and dangerous! What if he'd caught you at it?"

"But he didn't. Besides—"

"And she promises to be careful!" he cried, bounding up from the bed and pacing restlessly back and forth. "Christine, what am I going to do with you?"

I gazed around at the disaster area my room had become. "Well, for now, you could help me clean all this up."

I woke Saturday morning with bright light beating at my tired eyelids. I'd forgotten to close the curtains and the morning sun was streaming in. Cupping my hand over my eyes, I slowly opened them to find the brightly illuminated room looking quite normal; the only reminder of the previous night's misadventure was a bag in the corner containing my ruined dresses, books, and purse.

I reached a sleepy hand toward the bedside table, searching for my watch. I brought it close to my bleary eyes. Eight-forty. As I hadn't gotten to bed until after three, it was much too early. I rolled over and buried my face in the pillow, but sleep wouldn't come. A sudden nagging thought drove it away.

I jerked upright and turned to stare at the bureau, suddenly remembering what I'd forgotten the night before: Demetra's purse. When I'd left for dinner, it had been propped up against the mirror. Now it was gone. Had someone taken it? The someone who had ransacked my room?

I picked up my wallet and peered behind my driver's license. The piece of paper was still there. I stared down at the date I'd written down, feeling a strange prickling along my arms. What significance could a doctor's appointment have, even a doctor's appointment on the very day of William Redfield's death? I shook my head, resolving to ask Geoffrey about it.

Distracted, I was rather slow about getting dressed and was just slipping on my sandals when someone knocked loudly on the door. Fumbling with the strap on my left sandal, I finally managed to buckle it, but not before the knock had been repeated three or four times. I stood up and started toward the door, but before I could reach it, it was pushed open and Helen walked in.

She stopped when she saw me, her eyes widening in surprise.

"Yes?" I said, irritated at the intrusion. "What is it? If you're looking for Michael, he's not here."

Her disbelieving gaze swept the room.

"Perhaps you'd like to search the closets? Or under the bed?"

Slowly she shook her head and then frowned. "I am to ask you if you wish to take breakfast."

"Oh," I said, taken aback. "I see. Uh, thank you."

She turned and started walking down the hall. Closing the door quickly behind me, I followed.

We entered the dining room to find Spiro seated at the long table alone. He motioned for me to sit down next to him as Helen crossed to pick up a tray of food from the sideboard.

"Where are your sister and Michael? Have they eaten already?"

"Demetra takes only coffee in the mornings. Michael will be eating breakfast in his room."

"Couldn't he eat out here, with us?" I asked.

Spiro, his eyes looking a little pained, turned to me, the corner of his mouth curving up into a ragged smile. "Of course," he said reluctantly, "if you wish it. Though I hope you will ask the boy to speak softly. I am not feeling my best this morning."

I tried not to smile. "I'll see he's as quiet as a mouse."

Spiro acknowledged this with a slight lift of his brows that caused a look of discomfort to flutter across his face. "Helen," he said carefully, "leave the tray, and bring the boy here to us."

She set it down with a tight-lipped look of disapproval and left the room.

"She doesn't like me much," I said.

Spiro glanced at me in surprise. "She can have no reason to like or dislike you. She is merely a servant here."

"I suppose servants don't have feelings like everyone else?"

He winced and held his head. "Of course they have feelings," he replied in a low voice. "But they save them for their friends and family; they do not waste them on their employers, or their employers' guests."

Maria came bustling out of the kitchen carrying a platter of *tyropitas* and a carafe of strong, aromatic coffee. Aphrodite followed with a bowl of fresh grapes and a tower of *loukomathes* smothered in honey and cinnamon. Maria began pouring the coffee.

"Please," said Spiro, "I do not wish to argue with you this morning. I am anxious to make amends for my behavior last night."

"Do you even remember your behavior last night?" I asked, causing Aphrodite's eyes to widen as she placed a *tyropita* on my plate.

"You need not sound so disapproving. Perhaps I drank a little too much ouzo—"

"A *little* too much? It took three grown men to—"

"Good morning, Uncle Spiro!" Michael exclaimed, appearing suddenly at our elbows. "Miss Stewart!" He grinned widely, obviously pleased by the change of venue for his breakfast.

Spiro gave me a baleful look. I took the hint and cautioned, "Michael, we have to talk softly this morning and be very quiet. Your uncle has a headache, and loud noises hurt his head."

"Sorry," Michael whispered solemnly. "Is this better?"

I grinned. "That's fine."

Helen pulled out a chair on the opposite side of the table and motioned for Michael to sit down. He studiously avoided seeing her gesture, instead fixing his owlish gaze on me and solemnly seating himself in the seat next to mine. Helen sputtered, but Aphrodite—taking things as settled—began laying a place for him there. Helen stalked from the room.

The meal passed pleasantly enough, and I noticed with surprise that Spiro and Michael seemed to get along pretty well. Spiro, despite his aching head, made an effort to include Michael in the conversation, and Michael, for his part, did his best to keep his voice low and his boyish energy under wraps. The two almost seemed of an age as Spiro told Michael an amusing if totally false tale of our adventures in Ypsos the night before, and I found it suddenly difficult, with the sun streaming down on their laughing faces, to imagine Spiro cold-bloodedly climbing behind the wheel of a car and trying to run this little boy down.

Then Demetra Redfield glided into the room, and the laughter abruptly stopped. She seated herself across the table from us, in the chair Helen had held out for Michael, and motioned for Aphrodite to pour her some coffee.

"*Kalimera*, Stepmama," Michael said politely.

"Good morning, Mrs. Redfield," I echoed.

She inclined her head in acknowledgment of our greeting, and then turned to address her brother in Greek. "So," she said with a nod in my direction, "she is still here? I thought after last night she would be gone."

Spiro flashed his sister a warning look. "Mind your manners, Demetra, and speak in English. While it is true Miss Stewart *speaks Greek fluently,* it is not polite to exclude the boy from our conversation."

Her eyes widened. "You speak our language, Miss Stewart? I suppose you did not inform us of this because it made it easier to spy upon us?"

I smiled at her and replied sweetly in Greek, "I didn't mention it because no one asked me. But surely it doesn't matter? Only a very rude person would whisper in another language behind a guest's back."

Her cheeks went pink. "Spiro!" she cried in a high voice. "I will not sit here and be insulted at my own table!"

Spiro flashed me an irritated look. "I am sure Miss Stewart meant no insult."

"No, of course not," I murmured.

"There, you see? Now drink your coffee and be calm."

"I will not."

"Then perhaps you should leave us," he said coldly.

Demetra surged to her feet. "Need I remind you that this is still my house?"

Spiro, too, rose and addressed her across the table. "Need I remind you," he said softly, "of all that I have done for you?"

Their eyes met and locked. Demetra was the first to look away. "Very well," she said in a subdued voice. "I will go—this time. Have Aphrodite bring my coffee to my room."

As I watched her turn and make her regal way to the door, I wondered what precisely Spiro had done to merit such unwilling but total obedience from his sister.

After breakfast, Dr. Aristides telephoned to suggest I come by his office to have the stitches in my cheek taken out. Spiro offered to drive me. As I couldn't think of any easier way to get to town, and as I thought I'd insulted the Skouras family enough for one day, I accepted.

Dr. Aristides's office was located in a quiet, residential section of Corfu Town. The street, barely wide enough for three people to walk abreast, was too narrow for cars, so we left the

Lamborghini parked in a distant square and walked to the pretty building which contained both the doctor's office and home.

Spiro stopped in front of a black-painted door marked with a brass plate bearing Dr. Aristides' name and profession. He lifted the knocker and gave the door several loud taps. The door opened to reveal a tall, grey-haired man wearing a white lab coat over a wrinkled blue suit. His glance went from Spiro to me. "And how is my pretty patient? How is the cheek? It is healing well?"

I told him that I thought it was, but that he was the expert. He nodded agreement with an amused look. "Yes, but it is you who must live with my handiwork. Spiro, make yourself comfortable. Young lady, come with me." He led me down a long hallway to an old-fashioned examination room whose one saving grace was a view looking out on a rose garden in glorious bloom.

Dr. Aristides read my expression and laughed. "Don't worry, my dear. The room and I are old, but this"—he pointed toward his head—"is young. Now let me see if my work was as good as I think it was." He removed the bandage with gentle fingers and, after remarking that I was healing nicely, announced it was time to remove the stitches.

Fixing my attention on the roses, I told him to go ahead.

The process wasn't painless, but it didn't hurt as much as I had expected, so though I continued to gaze out at the garden, my body began to relax under the doctor's careful ministrations. He'd almost finished, when I suddenly jerked my head in surprise.

Dr. Aristides suppressed an oath. "What? Did I hurt you?"

I quickly assured him that he hadn't.

"Then please, do not move again! I could have cut you!"

I promised to stay still. After watching me several seconds through narrowed eyes, he believed me enough to continue. When he'd finished removing the stitches, he rebandaged my cheek and handed me a salve he claimed would help it heal without leaving a scar. "You will be as good as the new," he promised, patting me on the back and helping me off the examination table.

"Thank you," I replied absently, finally allowing myself another look out into the garden. I needn't have worried about reacting again, however. The man I'd seen signaling to me from among the roses was gone.

As Spiro and I said our goodbyes to the doctor, I racked my brain for an excuse not to accompany Spiro back to Ithaki. In the end, all I could come up with was that I wanted to visit several shops before they closed for the weekend. To my relief, Spiro didn't question the strange timing of my shopping urge and offered to meet me at a café in the Esplanade in two hours.

He headed off in the direction of the car. I strolled off in the opposite direction, trying to look nonchalant as I glanced over my shoulder every twenty or thirty feet to make sure he wasn't following me. When I was confident he'd really gone, I backtracked to the alley bordering the doctor's garden. Geoffrey stepped in beside me.

"I was beginning to wonder if you were coming," he said.

"I don't know why you worried. I mean, anyone seeing you wave wildly in that garden would have realized you were trying to arrange a secret and confidential rendezvous, wouldn't they?"

"Believe me, Christine, I felt every bit the fool you think I appeared, but I had to find some way to speak with you before I left, and I didn't know how else to go about it.

I stumbled on the uneven pavement. "You're leaving?"

"Yes, this afternoon. I have a five-thirty flight."

We'd arrived at the intersection of the alley with a wider street. I stared up at the white, hand-painted sign bearing its name, but couldn't seem to concentrate enough to read the Greek letters. "And what about Michael?" I heard myself say.

"With luck, he won't even know I've gone."

"Oh, I see." No longer caring about the street's name, I quickly turned down it, driven by the sheer necessity to move.

"Christine!" he called out as he hurried to catch up with me. "Christine, what's the matter? Is something wrong?"

All the churning, pent-up emotion of the past month seemed to ignite and blaze inside me. "You're ready to give up, fly home, wash your hands of Michael, and me, and this whole messy business, and you have the nerve to ask me what's the matter?"

He seized my arm and jerked me round to face him. "Do you actually think I'd abandon him like that? That I'd abandon you?"

I realized with a sigh that my own anger had blown itself out. I said wearily, "What am I supposed to think when you say that you're leaving?"

His tone softened. "Why, that I'm coming back, of course." He reached up and cupped his hand over my bandaged cheek. "With luck, I might be back to wave at you from another garden as early as Monday." There was barely concealed excitement in his voice.

"Geoffrey, what's happened?"

He grinned. "Something wonderful, something unbelievable, something that may slice through our own particular Gordian knot and guarantee Michael's safety once and for all."

"Geoffrey!" I exclaimed. "Will you please get to the point!"

"The point, my dear, is that this blasted custody fight for Michael may be over. My solicitor rang from London this morning with some remarkable news. You know that we thought Michael's mother had been killed in an aeroplane crash three years ago?"

Impatiently, I nodded.

"Well, it seems we may have been wrong."

I stared at him. "You mean she's alive?"

He nodded, his green eyes glittering. "Alive, and well, and living—of all places—in Monaco."

THIRTEEN

Despite Geoffrey's obvious excitement, or perhaps because of it, I had mixed feelings about the news Elizabeth Redfield Conner was alive. I was glad Michael was going to have his mother restored to him, but I wondered about Geoffrey. What did her reappearance mean to him? He'd loved her once. Did he still?

It's none of your business whether he does or not, I reminded myself. In four days, I'd be flying home. I looked around, trying to remind myself I was just a tourist on vacation.

"Geoffrey," I said, striving to keep my tone matter-of-fact, "I remember the news about Jesse Conner's jet crashing in the Rockies. All the news reports said there were no survivors."

"There were none," he said.

"You mean Elizabeth missed the flight? Her husband was really travelling alone?"

"Yes—and no. Conner boarded the flight with his wife."

"But Elizabeth got off before the crash?"

Geoffrey shook his head. "It's a bit more complicated than that. Elizabeth was never on the plane."

I grimaced at him. "Is this some kind of riddle?"

"It's rather like one, isn't it?" he agreed. "It took my solicitor a great deal of investigation to make any sense of it, but he wanted to be sure of the facts before he contacted me."

"And what did he find out?" I asked.

"The story goes something like this: some months before the accident, Elizabeth and her husband had a falling out. He was in love with a showgirl and wanted a divorce. Elizabeth had signed a prenuptial agreement and would get no money, but she threatened to go to the newspapers. Conner was in the midst of delicate financial negotiations and was anxious to avoid public scandal. He offered Elizabeth two million dollars to give him a quiet divorce, if she agreed to leave the country and keep the details of the divorce secret for a year."

"Elizabeth accepted and went to live in Monte Carlo. Conner, his delicate business deal completed, married his show-girl and boarded the ill-fated flight with his new bride, not his old."

"Why didn't any of this come out at the time?" I asked.

"Very few people knew about it, and the truth was carefully suppressed by Conner's family. His new wife was an orphan, with no relatives to raise a fuss, so his family felt justified in glossing over the poor girl's death to avoid untoward publicity."

"And Elizabeth?" I said. "Why didn't she speak out? Why didn't she protest being reported dead?"

"Conner's family threatened to cut off the payments of the settlement if she said a word about it to anyone."

"Even you and your brother?" I exclaimed in disbelief. "She didn't think you deserved the truth?"

"I doubt she felt she owed anything to William—or to me."

"What about Michael?" I demanded.

He avoided my eyes. "You don't understand, Christine. When William and Elizabeth divorced it was … messy. William kept Michael, and Elizabeth—well, she wanted to marry Conner, and Conner was in America. She and Michael lost touch."

"I see. So she figured why risk a cushy settlement for a son she'd already written off?"

"You're very quick to judge a woman you don't even know."

He was right. I didn't know her, yet I thoroughly disliked her. It was hardly fair. But truth was, I didn't feel like being fair. "Why didn't she contact Michael after your brother's death?"

"She probably doesn't know William is dead. There was little news of the accident outside of England, and Robert and my brother's other lawyers didn't know to contact her."

"So that's where you're going? To see her and break the news?"

"And to ask her to take Michael," he said.

"Do you think she'll be willing to do that?" I asked.

He stared at me. "Once she realizes the danger Michael's in? Of course! She'll be eager to take custody from Demetra."

I wasn't so certain, but said nothing. We walked along in uneasy silence. Then Geoffrey turned down a small alley.

"Why are we turning here?" I asked.

"Didn't you tell Skouras you intended to do some shopping?"

"Weren't there plenty of stores on that street?"

He made a dismissive sound. "Lumber for poor tourists who don't know better. Wouldn't you rather have something useful? A new handbag, perhaps? There's a good leather shop down this way."

"I guess I do need a replacement," I admitted, patting the ungainly bulges in my skirt. "Pockets just don't cut it."

He flashed me a sudden smile that dissolved the tension between us. "We men make do, but then we aren't expected to carry about the odds and ends you women are."

I would have liked to have floated along in the warmth of that smile indefinitely, but he was leaving, and there were things we had to discuss. Reluctantly I said, "Speaking of odds and ends, Geoffrey, there's something I need to tell you. The night Spiro and I went to the Achilleon, he lent me his sister's purse. There was an old doctor's appointment card in it." I paused, and then added, "It was for the day your brother died."

His smile faded. "So?"

"Demetra's appointment was at a fertility clinic." I paused. "I know this is a rather delicate question, but were your brother and Demetra having trouble having a child?"

"That's no one's business but their own." His tone was icy.

"But what if she went to that appointment and found out she couldn't have children?" I said. "She might have been afraid your brother would divorce her."

"Christine! My brother had his faults, but he was no Henry VIII. He wouldn't have divorced Demetra simply because she couldn't give him a child. After all, he already had Michael."

"But—"

"Sorry," he said. "You're barking up the wrong tree."

I didn't press further. Instead I said, "There's something else

I've been thinking about. If the attacks on Michael are related to your brother's death, then there's someone else who might be a suspect."

Now I had his full attention. "Who?"

I felt a sudden reluctance. After all, I liked the guy. Still it was important to consider all the possibilities. "Robert Humphreys." Seeing Geoffrey's astonished stare, I added defensively, "Well, he *was* your brother's lawyer. What if he was embezzling from your brother and your brother found out about it?"

"Robert is—was," Geoffrey grimaced at his error, "one of William's oldest and closest friends. He didn't handle the business side of my brother's legal affairs, only the personal ones. He had very little access to my brother's money, and my brother always went over his personal accounts very carefully. Robert would never have had a chance to steal from him." Suddenly an arrested look came over his face.

"Geoffrey? What is it? Have you thought of something?"

Slowly he nodded. Then suddenly he took my arm, swung me around, and kissed me long and hard.

"What was that about?" I demanded breathlessly when he finally set me free.

"Consider it a thank you," he said. "Robert might not have stolen from my brother, but you've just reminded me that someone else could have. According to Robert, my brother completed an audit of his foreign holdings right before he died."

"And?" I asked impatiently, wondering where this was leading.

"Spiro Skouras ran several of my brother's Greek operations."

I let out a low whistle. "So if your brother found out Spiro was stealing from him, Spiro might have had a motive for murder."

"Precisely. It shouldn't be too hard to find out the results of the audit. I'll look into it after I see Elizabeth."

Reminded of the imminent reunion, I fell silent, but Geoffrey, caught up in his own thoughts, didn't notice. The alley we had entered was narrow and empty of the signs of commerce. I was beginning to wonder if we were lost, when we emerged into a small and pretty courtyard surrounded by six buildings in the Venetian style, each with moldings carefully restored, paint freshly applied, shutters brightly colored, and banners fluttering in the wind.

The first floor of each building was occupied by an exclusive-looking boutique. Geoffrey led me past a burbling fountain to the nearest of the six. I gazed through the window at the handbags, attaché cases, and suitcases carefully displayed and agreed with his assessment; they were beautiful. They also looked terribly expensive. I tried to pull back, but he was already through the door and drawing me along with him.

The well-dressed saleswoman was elegant and aloof. She remained seated at her small mahogany escritoire, acknowledging our entrance with a small inclination of her head. Geoffrey began browsing through the displays.

"What about this one?" he asked, lightly tapping a handbag that was superficially similar to my old one, but which had better lines, richer color, and leather that was both soft and supple.

"It's lovely," I admitted, running my fingers over it, "but I suspect it's out of my price range."

Geoffrey glanced at the silver tag tied to the strap, then walked over to the woman at the desk. As he spoke, her expression became less frigid, and after he'd finished, she rose and disappeared into the back room. She returned with a large silver box and sheets of tissue paper imprinted with the store's name.

Nervously, I twisted the silver tag to see the price written there. Swearing under my breath, I set the purse down on the counter and retreated toward Geoffrey.

"I can't afford to spend that kind of money on a purse!"

"You like the thing, don't you?"

"Of course I like it. I love it! But that doesn't mean I can afford to buy it. You shouldn't have told her I would!"

"I didn't."

"Then why is she wrapping it up?"

"Because a gift should always come wrapped."

I stared at him. "A gift? But, Geoffrey, you can't! It's much too expensive."

His jaw set in a stiff line. "If you don't feel comfortable accepting it as a gift, think of it as partial reimbursement for the damage done to your things last night."

"But everything together wouldn't have cost this much! Besides, why should you be the one to pay?"

"For heaven's sake, Christine! Don't you think I owe you this much at least?"

I wondered if he wanted to buy me a lavish gift so he could say goodbye with a clear conscience. "You don't owe me anything."

"Why is it so difficult for you to accept this from me? You don't appear to have any difficulty accepting any number of things from Skouras."

"I suppose you never had trouble getting Elizabeth to accept expensive gifts," I countered.

"At the time I first knew Elizabeth," he said slowly, "I wasn't able to afford gifts, expensive or otherwise. My brother, however, had no such difficulty, and you're right. He had no trouble persuading her to accept the best money could buy."

I stood there desperately wishing I'd kept my mouth shut. "Geoffrey, I'm sorry. I didn't mean—"

The saleswoman had been hovering impatiently in the background. She came forward now, carrying the wrapped purse in one hand and the handwritten bill of sale in the other. With an angry shake of his head, Geoffrey informed her the sale was off. "The lady has changed her mind," he snapped. Then he turned and left the shop, leaving the two of us to stare after him in dismay.

Fourteen

The Esplanade was full of people, but there was little bustle or even movement in the sun-drenched square. Shops had closed, the last air-conditioned buses loaded with tourists were pulling out on their way to distant beaches, and native Corfiotes sat sipping drinks at café tables under the trees. I strolled along the Liston, the arcade lining the square, where most of the cafes are located, and scanned the seated throng for Spiro.

I was gazing at the last clump of tables, well shaded under a large plane tree, when I finally spotted him. To my astonishment, Michael was sitting next to him. "Well, this is a pleasant surprise," I said as I approached the table.

"I thought it might please you," Spiro remarked.

"Are you thirsty, Miss Stewart?" Michael asked. "We can vouch for the lemonade: it's quite good."

"We?" I said, surprised to note the empty lemonade bottle by Spiro's glass.

Spiro raised an eyebrow. "And here I assured you I meant to reform after last night. I see I must do more to assure you of my good intentions. Let me see. Perhaps an excursion to the western coast? Maria has packed a lunch, and after we eat we can make a swim. I know a beautiful beach not so crowded with tourists."

"But I don't have a swimsuit with me," I said.

"Ah, but you see, Maria was kind enough to pack one for you, so we will not need to seek out one of those naked beaches that the tourists love so much." He flashed me a look, and I knew he was thinking of the previous night. "Well, what is your decision? Does such an expedition appeal to you?"

I was still smarting from my clash with Geoffrey and wanted to go off by myself and mope, but I wasn't the only one involved. This was a chance for Michael to get out and have some fun. One look at his eager face and all I could say was, "It sounds wonderful."

Our drive across the island was, by Spiro's normal standards, sedate, and we had a chance to enjoy the pretty scenery. Near Paleokastritsa, we turned north, toward hills covered with olive trees. The road narrowed, twining its way through small villages and across long stretches of open country. It was almost three before we finally arrived at the small town of Agios Stephanos, which was set on a curved bay with a lovely sand beach.

To my surprise, however, the Lamborghini did not head toward the water, but instead climbed a gravel road up to the cliffs above the bay. I was about to ask Spiro where we were going, when we turned into the driveway of a small white house and stopped.

"The home of a friend who is away on business," Spiro explained, as he came around to help me out of the car. "We will eat here and change before we go down to make our swim."

We could see the beach from the patio where we ate our lunch, and I marvelled at how different it looked from the one at Ithaki. Instead of grey shingle, arching pines, and water the color of lapis lazuli, this beach was bleached and treeless, the warm, golden sand stretching in a gently-curving arc next to water the color of milky-turquoise.

After lunch, Spiro disappeared into the house and reappeared with a small gold foil box which he set down on the table with a flourish. "Look what I have found," he said, casting a sidelong glance at Michael. "A box of chocolates from *Evyeneia*. Shall we open it?" Without waiting for an answer he lifted off the lid, revealing three short rows of the most delectable looking chocolates I'd ever seen. Their aroma wafted up into the air and smacked me right in the nose. Spiro saw my look and smiled. "The chocolates of *Evyeneia* are famous throughout the island, Christine."

"I can understand why," I murmured raptly.

He chuckled and held out the box. "You had best take one now, before they disappear, as they have been known to do around that one." He gestured at Michael with his chin.

They all looked the same, so I selected one from the end. I held it in my hand for a moment inhaling the lovely scent, then bit deep. Sadly, though the chocolate was heavenly, the hazelnut cream inside was a disappointment. It tasted chalky and a little bitter compared to the lusciously sweet shell. Spiro was watching me expectantly, however, so I smiled and said how much I liked it.

He nodded and pushed the box over to Michael. "All right, you may have some now, but try not to eat the whole box. Christine may wish another. Now, if you two will excuse me? The butler must clean and put away the dishes." He made a wry face and departed for the kitchen.

After he'd gone, Michael made no move to take a chocolate. Watching him, I said, "I gather you don't care for those quite as much as your uncle thinks you do."

He looked sheepish. "Actually, they're my favorites, but last week I had Paul buy me a large box of them and I'm afraid I ate them all and got quite sick. Now just the smell of them makes me feel a bit queer."

I grinned. "I see."

His brow wrinkled up in concern. "What do you think I should do? Uncle Spiro will be insulted if I don't have some."

"You could tell him the truth."

He shook his head. "It might get Paul in trouble." He turned a pleading face toward me whose angelic quality was marred by the mischievous grin tugging at the corners of his mouth. "I don't suppose you'd like to eat four or five more—for me?"

I shook my head. "No, I've had quite enough, thank you, but if you're really desperate you could toss a few off the balcony. I doubt anyone will notice them at the bottom of the cliff."

"What a smashing idea!" he said, grabbing up a handful of chocolates and crossing to the balcony railing. He lobbed them over the edge with the vigor of a soldier disposing of live grenades, then trotted back to the table and plunked down next to me. "I say, I like the way you think. I'll have to remember that trick next time Maria serves eggplant!"

"Just so you don't blame it on me when you get caught."

"No fear," he said with a grin. "I'm good at keeping secrets."

I felt the smile fade from my face. "Michael, sometimes secrets can be dangerous."

He avoided my eyes. "Spy secrets, you mean. James Bond. MI-6. That kind of thing."

"Other kinds of secrets, as well," I said, reaching out and touching his arm. "Michael, won't you tell me? Why did you say you wanted a detective that day at the Old Fort?"

"I'd rather not talk about it."

"But Michael—"

"It's nothing like what you were saying, I promise. It's not a dangerous secret. It's just … a secret." His cheeks grew red, and he jerked to his feet. "I'd best go change now." He hurried away into the house, leaving me alone.

We headed for the beach shortly after four. It was pleasant to be on sand again, and as I waded into the amazingly clear water, I reveled in the soft feel of the sand squishing through my toes and eddying around my feet in small, dark clouds.

Despite the hot sun, the water was cold, so I decided to speed my entry and run for deeper water. Michael, laughing, followed, and so did Spiro, but though we waded and waded farther and farther out, the water refused to rise above our shoulders, and only Michael managed to lose touch of the bottom.

Spiro smiled at my expression. "It remains shallow for another hundred meters, I am afraid."

"You might have told me."

"But then you would have stopped, and it was very pleasant watching you race ahead of me."

"Oh, was it?" I said, splashing him hard in the face. I dove into the shallow water and started swimming toward where Michael was standing on tiptoe, twirling slowly in a circle like a lighthouse beacon.

"Shall we race?" I called to him. He nodded and flashed me a grin, then launched himself off with a quick arching dive followed by smooth, curving strokes that gave him an immediate lead.

"He's not a boy, he's a fish," I exclaimed, diving after him. I hadn't gone twenty feet, however, before something grabbed my ankles and pulled me under the water.

"Hey, let go!" I burbled, spitting out water and wrestling with my captor.

"I am merely trying to insure the boy has a fair chance," Spiro said calmly.

I stopped struggling, and Spiro loosened his hold. "You're showing uncommon concern in his welfare today," I snapped. "Why the sudden change of heart? You must have had a devil of a time getting your sister to agree to your bringing him on this outing, especially with me along."

"Devil of a time? Ah, you mean it was difficult. Yes, that's true, though perhaps not as difficult as it might have been had Mr. Humphreys not given my sister a lecture last night about the proper treatment of energetic young boys. It was also of help that my sister had no notion you were to join us on this excursion; she thinks you are spending the afternoon in town."

"But Maria—"

"I instructed her to say nothing until after we had left." He paused and looked at Michael's distant figure. "I think the boy has a sufficient start. You can go."

"Are you kidding? I'll never catch up with him now!"

"No? Well, then perhaps I shall go in your place." Without another word he shot through the water, and with long, sure strokes began rapidly closing the distance between them. A vague sense of uneasiness gripped me as I watched Michael's graceful motions and Spiro's determined ones. I scrambled to catch up to them, kicking and slicing through the clear water faster than I had ever swum in my life.

But it wasn't fast enough. I was still almost thirty feet away when the long, dark form caught up with the small, fair one. My breath caught in my throat when both suddenly disappeared. "No!" I yelled frantically.

Then nightmare dissolved into farce. Spiro, Michael in his arms, burst to the surface and tossed the giggling boy up into the air. Michael, landing with a splash, disappeared beneath the surface, and Spiro suddenly lost his footing and with an incredulous expression collapsed into the water as if someone had just pulled a chair out from under him.

As the tension poured out of me, I was left feeling like a deflated balloon. Weakly, I turned and began stroking slowly toward shore. The water was shallow enough to have waded out, but I wasn't sure my shaking knees would hold me.

"Miss Stewart!"

Michael swam over to ask if something was wrong. I told him I was just feeling tired and wanted to lie on the beach awhile.

The air was warm, the sand soft. I unrolled my mat and collapsed onto it, feeling a bit dizzy. I closed my eyes and the queasy waves receded. The sun beat down, wrapping me in a cocoon of warmth, and I felt as if I were still floating in the warm Ionian sea....

I woke with a start to find Spiro standing over me, shaking me. "At last!" he exclaimed as I opened my eyes. "You sleep like a stone. I was beginning to wonder if I would ever wake you."

I tried to bring his face into focus. "Where's Michael?"

His eyebrows rose at the urgency of my voice. "There," he said, gesturing toward a small, splashing figure cavorting in the sea with two other boys. He frowned. "Those two came along almost as soon as you left the water."

I closed my eyes in relief. "Sorry," I murmured weakly. "I didn't mean to leave you alone to play nursemaid.

"You intend to sleep again?"

"Of course not." I forced my eyes open and rose unsteadily to my feet. Drowsiness consumed me, so I stumbled down to the sea's edge and splashed water on my face. The salt stung my eyes.

Spiro came up and took my arm. "I see I am not the only one who should be drinking lemonade," he said. "Obviously, I served too much wine at lunch."

I pulled my arm away and frowned at the lowered position of the sun. "What time is it?"

"Almost seven. We should be going soon."

"Seven! You mean I've been asleep nearly three hours?"

He nodded, his face studiously bland.

"I don't understand," I said. "I don't even remember falling asleep, and now I feel so groggy I can barely keep my eyes open. The only time I ever felt like this before was when I had a brief bout of insomnia and my doctor gave me double-strength sleeping pills by mistake...."

My voice trailed off. Sleeping pills? No, it couldn't be. But why had the filling of the chocolates tasted so bitter? I cast a sidelong glance at Spiro. He was watching me closely.

I forced myself to smile, and gave a little shrug. "Well, I guess you're right. No more wine at lunch."

He nodded, his gaze still fixed on me. "We should be going. If you would call the boy?" I said I would, and he turned away. "I will fetch an extra towel from the car so that he may dry himself properly. I do not wish him dripping on my leather seats all the way back to town." He started toward the road where the Lamborghini was parked.

I called out after him. "Wait, Spiro, I'll come with you. I've got a hankering for one of those chocolates."

He stopped and turned. His expression was unreadable. "I am sorry, Christine. I do not have any to give you."

"But there were six still in the box when I went to change."

"True, but I threw the box in the dustbin before we left."

"May I ask why?"

He shrugged, as if the answer was obvious. "In this heat? The chocolates would have melted and made a mess in my car."

"Did you have one yourself before you threw them away?"

He shook his head. "Me, I do not care for sweets much. Chocolate is for women—and children," he flashed me an odd look, "though today the boy seems to have lost his taste for it." He turned and started again for the car.

I turned as well and stared out at the sea, where Michael was paddling around by himself, his two companions having been summoned to shore by their mothers. Was I letting my imagination run away with me? Drugged chocolates—what would have been the point?

Yet suddenly I could imagine a point. If one chocolate had been enough to knock me out for several hours, what would three or four have done to Michael? And what would have happened to him if he'd been out in the water, with only Spiro there to help him, when the drug started to take effect?

I shivered. And when Michael came cheerfully scampering out of the surf in response to my wave, I threw my arms around him and gave him a tight hug. He bore it with good grace for some time before he backed away with an embarrassed smile and exclaimed, "Lord's sake, Miss Stewart! What was that for?"

"That," I said in a voice that was not altogether steady, "is for making yourself sick last week and for throwing your chocolates over the cliff."

When we arrived back at Ithaki, Demetra was waiting for us.

As soon as we entered the villa, a subdued Maria ushered us into the drawing room where Demetra was pacing up and down, wearing a dark tread in the blue carpet. I expected some sort of storm to break when she turned and saw us standing there, but instead she stopped still, her gaze fixing first on me, then her brother, and finally on Michael. Strangely, the intensity of that gaze worried me more than any loud histrionics might have. Seeing her pale face and those smoldering eyes, I felt a strong wave of uneasiness, and it was a relief when Spiro curtly ordered us from the room saying he wished to speak with his sister alone.

I'd planned to escort Michael back to his room, but Helen was waiting for us outside the drawing room, and I was forced to relinquish him to her keeping.

Left alone, I decided to take the opportunity to speak with Maria. I found her in the kitchen preparing dinner. She lifted her head and flashed me a brief, questioning look. Unsure where to start, I thanked her for the lunch she had packed us. She nodded, her attention focused on the cucumbers she was slicing.

"You liked it?" she asked, reaching for a tomato. "I am glad. The young master, he ate well?"

"Very well," I assured her. "We all did. Those chocolates—they were especially good. Where did they come from?"

Her hand slipped and she pricked herself with the knife. "*Moré!* I am clumsy tonight!" She seized a dishtowel and wrapped it around her finger. "Aphrodite," she called, "here, finish the salad for me." Then she disappeared into the pantry. I followed her. She pulled down a box of bandages, and a dark bottle of some concoction that she dabbed on the cut before bandaging it.

When she had done, I reminded her gently, "The chocolates, Maria? Where did they come from? Did Mr. Skouras ask you to put them in as a special treat for Michael?"

She shook her head. "I do not know, Thespinis. I packed no chocolates. Perhaps you should ask the mistress. She said she wished to put a surprise in the basket for the young master."

Maria turned and started back to the kitchen. I watched her go, wondering about the surprise Demetra had planned for her stepson. Was that why she had looked so angry? Had she expected the afternoon to end differently?

There was a surprise of a much more pleasant nature waiting for me when I got back to my room. Sitting in the middle of my bed was a silver box tied with a white satin ribbon.

I crossed to the bed and sat down, picking up the package and setting it carefully on my lap. There was no card attached, but I hardly needed one to identify who it was from. I recognized the box and shop name all too well.

To my consternation, my fingers trembled a bit as I tugged at the elegantly tied bow and slid off the lid. Pushing back the inscribed tissue paper, I lifted out the purse Geoffrey had sent me as a gift. It was prettier even than I remembered.

I was about to set the box aside, when I noticed a card edged in silver lying on the tissue beneath the purse. I picked it up. There was a brief note written in an angular scrawl.

Christine—

My apologies for the row and for storming out like that. I'm afraid Elizabeth is still a touchy subject—rather like a sore tooth that won't stop aching. Anyway, please forgive me for behaving like a fool, and accept the purse as a token of my remorse (since I know you won't accept it as a token of anything else.)

Yrs.

G—

When I'd finished reading the note, I picked up the purse and ran my fingers caressingly across the highly polished leather. Then, with a smile tugging at the corners of my mouth, I walked over to the bureau and began slipping passport, wallet, makeup and hairbrush into my brand new handbag.

I had my first opportunity to wear it in public the next morning, when I accompanied the household to town to attend the Divine Liturgy at St. Spiridon's. Demetra seemed at a loss to explain my presence in church, and her perplexity increased during the service when, expecting to find me unfamiliar and ill at ease with the ritual and content of the Liturgy, she instead found me chanting prayers, singing hymns, and reciting the Creed right along with the rest of the congregation.

As we filed out of the church, Michael sidled up to me and whispered, "I say, you did that jolly well! Just like a native! Stepmama was ever so startled. She was watching you, you know, and her eyes kept getting bigger and bigger. I kept expecting them to fall right out and go bouncing across the floor!"

I tried hard to hide my smile, and we caught up to Demetra and Spiro in the courtyard where they were greeting an exhausting number of friends and acquaintances. Nearly a half-hour passed before Spiro finally announced it was time for us to leave. Taking his sister by the arm, he started leading the way to the car, which as usual was parked some distance away.

I fell back to walk alongside Michael. "Penny for your thoughts."

He was silent a moment, then he directed his chin toward a sleek black ten-speed parked in a small bicycle-rental lot. "I used to have one like that once," he said.

Seeing the wistful look on his face, I spoke without thinking. "Would you like to take it for a spin?"

He nodded, an eager light suddenly blazing in his eyes. I was about to speak to the man at the lot, when I remembered the obstacles to the plan strolling up ahead. I rushed to catch up with them. "Mrs. Redfield, Spiro! There's a man renting bicycles back there. It looks like fun. How about we take a short ride around the Esplanade before we head back? My treat, of course."

"Thank you for the invitation," Demetra replied stiffly, "but as you can see, I am hardly dressed for such an adventure. However, if my brother wishes to accompany you—" Spiro flashed her a look that stopped her short. For a moment, she looked perplexed and then all the color seemed to drain from her face. "Forgive me, Miss Stewart, I am being stupid. Spiro cannot serve as your escort. He does not know how to ride a bicycle. I think we must postpone this entertainment until another day." She turned nervously away.

The two walked on, and I stood there, staring after them. Michael trotted up looking disappointed, but I was too distracted to do much besides tell him I was sorry. I didn't understand why my innocuous suggestion about renting bicycles had caused such turmoil, but I was fairly certain the look Spiro had flashed his sister had been a warning, and her reaction had been naked fear.

FIFTEEN

I had trouble sleeping that night.

In part, it was the weather. As evening fell, the air—instead of cooling—grew heavy and sticky with moisture. By the time I climbed into bed, the heat in my room was oppressive, and though I opened the French windows to their full extent, not a single cooling breeze wafted in.

In part, it was restlessness. This was my fourth night at Ithaki, and what had I accomplished? Learned a few stray, awkward secrets that might or might not have something to do with the danger that threatened Michael. Gotten my room torn up. Started to fall for a man who still loved a woman he'd been thrown over by nearly a decade before. Angrily, I punched my pillow.

This was crazy. By Thursday I was going to be back home, hawking graphic systems and pattering around my large, solitary apartment with Geoffrey and Michael out of my life forever.

The thought was more oppressive than the air. Slipping on a robe, I went in search of something to drink.

The kitchen, I knew, was at the far end of the house, but as I navigated my way through darkened rooms and hallways, I must have made a wrong turn, because instead of finding myself at the kitchen, I found myself in a long hallway that looked exactly like the one outside my own room. Wondering how I could have possibly gone in such a complete circle, I soon realized my mistake; I was not back where I had started, but in the other wing of the house, the wing where Michael and his stepmother had their rooms.

Suddenly, I heard the faint sound of crying. Fairly confident it was not Demetra's weeping I was hearing, I padded over to one of the doors, quietly opened it, and went in.

The curtains were drawn back, and light from the waning moon cast a faint bluish-white glow over the boy curled up on the bed crying into a pillow hugged tightly to his chest. He didn't lift his head as the door opened; instead, in a low, hiccuping voice he told me to go away.

"I will if you want me to," I said gently, "but are you sure you couldn't use the company?"

Now he did turn to look. "Miss Stewart! I'm sorry. I thought you were Helen." He sat up and wiped his eyes with the back of his hand. "She's always bursting in without knocking." His eyes suddenly opened wide. "Not that I meant that you—"

"No, you're right. It was rude of me. I'm sorry I didn't knock, but it's so late I was afraid I might wake someone."

"I don't mind your being here," he said. "Though I don't want you to think I usually do this. Cry, I mean."

"I figured it was an aberration," I assured him. "Mind if I stay awhile? Or are you anxious to get back to sleep?"

"No! I mean, no, I'm not really tired."

I nodded. "Probably this weather. It's hard to sleep when you stick to everything."

Michael's green eyes began to glisten. "Actually, I did sleep a little, but I had a rather unpleasant dream and woke up again." He ran his closed fist across his damp and tousled hair in a childish imitation of his uncle's familiar gesture, and I felt a strange clamping pain in my chest. I wanted to put my arms around him and comfort him and tell him everything was going to be okay, but feared that if I did so, I'd injure his boyish pride.

A large painful tear slid down his cheek. He wiped it away with the inside of his wrist.

"Would it make you feel better to talk about it?" I asked.

He opened his mouth to speak, but then closed it again as more tears came. Then the tears turned to shaking sobs. Forgetting to worry whether it was wise or not, I held out my arms. He shot into them and I hugged him tight, stroking his hair and patting his back until the sobs quieted into gentle snuffles.

"Better?"

He nodded.

"Feel like telling me about this dream?"

He hesitated, then whispered into my shoulder, "It was late at night. There was a man in a car, and he had my new bicycle with him. Only it wasn't my bicycle, it was me, and he was driving toward a cliff so he could throw me over." He lifted his head and looked up at me with frightened eyes.

"That sounds pretty scary," I said, forcing my voice to be calm and steady, "but it was only a dream, Michael. It's not real, and never was. You're here, safe, and I'm with you, and I'll stay with you tonight as long as you want me to."

"I'm not usually a coward, you know, and I seldom ever cry," he assured me in a low, stricken voice.

"Michael, I know you're not a coward, and as for crying, well, what you've gone through these past few months would cause more than a few grown men to shed a tear or two, so please don't feel you have to apologize."

He gave a relieved sigh and nestled more tightly in my arms. We sat like that in silence for so long, I thought he'd fallen asleep, until a muffled voice said, "It was *partly* real, you know. That's what made it so terrible."

Startled, I pushed him away from me a little so I could see his face. "What was partly real?"

"My dream. The bicycle. I saw him drive away with it." He swallowed hard and went on. "I think that's why he went out that night. Why he drove on that road near the cliffs. When the fog rolled in...."

I felt the hairs rise on the back of my neck. "Whoa! Let's back up a little here. First of all, who did you see?"

"My...father. I looked out the window and saw him drive off. Well, I mean, I didn't actually see him, but I saw the car, and he never let anyone else drive the Rolls. Anyway, the bicycle was sticking out the boot, and I knew he was taking it somewhere to get rid of it."

"The car?"

"The bicycle."

"But why should he do such a thing?" I asked.

Michael colored. "He was angry when it arrived at

Christmas. He said Uncle Geoffrey shouldn't have given it to me, and he threatened to send it back. In the end, he let me keep it, but I suppose after that terrible row he and Uncle Geoffrey had—"

I said sharply, "Your father and your uncle had an argument?"

He nodded, looking miserable.

"When?"

"That day. In the afternoon." Dismay must have shown in my face for he quickly added, "I didn't mean to listen, honestly I didn't, but I was coming down the stairs and they were yelling at each other so loudly I couldn't help but hear some of it."

"It's all right, Michael," I said numbly. "I'm just trying to understand. I thought your father was alone in the house the day of his accident; I didn't know you were there, too."

He shook his head. "Will Guyshull's father arrived a day early to pick him up for Easter hols and he offered me a lift, so I came home early, too. But when I got home no one was there, not even Bennings or Sarah or any of the other servants. I didn't have a key, so I climbed up the old chestnut tree and slipped in through my bedroom window. About an hour later I heard the Rolls come up the drive and saw Father get out by himself, but I thought it might be best to wait a bit before putting in an appearance."

"Why?"

"The old chestnut tree's a bit rotten, and while I was climbing up to my room one of the branches broke off and crashed into one of his favorite rose bushes. When he got out of the car, he was already looking bloody—I mean, awfully—angry, so I wasn't keen to test his temper any further."

"I see. So what made you finally decide to venture downstairs?"

He paused and looked away. "I saw Uncle Geoff's car turn up the drive, and I didn't want to miss him." It was clear from Michael's voice that visits from his uncle had been much-cherished events.

"So you started down the stairs and you heard them arguing. Did either of them see you?"

"No," he said tightly.

"Are you sure?"

"Yes."

"What were they arguing about?"

He shook his head and stared down at his hands. I gently tipped his chin up so I could see his face, and found his eyes brimming with tears.

"Never mind. It doesn't matter," I told him softly, brushing a recalcitrant elf-lock back off his brow. "What happened next? Did you slip back upstairs?"

He nodded. "I went back to my room. After a while, I must have fallen asleep. It was dark when I woke. I heard the Rolls starting up. I went to look out the window, and I saw it disappear down the drive with my bicycle sticking out the boot. I slipped downstairs and looked around. The house was empty, so I got something to eat, watched some telly, and went back up to my room. When I woke the next morning, the servants were back, but there was no sign of the Rolls."

"Michael," I said gently, "we don't have to talk about this anymore if you don't want to."

"No, it's all right. I'd like to tell you, if you don't mind."

I assured him I didn't, and he described how he'd crept back down the chestnut tree and pretended to be arriving from the station. His stepmother had arrived soon after, followed by the police with news of the accident. She had gone off to identify the body, Spiro had arrived later in the day and had immediately rushed off to comfort his sister, and Michael had been left alone with only the servants for company because the police hadn't been able to reach Geoffrey until late into the night.

When Michael finally felt talked-out, we adjourned to the kitchen and I made some chamomile tea. By the time we returned to his room, he was already drooping, and soon after I tucked him back into bed, he was asleep.

Feeling more than a little worn myself, I dropped a light goodnight kiss on his forehead and tiptoed quietly out of the room. Climbing into my own bed, I sank against the mattress as if I were made of stone.

By morning, the humidity had dropped, the air was light and cool, and my mood was…darker than the wine-dark sea.

It didn't help having Demetra Redfield offer me eye cream to help cover the dark circles she so kindly pointed out had developed under my eyes; or to find out Spiro had disappeared to the mainland on business and that no one, not even his sister, knew when to expect him back; or to be told with obvious relish by Helen that Michael was feeling under the weather and would be spending the entire day in his room.

Which is perhaps why, when I met Paul on my way down to the beach and he asked me if I were going for a swim, I turned to him with perfect aplomb and snapped, "No, actually, I thought I'd just go down and drown myself." I was momentarily cheered out of my black mood to see a look of startled incredulity flash across his normally imperturbable countenance.

Later, however, as I paddled listlessly about in the water, I began to wonder if Paul had taken me seriously. I caught the glint of sunlight off a pair of binoculars, and, with that strange sixth sense that comes into play when you know you're being observed, I knew for a certainty that the binoculars were trained on me, watching my every move. Feeling first uncomfortable, then irritated, then downright angry after minutes of unceasing scrutiny, I scrambled out of the water and started up the path towards the garden.

Paul, no doubt seeing me come, was innocently picking tomatoes when I arrived, dripping and furious. "How dare you do that to me!" I yelled at him in Greek.

He straightened slowly. "Do what?"

"You know very well what! I'm warning you. I won't be stared at through those damn binoculars like some bug under a microscope! Do you understand?"

He shook his head. "No, I'm afraid I don't. Do you mean to say someone's been spying on you with binoculars?"

"Yes! Just now, while I was down swimming. Are you claiming it wasn't you?"

"Of course it wasn't me." He set the basket of tomatoes down on the ground. "You'd better stay here."

"Stay here? Why? Where are you going?"

He was gazing off in the direction of the house. "Why, to find your spy, of course."

He was gone for what seemed an inordinately long time, and when he returned he tossed a towel to me and said, "Nothing. I searched everywhere. I couldn't find a sign of anyone."

I wrapped myself in the towel and said coldly, "I don't care what you found or didn't find. Someone was up here watching me, and I'm still not convinced it wasn't you."

He didn't argue. "Your things are still down at the beach?"

"Yes."

"I'll get them for you; meanwhile, I think it would be best if you went back to the house. No one will bother you there."

"And why shouldn't I just stay here?"

He looked back over his shoulder. "I don't want you standing there dripping saltwater on my plants and killing them."

Geoffrey had said he might be back on Corfu as early as Monday, so when Maria knocked on my door after lunch and said there was a man on the phone who wished to speak to me, I ran to the telephone in the library and snatched up the receiver.

"Miss Stewart?" inquired a voice I didn't know.

"Yes?" I snapped, disappointed.

"Ah, Thespinis, I am Yiannis Andriatsis, from the Hotel Kerkyra. My grandmother asks that I telephone to you and inform you that a letter has arrived to you from overseas."

"A letter? Can you tell me where it's from?" I knew, even as I said the words, that it couldn't possibly be from Geoffrey. A letter could never arrive so quickly.

"Yes, of course. One moment. It is from the United States. From California."

"I see. Well, thank you."

"Wait, Miss Stewart! You would like the letter to be sent to you at the house of your friend, or would you like to come receive it yourself?"

"I—I'll come get it this afternoon." The letter wasn't from

Geoffrey, but at least it would give me an excuse to go to town. Perhaps I could stop by the Corfu Palace and see if they knew when he was expected back.

"That will be excellent, Thespinis. Goodbye."

"Goodbye, Kyrios Andriatsis."

The phone clicked as he hung up. I stood there for a moment with the receiver still absentmindedly pressed against my ear, wondering how I was going to get a ride into town. Then I heard a second, softer click, and I was suddenly grateful the message had not been from Geoffrey after all. Someone had been listening in on the conversation. Someone in the house.

I told Demetra about the letter waiting for me at the Hotel Kerkyra, and asked her if it would be possible for Paul to drive me into town. As luck would have it, she was already sending Paul into Corfu on an errand, so I was given permission to ride along.

Paul was a taciturn companion, but he drove smoothly and at a more relaxing pace then Spiro, and I found myself enjoying the ride. It was pleasant to let my gaze wander idly on the vistas flashing by. As the blue Fiat pulled up before the cream-colored façade of the Hotel Kerkyra, Paul asked me whether I'd be right out or whether he should start searching for a parking space.

"Oh, you can just drop me here, thank you. You don't have to wait. I may do a few errands myself after I pick up the letter, and I can catch a taxi back."

I expected he would be glad to be rid of me, but instead he seemed dismayed by this sudden change of plans. "It will not be easy to find a taxi to drive so far without a return fare."

"I've already done it twice before."

His face evinced disbelief. "Then you were lucky. Anyway, it is no trouble. If you wish to go someplace, I will take you."

"But you have that errand to do for Mrs. Redfield."

"It can be done in an instant, and at any time." The determined set of his mouth and the slight gleam in his eye made it clear he was not about to be bested in this test of wills.

"Oh, very well, do what you want," I said irritably, opening the door and climbing out. "Stay or go, as you please. I may be a while." I slammed the door shut and climbed the stairs. The Fiat suddenly slipped into gear and roared off down the street, but any hopes I had that Paul had changed his mind faded when I saw him maneuver the Fiat rapidly and deftly into a tiny gap between two parked cars.

Kyria Andriatsis came bustling out to greet me as I entered the cool, high-ceilinged lobby and led me back behind the counter and down a corridor to the family's rooms. There she sat me down, served me baklava and coffee, and asked me whether I was enjoying the visit with my friend. I assured her I was, but my assurances didn't seem to convince her; she kept darting troubled looks at my face. In an effort to shift her attention, I thanked her for letting me know about the arrival of my letter.

She took the hint, and went off to retrieve it for me. To my surprise, she returned to the room not with one envelope, but with two: an ordinary-looking airmail envelope with American stamps and a small cardboard envelope with no stamps whatsoever, but numerous labels and markings from some French express delivery firm.

"Why do you not open them?" Kyria Andriatsis asked, watching me closely with those dark raisin eyes.

"I'm afraid I have to get going," I replied, slipping both envelopes into my purse and rising to my feet. "Someone is waiting for me outside, and he's probably getting impatient." I thanked her for the coffee and baklava as she walked me out.

She smiled, but the anxious lines remained around her eyes. "Remember, *koritsi*, there is a room for you here—anytime."

"Thank you, Kyria," I said, touched by her concern.

Paul was waiting across the street in the narrow strip of shade provided by the buildings. He was leaning carelessly against a wall, his muscular arms crossed, his head cocked to one side. When he saw me emerge from the hotel he crossed to meet me. "Where do we go now?"

"*We're* going nowhere. *I'm* going for a walk."

"As you like," he said, falling into step beside me. "Perhaps the new saying should be, 'Mad dogs and Englishmen and young ladies from California'?"

"It's not midday, it's nearly two."

He made a harrumphing sound.

"If it's too hot for you, you're welcome to go back to your car and drive away. I'm perfectly capable of getting back to Ithaki on my own." He didn't answer or even seem to hear me. "Why are you so determined to make a pest of yourself?" I demanded. "Haven't I made it clear? I prefer to be alone."

"You return soon to America?" he asked in a conversational tone.

"Yes, Wednesday," I replied meaningfully. "And there's still a great deal I haven't yet had a chance to see."

"That is a pity."

I scowled at him, but it had no effect; no doubt Demetra had given him orders to stick with me. I pulled out a street map of Corfu Town and stared at it, trying to see if there was some way to lose him in the streets and alleyways. Then I noticed something on the map and came up with a somewhat simpler plan.

"I hadn't realized it was quite so far away," I murmured, allowing my shoulders to droop, "and it is awfully hot." He said nothing, merely waited, and I let out a long sigh. "Oh, all right. Let's go back to the car and you can drive me there."

"Where?"

"The Archaeological Museum. I still haven't seen it, and this might be my last chance. After all, how can I leave Corfu without seeing the…" I struggled to remember what I'd read in my guidebook about the museum. "The Gorgon pediment." It sounded unconvincing to my ears, but Paul merely nodded.

Climbing into the Fiat after it had been closed-up in the hot sun was a bit like climbing into an overheated pizza oven, but as Paul maneuvered us out of the maze of small streets and onto the main road circling the town at the water's edge, sea air blew in through the rolled-down windows and cooled the car down. I was enjoying the feel of the wind against my heated skin, when the car came to an abrupt halt at the corner of a small side street.

"The museum is up there, on the right," Paul said, pointing. He reached across me to unlatch the door and push it open.

I quickly climbed out, relieved he hadn't insisted on going to the museum with me. I headed in the direction he'd pointed, watching out of the corner of my eye as the Fiat zipped away, circling around a small traffic roundabout to head back downtown.

Pulling out my map, I turned the opposite direction, back toward the long, wide avenue called Dimokratias which curves in a panoramic arc around Garitsa bay. If the map was right, I was only three or four long blocks from Geoffrey's hotel.

After the heat of the walk, the outflung terraces of the Corfu Palace were a welcome sight. I entered the cool and subdued lobby and for a moment just enjoyed being out of the hot sun, then I crossed to the reception desk and asked the desk clerk if Geoffrey had returned yet. He reached down and flicked through his files, then gave the faintest shake of his head.

"No, he has not."

"When do you expect him back then?"

He glanced down at the white card in his hand. "I cannot say. When he left, he was unsure of the precise day of his return. He continues to pay for the room, so there was no need for him to give us an exact date."

I sighed with frustration. "Did he leave an address he could be reached at? Or a telephone number?"

His expression grew slightly more sympathetic. "I am sorry, no. It is important? You are anxious to speak with him?"

"Yes."

"Then perhaps you wish to leave a message? It is possible he may telephone, and if so, he would know to contact you."

It was a good suggestion, and I was about to take him up on it, when someone behind me called my name. I spun around guiltily.

But it was only Robert. "Oh, hello!" I said in relief.

"Hello," he echoed with a smile. The smile faded as he added, "I suppose you're here looking for Geoffrey?"

I hesitated for a moment, then nodded.

"I'm afraid you won't find him in," he said.

"Oh," I replied, trying to sound both surprised and noncommittal.

"Seems he's done a flit," Robert continued, his tone openly critical. "No one knows where he is or when he'll be back."

The instinctive urge to defend Geoffrey tickled in my

throat, but I was not about to be the one to break the news about Elizabeth to Robert. Those hazel eyes of his saw all too much, and I was in no mood to answer the questions he would no doubt ask about Elizabeth's miraculous survival and Geoffrey's reaction to it.

"It's okay," I said. "Nothing urgent. I was just in town and thought I'd stop by and say hello."

Robert frowned, as seemingly unconvinced by my words as Kyria Andriatsis had been. "I see. And how have things been at the Villa?" he asked. "Quiet, I hope?"

I considered telling him about the drugged chocolates, but without any proof, what was there to tell? "Quiet enough, I guess."

He regarded me for a long moment in silence. Then he said, "I could wring Geoffrey's neck for abandoning you and Michael at a time like this."

His words were dangerously close to my own feelings, but I ignored the surge of anger rising up my throat and said meekly, "I'm sure he'll be back soon."

"Well, in the meantime, I'm here," Robert said, "and I'd like to help if I can." He reached out and touched my arm in a gesture of concern that almost undid me. "Please, Christine, won't you tell me what's wrong?"

I replied more out frustration than out of any real belief he could give me the answer I so desperatedly craved. "What's wrong, Robert, is that I've found out Geoffrey and his brother had a bad argument the day his brother died, and I don't know what the argument was about." I paused. "You don't know, do you?"

Slowly, he shook his head, his sandy eyebrows forming two worried arcs over troubled hazel eyes. "Who told you about this supposed row?" he demanded. "Skouras?"

I wasn't sure how to answer. I didn't want Robert thinking I was bearing tales from Spiro, but I didn't want to admit Michael had been in the house the night of his father's accident, either. Suddenly, I was rescued from my quandary by the approach of a small, birdlike woman of about sixty.

"Why, it is you!" she chirped happily, beaming up at Robert as if he were a long, lost friend. His expression, however, as he regarded the small plume of extravagantly coifed white hair, the bright china-blue eyes, and the bejeweled finger coyly tapping his chest, was completely blank.

"Now don't tell me you don't remember me, Bobby Humphreys! Last December, outside Nice? You and your new bride gave me a ride back to town when my rental car broke down?"

Recognition dawned. "Of course, I remember you, Mrs. Baxter," he replied at last. "You are a woman quite impossible to forget."

I bit my lip to suppress a chuckle.

She frowned. "Trying to make me feel like an old woman, Bobby? Call me Elsie!" Suddenly she noticed me standing there, and her eyes narrowed. "And who is this?"

He made the necessary introductions, and I held out my hand politely. She gave it a single limp shake and then turned back to him and demanded archly, "And where is your dear wife?"

"At home," he replied politely. "She'll be sorry to have missed you."

"She should know better than to let an attractive man like you roam Corfu on his own," she said, her china blue gaze boring into me like a reproving laser.

"I'm here on business," Robert replied stiffly. "Miss Stewart is the friend of a client of mine."

She gave a small shrug of her narrow shoulders. "If you say so, Bobby. Now tell me, what have you got planned for today?"

For a fleeting moment, a look of pure horror passed over Robert's face. Then in a determined voice he said, "You'll have to excuse us, Elsie. We have a meeting to get to and we're running late." Before she could protest, he hauled me out of the lobby, and we started up Dimokratias at a breath-robbing pace.

"Would you mind if we slowed down a little?" I puffed.

"Of course not," he said apologetically. "Shall we sit?" He led the way to a wooden bench set against a wall. "I'm sorry for our abrupt exit, but I was afraid in another minute she was going to invite herself to spend the rest of the day with us. "

"Is that what happened on your honeymoon?"

He nodded grimly. "She attached herself to us for a week

and wouldn't let go. "

I couldn't help smiling at his morose expression. "Aw, come on, she couldn't have been that bad."

He gave a faint shudder. "You've no idea. The one mercy is that I'm not staying at the Corfu Palace, so she'll be hard put to find me again."

I giggled.

He frowned and then reluctantly began to smile. "Yes, I suppose it does sound a bit ridiculous." For a moment, we sat in amicable silence, then his expression sobered. "Now about this supposed row between Geoffrey and William—"

Inwardly I sighed. So much for Mrs. Baxter's value as a distraction. "You know, on second thought, Robert, let's just forget about it."

He shook his head. "No, Christine. Whoever told you about this argument is trying to make trouble for Geoffrey. "

"And what if they're telling the truth?" I asked tensely.

His expression grew stark. "Then I have some serious thinking to do. You see, the day of his accident, William rang up my office wanting to change his will. I was out when he telephoned, and when I rang back later there was no answer. I never found out what changes he intended to make."

A sudden breeze blew past, chilling me. "Go on."

"When William's death was ruled an accident, I gave no more thought to the matter, setting it down as mere bad luck that William died before he was able to alter his will as he wished. But the events of the past few days have caused me to reconsider." He paused, as if reluctant to go on, but it was clear what he was leading up to.

"You think William might have been killed to prevent him from changing his will?"

Robert nodded. "It's a possibility, which is why it's so important for me to know who told you about this row. I have to know if the source is credible. If Geoffrey really did have a falling out with his brother the very day his brother rang up wishing to alter his bequests, well…I am an officer of the court." His voice grew somber. "The proper authorities would have to be informed."

I shook my head. "Sorry, Robert. I've already told you all I'm going to."

"Christine, please! I understand your desire to protect Geoffrey, but this isn't the right way to go about it.

"You don't understand," I said, rising to my feet and walking away. "It's not Geoffrey I'm thinking of."

Despite my parting comment to Robert, Geoffrey was very much on my mind as I wandered through the small park of the Esplanade and plopped down, distracted, onto a shaded bench to think. Once again Geoffrey seemed to be proving right: his brother's accident was looking more and more like murder. Unfortunately, Geoffrey also seemed, once again, to be the only one with an obvious motive. *Why aren't you here to give me some answers?* I railed silently. The only answer I received was the grumpy chirrup of a bird waiting for me to throw it some crumbs.

Then I remembered the two letters in my purse.

I read the one in the airmail envelope—the one from California, the one that couldn't be from Geoffrey—first, to get it out of the way. It was from my sister. It was a nice letter, friendly and chatty, full of the news and gossip from home since I'd been gone. For a little while I was able to imagine that going home wasn't going to be so bad after all.

Then I opened the second letter. It contained just three hastily scrawled lines: *"Business in Monaco not going as expected. Returning Wednesday. Looking forward to seeing you then."* It wasn't signed and indicated no return address at which the writer could be contacted.

My flight was scheduled to leave Wednesday morning at ten. In all likelihood, by the time Geoffrey returned to Corfu, I'd be gone. Lost in contemplating this dismal vision, I didn't notice the Fiat pull up until Paul got out to open the door for me.

Somehow I wasn't even surprised to see him. I slipped the letters into my purse and rose to my feet. "I suppose you followed me?"

He shrugged apologetically, but held the door open, waiting. "The Archaeological Museum is closed on Mondays." After a pause he added, "You are ready to return to the villa?"

"Why didn't you tell me about the museum being closed before?"

He cocked one eyebrow at me in surprise. "I did not think it mattered. I assumed there were other sights you wished to see. I hope you were not overly disappointed to miss the Gorgon?" His expression was bland, but his blue eyes mocked me.

I bit my lip and for a moment considered the pleasures of being able—like that most famous Gorgon, Medusa—to turn a man to stone with a single look. Unfortunately, my glance was not withering enough. Paul, still flesh and blood, asked me again if I was ready to return to Ithaki.

Growling my assent, I let him hand me into the car.

We stopped at a small shop in the center of town so Paul could complete his errand for Demetra, then wove our way back toward the road leading north. When we reached the outskirts of the city, however, we found the road closed, forcing us to turn back. Paul was not pleased by this mandatory detour, and swore under his breath when he saw that we were being detoured back toward the port where the ferries from Italy and Yugoslavia dock. As we approached the perspiring man direct-ing traffic, Paul rolled down the window and began arguing with him, insisting that there had to be a better route to take. Calling the man an idiot, Paul gestured angrily to his watch: didn't the fool realize that it was time for the Brindisi ferry to arrive? The red-faced man made a rather rude comment about Paul's antecedents, and a policeman strolled up to ask Paul in an icy tone if something was wrong. Paul, grumbling, shook his head, rolled up the window, and reluctantly turned the Fiat in the direction of the port.

The ferry from Brindisi had indeed just arrived, and was dis-gorging a seemingly endless line of cars, trucks, and passengers as we approached. The traffic quickly slowed to a crawl as all the new arrivals tried to merge into the relatively narrow street, and I began to understand why Paul had grown so upset. The hot, still air began to stink with the smell of exhaust and vibrate with a cacophony of blasting horns, squealing tires, and shouted curses. I wasn't even driving, yet my nerves were still stretched tight with the desire to break free, somehow, and get out of there.

Unfortunately, everyone else on the dock felt the same way. During a brief surge forward in the traffic, a red Fiat Spider suddenly dashed through a nonexistent gap in front of us. Paul had to slam on the brakes and jerk the car hard to the right, onto a fortunately empty section of sidewalk, to avoid hitting it. We were both wearing seatbelts, so neither of us was really hurt, but Paul jumped out of the car and yelled curses in Italian at the driver of the Spider. The other driver was apparently in no mood for a fight; the red car darted through another gap and roared away, leaving Paul standing there shaking his fist at a cloud of exhaust.

Some of the passengers from the ferry had noticed our close call, and several came forward to ask if we were all right. Paul assured them we were fine and climbed back into the car. They drifted away and I watched them go, touched by their concern. Several of them were approached by other passengers curious to know the news.

With a strange feeling in the pit of my stomach, I watched as one of the curious, a man dressed casually in a blue knit shirt and khaki shorts, stopped to ask a woman about us. Apparently he was satisfied with the answer she gave him, for he quickly walked off, not bothering to glance a second time in our direction. But he didn't have to turn again for me to recognize him.

It was Geoffrey.

Paul maneuvered the Fiat back into traffic, which was still moving as slowly as molasses, and I turned around and settled back into my seat, staring blindly ahead at the dusty line of cars.

I'd been so worried that I might never see Geoffrey again.

Obviously my fears had been premature.

SIXTEEN

I spent the rest of Monday waiting for some word from Geoffrey, but none came. No voice whispered to me as I wandered the outskirts of the villa property before dinner. No note was to be found any of the many times I checked my room during the long evening I spent in Demetra Redfield's silent company. No reassuring figure emerged from the rustling, sighing shadows when I ventured down after midnight to the beach. No green-eyed interloper intruded on my dream-tossed sleep.

Disappointed, angry, and depressed, I woke Tuesday morning convinced I was glad this was my last full day in Greece. I might have remained convinced of it, too, if Demetra hadn't—in her relief at my imminent departure—let me spend the entire day in Michael's company.

We ate breakfast together and picked tomatoes together and after lunch we walked to Koussaki and shared a lemonade at the small café on the square. It was Helen's day off, so Paul accompanied us as watchdog. Though not much more talkative than Helen, he wasn't such dampening company, with the result that Michael and I talked and laughed and giggled enough for three.

By the time we returned to the villa, we were hot and dusty and ready for a swim. Michael and I went to change, and Paul disappeared on some errand, apparently deciding a watchdog wasn't necessary for such an innocuous activity.

"Last one in is a rotten egg!" I yelled to Michael as we ran down the path toward the azure water. He made a disparaging remark about the antiquated nature of my taunt and then flew by me with a mischievous grin and cry of triumph. I heard him splashing up ahead and arrived on the beach in time to see him slide into the water like a pale-skinned otter.

Treading the algae-covered stones at the sea's edge more gingerly, I slipped in after him and paddled lazily around, waiting for him to surface. There was a small, crashing burst near my shoulder as he popped buoyantly up, water streaming down his face and hair. He tossed his head back, throwing the wet locks out of the way and revealing green eyes—so like his uncle's—which sparkled in the sun with pleasure.

"Shall we race to that rock?" he asked eagerly.

"All right, my little fish. Just don't beat me too handily."

He shook his head. "No need to worry. Uncle Spiro isn't here to slow you up." So saying, he burst away, the bright red and purple of his swim trunks diminishing rapidly into the distance. Shaking my head at his speed, I swam after him.

The race ended in a tie, and after the race we paddled companionably around. I showed him how to swim in the direction of his feet, he showed me how to sink while holding my breath, and together we experimented with various configurations for floating on the surface while hooked together by our hands and feet.

"This has been a fun day," murmured Michael as we floated along, the sun shining warmly, the gentle current rocking us as if we were in some giant cradle. "I wish you didn't have to leave."

"But I do," I replied, realizing I disliked the prospect as much as he. Saying goodbye to him was going to be painful, and not getting the chance to say goodbye to his uncle even more so. "It's always hard when vacations come to an end, and you have to leave new friends behind, but that's just the way it is, Michael. People have to go home."

It was a speech intended to convince myself as much as him that leaving was a sensible necessity, but it didn't work—on either of us. For a minute or two we floated on in silence, and then the delicate balance that had been keeping us connected and afloat gave way, and we broke apart to avoid sinking. While I fanned the water to stay in place, Michael began swimming out toward the mouth of the small cove. Sensing his hurt and wanting to make amends, I made to follow, but when I began swimming in his direction, Michael moved off another way, making it clear my company was no longer welcome.

Stung by the rebuff, I left the water and went to sit on my mat in the shade of a large pine tree. I sat there some time lost in thought—mostly of a self-pitying sort, watching distractedly as Michael angrily practiced diving beneath the surface and remaining there brief periods holding his breath. Since he had already demonstrated his considerable talents in this area, I found nothing worrisome in his short disappearances from view.

So I watched Michael absently, complacently.

I was lost in an entirely satisfying—and unfortunately imaginary—harangue of Geoffrey when on some subconscious level an alarm went off. Michael had been underwater for an awfully long time, hadn't he? Abandoning my tirade, I scanned the cove. How long had it been since Michael's last dive? Angry with myself for my inattention, I realized I didn't know.

Feeling a sudden tensing in my stomach, I rose hastily to my feet and started toward the water, keeping my eyes fixed on the point where I last remembered seeing him. But despite my attempts to will him into view, there was no reassuring jack-in-the-box burst to the surface.

"Michael!" I called out. "Michael, can you hear me? Where are you? *Michael!*"

There was no answer, no movement. The deep blue water lapped calmly at my legs, mocking my growing fear. I plunged in, swimming hard toward the spot where I thought he'd disappeared. As I drew close, I dove, searching for some sight of him. Despite the stinging in my eyes, I could see the cloudy outlines of rocks and seaweed and small moving shadows that might have been fish, but no Michael. I was forced to the surface for air, and then dove again further on, but again I burst gasping to the surface without any sign of him.

Murmuring a brief prayer, I swam a little to the right and dove again. Then I tried to the left. My eyes were smarting and I began to despair as my view became blurrier and blurrier. Then I saw it. A glimpse of red too bright to belong to the sea. Rising to the surface for a brief gulp of air, I dove down toward the patch of red, repeating my prayer and adding to it, "Please, God, let me find him—and let him be alive." The stillness of that patch of red frightened me.

As I dove down, the red patch resolved into a blurry red and purple rectangle from which cream-colored shapes protruded top and bottom. Kicking hard, I drew close and gathered the small body in my arms. Frightened and angry, hopeful and despairing, I burst to the surface desperate for air and a closer look at him. He felt so limp in my arms.

I carried him out of the water and onto the beach, and set him down gently on the warm, smooth stones. His eyes were closed, his lips tinged with blue, and his chest was not moving. I stared down at him, terrified he was going to die, was dead already.

"Help! Somebody, help!"

I tried to scream the words, but no air seemed to come from my lungs; my cry for assistance came out a faint whistling wheeze. I took a deep breath and tried again, but though this time I managed to call out weakly, I knew no one up at the villa could possibly hear me. It was too far away. I looked down at Michael. He would only live if someone helped him, and I was the only one around to do it. Trembling, I knelt down beside him and felt for a pulse. It was faint, but it was there. His heart was still beating. Now, if I could just get his lungs to work again.

Lift the neck. Tilt the head. Pinch the nose. Four quick breaths.

Somewhere above and behind me there was the sound of clattering stones, but I didn't turn; instead I inhaled quickly, pressed my mouth against Michael's, and blew. The small chest rose. I pulled away, took a breath, and repeated the process. The small chest rose, then fell, but Michael didn't stir. I repeated the process again, and again, and again. My strength began to falter, but I had to go on; there was no one else.

I lifted my head to take a breath, and someone pulled me away. Paul said roughly, "I will breathe for him now." He slipped into my place and blew the next breath into Michael without missing a beat, and I sagged against an arm that was suddenly there, bracing me. I turned. Maria stood next to me, holding me up, her anxious gaze fixed on the man and boy crouched on the ground.

The distressingly monotonous process continued for what seemed an age, before a strange choking noise broke the steady soughing of Paul's donated breath. Michael began coughing, then heaving, and Paul turned his head so he could safely be sick. Eventually the violent coughing subsided into gentler and more sporadic bursts, and I realized that Michael was going to live.

The knowledge surged through me, sending waves of relief and exhilaration cascading down to my fingertips. Without thinking, I threw my arms around Maria. "We did it! He's safe! He's going to be all right!"

"Yes," she agreed somberly, "he is safe. But for how long?"

"I still do not completely understand," Lieutenant Mavros said. "What triggered your sudden anxiety for the boy? Why did you return to the sea and search for him?"

Fighting the urge to say something rude, I glared up at an innocent patch of peeling green paint—well, not all that innocent, the bilious color did nothing to soothe my temper and the dirty, curling strip was a reminder that Michael was a patient in a hospital that looked like a rundown bus terminal—and replied impatiently, "As I've already explained to you several times, Lieutenant, I grew alarmed when Michael didn't surface for air after what seemed to me an unusually long time."

"Your attention was fixed on the boy?"

"Not fixed, but yes, I was keeping an eye on him," I said.

The policeman frowned. "I beg your pardon?"

"I was watching him."

"And yet you did not see the boy attacked?"

"So this time you believe there was an attack?" I said. "You don't think it was another accident?"

He shook his head. "The boy says someone swam up behind him. At first, he thought it was you, but as he started to turn, he was seized by the throat. He remembers no more."

"He was knocked out?" I asked.

"You mean struck? No, his attacker was not so clumsy. Two slight bruises only—hardly visible unless a person is looking for them—have been found on the boy's neck, as if a someone pressed their thumbs against the carotid arteries."

"But that would cut off all blood to his brain!"

The lieutenant nodded. "Yes, once rendered unconscious, the boy had merely to be left where he was to drown."

My fists clenched in anger, but I was also afraid. "Did Michael see his attacker?"

"Unfortunately, he did not."

I slowly let out the breath I'd been holding. "So where does that leave us?"

"Me, it leaves with a murderer to find, and you? Under the circumstances, Miss Stewart, I am afraid I must ask you to cancel your airplane reservation for tomorrow. I would like you to remain on Corfu for a few more days as your part in all this—you will forgive me—seems to me still unclear." He turned and walked away, leaving me with a strong desire to kick one of the ugly, orange plastic chairs that circled the waiting room.

Instead I climbed the dark, dingy staircase to the third floor, and the single-occupant room that Demetra Redfield had insisted on for her stepson. For once, I was grateful for her patrician attitudes; most of the rooms I'd seen had patients packed in six deep.

I found Paul on guard duty outside Michael's door, Demetra having deputized him to keep undesirables—namely Geoffrey and me—out in her absence. Having saved her stepson's life twice did not redeem me in her eyes; after all, he would not have been in the water but for me. I thought that after our cooperative effort at the beach, I might be able to coax Paul into allowing me in to see Michael for a minute or two, but Paul was clearly unwilling to risk his employer's wrath on my behalf.

"He will be fine," he assured me, "but the doctor says he must rest. Do not worry, Thespinis. Go home and prepare you things. After all, tomorrow you are leaving."

"Actually, I'm not. Lieutenant Mavros's orders. He wants me to stick around for a while."

"He suspects you?"

I nodded. "But then I guess he suspects just about everyone. I bet he's already asked you why you were in swim trunks and dripping wet when Maria called you to help me with Michael."

The turquoise eyes blinked. "I thought I saw a trespasser swimming in the next cove," Paul said in a flat voice. "I went to chase him off."

I nodded. "And did you?"

"Unfortunately, he was gone by the time I arrived. I could not find him."

"Too bad."

"Yes."

We regarded each other in silence for a moment. "Will you remain at Ithaki?" Paul finally asked.

"Unless Mr. Skouras returns soon, probably not. I suspect Mrs. Redfield will consider this an excellent opportunity to kick me out. I don't suppose you happen to know where Mr. Skouras is, by the way?"

Paul shook his head. "Somewhere on the mainland."

Somewhere on the mainland. A conveniently vague location, and worthless as an alibi for the attack that afternoon. Ferries ran almost hourly between Igoumenitsa and Corfu. Had Spiro slipped across on one and tried to murder Michael? Though it was a more palatable solution than the one which worried at my peace, I still knew of no definite motive to explain why he should.

Which left Geoffrey.

Geoffrey, who had had a violent quarrel with his brother on the very day his brother died and who would inherit millions if Michael died, too.

Geoffrey, who knew the Old Fort, scene of the first attack, like the back of his hand, and who knew the cove at Ithaki, scene of this last, like the front of it.

Geoffrey, who frequently seemed as anxious as Demetra for me to quit the villa and Michael's company, and who had been back on Corfu for more than a day without so much as a word to me.

Suddenly, from down the hall, a man's voice called out my name. I turned.

Geoffrey.

Seventeen

"Of course, Paul, I'll be happy to take Miss Stewart home." Ignoring my angry scowl, Geoffrey slid his arm through mine and led me away down the dim and dreary corridor as if I were a recalcitrant child.

I pulled my arm free as soon as we were out Paul's sight. "I don't understand you at all. You're Michael's uncle! How can you let your sister-in-law's *gardener* prevent you from seeing him?"

"From what I've been told, that gardener helped save the boy's life this afternoon. Besides, what did you expect me to do? Throw him aside and burst into Michael's room unbidden?"

"No, of course not, I just...." My voice trailed away as I realized that despite what I'd said, that was exactly what I'd wanted him to do. I'd wanted him to challenge Paul—to fight him, if necessary—to see Michael. I'd wanted him to throw his weight around and yell and curse and prove in some tangible way that he was upset, that he cared. Michael had been attacked and nearly killed, yet Geoffrey was acting as if he didn't give a damn.

I bit my lip and stared up at the peeling paint. "You don't have to worry about driving me back. I can take a taxi."

He frowned. "I see. Gone three days and you've already lost the taste for my company. Well, I'd be happy to leave it to Skouras to squire you back, but he doesn't appear to be about. As for taking a taxi, I doubt you'll find one around here at this time of night. The hospital isn't exactly a tourist stop."

He was right, and I knew it. "In that case," I said stiffly, "I suppose I'll have to take you up on your offer."

He flashed me a searching look, then gave a grim nod. We

started down the stairs in uneasy silence.

"Have you spoken to Lieutenant Mavros yet?" I finally asked.

"There's been no time. My flight arrived an hour ago, and when I arrived at my hotel there was a message that there'd been another 'accident'. I came straight here."

"Your flight?" I exclaimed. "Are you trying to tell me you've just now returned to Corfu?"

"Of course." He shot me a sideways glance. "Didn't you get my letter?" He paused, then added, "Things didn't go as smoothly with Elizabeth as I'd hoped."

"She doesn't want custody, does she?"

"It didn't get that far. She wouldn't listen to me, refused to hear me out. When I tried to explain to her that Michael was in danger, she insisted he was quite safe where he was."

"Perhaps she doesn't want to get involved."

"She's his mother, Christine! Do you think she'd simply stand by if she truly believed he was in danger?"

"She abandoned him when he was two. That's hardly the act of a woman overburdened by maternal instinct."

He shook his head. "The problem isn't Michael, it's me. Someone's convinced her I'm not to be trusted. Considering our past relationship, that probably wasn't hard to do."

"Considering your past relationship," I snapped, "you were crazy to think she'd be of any help in the first place." I hurried down the last of the steps and out the main entrance.

"May I ask why you're in such a blasted hurry?" he demanded as he caught up with me near the hospital gates. The dwindling twilight left his face swathed in shadow.

"I want to get back to the villa. I have to pack my things."

"Of course," he said, his voice sounding strangely hollow as it echoed in the courtyard. "I'd forgotten. You're leaving tomorrow, aren't you?"

I didn't bother to correct him. With his rekindled feelings for Elizabeth, I doubted it mattered much to him whether I stayed or went. As if to confirm this, he added abstractedly, "Yes, I suppose that's for the best."

"I'm glad you think so." I started to walk away.

Once again he followed me. "Where are you going?"

"I told you. Back to the villa to pack."

"But first you're dining with me," he insisted.

I shook my head. "I'm not hungry."

"Have you forgotten? I'm your lift back. And anyway, you promised to have dinner with me again before you left the island. Are you going back on your word?"

I gazed up at the darkening sky and sighed. "No."

The Bella Roma is a small outdoor restaurant clinging to the cliffs which overlook the sea near Kassiopi. Though the decor has a distinctly Italian feel, the specialty of the house is sofrito, that most Corfiote of dishes. "It serves the best on the island," Geoffrey assured me, after I'd asked why we needed to drive so far for dinner when there were so many places to eat right there in town. It was a little after nine when we arrived, and the restaurant was not yet crowded. Geoffrey led the way to a small table near the railing at the cliff's edge, and soon after we sat down, a short, strongly-built man wearing a red polo shirt and jeans appeared at our table and greeted Geoffrey with a grin.

"Hello, stranger," Geoffrey said. "*Ti kanete?*"

"Not bad. Not bad at all. The old man's out with a bad back, so I've been running things solo, but I can't complain."

I must have been staring, because Geoffrey laughed. "George, this is Christine Stewart. Christine, this is George Dinatakis. He and his father own the Bella Roma."

"Pleased to meet ya," George said, thrusting his right hand forward.

I took it. "Pleased to meet you, too," I echoed faintly, trying not to wince at his strong grip. "You're from New York?"

"South Bronx, born and raised. My dad grew up here on the island, but emigrated to the States in '52. Twelve years ago he got homesick and decided to come back and start a restaurant." George shrugged. "I came, too."

"Don't you ever get homesick yourself?" I asked.

"Sometimes. But life here has its compensations." Just then a moped swerved to a stop on the gravel of the Bella Roma's parking lot, and George's gaze swiveled to follow the two attractive blondes who climbed off the Vesta and slowly strolled in.

"Excuse me—" he murmured, hurrying off to offer the women a table.

"You'll have to forgive George," Geoffrey commented, his lips twitching. "I'm afraid he has a weakness for Scandinavian women."

"How do you know they're Scandinavian?"

"George's reaction, of course. He has an uncanny intuition for such things, rather like an overgrown bloodhound."

"He did look a bit like a dog going on point," I agreed with a smile, but the smile faded abruptly as I became conscious of the sound of waves crashing on the rocks far below us. For a moment I had actually forgotten what had happened that afternoon, but now memory came rushing back like the incoming sea.

I gazed out at the blackness: the black sea, the black sky, the black, barely discernible silhouette of the Albanian coast only a mile or two away. Where had the moonlight gone?

"Christine?"

I looked across the table at him. In the romantically dim light, it was difficult to read his expression. The candle on the table cast flickering shadows across the surprisingly jagged planes of his face, and I realized how tense he was, like a taut wire ready to snap. I could imagine running a finger along the curve of his jaw and feeling it vibrate.

"A penny for them," he said sharply.

"For what?"

"Your thoughts. You seem quite lost in them. You've scarcely spoken a word in five minutes."

"Since you didn't speak to me the entire drive up here, I don't think you're in a position to complain. I spent the whole time staring out the window at scenery it was too dark to see."

"I'm sorry," he said stiffly. "I was lost in some unpleasant thoughts of my own. But you'll find me quite attentive now."

"I suppose you were thinking about Michael?"

He shook his head, but remained silent.

"Hmmm, you pique my curiosity," I said, twirling the stem of my empty wine glass. "Now let's see. You weren't thinking about your accident-prone nephew. Perhaps you were thinking about the strange coincidence that he almost got himself drowned the very day of your return?" I paused, then added, "Of course, you'll be quite in the clear with Lieutenant Mavros this time, won't you? Since you were safely in the air when it all happened. Though speaking of coincidences, I could swear I saw a man who looked exactly like you getting off the ferry from Brindisi yesterday."

The wire seemed to snap, but the only change in Geoffrey's expression was that his mouth curved into a slightly bitter smile. "Actually, my thoughts were focused on a matter of considerably less consequence," he said quietly. "I was merely reflecting that tonight might be the last time I ever see you."

I stared at him, my lips forming a silent "oh."

Suddenly George appeared with our dinners. "Here ya go," he said cheerfully, sliding the heaping plates in front of us. He seemed blissfully unaware of the charged atmosphere at the table. "*Bon appetit*, you two! I'll be right back with your wine."

After George had gone I said in an uneven voice, "You haven't bothered to deny it."

"Deny what?" he replied coolly.

"That you lied to me! You came back yesterday, not today, and by ferry, not by plane."

A gust of wind caused the candle flame to sputter and then flare, illuminating his face. "Yes."

A sudden knot in my stomach tightened. "So I guess I have to ask: where were you this afternoon, Geoffrey?"

He looked as if I'd slapped him. "Where do you think I was, Christine? At Ithaki's cove throttling Michael into unconsciousness and leaving him to drown?"

Suddenly, I felt rather dizzy.

George returned, brandishing a bottle at us. "This is from a friend's private cellar at Ypsos." He carefully uncorked the bottle and poured generous portions of the wine into our glasses. Then he reached over to another table, picked up a wineglass, and poured some for himself. "*'Igeia sas!*" he toasted. Reluctantly, Geoffrey and I joined in, clinking our glasses against his. I took a sip. The wine trickled down my throat like a caress.

"You like it?" George asked.

I nodded and drank deeply. "It's wonderful," I murmured, setting the empty glass down on the table.

George beamed at me and splashed more wine into my glass, setting the bottle down within easy reach. "This girl of yours has good taste, Geoff, at least in wine, that is!" He slapped Geoffrey on the back.

"Shouldn't you be seeing to your Scandinavians?" Geoffrey inquired tensely.

George cast a quick glance over his shoulder and saw that the two ladies were indeed looking put out at his neglect. "Pays to keep the customers satisfied," he said with a wink. "Geoff, Christine, enjoy!"

Happy to oblige him, I drank up, wondering fleetingly how much of the delicious wine I'd have to drink to forget that Geoffrey couldn't know Michael had been rendered unconscious by being throttled unless—I emptied my glass a second time—unless he'd been the one doing the throttling.

"George must really like you to serve you this," I said, setting my glass down a bit unsteadily and splashing more of the lovely crimson wine into it. "I wonder why?"

Geoffrey plucked the bottle out of reach. "I think you'd best go easy on that until you get something else in your stomach." He pushed my plate toward me.

"I'm not hungry."

He said more gently, "Christine, I'm sorry I lied to you, but please believe me, I have a good reason for not wanting it known that I returned yesterday, rather than today." He reached across the table and placed his hand on mine.

"But you're not going to tell me what that reason is, are you?"

He shook his head. "I'm afraid I can't."

"You mean won't!" I corrected him angrily. "Strange, I thought we were in this together, that we were on the same side."

"We are! I owe you a great deal, you know. You were right about Michael needing someone on the spot to protect him. My God, if you hadn't been there this afternoon—" His hand tightened convulsively on mine.

The emotion in his voice sounded genuine. I wanted to

believe him. Needing time to think and a safe place to look, I pulled my hand away and began absently slicing away at my sofrito.

"You know," he continued in that same gentle and persuasive voice, "I haven't yet heard the whole story of what happened. Would you mind telling it to me, from the beginning?"

I hesitated for a moment, then I told him. When I'd finished, I looked up to find him staring out at the blackness. The moon was rising over the sea, casting threads of light on the rippling water, but none of the light was reflected in his eyes. They were dark and stormy and…dangerous. He turned to me and said in a voice no longer gentle, "When do you leave tomorrow?"

"My flight's scheduled for eleven, but—"

"You should be at the airport by nine."

"But I'm not going."

His eyes grew stormier. "Christine, I want you on that plane tomorrow. I want you thousands of miles from this bloody mess as soon as possible."

"I'm afraid that what you want doesn't matter. Lieutenant Mavros is finally taking this thing seriously, and he seems to consider me one of his prime suspects. I have been warned, as they say in all the B-movies, not to leave town."

"He has no evidence to charge you, and no authority to keep you. There's no reason why you can't be on that flight."

"Why so anxious to get rid of me?" I demanded, the wine loosening my tongue. "Afraid I may tell someone about your early return to the island?"

He slammed his fist down, rattling the silverware, and reached across the table to seize my wrist. "You must give me your word you'll say nothing about that to anyone, *especially* the good Lieutenant."

"Why?"

"Your word, Christine!"

His grip on my wrist hurt, but what hurt more was the frightening stranger he'd suddenly become—had always been? Up to that moment, despite my doubts and suspicions, a part of me hadn't really believed him a man capable of true violence. I hadn't believed he could hurt Michael—or me. But suddenly there was something dangerous, something terrifyingly determined about him. I forced myself to stay calm, to speak quietly, not to let my voice betray the sudden fear I felt inside. "Very well, I promise. I won't tell anyone that I saw you down at the port yesterday. Now will you please let me go?"

He acquiesced immediately. I rubbed the red mark on my wrist and his gaze followed the motion. "I'm sorry," he said roughly. "I didn't mean to hurt you."

"Didn't you?" I pushed back my chair and stood up. "Now, if you'll excuse me, I'd better get back and pack my things before your sister-in-law decides to dump them by the side of the road."

I started to walk out, but as I passed the last table I was waylaid by George. "You're leaving?" he exclaimed in surprise. "Something wrong with the food?"

"No, of course not. It was delicious. It's just—"

"It's just Christine has had a long and trying day and is feeling all done in," Geoffrey said, coming up behind me. "Please excuse us, George, but I'd best get her back before she drops in her tracks. How much do I owe you for our delicious repast?"

George refused to produce a bill, claiming the whole thing was on the house, and Geoffrey didn't argue, merely thanked him and assured him they'd settle up later. Sliding his arm through mine, Geoffrey led the way toward the car. I would have pulled away, but George's delicious and deceptively potent wine was affecting my locomotive skills, and before I knew it, Geoffrey had eased me into the black Mercedes and slammed the door shut.

He jerked open the driver's side door and slid in next to me, flashing me one brief but searching look. Then he started the engine and sent the car roaring down the highway toward Ithaki.

We drove for some minutes without either of us saying a word. Then I did something amazingly stupid. I don't know if it was the wine, or the accumulated stress of the day, or just my desperate desire to know regardless of the consequences, but I suddenly blurted out into the thick, warm air between us, "What did you and your brother argue about on the day that he died?"

Silence. Geoffrey greeted the question with absolute silence. If not for his white-knuckled grip on the steering wheel and his foot slamming down on the accelerator pedal, I would have wondered if he'd heard me at all. The already speeding car flew forward.

We skimmed round sharp curves accompanied by the sound of screeching rubber. "Are you going to answer me?" I asked over the pounding in my throat, "or are you simply planning to run us off the road?"

His breath caught sharply and the car slowed to a safer pace as we navigated the last of the curves and descended to a wider stretch of highway. "Who told you about this supposed argument?"

"What does it matter?" I hedged, realizing too late that I might be giving him a stronger motive than money for wanting Michael out of the way. "Did you or did you not have a violent fight with your brother that day?"

He nodded almost abstractedly as he guided the car off the road and brought it to a halt.

"Why have we stopped?" I demanded tensely.

"I need to find out who told you about that row and precisely how much they know."

"There's something else," I said, playing for time. "After you and your brother fought"—my left hand slid stealthily toward the seat belt release—"your brother called up Robert Humphreys's office saying that he wanted to change his will." I pressed the button softly. There was the smallest of clicks.

"So it was Robert who told you that my brother and I argued?"

The seat belt began slipping back across my waist. "You still haven't told me what the argument was about," I countered, easing my right hand onto the door handle. "Did your brother tell you he'd decided to disinherit you?"

He stared at me. "Dammit, Christine, just how much do you know?"

I didn't answer. Instead, I threw open the door and started running, ignoring the exclamations of the man behind me.

At first I ran straight, like a horse bolting from the starting gate, but soon I noticed a hulking, dark silhouette looming up ahead and realized I was running straight toward the foot of a cliff.

"Christine, wait!" he called out behind me. "Come back!"

I veered to the left, making a wide turn back toward the road. Perhaps a passing car would see me.

"Christine!"

He was gaining on me and I was starting to tire. I pushed to go faster and stumbled, got up and kept running. My muscles began to protest. Only adrenalin kept me going. He was only yards behind me now. I burst through a thicket of bushes and felt my sandals slap firm, flat asphalt. Then I heard the sound of an approaching car. Help at last.

I waved my arms frantically, but though the car's headlights spilled over me, illuminating my flailing signal for help, the car did not slow or veer, but rather seemed to gather speed and aim directly for me.

"*Jump!*" yelled a voice behind me, but somehow I couldn't seem to move. I suppose my overtaxed system had had enough; I just stood there, transfixed. I closed my eyes, and was hit with a force that sent me rolling off the road into a small trench as the car went roaring by.

It didn't take me long to realize what had hit me. It was lying flat on top of me, angrily demanding to know if I was alive.

I squeaked out a faint affirmative with what little air was left in me.

"Well, you don't deserve to be," Geoffrey growled into my neck. "Why the bloody hell did you go haring off like that?"

I emitted a faint wheeze in reply.

"I suppose I'm squashing you," he said, rolling off me. His face, streaked with dirt and marked by several cuts, was only inches from my own. "Are you hurt?" he asked.

I shook my head slightly. "You?"

"I'll live."

So will I, I thought, *but only because you risked your life to push me out of the way in time.*

His eyes searched my face. "You do realize, don't you, that you came within a hairsbreadth of getting yourself killed?"

"I know," I said, staring remorsefully at his torn shirt. I touched the ragged edge of the tear, my fingers lightly tracing the rise and fall of his chest. "I'm sorry."

"And well you should be," he muttered reprovingly, reaching out to pull me tightly against him. He rested one hand warmly in the small of my back; the other stroked my hair and then tilted my face toward his. "You turned my blood to ice when you ran out in front of that car," he said in a low, deep voice that seemed to ripple along my skin like a touch. "The least you can do is turn it back again." He ran caressing fingers down the side of my face, then with a fierce swoop of his mouth he kissed me.

His blood may have been frozen, but his lips were warm and tasted faintly of wine, which perhaps explains why I felt as if an entire bottle of George's finest was being poured directly into my veins. Intoxicated by his mouth and the feel of his body pressed against mine, it was some time before I finally opened my eyes to find Geoffrey staring at me, a dazed expression on his face.

"Defrosted yet?" I asked breathlessly.

"Melted to a puddle."

"You don't have to sound so glum about it."

He grimaced. "Forgive a man his frustration. You're leaving in the morning, and tonight—well, the truth of it is I must be getting back to town soon." He brushed my lips lightly with his own once more and then pulled away.

Silly to feel rejected. Especially by a man from whom, ten minutes earlier, I had thought it necessary to flee. "A prior engagement?"

"In a manner of speaking."

"Well, then, I guess we'd better get going."

Avoiding my eyes, he nodded. He helped me to my feet, and together we started down the road. I was surprised to find how far back the abandoned Mercedes was parked; I had run quite a distance without knowing it. So had my thoughts, I realized, as I climbed back into the car and remembered the utter panic in which I'd left it. I had plenty of reasons to mistrust Geoffrey, even to suspect him of the attacks on Michael, but I also had reasons to believe him, to give him the benefit of the doubt, not least of which was the fact he had just saved my life by risking his own.

Yes, but why did he lie to you about which day he returned to

Corfu? a doubting voice in my head demanded. *Why didn't he tell you about the fight with his brother or about the will?* I yanked the seat belt across my chest and shoved the latch into the buckle.

Geoffrey flung himself into the seat next to me and started the car. The Mercedes slid onto the highway, its strong engine purring, the beams from its headlights ricocheting off cliffs and curves and occasionally a car coming the other way.

We drove for miles in silence. Geoffrey kept his gaze fixed on the road, and I kept sneaking glances at his profile. He must have sensed my scrutiny, for he turned his head abruptly, and our eyes met and locked. "You still haven't answered my question," he said.

"I'm sorry, but I'm not going to tell you who told me about the fight with your brother. In the first place, it's not my place to tell, and in the second, even if it were, I'm not sure telling you would be a good idea."

Slowly, he shook his head. "That wasn't the question I meant, Christine."

"Then what—"

"I wanted to know why you ran away from me. But I suppose you've already given me the answer to that, haven't you?"

I suddenly felt my throat tighten. "Geoffrey, I—"

He cut me off. "I can't say as I blame you. I'd probably think the same if I were you."

"If you'd only just explain—"

"But I can't." His voice was rough. "So that's that. Anyway, we've arrived." Startled, I saw the headlight beams hit Ithaki's gate. The Mercedes turned off the road but not down the drive. Geoffrey got out and came round to open my door. "You'd best get out here and walk down," he said. "That way there won't be any awkward questions for you to answer."

I nodded, and reluctantly got out of the car.

"Christine—"

"Yes?"

"You will be on that aeroplane tomorrow, won't you?"

"I don't know. Lieutenant Mavros was pretty adamant."

"Blast Mavros! Don't you see? The danger to you is no longer hypothetical. That car that almost ran you down: did you stop to wonder where it came from?"

"I don't know. I suppose from the direction it was going it must have come from Kassiopi."

"That would mean it would have had to have been behind us. But there was only one car behind us the entire time, and it passed us right after we pulled off the road."

"Another car must have come along then."

He shook his head. "No, there was no sound of an engine. There were no headlights, either. You've seen how they shoot ahead. In this darkness, you can see someone coming for miles. There was only the one car behind us all the way from Kassiopi."

"We were being followed?"

"I think so. When we stopped, the other car must have passed us and pulled over as well. When you got out and started running, whoever was in the car waited to see what would happen. When you ran out onto the highway...."

"You think someone deliberately tried to run me down?"

"I think it's a distinct possibility. Which is why I want your promise that when your flight leaves tomorrow you'll be on it. I realize you don't trust me, I realize you're afraid of me, but if you're thousands of miles away, there's nothing I or anyone else can do to harm you."

"Geoffrey, you saved my life!"

His mouth curved bitterly. "Yet you still wonder if I was the one who tried to drown poor Michael like a kitten."

I wanted to deny it, but couldn't. "If you would just explain—"

"I'm sorry. I can't." He regarded me in silence for moment, and then said, "You'll be on that flight tomorrow, won't you?"

He was so obviously anxious to be rid of me, and Michael—well, Michael had Lieutenant Mavros and the Corfu police to look after him now. Besides, the memory of standing transfixed in the path of stampeding headlights was enough to drain away my resistance. I was tired of being afraid.

"All right," I said wearily, "you win. I'll go."

Eighteen

When I arrived at the house, I found Demetra had already retired for the night. My bags weren't out in the drive, and there was no message pinned to my pillow telling me to clear out, so I collapsed into bed, pausing only to strip off my dirt-stained clothes and kick off my sandals.

Next morning I rose early and packed, then went in search of breakfast and information about Michael. The dining room was empty and only a single place was set at the table; Aphrodite soon bustled in to tell me it was set for me, as Demetra was still in bed and Spiro had not yet returned. I asked about Michael, and was relieved to hear that the doctor had phoned to say he was doing fine and would be coming home that afternoon. I realized with a pang that I'd be gone by the time he returned.

To my surprise, Maria seemed genuinely upset to learn I was leaving, and made me a large feta-filled omelette to insure I wouldn't starve on my journey. While she bustled off to the kitchen to wrap up the remainder I couldn't eat, I asked Aphrodite if she knew the number to call to order a taxi. She told me I shouldn't waste my money, as Paul could drive me to the airport.

Entering with a pot of coffee, Maria shook her head at the suggestion. "He cannot. He is not here. Last night they call from Ioannina; his mother has fallen and broken her hip."

Aphrodite expostulated and made her *stavros*.

"That's too bad," I echoed politely.

Maria nodded. "When I telephoned to the hospital and told Paul, he left and took the boat to Igoumenitsa. He will not return before one week, so I must care for the garden now."

"And what about Mr. Skouras? When will he be back?"

Maria shrugged and poured some fresh coffee into my cup. "Who can say?"

"I'm surprised he didn't rush back here when he heard the news about Michael," I said.

Maria ignored the bait. "I will make you some lunch for the airplane," she said, setting down the pot of coffee and gathering up the dishes from the table onto a tray.

I tried to convince her I didn't need more food—that her omelette would probably last me the rest of the day—but to no avail. She headed for the kitchen. Aphrodite remained behind.

Her pretty face was unusually pale. "Kyrios Skouras does not yet know what happened to the boy," she confided in a low voice. "The mistress tried to telephone him last night, but he was not at his hotel. No one knows where he is." Her eyes opened wide and she bit at her lip. "I am afraid, Thespinis. Perhaps he has been attacked like the boy and is lying somewhere injured—" Her voice faltered. "…or dead." Her blue eyes suddenly filled with tears.

Whatever my concerns about Spiro's role in the attacks on Michael, I had no worries that he, himself, was in any danger. I was about to reassure her on that point when Demetra Redfield walked into the room.

As always, she was stylishly turned out and perfectly groomed, but her face looked haggard and there were dark smudges under her eyes. "Thank you," she murmured as Aphrodite pulled out a chair for her and then hurried to set a place at the table. "So, Miss Stewart, this morning you go."

"Yes, my flight leaves at eleven."

"You have telephoned for a taxi to take you to the airport? Paul is not here to drive you."

"I haven't yet, but I will after breakfast."

She nodded, and poured herself some coffee with a hand that was not altogether steady. For a few minutes we sat in silence. Then I thanked her for her hospitality.

This brought a ghost of a smile to her face. "You are very polite. Your stay with us cannot have been what you had hoped."

I shrugged. "It had its moments."

Her beautifully-shaped eyebrows arched briefly and then sank back down wearily over her eyes. "Yes, my brother is a man of great charm—charm enough to make one ignore, even forget, that which is unpleasant."

"It's too bad he wasn't here yesterday to help you with all this mess with Michael," I said. "It must have been hard for you to deal with on your own."

She looked up at that, and her dark gaze locked with mine. "I am touched by your concern, but do not worry for me. The women of my island are strong. We do not submit meekly to fate."

There was something at once both magnetic and chilling about the expression on her face as she spoke the words. It was the sort of determination one could imagine finding in the countenance of a Joan of Arc—or a Medea.

After breakfast, I phoned for a taxi, then retreated to my room to gather up my things and prepare to go. As I did so, I pondered the news that Spiro was not where he was supposed to be. Had he really gone to the mainland, I wondered, or had he remained on Corfu, waiting for the moment when he could swim up behind Michael unnoticed and throttle him into unconsciousness?

The problem with that scenario was why? Even if Geoffrey was right, and William Redfield had discovered his brother-in-law was stealing from him, Spiro had a solid alibi for the day of William Redfield's death. And if Spiro had not killed William, what possible reason could he have for wanting to kill William's son?

I could think of none. Yet my stay at Ithaki had convinced me Geoffrey was right about one thing, Spiro *was* hiding something. I just had no idea what it was. And time had run out to find out.

I went into the bathroom and looked around to make sure I hadn't forgotten anything. My glance fell on the door leading to Spiro's room. Perhaps there was still a chance....

I crossed to the door and slowly turned the knob.

Fortunately, Spiro hadn't bothered with the lock. I eased the door open, listening for any sound that might indicate someone was in the room. I opened the door wider. The room was empty. All I had to do was walk in. I started toward the dresser, but suddenly I heard footsteps.

I retreated to the bathroom, but didn't have time to completely close the door before someone entered Spiro's room from the hall. I heard the click-clack of high heels crossing the floor. Deciding to make necessity a virtue, I peeked out the slightly open door and saw Demetra go to Spiro's dresser, pull open the top drawer, and take something out of it. She had her back to me, so I couldn't see what it was.

She crossed to the small desk by the window. Her hand slid down along the right side of the desk and then stopped; a moment later a small drawer popped out in front. She slipped whatever she had removed from his bureau into the drawer and pushed it closed. It disappeared into a façade of marquetry decoration. Then, her mission apparently accomplished, Demetra left the room.

After her footsteps had safely faded away, I eased the door open and walked over to the desk. I looked in vain for the button or latch she had pushed, however. The marquetry on the side was just as elaborate as the front, and the opening mechanism was as well-camouflaged as the drawer itself. I decided to try to find it by feel, and ran my hand along the side as I'd seen her do. Twice I tried and twice I failed, but on my third try I felt a diamond-shaped piece of wood that seemed slightly recessed. I pressed it. The secret drawer popped out.

Inside it lay Spiro's passport.

I stared at it in surprise. Why had his sister hidden it? Was there, perhaps, something concealed inside? Picking it up by the spine, I shook it vigorously, but nothing fell out. So it had to be the passport itself. There was something in it Demetra wanted to keep secret. But what? I held the small blue book in my hands and thumbed through it. Date stamps in various colors and shapes decorated a surprising number of the pages. The man certainly got around. Rio de Janeiro. Monte Carlo. Rome. Birmingham.

Suddenly I started, my attention caught and fixed by the date of this last stamp. The green ink was blurred a little, but the date stood out clearly, the extremely legible fifteen impossible to mistake.

But the police had checked....

I searched through the passport again more closely. Two pages further along there was another green entry stamp—this time from Heathrow Airport and dated March 16.

Two entry stamps dated a single day apart. Two arrivals in England, but the police only aware of the second one, the safe one, the one occurring the day after William Redfield's death.

"You should not be in here!" exclaimed an angry voice behind me.

I whirled around to find Helen standing beside the bureau. I wondered for a moment why I hadn't heard the door to the hall open, then realized she had entered the same way I had— through the bathroom from my room.

"What have you got there?" she demanded.

I looked down at the passport, forgotten in my hand. I turned toward the desk, dropped it into the secret drawer, and slammed the drawer shut. "Nothing," I said, swinging back round to face her.

She glared at me, then her eyes narrowed, as if she were calculating something. "You will be in big trouble if I tell Kyrios Skouras what I have seen. If I tell him what you have been doing. "

"Go right ahead," I said, trying to sound calm. "I'll be in California by the time you do, and I don't think he'll care much by then."

"Then I will tell the mistress. She will call the police."

I shook my head. "Actually, I don't think she will, but you're welcome to try. If you like, I'll talk to her myself, and perhaps, while I'm at it, I'll also tell her about your meeting last week in that pretty little church in Koussaki."

Helen's eyes widened and her face went pale.

I pressed my advantage. "But then again, perhaps neither of us should bother her with such trivial details when she has so much on her mind right now." I paused, regarding her with a steady look. "What do you think, Helen?"

She stared at me, her expression a mixture of animosity and fear, and then slowly, reluctantly, she muttered, "I think that you are right."

Nodding, satisfied, I walked past her back to my room. I closed the door behind me and made it all the way to a chair before my legs gave out completely.

My luggage and I were standing out in the drive when the sound of flying gravel announced the arrival of a car. I assumed it was my taxi, but as it swooped down the driveway and slid to a stop in front of me, I realized my mistake. Spiro stepped out of the Lamborghini with light-footed grace and crossed to my side.

He gave me a long, considering look. "This is hardly how I expected you to repay my hospitality, Christine."

My heart began to thump a double-time beat. "I don't know what you mean," I replied nervously.

"I think you do," he said, his dark eyes full of reproof.

I tensed, wondering if I could outrun him back to the house. After all, he wouldn't try anything in front of Maria and Aphrodite.

Then he gestured toward my feet with his chin. "Once again I find you on the doorstep surrounded by baggage. Can it be that you are planning to leave without saying goodbye?"

I lowered my heels and took a few calming breaths. "I said goodbye to your sister."

"But not to me."

"You weren't here to say goodbye to."

He shrugged to acknowledge that it was a valid point. "Yes, my business proved more arduous than expected." His well-shaped lips twitched at some private joke. "I was away longer than I intended. Now, however, my work is finished and all is well." He flashed me a triumphant smile. "What a pity you cannot remain and help me celebrate my victory."

His palpable exultation made me uneasy, but before I could reply, Demetra called out behind me.

"Miss Stewart, you cannot leave!"

As I whirled around at her words, she spotted her brother.

"*Spiro!*" she cried. "I did not know you had returned!"

"I have just arrived," he said, stepping forward to take her hands.

"And what of your business?" she inquired anxiously.

He slid an arm around her shoulders. "It has been concluded successfully."

"Has it?" she asked, hope and wariness vying on her face.

"Yes," he replied, lifting his hand and brushing his bent knuckles gently against her cheek. "You need fear no longer."

She closed her eyes for a moment, and then both brother and sister turned to look at me.

I said, in what I hoped was a cool and calm voice, "Mrs. Redfield, I don't know what you meant before, but my taxi should be arriving any minute, and when it gets here I *am* leaving—for the airport."

Demetra Redfield shook her head. "You cannot."

"Why not?" I demanded.

"Because Ari Mavros wishes to speak with you, with me, with all of us in his office as soon as possible."

"Lieutenant Mavros wants to see us?" I said. "Why?"

She turned and her eyes sought out Spiro's as she replied in a low, tense voice, "It seems my stepson has disappeared."

Nineteen

The small office was full of people.

Lieutenant Mavros gestured for the newcomer to be seated. Geoffrey crossed to the last empty chair and sat down, while the officers escorting him were dismissed with a single thrust of the lieutenant's chin. They scurried from the room, no doubt relieved to escape their superior's poorly concealed wrath.

"Good." The word was almost a growl. "Now that you are here, Mr. Redfield, we can begin." The lieutenant settled back in his seat and his angry blue gaze swept the semi-circle of chairs gathered around his desk. "Before we begin our discussion," he said, "I would like an account of how each of you spent the night, and where you were at approximately six-thirty this morning."

Demetra began to protest, but was quickly silenced by her brother, who sat next to her. Meanwhile Robert, seated to Spiro's left, gravely inquired, "Do I gather, Lieutenant, that you suspect one of us of having engineered Michael's disappearance?"

"At this point, I have no evidence to suggest such a thing, which is why we are discussing the matter informally. However, if I learn one of you has lied to me," his gaze swept past each of us in turn, "then our next interview will be considerably different. Mr. Redfield, perhaps you will begin? And since I have not yet had an opportunity to question you about yesterday's swimming mishap, perhaps you will also tell me where you were yesterday afternoon—shall we say around four?"

"I believe," Geoffrey replied coolly, "at that time, I would have been about 30,000 feet in the air. My flight from Paris arrived in Rome a little before five; the connecting flight to Corfu got in about seven." He paused and withdrew a small leather pocketbook from his jacket. "Perhaps you'd care to see the cancelled boarding passes, Lieutenant?"

Mavros shook his head. "That will not be necessary. I have already had a report from the airport, and Alitalia confirms you were on the passenger list for the Rome flight, or—at least— someone travelling under your name and with your passport."

Geoffrey slid whatever he'd been about to take out of his pocketbook back in and closed it with a soft thump, a sound that echoed in my chest as I remembered once again to breathe. "After learning Michael was in hospital," he resumed, "I went straight there." He flashed a look at Demetra. "I wasn't allowed into his room to see him, but I was assured he was well and rest- ing comfortably.

"After I left the hospital"—Did he pause faintly?—"I drove to Kassiopi to have dinner at a friend's restaurant. Then I returned to my hotel. I went to bed sometime after one and woke before eight, but was alone from the time I left the restau- rant until your men swept down on me in the lobby of my hotel this morning, so I can't really prove where I was at six-thirty."

His tone was faintly apologetic. I wanted to sock him one.

He had lied about the flight and his return to the island and had neglected to mention that I'd been with him at dinner. Now I was put in the position of having to lie as well, or risk seeing him arrested on the spot.

The lieutenant shrugged his shoulders. "At the moment I find it hard to believe yesterday's attack and today's disappear- ance are unrelated, so for now, your word is sufficient." The implication that this state of affairs might not last was clear.

Hesitantly, I began a similarly specious version of the evening's events, saying that I had run into Geoffrey at the hos- pital, that we had walked out together and parted outside, that I had had dinner in some small restaurant—no, I was sorry, I couldn't remember the name or what street it was on—and that later I'd caught a taxi back to Ithaki and gone straight to bed.

Safely past the treacherous waters of the previous evening's events, I continued in a firmer voice, "I woke up early this morning, probably around six; I was planning to catch a flight home at eleven."

The lieutenant bent his head slightly in acknowledgment. "I appreciate your changing your plans to accommodate me."

"I didn't stay because of you, Lieutenant. I just couldn't leave without knowing Michael was okay."

That he might *not* be okay was a thought I kept pushing away with the frantic energy of the truly frightened. Still, my churning stomach knew the grim odds. I bit down hard on my lip and forced myself to continue.

"After I got dressed, I packed and then went to breakfast. I was getting ready to leave for the airport when Mrs. Redfield came out to tell us—Mr. Skouras and me—what had happened."

At the mention of Spiro's name, Geoffrey turned and glanced my way. I looked into his eyes, hoping to find reassurance there from the man who had saved my life, but his expression was stony, and he gazed at me with the detachment of a stranger.

Robert went next, saying he'd spent the evening alone, had dined out, risen early, and at the time in question—six-thirty?—had been having coffee with a Greek colleague whose name he would be happy to provide.

"Isn't that rather early for such a meeting?" the lieutenant asked.

"On a normal day, yes, it would be," Robert agreed, "but as I said, I had risen early. As for my friend—he had not yet gone to bed."

Mavros nodded and turned his attention to Demetra. A charged look passed between them. Then she began to speak, giving a description of events that was terse in the extreme. She had dined at home, gone to bed early, and risen late. At his prompting she admitted that yes, she had seen me at breakfast.

Finally, it was Spiro's turn to be quizzed. Five listeners turned their attention to him, waiting to hear his answers. Robert seemed expectant, Demetra anxious, Lieutenant Mavros tense, while Geoffrey sat grim-faced and aloof. And I? I'm not sure what expression I wore; my emotions were as roiled as the sea had been that first morning, when the storm had blown in and brought Michael.

"Spiro, I am waiting," Mavros repeated. "I must know where you have been the past few days, and where you were at six-thirty this morning."

Spiro regarded him steadily for a long moment and then said, "I am sorry, Ari, but I cannot answer your questions."

A palpable stillness filled the room. "This is a serious matter," Mavros snapped in Greek. "The events of yesterday make that clear. The boy was attacked and now is missing. You are my friend, but I warn you: I will do whatever is necessary to discover who has taken the boy and ensure he returns safely."

Demetra whispered something under her breath, but Spiro shook his head impatiently. "Ari, I give you my word that I did not kidnap the boy. For God's sake, why should I?" His voice grew scornful as he switched back to English, "What do I gain from his disappearance? Nothing. What do I inherit if he dies? Nothing." He gestured at Geoffrey. "Can that one say the same?"

The stark words hung in the air like a challenge. Attention swiveled back to Geoffrey, but he just sat there quietly, refusing to be baited. It was Robert who broke the silence.

"Look here, Mavros, you haven't yet explained how anyone could have taken the boy from right under your nose. I thought I understood from our conversation last evening that you intended to station one of your men by the boy's door throughout the night."

"And so I did," the lieutenant replied, tight-lipped. "But early this morning, near to the time when my man was due to be relieved, he received a phone call telling him to report back here and not wait for his replacement. The boy's room was unguarded for only ten minutes, but it was enough. When the day officer arrived he found the room empty and the boy missing."

"But surely somebody must have seen something!" I exclaimed.

The policeman shrugged. "It was early and there were few people in the halls. The nurse who knew about the boy's case had gone home for the night, and the morning nurse saw nothing unusual. An orderly saw a young boy walking toward the entrance at about the right time, but the boy was alone, and when the orderly asked him what he was doing there so early in the morning, the boy told him he was visiting a sick sister."

"Hardly the behavior of a boy being abducted against his will," Spiro murmured.

Mavros nodded. "My thoughts also," he agreed. "Indeed, I did not think it could be the same boy. However, I sent someone to show the orderly young Redfield's photograph just in case."

"And did the man recognize him?" Robert asked.

"Yes," Mavros said. "Which unfortunately leaves us with an even greater mystery than before."

"This orderly," I asked, "he's sure Michael was alone?"

"Very much so, Miss Stewart."

"There couldn't have been someone else he didn't see? Someone who threatened Michael and forced him to say what he did?"

"It was an empty hallway," he replied patiently. "If anyone had been hidden, he would have been too far away to threaten the boy in such a way."

"But the answer is obvious!" Demetra exclaimed impatiently. "The boy was not kidnapped. He simply ran away!" Her voice shook with satisfaction at this solution, and she gazed around the room in surprise that we did not all immediately accept it.

"I'm afraid it's not quite that simple," Robert said quietly. "There's still the telephone call to the policeman to be explained. Isn't that right, Lieutenant?"

Mavros, who was gazing apologetically at Spiro's sister, nodded. "I'm afraid that is so, Demetra. Otherwise, I would never have—" He was interrupted by a knock on the door.

"*Embrós!*" he snapped impatiently.

An unhappy-looking policeman with drooping mustaches and a wrinkled shirt entered the room. He crossed to his superior's desk and murmured something that caused the lieutenant to snap in Greek, "Then she will have to wait. I am not finished with Mr. Redfield yet." The policeman bent over and murmured something else. A look that was part irritation, part resignation crossed Mavros's face. "Oh, very well. Send her in!"

The mustachioed policeman hurried out the doorway, and a

moment later a woman appeared, gazing in at the room and its occupants. Even in the ugly light from the hallway it was apparent she was beautiful: tall, blond, slim, with skin smooth as velvet and eyes the color of a lion's mane. For a moment, as those golden eyes scanned the room, I thought I saw a startled flicker of surprise cross her beautiful face, but before I could think to wonder what had caused it, Geoffrey called out her name.

"Elizabeth!" he exclaimed in a stunned voice.

The golden eyes turned his way and the perfectly-shaped coral lips curved into a smile.

TWENTY

"Forgive me for interrupting your meeting, Lieutenant," Elizabeth said, "but I've come a long way to see my brother-in-law, and when I overheard some of your men say that Geoffrey was to be brought here—"

Mavros interrupted sharply, "One moment, please, Miss Conner. I wish to understand. How exactly is Mr. Redfield related to you?"

"It's *Mrs.*, Lieutenant. Mrs. Elizabeth Redfield Conner. I was married to Geoffrey's brother, William, a long time ago."

"But it cannot be!" Demetra exclaimed. "William's first wife is dead! She was killed in an airplane crash!"

Elizabeth glanced briefly at her and then turned away—obviously uninterested in the successor to her first husband's affections. "An unfortunate misunderstanding. I think it's obvious I'm very much alive."

"Quite obvious, madame," replied Mavros drily. "And now, so that I may be clear on the details, may I ask a few questions?"

"Of course."

"You were the late Mr. William Redfield's first wife?"

"Yes."

"And the boy, Michael Redfield—he is your son?"

She nodded.

"For several years, then, you have allowed your family to believe you dead?"

Her eyes narrowed. "If you refer to my late husband, yes, I let him think I was dead. Ours was not an amicable divorce, and I didn't really think he'd care one way or the other."

"But your son? He did not deserve to know the truth?"

The golden eyes glittered. "You'll excuse me, Lieutenant, but I don't quite see how any of this is your business."

"Ah, but you see, your son has disappeared, and on the very day you decide to reappear into his life. It is quite a coincidence, that, is it not?"

"Stop it, Mavros! You have no right!" Geoffrey crossed to Elizabeth, took her arm, and led her to sit down in the chair that Robert had gallantly vacated for the purpose. "Don't you realize what a shock you've just given her?"

"Disappeared? Michael?" she murmured faintly, her left hand clutching at Geoffrey's arm, her right flying dramatically to her mouth. "But how? When?"

"This morning, I'm afraid," said Robert. "It seems he wandered out of the hospital, and there's some worry someone may have abducted him."

She looked up at that, and despite my skepticism about her maternal instincts, her face looked quite pale. She said, in an almost accusing tone, "What was he doing in the hospital?"

This time it was Lieutenant Mavros who answered, but I didn't pay much attention to his explanation. I was too busy staring at Elizabeth's possessive grip on Geoffrey's arm. Her tight hold on him seemed to generate an ache deep in my chest. I gazed at her long, tan fingers. They were as beautiful as the rest of her, the only flaw in their appearance being a slightly reddened knuckle on one of the fingers of her left hand. Had the lovely Mrs. Conner been brawling? It was a tempting thought, especially as I realized I wouldn't mind squaring off with her myself.

Sensing my scrutiny, she glanced over at me. Seeing my expression, the corner of her mouth tightened into the faintest of smiles, and with an exaggerated sigh she leaned toward Geoffrey, resting her head against his side. As she nestled there, she flashed me a look that made me grit my teeth. It was the look of a woman staking her claim, and it hinted at such a level of confidence and assurance in her position that I was hard-pressed not to ball my hands into fists.

She acted as if Geoffrey was hers for the taking.

Perhaps she was right. I looked at Geoffrey's face. He was staring down at her, his expression almost painfully anxious.

Lieutenant Mavros finished up his description of Michael's disappearance, and Elizabeth recalled herself to the matter at hand. "But no one could have any reason to harm Michael. Don't you think it more likely he simply ran away?"

"That's definitely a possibility," Geoffrey assured her, flashing the rest of us a warning to be silent. "In which case, he's bound to show up soon. In the meantime, you need some rest." He took her hand and then turned to Mavros. "Can I be excused to escort Mrs. Conner back to her hotel? I'll answer more questions later, but in the meantime, the lady has suffered a considerable shock and I think she'd be more comfortable lying down."

Mavros threw up his hands in resignation. "Go, go, by all means go! We have accomplished little enough as it is. Take her back to her hotel. The rest of you may leave as well—except for you, Spiro. I wish to speak with you further." And with that pronouncement, he rose to his feet and stalked from the room.

Geoffrey led Elizabeth out, one arm around her shoulders, the other still clasping her hand. I turned away, trying to convince myself the only reason I was upset was that Geoffrey's trip to drop Elizabeth at her hotel would mean a further delay in telling him about Spiro's passport.

Robert joined me in the hallway outside. "Well, this has been a damnable morning, hasn't it?" he said grimly. "And this news about Elizabeth. I can't quite seem to grasp it yet. I thought she was dead, and then she walks in—big as life."

I wasn't in the mood to discuss Elizabeth's miraculous reappearance. Instead I asked, hoping I could be convinced, "Do you think there's a possibility Michael really did just run away?"

The question seemed to take him by surprise. But slowly he shook his head. "To be honest, Christine, I don't know what to believe. Every time I begin to feel I have a grip on what's going on, something comes along that changes things entirely."

"Have you asked the lieutenant what he plans to do?" I asked, figuring Robert, in his official capacity as Michael's trustee, might have some influence with Mavros.

Robert shook his head in disgust. "He's given me the usual police rigmarole about a search being made and official procedures being followed, but to be honest, I begin to wonder if his heart is really in it. You know that Skouras and he are old friends?"

I nodded. "I wish we could do something to find Michael."

For a moment we stood there in worried silence, then he said thoughtfully, "You know, perhaps there is. It seems to me the most useful clue to Michael's disappearance is the phone call that policeman received tricking him into leaving early. Perhaps you could try to find out the fellow's name and ask him about the call? He'd probably be less on his guard speaking with you than with me. You could learn what the caller actually said and how he sounded."

"And what will you do?" I asked.

"I think I'll toddle over to that barnyard that passes as a hospital here and see if I can locate the orderly who spotted Michael on his way out."

"Sounds like a plan," I said, relieved to have something concrete to do.

He flashed me a faint smile and reached out to clasp my hand. "Be careful, Christine. I don't want anyone else turning up missing."

"I'll be careful, Robert. Thanks for caring."

He disappeared down the hallway, and I made my way downstairs. My questions about the policeman who'd been stationed at the hospital the previous evening were met with considerable suspicion by the middle-aged officer manning the reception area.

"Why do you wish to know the man's name?" he demanded, his dark eyes sweeping over me with suspicion. "We do not usually give out such information."

I wracked my brain, searching for a reason he would find acceptable. "Well, you see…" I finally said, "…last night I was at the hospital visiting a friend, and I, well, this policeman and I began talking and—you see, I thought he was quite nice and he told me his name, only, you know, your Greek names are kind of hard to remember, and he told me to come by and see him tonight, but I don't want him to think I forgot his name, and so I—"

The officer's scowl had transformed into a bemused grin and he held up a hand, "Okay, okay, I find his name for you." He left for a moment and I heard him talking with someone in the next room, then he returned and picked up a small pad of paper. He wrote down a name in Greek and then English. "Okay, miss, here is the name of your boyfriend." He ripped off the top sheet and slid it across the desk to me. "His name is Yiorgos—in English you say George—Spy-ro-pou-los, and he comes in at eight o'clock."

"Oh, thank you. Thank you very much."

"*Parakaló*," he said, and winked. "I hope you will have a good evening."

"I'm sure I will," I replied, slipping the paper into my purse and heading out the door into blinding sunshine.

For a moment the heat and light cheered me, but as I started down the street towards the Esplanade and looked up at the Old Fortress glittering in the distance, I suddenly ached for grey clouds and stinging rain and Michael safe and sound, staring up at me like a grave little owl.

I trudged dispiritedly past the sun-dappled Liston and through the park towards Dimokratias and Geoffrey's hotel. When I finally reached the Corfu Palace, there was no answer at Geoffrey's room. I went back downstairs to the lobby and settled myself to wait.

I waited for one hour and then two. Still, he didn't come. It was almost three when I finally gave up. I was about to leave when I suddenly had an idea. I crossed to the front desk.

"Is Mrs. Elizabeth Conner registered here?" I asked.

The man checked his revolving file. "No, miss."

"What other hotels in town are of this class?"

"In town, only the Cavalieri. In Kanoni, there is the Hilton." He plucked a brochure labeled "Greece/Corfu" from a wooden rack and opened it on the counter to a listing of hotels. "If you wish to call, here are the numbers. You may use this telephone." He pointed to a grey house phone behind the front desk. I smiled at him gratefully, and he smiled back, motioning me toward a door through which I could come around to the back.

I had no luck with the Cavalieri; the dour woman who answered the phone frostily informed me she had no record of a Kyria Conner. The operator at the Hilton was more friendly—

and more helpful. Yes, Mrs. Redfield Conner was registered; would I like to be connected with Mrs. Conner's room?

"No, thank you," I said quickly and hung up. For a moment I stood there holding the receiver; then I came to a decision. Borrowing paper and an envelope, I quickly penned a note to Geoffrey, then took it upstairs and slipped it under his door.

When I returned to the lobby I had one more favor to ask my friend at the front desk. "Could you call me a taxi to take me to the Hilton?"

"Of course, miss," he replied obligingly. "It would be a pleasure."

The suburb of Kanoni stretches out on a small, hilly peninsula overlooking the airport to the south of town. It is a maze-like strip of land, threaded by narrow, twisty roads and packed with high-walled gardens, pretty hotels, and—as one nears the peninsula's southernmost tip—clusters of garden-terrace tavernas and neon-lit discotheques.

The Hilton was located near this southern tip, and it did look luxurious as we drove up the curving drive amongst the shady trees and well-landscaped gardens. As I paid the taxi driver, a doorman opened my door to help me out, and as I walked into the grand-looking lobby with its expensively frigid air, I was not surprised this had been Elizabeth's choice for accommodations. It had that extra air of luxury I suspected she would always require.

Unfortunately, mixed with the air of luxury was the air of caution, and my inquiries as to her room number were politely but efficiently rebuffed. The man at the front desk explained in irritatingly perfect English that it was the hotel's policy never to give out such information. If I wished he would ring Mrs. Conner's suite and I could ask her the room number myself.

"No, that's okay. Don't bother her. It's really not important, and I think she might be sleeping." The man shrugged and turned to help someone else, and I beat a hasty retreat.

I went and sat down in a small red and gold lounge and pondered how best to go about finding out what I wanted to know.

Unfortunately, this went beyond what room Elizabeth was in. I wanted to know why she'd come to Corfu, and whether she knew anything about Michael's disappearance, and—it was impossible to pretend I didn't care—whether Geoffrey was upstairs with her now getting, well…reacquainted.

The possibility hurt more than I wanted to admit.

Rehearsing various speeches in my head, I picked up the house phone and asked the operator to ring Elizabeth's room. When she picked up the receiver and said hello, however, my nerve deserted me. I mumbled, "Sorry, I must have the wrong room. Is this 201?"

"No," she said impatiently, "it's 512," and hung up.

Thus, almost by accident, I found out one of the things I wanted to know. Up on the fifth floor I found out another.

Elizabeth's suite was at the end of a long corridor on the side of the hotel that faces the sea. For several minutes I stood outside her door debating with myself. Then I heard the sound of a woman giggling—no, cooing is perhaps a better word—and a man murmuring something that sounded like an endearment. My hand, already balled up in a fist and poised to knock, dropped limply to my side, and I backed away, not wanting to hear more.

Then a bell rang and the elevator doors opened. A waiter pushing a room service cart started down the hallway toward me. On the cart was a silver ice bucket in which a bottle of champagne was chilling. Next to it, two champagne glasses, two small plates, a napkin-covered basket, and a crystal vase filled with red roses were distributed on a well-starched white linen cloth. Somehow I wasn't surprised when the cart pushed past me and the waiter lifted his arm to knock on the door of room 512.

The door opened. I turned to face the entrance of another room, delving into my purse as if I were looking for a key.

"The champagne's here, darling," I heard Elizabeth call out. Turning my head slightly, I saw her out of the corner of my eye. She stood in the doorway wearing a beautiful silk peignoir the color of ripe apricots. She flashed the waiter a dimpled smile which seemed to leave him rather dazed, for he merely nodded mutely as she drew the cart into the room and slammed the door shut in his face.

Feeling as if I'd just had one slammed in my own, I walked to the elevator and jammed my finger into the call button so hard it hurt.

Twenty-One

Not sure what else to do, I took a taxi back to Ithaki to wait out the hours until Yiorgos Spyropoulos came on duty.

Maria was pleased to see me. Spiro had not yet returned from town, and Demetra was not in the best of moods. Whether this was due to worry about her brother or upset over the prodigal mother's return I wasn't sure, though Maria hinted that her mistress had been storming around ranting about the "impostor."

"Do you believe the woman is an impostor," Maria asked in an anxious undertone, "or has Kyrios Redfield's first wife truly returned from the dead?"

"She hasn't returned from the dead," I snapped, "she just didn't bother to let anybody know she was alive. And yes, she is definitely who she says she is." I added under my breath, "Unfortunately."

"You do not like her much," Maria said with a faint smile.

"No," I admitted.

"The mistress does not either, I think. Perhaps you will go speak with her, Thesponis? She was very upset when she returned from town, and now that Helen has disappeared—"

"What?" I exclaimed, startled. "Since when?"

Maria shrugged. "Nobody knows. Aphrodite says she last saw her a little before noon."

"All right, Maria. I'll talk with Mrs. Redfield."

Maria looked relieved, but my thoughts were whirling. First Michael, then Helen. Was there a connection? I remembered Helen's pale face when I'd threatened to tell about her clandestine meeting in Koussaki. Was that the reason she'd fled?

I had to knock several times on Demetra's door before she responded with an impatient command to enter. She obviously had not been expecting me; her mouth tightened in an uneasy line when she turned to see who had entered the room.

We regarded each other in uncomfortable silence. "I came to see how you were doing," I finally said.

Her finely-shaped eyebrows rose skeptically.

"After all, you've had a pretty tough day," I added, realizing it was no more than the truth. The dark smudges under her eyes had developed into deep hollows, and the beautiful line of her jaw sagged wearily. She wore no makeup, and the olive skin of her face looked colorless and wan.

At my words, a flicker of surprise appeared in her dark eyes.

"It must have been quite a shock to find out she was alive that way," I continued sympathetically, hoping to forge a bond out of the one emotion we both shared: our dislike of Elizabeth.

"A shock?" she repeated slowly. "Yes, I suppose it can be called that. It is not every day one meets a ghost, and this is a ghost I have hated for several years now. Ah, now I have shocked you. Yet, how else could I feel, when the man I loved burned for someone else?"

I stared at her. "You mean even after she walked out on him, William still loved her?"

"Did you not see them today?" Demetra replied bitterly. "Even my own brother is not immune...." Her voice trailed away.

Biting my lip, I thought of Geoffrey's strained face and of Elizabeth, in her apricot peignoir, smiling her dazzling smile at the room service waiter. Of course, Geoffrey still loved her. He'd probably never stopped.

"I thought it might change when we had a child of our own," Demetra continued, "but while she, who never wanted to be a mother, was able to give William a son, I, who burned and ached and prayed to be one, could not."

I remembered the card I'd found in Demetra's purse. "You saw doctors?"

She tossed her head scornfully. "Doctors and doctors and more doctors. Not one of them could find what was wrong with me."

"What about the day your husband died?"

"What?"

"Didn't you go to see one of those doctors on the day of your husband's accident?"

Demetra shook her head dismissively. "You are mistaken. I finished with the doctors in January; I saw no one in March." Suddenly, her eyes narrowed. "Have you been speaking with Helen?"

"Strange how she's disappeared, isn't it?" I replied evasively.

Luckily, she was easily distracted. She nodded. "First the boy and now my maid. Who will vanish next, I wonder?"

"Do not fear, dear sister, it shall not be me," quipped Spiro from the doorway.

As we both looked around in surprise, he crossed to Demetra's side and slid his arm around her shoulders. She leaned gratefully toward him. "Spiridonaki," she murmured softly, "I am glad you have come."

Spiro smiled down at her, then lifted his head and regarded me coolly. "You will excuse us, Christine? My sister and I have much to talk about."

Frustrated by his timing, I reluctantly ceded the field and retreated to my room.

I lay on my bed for some time, staring up at the ceiling and trying to make sense of the chaotic jumble of facts and speculation that was spinning around in my head. Finally, I grew too impatient to lie still and went in search of pen and paper.

I decided to make up a chart titled "List of Suspects in Michael's Disappearance." I divided the page into five columns and labeled the last four: "Opportunity," "Motive," "Alibi," and "Incriminating Facts." Down the first column I wrote names.

The first name I wrote was Spiro's. *Opportunity?* Almost certainly. No one knew where he was at the time of Michael's disappearance, not even his sister. *Motive?* My guess was: fear of exposure. If Spiro had killed William Redfield and then learned Michael was home that night, he might fear Michael could incriminate him. *Alibi?* Spiro had none. Not for the attack on Michael, nor for Michael's disappearance, nor for the death of William Redfield. *Incriminating Facts.* Spiro needed money badly—a lot of it. He'd also gone to great lengths to hide the fact that he'd been in England on the day of William Redfield's death.

Next came Demetra. *Opportunity?* I wasn't sure. I'd seen her at breakfast a little before eight. Michael had disappeared at six-thirty. Was an hour and a half long enough to lure Michael out of the hospital, stash him somewhere, and then drive back to Ithaki? I didn't know. *Motive?* Probably the same as her brother, fear that Michael might be able to incriminate her in her husband's death. *Alibi?* It didn't look like it, though perhaps Maria or Aphrodite could provide her with one. *Incriminating Facts.* I still felt that the appointment card I'd found in her purse was important, but I wasn't sure how.

I added Paul next. *Opportunity?* If he was on the mainland tending his mother, it didn't look like it, but ferries crossed from Igoumenitsa almost hourly. *Motive?* Unknown, unless he was being paid to perform Demetra's dirty work for her. *Alibi?* Probably. *Incriminating Facts.* Again, I couldn't come up with anything concrete—only a nebulous feeling I had that Paul always seemed to be in the middle of things at critical moments. He was the one who had driven Michael into town the day he was attacked at the old Fort, he was the one who had arrived late the night Michael had almost been run down, he had already been in swim trunks and dripping wet when Michael had been attacked while swimming, and he was conveniently absent from the scene when Michael had disappeared.

Helen was a longshot, but I wrote her down anyway. *Opportunity?* I didn't know. I would have to check with Aphrodite and find out if she had seen Helen earlier in the day. *Motive?* Unknown, though she struck me as the type who could easily be motivated by money, anyone's money. *Alibi?* I didn't know. *Incriminating Facts.* Her clandestine visit with Geoffrey in Koussaki was yet to be explained, and her sudden disappearance the same day as Michael seemed suspicious.

Robert constituted an even greater longshot. *Opportunity?* It didn't look like it. *Motive?* Since Geoffrey seemed confident he wasn't involved in William's death, I couldn't think of one. *Alibi?* Yes. *Incriminating Facts.* Only that he was the one person I didn't have any reason to suspect, which was, of couse, suspicious. I grinned as I wrote this last down.

I debated for some time putting the next name down: Elizabeth. *Opportunity*? Possible. It depended on when she had arrived on Corfu. *Motive*? I couldn't think of one. She might not be the maternal type, but I couldn't really imagine her trying to hurt her own son. *Alibi*? Unknown. *Incriminating Facts*. Besides the fact that she was gorgeous and seemed to mesmerize every man she met? I grimaced at the page. Only that she had kept her survival of a deadly plane crash secret.

Finally I had to write down the name I had been dreading: Geoffrey. *Opportunity*? Very possible. Geoffrey had lied to Mavros about when he'd returned to the island and about his movements the night before; it was perfectly possible he had also lied about being in his hotel room at the time of Michael's disappearance. *Motive*? Money. He would inherit the Redfield millions if Michael died. *Alibi*? None. *Incriminating Facts*. I was trying to decide what to write down in this column, when my eyes strayed back to Geoffrey's motive.

A sudden lightness filled me. I had it all wrong.

What had Robert said? Michael's heir would be his closest blood relative. We had all assumed that was Geoffrey, but that had been before anyone knew Elizabeth was alive.

Elizabeth, not Geoffrey, was Michael's closest blood relative, and Elizabeth, not Geoffrey, would be his heir.

Geoffrey had no motive to harm Michael. What was more, he had *known* he had no motive before he returned to Corfu and before someone tried to drown Michael, because he'd already been to see Elizabeth and knew she was alive.

I closed my eyes, feeling a bit giddy.

Suddenly there was a knock on my door. I quickly folded closed the paper I'd been writing on and slipped it into the pocket of my skirt. It wasn't a moment too soon; without waiting for me to answer, Spiro turned the knob and walked in.

"So, Christine, you are still here, and it seems the sword I thought I had eliminated still hangs above my head. The day has not turned out as either of us planned, has it?"

"I guess not," I said warily, trying to gauge his mood. Though he spoke in his usual bantering tone, his expression was grim.

"You are no doubt wondering why I am here," he said, his

dark eyes regarding me with unaccustomed seriousness.

I shrugged. "It's your house, Spiro, not mine. I suppose your sister wants me to leave?"

"Quite the contrary. She has sent me to apologize for my abrupt dismissal of you before. The events of the day have put a great strain on her, and our latest domestic crisis has only made things worse. She was touched by your concern."

This speech made me feel more than a little guilty. With my written suspicions of both him and his sister burning a hole in my pocket, I hurried to change the subject. "So your sister told you about Helen?"

He nodded.

"Don't you find her disappearance a little strange?" I asked.

"Of course I find it strange. What has not been strange these last days?"

"But the timing of it. First Michael is kidnapped, then Helen disappears. Isn't it possible there's a connection?"

Spiro shook his head. "Please, Christine, do not become like my sister, seeing conspiracies under every bush. Helen has probably grown tired of this household and her work, and has simply gone off to work somewhere else."

"On the very day Michael disappears?"

"Yes, I agree, the timing is bad. The house is already in chaos; we do not need this additional aggravation. Still, we must do our best. Which reminds me. Aphrodite tells me you have asked for a taxi to be summoned at seven to drive you into town."

"Yes, is that a problem?"

"No problem. However, as I have some business in town, I thought I would drive you myself and save you the taxi fare."

Driving into town with Spiro was the last thing I wanted to do, but I couldn't think of a way to turn him down that wouldn't either insult him or make him suspicious. In the end, I just agreed quietly, "Sure. That will work out fine. I have a small errand of my own to see to."

Yiorgos Spyropoulos was a short, solemn-looking man with

thick black hair and pale eyes fringed by long, dark lashes. He seemed to be watching me from behind those lashes as I asked him a second time if he was the policeman who'd spent the previous evening at the hospital guarding a young English boy named Michael Redfield. Slowly he nodded.

"Why do you wish to know?" he asked warily.

"I'm a friend of Michael's and I'm worried about him and what's become of him. I hoped you might tell me about what happened at the hospital while you were there."

He frowned. "Nothing happened while I was there, only after. That is the problem."

"You received a phone call?"

"Yes."

"Did you recognize the voice?"

"No," he said, "but I did not suspect a deception. There was no reason to think ten minutes would make a difference. It had been a quiet night." He regarded me balefully across the desk.

I nodded silently, wishing I could think of something to say that would make him feel less defensive. "When you first came on duty, was there anyone keeping an eye on Michael's room?"

"Yes," he replied, his tone more relaxed. "A tall fellow who works for the boy's family. Paul, I think his name is."

"Paul was still there?" I exclaimed, surprised. "What time was this?"

"About ten o'clock."

I frowned. "Did he seem in a hurry to leave? Had he been waiting there for you to arrive?"

"I don't think so," the policeman said. "He seemed a bit surprised when I told him who I was and why I was there, but he was friendly enough and seemed in no hurry to leave. In fact, he went off and got us both some coffee, and we sat talking for nearly an hour. He left, oh, a little after eleven."

"Did he get any phone calls while you were there?"

He wrinkled his forehead in thought. "I don't remember any."

"Did he mention receiving any bad news about his mother?"

He shook his head in surprise. "No, nothing. Why, has something happened to the lady?"

"You know," I said, "I'm beginning to wonder."

Spiro and I had arranged to meet at one of the cafés in the Liston at nine, but it was only eight-twenty when I left the police station and started strolling slowly toward the square. When we had parted, Spiro had been more than a little curious about my plans, a curiosity I had temporarily deflected by offering to invite him along on my business if he would invite me along on his. He had been in no mood to share secrets then; I was in no mood to share them now. Yiorgos Spyropoulos had given me a great deal to think about, and I preferred to do so outside of Spiro's inhibiting presence.

"Hello there!" called out someone to my right.

"Hello," I replied automatically, turning to see who had addressed me. It took me a moment to recognize the small, white-haired woman smiling up at me from beneath an immense straw hat, but then the bird-like tilt of her head as she waited for me to remember brought it all back. "You're Robert's friend—Mrs. Baxter, isn't it?"

"How clever of you to remember, dear. I must confess I don't remember your name, though Bobby did introduce us."

"It's Christine, Christine Stewart."

"That's a pretty name," she said, smiling. "It's nice to meet you again, Christy."

"Actually, it's Christine."

"Of course, dear. Now, tell me, Christy, what are you doing out here all by yourself at this hour? You have to be careful, you know; these Greek Lotharios consider any woman strolling alone after dark fair game for their overtures. Why there's one leering at you now—and he's coming this way!"

I followed her gaze. I couldn't spot the Lothario, but I did see someone familiar in the distance. *Demetra?* What in the world was she doing here?

Mrs. Baxter slipped her arm through mine and began pulling me along. "Come, my dear! We'll show him."

I looked back, but Demetra was gone. Was that her, disappearing into the shadow of an alley? "Please, Mrs. Baxter," I exclaimed in frustration, "I'm waiting for someone—"

"Bobby?" she demanded sharply. She shook her head and kept pulling. "He's a married man, Christy. Take it from me: these holiday flings only bring pain. Come on. We'll go sit by the water, drink some lemonade, listen to the crickets—"

"Cicadas," I corrected through clenched teeth.

"— whatever, and have a nice girl-to-girl chat."

"But you don't understand—"

"Christy, take it from me, you're not the home-wrecking type."

My fists began to clench. How did one get through to this woman? I had to find out what Demetra was doing in town, but she kept dragging me farther and farther from where Demetra had disappeared.

"Just wait 'til you get home," she rattled on obliviously. "You'll meet some nice, clean-cut American boy who'll make you forget all about Bobby and—"

I stopped and jerked on her arm. "Mrs. Baxter, please! *Listen to me!* I'm not interested in Robert Humphreys, and I'm not having an affair with him!"

Still she clung to me, so I swung her around to face me. I felt something whiz past, stinging my arm. Mrs. Baxter stared up at me with a look of astonishment. Then she cried out faintly and crumpled to the ground. Horrified, I knelt down by her, wondering if she'd had a heart attack or stroke. It was then I saw the dark stain spreading across the bright yellow of her dress.

Remotely I heard the sound of running feet and a man calling my name. "Christine, is that you?" Spiro exclaimed from somewhere far above me. "Good God! What has happened?"

I swallowed hard, trying to get enough moisture into my mouth to speak. "Tell someone to call an ambulance. I think she's been shot."

Once again I was in a hospital corridor staring up at peeling green paint while Lieutenant Mavros asked me questions. This time, however, I was sitting in an ugly orange chair with a bandage on my arm, and this time the lieutenant's voice was almost gentle as he asked me if I would rather answer the rest of his questions in the morning.

I nodded wearily.

A nurse came up and murmured something in his ear. He nodded and turned to me. "She is out of surgery now. It's difficult to predict, but the doctors think she has a good chance to recover."

"Thank God!" I exclaimed, sinking my face into my hands.

"You will excuse me for saying so, but you seem to take the situation very much to heart, considering she is a stranger to you."

"I feel responsible," I said. "After all, that bullet was meant for me. I keep thinking perhaps, if I hadn't jerked her back like that...."

He frowned. "Perhaps what? Perhaps the bullet might have missed her? It is possible. It is also possible that the bullet might have struck a more vital place killing her on the spot, or killing you. Would that truly have been better?"

"No," I admitted. "Though I can't help feeling it would be fairer for me to be lying on that recovery table instead of her."

He shook his head. "Can one wrong truly be considered more just than another?"

I smiled faintly. "A philosopher-detective?"

"You are surprised?" he replied with a shrug and a grin. "I am Greek, after all."

I found myself grinning back.

"That's better," he said. "And now it is time to send you home." He motioned to one of his men stationed at the end of the hall. "Is Takis back with Kyrios Skouras, yet?"

"I think so."

"Have them both sent up then." The man nodded and hurried off. Mavros turned back to me and said, "You realize you may still be in danger?"

I nodded.

"I will have a man stay at the villa tonight. Be sure to lock all the doors and windows of the room where you sleep. Tomorrow we will decide what further arrangements need to be made for your protection."

"Thank you."

He bowed his head. "You are welcome." Seeing my expression, he added, "Is there something else troubling you?"

"Lieutenant, about Spiro…. I was supposed to meet him in the Liston, but not until nine. I can't help wondering how he happened to show up so quickly after Mrs. Baxter was shot."

Mavros's expression lost some of its friendliness. "He has said that his business concluded early," he replied stiffly. "In any case, you have no cause for concern. On my orders, Spiro's hands and clothing have been tested. No gunshot residue was found. He did not fire the weapon that wounded you."

"What about the attack on Michael?" I persevered. Has Spiro told you where he was when that was made?"

"Yes," he replied tersely.

"So? Does he have an alibi?"

He grimaced. "Of a sort."

"What does that mean?"

"The one witness to Spiro's alibi refuses to confirm it."

"Why?"

"She is a married woman and is not eager to have it known that she spent two days with a man who is not her husband."

"That's rather convenient, isn't it?"

The expression in his blue eyes turned cold. "For Spiro? No, I do not think so. Now, Miss Stewart, you will excuse me?"

He strode away down the hallway to where Spiro and another man had just emerged from the stairwell. I'd meant to tell him about seeing Demetra, but decided he was irritated enough with me at the moment. The questions about Demetra could wait. Mavros exchanged a few words with the man I didn't recognize, then led Spiro back to me. "Spiro will drive you home, and Takis will follow in another car. Until tomorrow, Miss Stewart."

I nodded in acknowledgment. "Until tomorrow, Lieutenant."

It was a short and mostly silent drive back to Ithaki, for which I was grateful. Despite the lieutenant's assurances, I was uncomfortable in Spiro's company and too exhausted to hide the fact behind small talk. Fortunately, Spiro was in no mood to talk either and invested all his attention in driving very, very fast—much to the chagrin of the policeman, Takis, who struggled to keep pace with us in his beat-up Renault.

Once we arrived at the villa, however, it was Takis who took the lead. He escorted us into the darkened house, and insisted on entering my room first to make sure that "all was as it should be."

Apparently it was. Finishing his inspection behind the curtains, inside the armoire, and under the bed, he nodded his head and motioned for me to enter. "It is okay, miss. You will lock all doors and windows, please?" I assured him I would, and he turned to Spiro. "May I see the rest of the house now, sir?"

The two men moved off together, and, feeling thoroughly exhausted, I locked up and began to get ready for bed. I slipped out of my clothes—trying to ignore the reddish-brown stains on my skirt and the jagged black hole in the sleeve of my blouse—and pulled on a sleeveless nightgown of thin pink cotton. With everything shut up tight, it was going to be a hot night. I pulled the coverlet off my bed and folded it on the chair in the corner. Then I began to climb under the sheets.

There was a knock on the door.

Wearily I climbed back out, crossed to the door, and opened it. There was no one there but the policeman, Takis, sitting on a chair perusing a newspaper. He glanced up at me and nodded, then returned to his reading. Embarrassed, I closed the door.

There was another knock followed by the sound of someone calling my name. Realizing my mistake, I crossed to the bathroom door, and called loudly into it. "What do you want?"

"Open the door. I wish to speak with you."

"Can't it wait until morning, Spiro?"

"No."

"But you heard my orders. I'm supposed to keep everything locked."

"I have a proposition for you."

I didn't answer.

"Christine, please, this is ridiculous. That fellow, Takis, is right outside. I simply wish to speak with you a few minutes."

He had a point. Reluctantly I undid the latch. "All right. What's so important?"

His expression of irritation transformed into amusement as he gazed up and down at me. Suppressing a surge of irritation, I asked coolly, "Is something funny?"

He shook his head. "No, that night dress is quaint, but also charming."

"Spiro, I'm tired, I've had a lousy evening, and I want to get to bed. Is there anything besides my nightgown you want to discuss?"

He shrugged. "I have been thinking. I do not like the way events have been proceeding. I think you and I should exchange rooms tonight. That way, if you receive any visitors, I shall be the one to greet them." His voice was bland, but a dangerous light burned in his brown eyes.

"It's nice of you to offer," I said uneasily, "but visitors shouldn't be a problem with a policeman right outside my door."

"The boy also had a policeman outside his door, and he has disappeared."

I flinched at the reminder. Michael had been missing almost a full day. Thinking of that somehow made my worries about switching rooms seem petty. "All right, Spiro, I'll do it," I said, "but only if we tell Takis what we're planning. If he's going to guard me, I want him guarding the right room."

Spiro nodded his acquiescence.

Takis was at first reluctant to sanction the change, but after he had searched Spiro's room and examined all the locks, he finally gave us the okay.

Yet despite the policeman's thorough inspection of the room, I was decidedly uneasy as I climbed into Spiro's large bed. Perhaps Mavros was right and I didn't have to worry about Spiro.

But what about Demetra?

TWENTY-TWO

I slept fitfully that night, woken several times by scary dreams I couldn't remember. So I was more than a little groggy the next morning when the sound of banging furniture and raised voices finally penetrated my consciousness and sent me stumbling out of bed.

"Dammit, Skouras, where is she?"

"Remove your hands from me! You are the one who should be answering questions, not I! You have broken into my house—"

"Michael's house!"

"I do not think the police will consider the difference," Spiro said coldly.

"Why were you creeping into her room at this hour?"

"What business is it of yours?"

My nervous fingers finally managed to undo the lock, and I swung open the door. Geoffrey and Spiro both turned at the sound.

"Christine!" Geoffrey exclaimed, releasing his hold on Spiro and rushing forward. "Are you all right?"

"I'm fine," I assured him, noticing how very haggard he looked. Spiro gazed at us speculatively. For a moment I tried to think of some way to salvage the situation; then I realized it probably wasn't possible. Geoffrey was in no mood to be discreet, and to be honest, neither was I. I was sick and tired of pretending.

"Where the bloody hell have you been?" Geoffrey demanded in a low voice, his hands reaching out to seize mine. "I was about to go mad with worry. First I find him—" he jerked his head in Spiro's direction, "— stealing into your room, then you aren't in your bed, or anywhere else for that matter."

"I slept in Spiro's room last night," I said, too distracted by the look in his eyes and the warmth of his fingers to pay attention to my words or to realize they were prone to misinterpretation.

He abruptly released my hands. "I see," he said tightly.

"No, you don't," I began, ready to clarify the situation. Then I remembered the nature of his reunion with Elizabeth. What right did he have to explanations? Biting my lip, I fell silent.

"You've not yet explained what *you're* doing here," Spiro reminded him. "Your presence seems rather suspicious after the attack upon Christine last night."

Geoffrey swung around at that. "What attack?" he exclaimed.

"You do not know?" Spiro said skeptically. "Someone took a shot at her."

Geoffrey turned back to me and his gaze focused on the small, rumpled bandage on my upper arm. His eyes slowly rose to my face.

"It's nothing, really," I said quickly. "Just a scrape."

"The woman standing next to Christine was not so fortunate," Spiro remarked. "The bullet struck her in the chest."

Geoffrey paled. "What's that fool Mavros about? Why doesn't he have you safe under lock and key?"

"I assure you, Mr. Redfield," said a voice from the doorway, "I am as concerned with Miss Stewart's safety as you are. That is why I assigned one of my men to guard her."

All three of us turned to face Lieutenant Mavros. "Well, he's not doing a very good job of it, is he?" Geoffrey snapped. "Where is he?"

"I had hoped you might tell me." The lieutenant's tone was grave.

"Sorry," Geoffrey snapped. "I haven't seen him."

"Spiro?"

Spiro frowned. "He is not in the hallway?"

Mavros shook his head. "Nor anywhere in the house. I've had the housekeeper looking."

"Perhaps he has gone back to town?" Spiro suggested.

"Takis had orders to remain here until I arrived," the lieutenant said. "He was also to report in every two hours. His last report is overdue. I think we must begin a search of the grounds."

"Give me a few minutes to get dressed," I said. "I'd like to help you look."

"Thank you, but for the time being I think it would be best if you remained here. Spiro can help with the search. Mr. Redfield, I think you should stay with the young lady. There may still be danger for her, and I do not wish her to be alone."

Spiro began to protest, but Mavros cut him short. "Do not concern yourself, Spiro. Mr. Redfield is an intelligent man. He understands I will hold him personally responsible if any harm comes to the young lady during our absence. Is that not so?"

"She'll be quite safe with *me*," Geoffrey replied coolly.

Lieutenant Mavros raised an eyebrow at his emphasis on the second pronoun. "I am pleased to hear it. There is perhaps one other small detail I should mention, however. There is a man stationed in the driveway with orders to shoot anyone who tries to leave the villa without my express permission, so I trust I may depend on you to remain here until Spiro and I return?"

"Of course, Lieutenant. You don't think I'd leave Miss Stewart alone in this lion's den, do you?"

"But I wonder, Mr. Redfield," said Mavros with a shrug, "who is the lion?" With that he motioned to Spiro and the two men exited, leaving Geoffrey and me alone in the room. We stood there in silence until I escaped to the bathroom to get dressed. When I emerged, Geoffrey was sitting in a chair, his head resting wearily in both hands.

"You look exhausted," I said.

He gazed up in surprise. "I'm afraid I didn't get much sleep last night."

Thinking of Elizabeth in her apricot peignoir, I ground my teeth. "I suppose you were too worried about Michael?"

He stood up. "It seems I should have been more worried about you. Why didn't you leave yesterday as we agreed?"

"With Michael missing? How could I?"

"Are you sure Michael was the only reason you stayed?"

"Of course. What other reason could there be?"

His gaze traveled in the direction of Spiro's room. "One obvious possibility springs to mind."

The thought that he might actually be jealous was balm to my battered ego. "Is that why you came bursting in here this morning?"

"I came 'bursting in here,' as you put it, because I found your note and thought perhaps you were in some sort of trouble."

"It's just as well I wasn't, since I slipped that note under your door yesterday afternoon. I suppose with your busy night you only just found it?"

"My busy night?"

"Never mind." I took a deep breath. "The reason I wanted to see you and the reason I wrote that note is that I've found out something I think you should know: Spiro was in England on the day your brother died."

"But that's impossible!" he exclaimed. "The police checked. He arrived in England on the 16th."

I nodded. "He also arrived on the 15th. I've seen his passport. There are two dated entry stamps: one dated March 15th from Birmingham and another dated March 16th from Heathrow."

Geoffrey flashed me a strange look. "You realize what this means?"

"Of course," I snapped, feeling an illogical sense of guilt. I reminded myself that the rules of hospitality could hardly apply when murder was involved. "It means Spiro manufactured an alibi for himself. More importantly, it means he manufactured an alibi for himself before anyone could have known he would need one."

"Anyone," Geoffrey corrected grimly, "except the person who sent my brother over that cliff."

"What are you going to do now?" I asked.

"Give this information to the police. There was an inspector who seemed less than satisfied with the verdict of death by misadventure. Perhaps with this she'll be able to persuade her superiors to reopen the case."

"But there's still no proof your brother's death was anything but an accident."

"Perhaps they'll find something new."

"Perhaps," I agreed slowly. "Of course, it might help if you told them the truth about what happened the day he died. What did you and your brother argue about that afternoon?"

"I'm sorry, Christine. I can't tell you."

Angrily, I bit my lip. "Did your brother threaten to disinherit you?"

His green eyes regarded me steadily. "Yes."

"And that made you angry?"

"No. I probably would have done the same in his place." He added quietly, "You still haven't told me how you come to know all this."

"I guess we both have our secrets," I said.

He frowned. "I thought William and I were alone in the house that afternoon. If someone else was there, lurking in the shadows, that person may be his murderer."

I shook my head. "No."

"How can you be so certain?"

"I just am."

He gave me a long look. "It was Skouras, wasn't it?"

I shook my head. "No."

"You've already admitted he was in England that day, despite what he told the police. It's obvious he must be the one who told you about the argument with my brother—I suppose he was hiding in my brother's house that afternoon and overheard us?"

I evaded a direct answer. "You still haven't told me why your brother was so angry with you. What had you done, that he felt compelled then and there to dispose of the bicycle you'd given Michael for Christmas?"

"What? What are you talking about?"

"That's the reason he went out that night," I said. "To get rid of it." Geoffrey stared at me and I added, "Wasn't Michael's bicycle found in the trunk of your brother's car?"

"No."

"Perhaps it was thrown clear?"

He shook his head. "The area was searched thoroughly. If Michael's bicycle had been in my brother's car when it went over that cliff, I assure you it would have been found."

"Perhaps your brother had already gotten rid of it?"

"Perhaps," he agreed, sounding thoughtful.

There was the sound of running footsteps, and Spiro burst into the room. His gaze immediately fixed on Geoffrey. "So," he said. "You are still here."

Geoffrey replied blandly, "Why shouldn't I be? It's my nephew's house, after all."

Something angry and more than a little menacing flared in Spiro's face.

"Did you find Takis?" I asked anxiously. "Is he all right?"

"He will live," Spiro replied. "I must phone the ambulance." He strode across the room toward the door to the hallway.

"Where's the lieutenant?" I asked.

"By the cliff." Spiro flashed me one brief, considering look, and then the door slammed after him.

Geoffrey started for the French windows.

"Wait, I'm coming with you," I called out. He paused and turned, holding out his hand. Oddly comforted, I took it.

We followed the path I'd followed my first day at Ithaki. We emerged from the thicket of pine to see Mavros kneeling beside a prone figure. My grip on Geoffrey's hand tightened.

As we drew closer, we could see the man lying on the ground was Takis. To my relief, his eyes were open. One hand cupped a large and rather nasty looking bump on the back of his head. My exclamation of dismay caused his angry scowl to change to a look of embarrassment.

"What happened?" I exclaimed.

"He was making an inspection of the grounds," Lieutenant Mavros replied, "when he thought he heard someone cry out."

"The sound came from this direction," Takis added, "so I ran here, but when I arrived I could find nothing. I started toward the cliff to look over and make sure no one was below, but before I could do so, someone struck me from behind and knocked me out."

"What about the cry?" I demanded, my stomach clenched in fear. "It wasn't Michael, was it?"

"No, it was not the boy," Mavros replied heavily.

"Then who?"

He stood up and led the way to the edge of the cliff.

Geoffrey and I followed. We stared down at the rocks below. A crumpled figure lay still on the mottled grey shore, one brown arm flung out, its hand tightly clasping a purse that glittered gold in the morning sun.

I quickly turned away feeling a little sick.

Helen was no longer missing.

TWENTY-THREE

The morning crawled by slowly and grimly.

For some time, Mavros was too busy with the routines necessary in a case of violent death to spare attention to the somber and uneasy group of people gathered inside the villa. Two ambulances, one for Takis and one for Helen, came and went. Policemen swarmed over the beach and cliff like ants. Ithaki's grounds were combed for any sign of the mysterious assailant.

Inside the villa, two policemen stood guard. To simplify their job, we were all gathered into the large drawing room, but we were far from a united group. Spiro and his sister set up camp on one side of the room and Geoffrey established his base on the other. Maria and Aphrodite, the only remaining representatives of the live-in staff, hovered in the corner looking dazed, and I—well, I wasn't sure where to go, so I sat by myself near the windows and watched the policemen scurrying to and fro.

The lieutenant decided to conduct his interviews separately this time, one person being summoned from the drawing room at a time. Demetra was called out first. Spiro was next, followed by Aphrodite and then Maria. Finally, it was my turn. Geoffrey, apparently, was being saved for last.

I was led to a room I had not before entered, a study lined with bookshelves and containing a large fireplace and leather chairs and a massive desk behind which Lieutenant Mavros sat, looking fiercer than I had ever seen him.

"Please be seated," he said, gesturing to the closer of the two chairs. He waited for me to do so, then said, "I do not think I need to remind you how serious this matter has become, Miss

Stewart. Murder has been attempted not once, but several times. A boy is missing, perhaps kidnapped. An innocent tourist has been shot. One of my men has been lured away from his post, another attacked, and now a woman lies dead, thrown from a cliff by a ruthless killer. There is no more time for games, evasions, or half-truths. There is no more time for lies, however well-intentioned. From this moment I expect—no, I require— your full and complete cooperation."

"Yes, Lieutenant."

"Good. Let us begin, then. First I would like your description of events from the time you left the hospital last night until my arrival this morning."

I told him everything, describing the drive home, Spiro and I swapping bedrooms, and waking to find Spiro and Geoffrey arguing loudly in my room.

"How long were the three of you together before I arrived?"

"Not long, maybe five minutes."

"You say Spiro and Mr. Redfield were arguing loudly. Could they have been arguing more than a few minutes before you awoke?"

"I don't think so, but I'm not sure. You'll have to ask them."

He nodded. "And you, did you leave Spiro's room during the night or at any time this morning?"

"No, though I can't prove I didn't."

"Tell me, were you surprised to find Mr. Redfield in your room so early this morning?"

For a moment I hesitated, then admitted, "I was at first, but he explained to me that he'd come because of a note I'd left for him at his hotel. He thought I was in some sort of trouble."

"Is he in the habit of coming to your rescue then?"

I felt my cheeks grow warm. "I think he feels a responsibility for me because I came to Ithaki to keep an eye on Michael."

"I see," he said, looking skeptical. "And that is why he stormed into your bedroom like a jealous lover? No, don't bother answering. How did he know which room was yours?"

I met his intent blue gaze. "He visited me there before," I admitted. "When I first arrived at Ithaki."

His dark eyebrows rose, but he moved on to another subject. "I understand that during your first evening here, Spiro loaned you a gold purse belonging to his sister. She tells me the purse was never returned to her."

"I meant to return it," I said, "but it disappeared before I had a chance to."

"Disappeared?"

"Yes, it was propped up on the bureau when I left for dinner Friday night, but Saturday morning I realized it was gone."

"Why did it take you so long to notice its disappearance, and why didn't you tell someone about it when you finally did?"

"I didn't notice it was gone, because I was distracted by other things when I got back to my room Friday night, and I didn't say anything about its being missing, because I assumed Maria had returned it to Mrs. Redfield. Look, I don't see what any of this has to do with—" I broke off, suddenly remembering the glittering object that had been clutched in Helen's lifeless hand.

"Oh, my God," I exclaimed. "So it was Helen who took it."

"Apparently, but why?"

"I don't know. But the reason I didn't notice the purse was missing Friday night was that my room had been trashed. There was nail polish on my dresses, my purse was slashed to ribbons, and someone scrawled a message on the mirror telling me to leave Ithaki."

His expression was grave. "Why didn't you tell me of this before?"

"I was going to," I said, "but I was afraid you wouldn't believe me. I thought you might think I'd done it myself. I decided to clean things up and not say anything."

His mouth tightened. "The purse disappeared from your room at the time of this attack?"

"Yes."

"And you think Helen was responsible for the attempt to frighten you away?"

"She never seemed happy with my being here, and when she came by my room Saturday morning she seemed startled to find me still there and the room looking normal. I wondered at the time, but I had no proof."

"I see." He paused, steepling his fingers together. "Perhaps Mr. Redfield took exception to such treatment of you?"

My head jerked up in surprise. "Come on, Lieutenant! You

don't really think Geoffrey would murder Helen just because she wrecked my room, do you?"

He shrugged. "I am still not satisfied with the explanation of his presence here this morning."

"What about Spiro?" I demanded. "What reason does he give for being up and about?"

"A perfectly reasonable one. He heard a strange noise and went out to investigate. When he returned to the house, he was set upon by Mr. Redfield."

"Kind of undermines your theory, doesn't it? Geoffrey tackling Spiro that way? I mean, if I'd just pushed a woman off a cliff, I wouldn't rush to the nearest house and pick a fight with someone. Would you?"

"Who can know what crazy things an Englishman may do?" he said, but something akin to respect flickered in his blue eyes. "Well, Miss Stewart, I have only one more question to ask you. "For what reason do you believe the maid, Helen, was murdered?"

"I've been thinking about that all morning, Lieutenant, and I just can't figure it out. My only guess is that she must have known or discovered something about these attacks on Michael. She disappeared yesterday. Maybe she was lying low because she knew she was in danger?"

"It is a possibility," he agreed with a small nod. He stood up. "Of course, then we are faced with the perhaps more important question: why did she return?"

I shook my head. "Sorry, Lieutenant, I haven't a clue."

"Well, thank you. You may go now."

"Wait! What about Michael?" I asked. "Have you found out anything?"

"No," he said, "there is no news, but that, in a way, is what I expected."

"What do you mean, what you expected? Haven't you at least been trying to find him? He's in terrible danger!"

"Is he?" replied the policeman. "I am not so certain."

"What do you mean you're not so certain?" I snapped. "He's in the hands of a murderer who's already tried to kill him at least three times—"

"It has been more than twenty-four hours," he interrupted,

"and—you will forgive the brutality of my words—we have found no body, which gives me hope that the boy is safe enough for now. You do not need to scowl at me that way, Miss Stewart. I do not say I have abandoned the search for him, only that I believe the discovery of his whereabouts may not be the most pressing problem. Judging from the events of last night and this morning, I fear our murderer is growing desperate."

"Exactly!" I cried. "That's why we have to do something."

He frowned. "The boy is not the only one in danger," he said, striding to the door and opening it. "Do not attempt to do my work for me, Miss Stewart. I do not wish to see you taken away in an ambulance like Helen."

After the lieutenant had finished with me, I returned to the drawing room to find Spiro anxiously urging his sister to retire to bed with some sleeping pills. I didn't blame him for his concern. Up close, I was shocked to see how haggard Demetra looked. Helen's murder had obviously taken a toll on her; she looked strained to the breaking point.

My eyes rose and met Spiro's, and I was startled by the open anger I saw there. When he spoke, however, his voice was frighteningly calm.

"Yes?" he said.

"I just wanted to tell you I'll be leaving today. I've already imposed on your hospitality too long, and after this morning I thought it might be best if I returned to town."

Demetra suddenly looked up in surprise. "You are leaving?" she said, almost as if the thought upset her. "Ah, I see, you are— how do they say it?—'abandoning the sinking ship.' My friends in England, my supposed friends, they did the same after my husband died and the police started coming around with their questions. Very well then, leave. We do not need you."

"Demetra, please," Spiro murmured softly in Greek, "do not upset yourself. Everything will be fine. Miss Stewart is leaving because she and I have had a personal disagreement, nothing more. It has nothing to do with this business of Helen. Do you understand? There is nothing to worry about." He motioned to

Maria, who was hovering in the doorway. "Now Maria will help you to bed, and I will be in in a few minutes to sit with you until you fall asleep. All right?"

Demetra nodded wearily and allowed Maria to guide her from the room. Spiro turned on me furiously, "Have you not done us enough harm?"

"I'm sorry," I said. "I didn't know. I thought she'd be glad to be rid of me."

"I want you out of this house as soon as you can pack your things and go. And not another word to my sister, do you understand?"

I nodded silently and started to turn away, but he seized my wrist. "So, my sister was right. All this, everything you've said and done, has been for Redfield."

"No."

"Then for whom?"

I hesitated for a moment, then said, "Michael. I was afraid he was still in danger."

"Ah, I see. Now I am a murderer of small children?"

"You haven't yet said where you were when Michael was almost drowned."

His eyes narrowed. "I see Redfield has indoctrinated you well."

"That doesn't answer my question."

He shrugged and abruptly released my wrist. "Perhaps you should go pack now," he said coldly.

"Where's Michael?"

"I have no idea," he said, turning away and striding toward the door. "Perhaps you should ask your dear friend, Geoffrey."

Back in my room, there wasn't much to do, as I hadn't really unpacked from the previous day. I was just gathering up my toothbrush and comb when there was a soft knock at the door and Maria entered with my laundered skirt and neatly darned blouse. She had managed to get the bloodstains out of both.

"Thank you," I said. "I wondered where those had gotten to." I took the clothes from her and put them in my suitcase, and then a thought struck me. "When did you come by for them?"

She shrugged and smiled a little, as if embarrassed. "This morning, I wake early, so I decide to make some laundry. I come, quiet, into the room to take the clothes, but you are already from the bed."

"The room was empty?" I asked.

She nodded. "I think you are like me and cannot sleep."

"What time was this?"

She shrugged. "I do not know. Perhaps seven o'clock?"

Seven o'clock. Roughly half-an-hour before I woke to the sounds of Spiro and Geoffrey scuffling. If Spiro had been gone from the room as early as seven, then his brief reconnoiter of the grounds hadn't been as brief as he'd hinted and he could well have been the one to push Helen over the cliff. "Did you tell Lieutenant Mavros this?" I asked.

She flashed me a look that revealed she knew quite well the implications of an empty room on this of all mornings. "He did not ask me," she replied simply.

Did she think she was protecting me? Or was it Spiro she was trying to protect? "I think you ought to tell him," I said.

Her eyes widened slightly in surprise. "You think so?"

"Yes."

We exchanged a long look and then she nodded. "I will do as you say." She looked down at my packed bags. "You are leaving?"

"I'm returning to my hotel in town."

"Goodbye then, and God go with you." She turned to leave.

"Wait, Maria, there was something I wanted to ask you— about Paul. What time did you call him the other night at the hospital with the news about his mother?"

She seemed taken aback by the question. "I do not know," she said hesitantly. "I think perhaps nine o'clock."

Nine o'clock. So Paul had heard the news about his mother's fall before Yiorgos Spyropoulos showed up to guard Michael. Why, then, had he hung around talking and drinking coffee with the policeman for another hour?

"Maria, do you know where Paul's mother lives in Ioannina? Do you have an address for her or a phone number?

"I am sorry, Thesponis. No. It is important?"

I shook my head slowly. "I'm not sure."

Twenty-Four

After Maria had gone, I got permission to leave the villa from one of the lieutenant's minions and left the house as unobtrusively as possible. Hefting up my suitcases, I started up the drive to wait for my taxi.

"Hold on a moment. I'll take those," said a voice behind me. My suitcases were slipped from my hands.

"You don't have to do that," I said. "I can carry them."

Geoffrey shook his head. "This isn't gallantry, my dear, it's leverage. Now you'll have to let me drive you into town."

"But I've already called a cab."

"I cancelled it."

"What is this, blackmail?"

"I prefer to think of it as bargaining from a position of strength. In any case, it doesn't seem fair to let you cart these all the way up the drive and the additional half-mile down the highway to where the car is parked."

I raised a questioning eyebrow at him.

He grinned. "My attempt at stealth. Tackling Spiro in your room rather put such efforts to waste, but I promise you, up until then I was trying to be discreet."

I snorted derisively. "You're lucky the lieutenant didn't arrest you on the spot. Of all the mornings to come blundering onto the scene."

His expression sobered. "Yes, poor Helen."

A heavy silence settled between us, and we started up the drive. After a while, I said, "Mavros considers you a suspect, you know."

He shrugged. "Under the circumstances, I don't blame

him."

It irked me that he didn't seem more worried. He drew ahead of me, and I watched the surprisingly tranquil set of his shoulders with growing annoyance.

"How can you act so calm after all that's happened?" I demanded.

He turned. "If you must know, I feel a good bit easier knowing you're safely out of that house."

I felt easier, too, but I was not about to admit it to him.

As we continued up the drive, Geoffrey slowed his long-legged pace until we were once again side-by-side. I found myself almost nostalgic for the view of his back, however, as the frequent sidelong glances he cast my way left me increasingly flustered. There was an intimacy in those looks I didn't want to acknowledge, but was incapable of rejecting. Finally, desperate to distract his attention, I blurted out, "You'll be pleased to know I didn't mention anything to the lieutenant about Helen being your inside contact at Ithaki."

That got his attention. He came to a full stop and I stumbled to a halt next to him. "What did you say?" he asked, his tone of mild inquiry belied by his suddenly white-knuckled grip on my suitcases.

"Please, Geoffrey, don't. I understand why you feel you have to deny it now, but I'm not going to say anything to Mavros, so you don't have to lie to me, okay? You always did seem to know a little too much about what was going on at the villa. Now I realize Helen was your source of information."

He stared at me, his mouth taut, his gaze filled with an intensity that made it impossible to look away. "I'm not going to ask how you came to this amazing conclusion, Christine. I just want to know one thing. Do you think I'm the one who killed her?"

I shook my head. "No," I said with conviction, "I know it wasn't you."

For a moment, his eyes closed, as if in relief. Then he was moving again, his demeanor almost cheerful. He turned out onto the highway and looked back at me, a small, mischievous smile playing over his lips. "You still haven't explained how I managed to bend the not-so-fair Helen to my will."

Something in his bantering tone buoyed my spirits. I hurried after him. "I don't know," I answered. "Perhaps you paid her, perhaps you exerted your not inconsiderable male charms upon her."

He gave a loud chuckle. I clung to the sound, wanting to hold on to the unexpected lightness of the moment like a child holds on to a treasured toy. But the reality of the morning's events could not be shut out for long. Darker thoughts bubbled up my throat and I had to give voice to the words, "I doubt it took much prompting to get her to trash my room."

"You think I'm responsible for that?" he exclaimed.

"I think you enlisted Helen's help to persuade me to leave— for my own good, of course. Though I don't think you were prepared for her to be quite as destructive as she turned out to be."

"You're wrong, Christine," he said quietly. "I never would have subjected you to that, no matter how much I wanted you to leave." He turned his head and flashed me a look that caused my stomach to do an odd flip. "I have a little more regard for you than that, you know," he added in a deeper tone.

I looked away, afraid of that look and that tone, until Geoffrey moved off again down the road. I followed, and at last we reached the Mercedes.

He set down my bags and unlocked the passenger door for me, but instead of helping me into the car, he drew me into his arms. "Mavros explained about you and Skouras switching rooms," he murmured against my hair. "Why didn't you tell me?"

I thought of him with Elizabeth. "I didn't think it mattered," I said tightly.

His arms dropped away. "No?"

I shook my head and ducked into the car.

He stowed my luggage in the trunk, then climbed into the driver's seat. He flashed me an inquiring look, but I turned away to stare out the window. He let out a sharp breath and started the car. We were gliding through Ypsos before he said, "Do you think you might tell me what's wrong now?"

"You mean besides the fact that Helen's dead, I've been shot at, and Michael may be in the hands of a murderer?"

"Yes," he said gently, "besides that."

I was tempted to tell him. Tempted to succumb to the tenderness I heard—imagined?—in his voice and lay myself bare. Confess my feelings. Admit my jealousy. Plead for some assurance that what I knew to be true, wasn't.

I was tempted, but then I remembered the last big risk I'd taken and how badly it had turned out. I wasn't sure I could bear a second such humiliation so soon after the first. Worse, I was afraid. Being rejected by a father I'd longed for most of my life suddenly seemed easy compared to being rejected by the man sitting next to me, whom I'd known a mere ten days.

"Christine?" he prompted, holding his right hand out to me as he kept his eyes on the road.

I ignored the proferred hand. "Nothing's the matter. I'm just worried about Michael, that's all."

He placed his hand back on the steering wheel. "I see."

I resisted the urge to touch his now taut arm or rest my cheek on his now tensed shoulder. Instead, I continued, "Mavros still doesn't seem to grasp the danger he's in. I think we've got to try to find him ourselves."

"What do you propose we do that the police haven't already done?" The gentleness was gone from his voice, replaced by edgy impatience.

"Track down Paul," I said.

"And how in the world would that help? He left the island before Michael disappeared. His mother broke her hip."

"Did she?" I said skeptically. "I'm not so sure. Maria says she phoned Paul with the news about his mother around nine. But he was still at the hospital at ten when the policeman assigned to guard Michael arrived. And he stayed there another hour acting as if nothing was wrong."

"That doesn't mean anything," Geoffrey said. "He probably knew he'd have a wait for the ferry and decided he might as well spend the time in comfort at the hospital as spend it down at the dock."

"Comfort is hardly the word I'd use to describe that place!"

"The point is—" he began.

"The point is," I interrupted, "if Paul stayed at the hospital for another hour, he *couldn't* have taken the ferry to Igoumenitsa that night. This morning, I asked one of the lieutenant's men. The last ferry leaves at ten."

"So he missed the ferry and had to cross the next morning. That hardly proves he's involved in Michael's disappearance."

"But whoever made the phone call luring the policeman away had to know when he was due to go off duty and when the morning man would be coming on. Paul had quite a chat with him that night. Yiorgos Spyropoulos might well have mentioned the hours of his shift—in passing, of course."

"You make quite a convincing case," he said. "I might almost believe Paul were the kidnapper if it weren't for one important point: *Michael wasn't kidnapped.*"

I stared at him. "What are you talking about? Of course he was kidnapped!"

"A boy walks out of a hospital and disappears. There's no indication of a struggle. He's seen walking toward the hospital's entrance alone, and when he's questioned about his presence in a hospital corridor so early in the morning, he lies and says he's visiting a sick sister. What evidence is there to show that he was taken against his will?"

"What about the phone call telling his guard to report back to the police station?" I demanded. "That's evidence."

"Is it? A man leaves his post ten minutes early and then, when the boy he's supposed to be guarding disappears, claims to have done so because of a fake phone call from his constabulary. Personally, I don't believe the call ever took place. I think he left early because he was tired and bored and mistakenly thought ten minutes wouldn't matter."

It was possible; I remembered Yiorgos Spyropoulos's wary face. "Are you saying Michael just ran away on his own?"

"Would it be so surprising?" Geoffrey said. "He's already had two close calls. If you were frightened and didn't know where the danger was coming from, what would you do?"

"But he's only nine years old," I said. "He has no money, no place to hide, and the police are looking for him. If he were doing this on his own, shouldn't someone have found him by now?"

"Perhaps. But he's a clever little fellow and fairly resourceful. Greeks have a soft spot for children. I'm sure he could have persuaded some family to take him in, give him a meal, perhaps even drive him to some other part of the island or give him a lift on the ferry to the mainland."

"But he doesn't have his passport."

"No," he said, "you're right. He can't leave the country. But he can get pretty far away and it might take some time to track him down. The way things stand at the moment, perhaps the longer it takes the better."

"You can't be serious! You like the idea of Michael wandering around Greece at the mercy of strangers?"

"He's safer with strangers right now than with those familiar to him, one of whom is a murderer. I need time, Christine. Time to use this news about Skouras being in England when my brother was killed to find evidence that will convince Mavros to arrest him. That's one reason you've got to give up trying to find Michael's imaginary kidnapper."

I tensed, suddenly realizing why he had been so insistent on driving me to town. "What's the other reason?"

A muscle along his jaw twitched, and he turned and flashed me an impatient look. "Do you really need to ask? One woman's dead, another's in hospital with a bullet in her chest. For heaven's sake, Christine, don't you have any sense of self-preservation?"

"Of course I do. I'm still alive, aren't I?"

"Let's be clear on this: your snooping days are over. Michael's missing, but probably safe. You're the one who seems in the most danger at the moment. Mavros has promised me there will be some men assigned to guard you by this afternoon, but in the meantime I plan to keep an eye on you and make sure you don't get into any more trouble."

"But what about Paul?" I demanded.

"Skouras is the problem, not his gardener. I don't want you going off on some wild goose chase that might prove dangerous."

"Let me get this straight. I'm to do nothing and say nothing, and you're going to hang around until the lieutenant's men arrive to make sure I do just that?"

We had entered Corfu and were turning toward the older part of town. Geoffrey eyed me warily. "That was my intention, but that chin of yours bodes ill for my plans. It's set at that particularly stubborn angle that proclaims 'I'll do whatever I think best, and no one's going to stop me.'"

"I'm still worried about Michael," I insisted, "and I still think Paul had something to do with his disappearance."

Geoffrey made an exasperated sound. "What if I agree to make discreet inquiries about him myself? Will that satisfy you?"

I lowered my chin to a more compliant angle. "Yes." After a moment, I added, "I suppose you want me to go straight back to my hotel and stay there?"

"For today at least, yes."

"Well, then," I said, "if that's the plan, can we stop on the way so I can buy a few books to read? There's an English bookstore I found the other day, up one of those streets behind the Liston."

He glanced at me suspiciously. He was, I thought, getting to know me a little too well. He suspected I was up to something, but didn't know what. Problem was, neither did I. I was determined to give him the slip, but I wasn't at all sure how to go about it. All I had for the moment was the nebulous memory that this particular bookstore had a back entrance.

We parked in a small but bustling square to the east of the maze of narrow shop-lined streets to which the Liston serves as a sort of gateway. After a mere twenty minutes and two wrong turns I managed to find the book shop, and we entered to find it unoccupied, save for a kneeling dark-haired woman making room on the shelves for the contents of a just-opened carton.

She glanced up as we walked in, smiled, and then returned to her work. I left Geoffrey to stare impatiently out the front window and began browsing the shelves, slowly working my way toward the back of the shop. There the room bent to the left into a small annex not visible from the front. At the far end of this annex was the door my hopes were pinned on.

When I disappeared from Geoffrey's line-of-sight, I half-expected him to come rushing back to see what I was up to. But though I stared unseeing at shelf after shelf and counted slowly to one hundred, he never came.

This was my chance. I crossed to the door and turned the

knob. It opened easily and noiselessly, and I was about to step out when I realized that the door did not, as I'd assumed, lead out to a back alley or another street, but instead opened on a small walled courtyard that had no other exit. Frustrated and disappointed, I returned to the front of the shop. Geoffrey was asking the kneeling woman about finding a telephone.

"I'd invite you to use ours, but I'm afraid it's on the fritz at the moment," she apologized in English spoken with a soft Australian twang. "There's a public one across the way," she pointed. "Over at the grocer's."

He thanked her and started towards me. Anxious to appear immersed, I grabbed up a book. Coming up behind me, Geoffrey leaned over my shoulder and read the title out loud. "Hmmm. *The History of Nudity in Greek Art*." He reached past me and began thumbing through large full-color plates illustrating the book's theme in eye-catching detail. Feeling positively adolescent, I felt my cheeks burn pink. "Why Miss Stewart, you never cease to amaze me," he chuckled in my ear. "I never dreamed you had such interesting tastes in literature."

I slammed the book shut and set it down on a nearby table, then turned to face him. "Was there something you wanted?"

He nodded, a trace of laughter still in his eyes. "I need to place a telephone call. I thought if you were still looking about," the green eyes glittered suspiciously, "I might dash across the way and do it now." His expression sobered. "I'll just be a moment. You'll stay put until I come back?"

I had trouble meeting his gaze. "You're still holding my luggage hostage, remember?"

He nodded and flashed me a smile that almost destroyed my resolve. After all, he was only trying to do what he thought best. But he was wrong about Michael—I could feel it. Whatever sixth sense I had about the boy was on alert and fairly screaming that he was in danger.

I waited until Geoffrey disappeared into the shop across the street, and then went up to the dark-haired woman and said, "I have a favor to ask. That man who just left for the phone—I need to give him the slip, but if I leave now he may see me when I pass by the grocer's. I know it's a lot to ask, but could I hide in the small courtyard out back and have you tell him I've gone?"

She stared at me. "Why on earth should I?"

"It's very important, I promise," I pleaded. "I wouldn't ask otherwise. I don't have time to explain, but I have to get away."

I could see her reluctance to get involved. She was about to say no when suddenly her eyes narrowed and she focused on the healing cut on my cheek. Her gaze drifted downward to take in the scrapes on my elbow and knee and the bandage on my arm. "Is *he* responsible for those?" she demanded.

I didn't deny it. Her lips clamped tightly together and slowly she nodded. "All right, I'll help you. But the courtyard's no good; if he decides to look for you there, there's nowhere to hide. The storeroom would be better. The door's hidden behind that tapestry there and there are plenty of boxes to hide behind. We've just gotten in our summer shipment."

There were indeed plenty of boxes in the dimly-lit room. Cynthia, as I learned she was called, pointed to a cluster that resembled the ruin of some box-based temple, and I retreated behind the unevenly stacked wall. She flashed me an encouraging thumbs-up and closed the door behind her. I heard the heavy slap of wool against wood as the tapestry dropped back into place.

Barely a minute later I heard the tinkle of bells at the door heralding Geoffrey's return. The voices in the outer room were muffled; all I could make out was that the man's voice sounded angry and disbelieving while the woman's remained cool and adamant. I held my breath as footsteps approached, then passed by. I caught a brief snatch of the conversation.

"She couldn't have left! I was watching the street the entire time!"

"I don't know about that, but there's nothing back there but an empty courtyard."

"I'd like to see that for myself."

They moved away and I didn't hear her reply. After what seemed an age, but by my watch was less than three minutes, Cynthia rapped softly against the door and whispered. "He's gone, but I think you should wait a while before coming out."

I agreed. To pass the time as I waited, I browsed through some of the open cartons, glancing at the books stored inside. My eye was caught by one containing a stack of children's picture books. I knelt down and gingerly lifted a few out to see the covers. My father had a new book out, and I wondered if by some chance I might find it there. Usually I avoided his books like the plague, fearing the roiling emotions I experienced seeing his work in print, but somehow things were different now; I didn't feel angry or bitter anymore, only curious.

Serendipity didn't cooperate with my mood, however. None of the books on top were his, so I lifted another handful out, but none of those was it, either. Eventually every book from the box was stacked in a pile in front of me, but none was what one reviewer had described as the "humorous tale of a frog forced to take the form of a prince until he can find a girl who refuses to kiss him." With a surprisingly strong sense of disappointment, I began to put them back.

I had almost finished doing so when a book of illustrated tales from *The Odyssey* caught my attention. I had passed over it quickly before, but this time my attention was caught and held by the cover, where a storm-tossed ship threaded its way through a narrow strait straddled by a monster reaching out to grab and destroy it. It was a gripping image, but far more gripping to me were the words which appeared underneath in small gold letters: "Illustrated by Geoffrey Redfield."

The stories of Odysseus's adventures and his struggles to return home had been favorites of mine as a girl, and I began leafing eagerly through the book, impressed by the literate text which accompanied the amazing pictures. When I turned the last page, it was with regret; it took a moment for the photographs of the artist and author on the book jacket's back flap to register.

I saw Geoffrey first. He stood on the steps of a temple overlooking a glimmering sea and grinned at the camera with a faintly self-mocking smile. The photograph was captioned, "*The artist, G. Redfield, at the Temple of Poseidon, Cape Sounion.*"

"Why didn't you tell me you were this good?" I demanded of the photograph indignantly, but Geoffrey just grinned back at me, disdaining to reply.

My glance dropped to the second photograph. It was of a man standing in a square pit, his shirt stripped off, sweat beading on his skin, his face the picture of concentration as he peered at a broken shard of pottery which a colleague held out to him. With a gasp of recognition, I stared at the caption below the photograph: "*The author, Dr. P. Stanathopoulos, at work at an archaeological site in Sicily.*"

It couldn't be, but it was.

Paul, Ithaki's mysterious gardener, was not really a gardener at all, but Dr. P. Stanathopoulos, archaeologist and author.

And Geoffrey had known it all the time.

Below the photographs was a brief paragraph: "*The Adventures of Odysseus* marks the fifth collaboration between Redfield and Stanathopoulos. Longtime friends, they have combined their talents for painting and storytelling with their love of Greek literature to produce an enchanting series of books enjoyed by children and adults alike. Other titles in the series include...."

I read no more. I was too angry to read more. Geoffrey had deceived me, had been deceiving me the entire time I was at Ithaki. He had had an inside contact at the villa, but it had been Paul, not Helen. No wonder he'd seen no need for me to keep an eye on Michael, to snoop around and learn what I could. He'd already had someone in place to fill that role—his old friend Paul.

But that left one question unanswered.

Where was Paul now?

TWENTY-FIVE

I had a hunch how to find out the answer to that question when I left the bookstore twenty minutes later with a copy of *The Adventures of Odysseus* tucked under my arm and the telephone number of Ionian University in my purse.

It was past one, and the torrent of people that had earlier poured down the narrow street was thinning to a trickle as the shops began to close for siesta. The grocer across the way was reaching up to pull down rolling metal shutters when I called out to him to wait because I wanted to buy something to drink.

Flashing me an irritated look, he motioned me into the store. As I made my way toward the small refrigerated case in the back where the drinks were kept, I beamed my most ingratiating smile, but to no avail. He was in no mood to be charmed by a tourist.

I pulled out a cool bottle of carbonated lemonade and carried it to the counter. "I'm sorry to keep you," I said lightly in Greek. "I was just so terribly thirsty in this heat."

"*Ellenida eisai*?" he asked in surprise. "You are Greek?

I nodded. "On my mother's side. I'm from California."

His mouth began to curl into a smile. "California?" he repeated. "I have a cousin in California. In Los Angeles."

"Really?" I said sweetly. "I'm from Los Angeles."

His smile grew broad. We chatted about L.A., and his cousin, and how much he wanted to see Hollywood someday, and finally I broached the subject I'd been waiting to ask him about.

"There was a man in here earlier, a tall man, English, with light-colored hair and green eyes. Do you remember him?"

"I did not notice the color of his eyes, *koritsi*," he said, flashing me a wry look, "but yes, I remember the man you describe. He wanted to use the telephone there." He gestured with his chin at the large red phone on the counter. "He is a friend of yours?"

I shrugged and made a face. His mouth quirked in amusement. "Ah, so that's the way of it, is it? You two have a fight?"

"You don't know what number he called, do you?" I asked.

He shook his head apologetically. "I'm sorry, no. Why? Are you afraid he was calling a girlfriend?"

"Did it sound like he was calling a girlfriend?"

He hunched his shoulders and spread his hands. "Who can say? The person he called was not at home. He tried a second time, but there was no answer, and eventually he gave up and left." He flashed me a rueful smile. "Now if you'll excuse me, I'd better be going. My wife will not be pleased if she learns I am late because I was talking with a pretty girl."

"I'm sorry to keep you, but can I ask one more favor? That phone," I pointed to the one on the counter, "is only for local calls, isn't it?" He nodded. "I need to call someone in Ioannina. Do you have a phone I could use to make that call? I'd be happy to pay you whatever you think it will cost."

"It is important?"

"Very important," I said.

"Very well. Come with me, in the back."

I took me three phone calls before I reached the right office, but finally a woman's voice answered with the words, "Department of Archeology, Professor Kuriakou speaking."

"I'm trying to reach Paul Stanathopoulos," I said quickly.

"I'm sorry. Dr. Stanathopoulos is away on sabbatical. Perhaps I can help you?"

"I hope so. You see, I work with Dr. Stanathopoulos's publisher"—I looked down at the book in my hand—"Raytham & Sons. I have some papers to deliver to him, but I'm afraid I've misplaced his address here on Corfu. I'm here on vacation, you see, so they kind of shoved this at me at the last minute. Anyway, I thought of calling up the office, but I'm new there, and I don't really want to admit I've been such a scatterbrain. I was hoping someone at the University might be able to help."

"Of course. Actually, I have the information right here. Someone else from your office called not too long ago. Let's see. Have you a pencil? There's no street number, but the name of the house is Alcinoos, and the mailing address is the village of Pagi. Pagi is on the west side of the island, by the way, near Paleokastritsa. The house is a mile or two north of the village."

I thanked her and asked about her other caller.

"Actually, I didn't speak with him myself," she said, "the secretary did, but I think he must have been from your office as well. He told her that he had some contracts for Paul to sign."

"I see. Well, thanks again."

"Say hello to Paul from me," she called out cheerfully.

"I will," I said, setting the receiver back in its cradle.

"You've had bad news?" asked the grocer when I returned to the front of the store.

"I'm not sure," I said, reaching into my purse and pulling out my wallet. "I'm afraid I made three calls instead of one. How much do I owe you?"

He shook his head and handed me a piece of paper. "This is the name and address of my cousin in Los Angeles. When you return home just drop by and tell him that I send my greetings."

When I left the grocer's, the street was almost deserted. Nearly all the shops were shuttered and closed, and the few stragglers left strolling along the colonnaded walkways were tourists. Still, I had a lot to think about as I wound my way back to the Esplanade, so it took me some time to notice that I was being followed by a short, dark-haired man in a white shirt and khaki pants. Belatedly, I realized he must be one of Lieutenant Mavros's men. I wondered if he'd been following me since I'd left Ithaki with Geoffrey.

Under other circumstances, it would have been reassuring to have a bodyguard in tow, but right now I had to find some things out, and find them out fast, and if what I suspected was true, the last thing I needed was a policeman along for the ride.

But how to get rid of him? There weren't any open shops to duck into. It was that time of day when only cafés and museums are open. A café wouldn't serve my purpose, but perhaps a museum would. I veered to the left, toward the Palace of St.

Michael and St. George. Five minutes later I was buying a ticket for the Museum of Oriental Art.

I'd had a faint hope that he wouldn't bother following me inside, but apparently he'd had orders to stick with me, and as I paused on the main staircase leading up to the second floor I could see him buying his ticket. Twenty minutes and dozens of display cases later, he was still firmly on my heels and I was beginning to wonder if I was ever going to give him the slip.

Then I entered a room filled with Japanese screens placed so closely together they formed a virtual wall. The guard had his back to me and was fully occupied watching a well-built blonde in the next room. Taking advantage of the opportunity offered, I slipped past the looped chain barrier and hid behind the screens. Peeking out between two of them, I saw Lieutenant Mavros's man stroll in casually a minute later. Seeing me absent, he dropped the lackadaisical pose and strode quickly toward the next room.

My luck was holding. The guard was still turned away, so I slipped out and hurried back toward the exit. Ten minutes later I was making my way through quiet residential streets congratulating myself on the fact that I was no longer being followed.

"And what do you plan to do now," Geoffrey murmured in my ear, "now that you've given that poor policeman the slip?" His arm slid through mine, capturing it in a grip that was anything but casual.

"You were following me, too?" I exclaimed in consternation.

"Since you left the bookshop. I noticed your escort, so I hung back a bit. When you turned into the Palace, I suspected what you were up to and waited outside. Which brings me back to my original question." He flashed me a look. "What do you plan to do now?"

I took a deep breath and turned to meet his gaze. "Actually, I'm on my way to find out how you managed to convince a respected university professor to be your accomplice in kidnapping."

His grip on my arm tightened, and I felt a certain satisfaction at the shock I saw displayed on his face. "How in the world did you find out?"

No explanation. No denial. Just a simple inquiry. I showed

him the book held open to the back flap and said bitterly, "It's a good likeness don't you think?"

He grimaced. "I'd forgotten about that. It's the first time they've bothered with photographs. This complicates things."

"Complicates things!" I cried angrily. "You kidnap your own nephew, lie to the police, leave me thinking Michael's in the hands of some desperate killer, and all you can say is *this complicates things?*"

"I'm sorry, Christine, but I thought you'd be on your way home before Michael's disappearance became widely known."

"You couldn't trust me with the truth?"

"It wasn't a matter of trust. I simply didn't want you mired in this any deeper than you already were. Abduction, even in the best of causes, is a rather serious offense. If something went wrong, I didn't want you charged as an accomplice."

"What about Paul?"

"I should never have involved Paul, but I was desperate to get Michael away, and to get him away quickly, before another attempt on his life could be made."

"So you kidnapped him to keep him safe? I suppose you came up with this idiotic plan when Elizabeth turned you down?"

He shrugged. "After she refused to take custody, I decided a more radical solution might be required. I returned to Corfu early and began making arrangements, but then Michael was attacked again, and I realized there was no time for careful planning. Paul offered his help, and I took it. I called the villa and gave them the message about his mother. Paul talked with Mavros's man and discovered when he was due to go off duty, then he slipped into Michael's room and gave him some clothes and a message to meet us outside the hospital the next morning at six-twenty-five. When it was time, I called the guard with the message to report back to his station early, and Michael walked out without a hitch. We had a car waiting, and Michael left with Paul while I returned to my hotel to await the inevitable visit from the lieutenant's men."

"So that's why you lied about when you got back. But where's Michael now?"

"He's safe with Paul."

I felt a prickling down the back of my neck. "At the house in Pagi?" I asked sharply.

He stared at me. "How do you know about that?"

Impatiently, I slapped at the cover of the book. "I called up his department at the University. One of his colleagues gave me directions to the place without a second thought."

Geoffrey swore.

"It gets worse. She told me that someone else, a man, had called earlier wanting to know the very same thing. Geoffrey, I think Spiro may have found out where Michael is."

"Come along!" he exclaimed, setting off at a run.

We veered through narrow alleyways and past countless streets before arriving, breathless, at a small and almost deserted square lined with parked cars. None of these, however, resembled Geoffrey's rented Mercedes, and to my surprise he led the way to an old brown and battered Renault with Italian plates.

"Is this why you came back to Corfu by ferry?" I asked as he threw open the door to let me in.

He nodded. "I purchased it in Bari. I thought it might prove useful to have a car the good lieutenant and his men knew nothing about."

I understood his caution, but regretted the loss of power and speed which the Mercedes would have offered. Fear was fluttering in my stomach, and I couldn't help feeling every minute counted.

"Don't worry," he said, seeing my face. "It may look a dilapidated piece of rubbish but under the bonnet there's a motor that sings." He turned the key in the ignition and the engine roared to life. "It used to belong to a mechanic who loved to tinker. I presume you don't mind a bit of speed?" I shook my head, and he sent the car catapulting from its parking space and hurtling down the street.

Our ride across the island was a streak of blurred scenery, rushing wind, and the poignant fragrance of wild rosemary, which still culls remembrance of that afternoon into a pungent bouquet of pure emotion. To this day, I cannot remember the roads we took, the things we said, or any other details of the time that passed in our race to reach the house in Pagi, but one whiff of rosemary is enough to flood my mind with the haunting apprehension I felt as we drove up the dirt driveway and stepped out of the car to be greeted by absolute silence.

There was no other car. The small, white-washed house stood in an open semi-circle surrounded by olive trees. Green shutters on the windows were thrown open and the front door stood ajar, but no one emerged to meet us. Geoffrey called out a greeting, but no one answered. He started toward the house, and I followed.

Inside, the house was cool, quiet, and seemingly empty. Geoffrey called out Paul's name, then Michael's, with no result. "I'm going to look about outside. See what you can find out in here."

I did as I was told, though I had no idea what I was looking for. As I went from room to room, everything looked normal—until I reached the back of the house and the kitchen.

By the look of the food that still sat untouched on the table, they had been about to sit down for lunch. A knife and a half-sliced loaf of bread stood abandoned on the sideboard. A bottle of wine had been dropped on the floor leaving a pool of broken glass and red liquid puddling near the sink. A chair had toppled on its side. And something had shattered a hole through the back window, something about the size of a bullet.

"*Geoffrey!*"

He came bursting in the back door and ran straight for me, gathering me up in an embrace so fierce it hurt. "What's happened? Are you all right?"

"I'm fine, but, Geoffrey, look!" I pointed toward the shattered window.

His face went white. His arms dropped away and he crossed the room toward the toppled chair. His gaze lowered to the floor where smeared drops of blood traced a trail from the chair to a tall, thin cupboard by the door. He pulled the cupboard open with a hand that shook. It was empty.

His eyes closed in relief. I fumbled for a chair to sit down. "Do you think they're still alive?" I asked weakly.

"I think there's a chance they may be. One bullet is unlikely to have hit them both, and after that first shot Paul would have gone for his rifle. He usually kept it here, in this cabinet. The fact that it's gone, and that his car is missing as well, gives me hope that he was able to get Michael away." Despite the brave words, his voice was bleak.

Startled to realize just how deeply he cared, I said softly, "You love your nephew very much, don't you?"

Violently, he shook his head. Fists clenched, he wheeled around to face me. "You don't understand, Christine. Michael's not my nephew, he's my son!"

Twenty-Six

"Well?" Geoffrey said heavily into the silence that ensued. "Have I shocked you into speechlessness?"

Feeling a bit dazed, I shook my head. "Actually, when I first saw you, I was sure you must be Michael's father. Then you said you weren't, and I accepted that, but you and he are awfully alike, you know." I paused, then said, "How did it happen?"

He flushed, avoiding my eyes. "Three months after my brother and Elizabeth were married, she turned up at my flat one evening, weeping. She told me that the marriage had been a mistake, that she was dreadfully unhappy, that I was the only man she really cared for. At first I was wary, but despite everything, I was still very much in love with her. When she asked me if she could stay the night, I said yes.

"By morning, however, she'd had a change of heart. I woke to find her gone, returned to William and her marriage. Michael was born nine months later, so of course I wondered, but she was adamant William was the father. I suspected she might be lying, but what could I do? I knew the truth would tear William apart, and I reasoned the child would be better off with a family that was whole. I kept silent and tried to forget.

"Time passed. As Michael grew older, people sometimes remarked on how much he resembled me, but that sort of thing happens in families, and I tried not to think too much about it. I didn't see Michael all that often, and I managed to dismiss the strong affinity I felt for him as merely an uncle's affection.

"However, when William married Demetra, Michael was sent off to school. Remembering how miserable I'd been during my own school days, I began visiting him there. We got on well from the start, and the more time I spent with him, the more attached I became, though I still didn't know whether he was my son or not."

"How did you learn the truth?" I asked.

"The day my brother died, he rang up and demanded I meet him at his home. At first, his imperious tone put my back up and I refused; then he told me that if I cared about Michael's future I'd better come. When I arrived he led me into the hall and asked me point-blank if I knew who Michael's real father was. Startled, I asked him what reason he had for doubting the boy's paternity. He replied he'd just come from specialists in London who'd informed him he suffered from a congenital malady that made it impossible for him to father children."

"So the appointment card was for your brother, not Demetra!" I exclaimed.

Geoffrey nodded.

"What happened then?"

"I told my brother the truth. I said if he wasn't Michael's real father, then in all likelihood I was, and I told him about the night I'd spent with Elizabeth. He was furious. He swore at me and said he was done providing for my bastard. I told him he had every right to wish me to the devil, but none to take out his anger on Michael. He yelled that he'd do as he damn well saw fit. I was afraid that if I stayed any longer we'd come to blows, so I left." He paused, then added bleakly, "I never saw him again—alive."

I reached out and touched his hand. "Geoffrey, I'm sorry." His fingers curled around mine. "Do you think your brother really meant to disinherit Michael?"

He said wearily, "At that moment, yes. Eventually, though, I think he would have seen reason and reconsidered."

"Does anyone else know about this?"

"I don't know. I can't believe Demetra does, or she'd be trying to use the information to contest Michael's inheritance. But if Skouras was in the house that day and heard us arguing—"

I shook my head unhappily. "It wasn't Spiro who told me about the argument. It was Michael."

For a long, frozen moment he stared at me in chagrin. Then we heard the sound of a car coming up the drive.

"Who—" I began.

"I don't know. Stay here!" He disappeared through the doorway toward the front of the house. The engine stopped and for a moment everything was still, then with a stifled exclamation Geoffrey threw the front door open and ran out. I followed.

A boxy green Fiat was parked in the drive and a man facing away from me was slowly getting out it. He had a rifle gripped tightly in one hand, and I was about to call out a warning when I saw Geoffrey hug a small, familiar figure to his chest. I realized belatedly that the man with the rifle was Paul.

Geoffrey saw me and let Michael slide down from his arms to the ground. Michael turned and, seeing me, came running.

"Oh, Miss Stewart, you'll never believe what's happened!" he exclaimed excitedly. "Someone fired a shot at us through the window, and it hit Paul in the shoulder, but he managed to get his rifle from the cupboard and fire back, and whoever it was drove away. Then Paul and I tried to follow, but we never even caught a glimpse of the car, so we drove to a monastery where a monk bandaged Paul up, and then we drove back here and here you are! It's awfully nice to see you, by the way." He flashed a brief, accusing glance at Geoffrey, then turned back to me. "I thought you'd gone back to California."

"Not yet," I replied, smiling at his breathless narrative. He was obviously relishing the memory of his most recent adventure with boyish gusto.

"It is indeed a surprise to find you here," echoed Paul as he directed a long, inquiring look Geoffrey's way, "but then this has been a day of unexpected visitors."

"And unexpected events," added Geoffrey, "of which we've all had our share. Michael, why don't you take Miss Stewart into the house and find her something cool to drink while I talk to Paul."

I was irritated to find myself so cavalierly dismissed, but then Michael slipped his hand in mine and said coaxingly, "There are two bottles of frightfully good lemonade left in the fridge."

The lemonade was good, and Michael, eager to fulfill his role as host, also brought out a roll of creme-filled cookies and a slightly melted chocolate bar to round out our repast. As we sat munching away, I found myself sneaking glances across the table at him, wondering what it was about him that seemed so different. With a start I realized the truth: for the first time since I'd known him, he seemed completely happy and content. Considering all that had happened to him the past few days, it didn't make any sense—unless.…

"Michael, you're fond of your Uncle Geoffrey, aren't you?"

Slowly, warily, he nodded.

"From what he tells me it sounds as if he used to visit you at school fairly often. I suppose you must have gotten pretty used to those visits, pretty used to being with him and knowing he was around to look out for you. If it had been me, I suspect I would have started thinking of him almost as a second father."

Michael's eyes fell and his cheeks went pink.

I said gently, "There's nothing wrong with that, you know. It would be a perfectly natural way to feel."

He shook his head and mumbled, "You don't understand—"

I reached across the table and caught his hands in mine. "Yes, I do. Your uncle told me what he and your father quarreled about the day of your father's accident."

He looked up, his eyes large and vulnerable and so like Geoffrey's that my heart lurched painfully against my ribs. "He did?"

"Yes."

"And it doesn't matter to you that I'm a b-bas—"

I interrupted forcefully. "That you're fortunate enough to have had two fathers instead of one? No."

He sighed softly. "Whenever Uncle Geoff came to visit, I hated for him to leave. I used to imagine what it would be like to live with him in his flat in London instead of at school. Sometimes I even wished he were my dad instead of Father. Then I heard them arguing and realized he really *was* my father. I couldn't believe it. It was upsetting at first, but then I was kind of glad—at least, I was until I heard about Father's car crash."

His small fists clenched against the table. "It was awful then. I was afraid the crash wasn't an accident. Father was such a careful driver, you see, and I just couldn't believe he would drive along that cliff in the fog unless…unless he intended to go over."

I stared at Michael's small, grave face unsure what to say. I longed to assure him his father hadn't committed suicide, but it was entirely possible William Redfield had, in a fit of anger or self-loathing, done precisely that. And if it wasn't suicide, would it be any kinder to Michael to hold out the possibility—up to now, unprovable—that his father had actually been murdered?

"Even careful drivers make mistakes," I finally said, "and if everyone accepts that it was an accident, perhaps you should, too."

Michael shook his head. "Last night I overheard Uncle Geoff and Paul talking when they thought I was asleep. Uncle Geoff doesn't think Father's death was an accident, and he doesn't think Father did away with himself either." His relief at this second conclusion was evident; the haunted look was suddenly gone from his eyes. He leaned closer and said in conspiratorial whisper. "You won't believe it, Miss Stewart, but he thinks Father was killed—by Uncle Spiro!—and that now Uncle Spiro's after me!"

I didn't have to feign being startled by this pronouncement, though it was actually his calm and almost cheerful acceptance of the situation that caused my eyes to widen and my mouth to drop open so effectively. He was boyishly gratified by my reaction, and hastily proceeded to assure me that I needn't worry about him. "Paul's a ripping bodyguard, and I'm certain Uncle Geoff will find all the evidence the police need to arrest Uncle Spiro."

"And you're not frightened, not even a little bit?"

"Well, perhaps a little bit," he admitted, "but it's rather exciting as well, rather like being the hero in a film."

Only in the movies, I thought anxiously, heroes—especially little boy heroes—aren't in any real danger of being killed.

Suddenly, his expression clouded. "Of course, it's a bit of a jolt to find out Uncle Spiro wants to kill me. I thought he sort of liked me and that we were, well, friends. Still," he said, with a small smile, "at least now I know Uncle Geoff hasn't washed his hands of me."

"Of course he hasn't! What made you think he had?"

"After Father died, I kept expecting him to come and take me to live with him, but he never did. Then when Stepmama and I left to come here to Corfu, he didn't even stop by to say goodbye. After a while, I began to wonder if he really was my father, or whether it had all just been a mistake, but I didn't know how to find out for certain." He paused and regarded me shyly from behind his lashes. "That's why I wanted to hire a detective." Once again my mouth fell open. "I'm sorry I didn't tell you before," he apologized.

I snapped my mouth shut and said gently, "It doesn't matter."

"Miss Stewart, may I ask you a question?"

"Of course."

"Do you think it's disloyal of me to want to go live with Uncle Geoff now that Father is dead?"

"No. I think it's only natural for you to want to be with him, just as it's only natural for him to want to be with you."

He flashed me an anxious look. "But some fathers don't care tuppence about being with their children."

"True," I admitted, thinking of my own. Strangely, the thought held no sting. "But he's not one of those. Otherwise he wouldn't be fighting so hard to get custody of you." Seeing Michael's look of surprise, I exclaimed, "Didn't you know?"

He shook his head dazedly. "No."

"Oh, Michael! Even before he found out the truth he wished you were his son. After the accident he went to your stepmother and asked her for custody, but she refused. When he tried to take her to court to force the issue, she brought you here to Greece. He's been trying ever since to get you back to England."

He searched my face for assurance I was telling the truth, and then, seemingly satisfied, relaxed against his chair. A moment later, however, he snapped upright. "You don't think he's asking for me simply because he thinks he has to, do you?"

I shook my head. "Have you ever known your uncle—I mean your father—to do anything simply because he thought he had to?"

Michael shook his head and flashed me a grin so wide the Cheshire Cat would have been envious.

By the time Paul and Geoffrey appeared in the kitchen, they had decided I was to return to Corfu with Paul, while Geoffrey and Michael went in search of a more secure place to hide out. Geoffrey eyed me warily as he announced the plan, and then drew me out into the hall. "Well?" he said.

"Well, what?"

"Haven't you something to say?"

"I don't think so."

"You've no objections to make? You don't mind being sent back to town with Paul?"

"I agree he needs to see a doctor," I said, "and that the only place he can do that without having awkward questions asked is on the mainland. With the injury to his shoulder, he needs someone to drive him to the ferry, and I can see I'm the obvious choice."

"And you'll be careful?" Geoffrey asked. "Once you're back in town you'll go straight to your hotel and stay there?"

"Will it make you feel better if I say yes?"

He made a face. "It might, if I actually thought you meant it. As it is, I suspect I'll be a nerve case by the time I see you again."

"And when will that be?"

"I don't know."

"Geoffrey, you can't keep Michael on the run forever." I stared down at my hands and added reluctantly, "Elizabeth's here now. Can't she take Michael back to England?"

He shook his head. "I doubt he'd be safe even there. Skouras is getting desperate. He's given up trying to make these attacks look like accidents. Michael won't be safe until we have enough proof to force his arrest."

"What about Lieutenant Mavros?" I said. "I'm beginning to think he already suspects it was you who took Michael; if you just disappear, he might think you murdered Helen, as well."

He shrugged. "With luck, in a few days I'll be able to prove to him that Skouras is the real killer. I've been thinking about what you told me this morning, and I have a theory I plan to pursue once I have Michael properly settled."

"Theory? What theory?"

"Let's just say I have a notion as to what may have happened to Michael's bicycle."

Paul, looking pale, ducked his head out from the kitchen. "Excuse the interruption, but I think we must be leaving soon."

Geoffrey nodded. "Of course. You're right." Paul's head disappeared again, and Geoffrey took my hands in his and said in a low voice, "Christine...."

I stared at the pulse beating strongly in the hollow of his neck. "Yes?"

"When you get back to town—you will be careful?"

I nodded.

His grip tightened. "Because I swear, if anything were to happen to you now—" Suddenly his arms were around me and his mouth was pressed possessively against mine.

I surrendered to the kiss without thought. I was incapable of thought. My rational mind had fled, along with any sense I had of separateness from this man who, with a single touch, could send me up in flames. I twined my arms around his neck, ran trembling fingers through his hair, shivered as his hands roamed over me and his mouth trailed kisses along my neck and up to my ear into which he whispered huskily, "My sweet, my darling—"

Darling. In one of those strange associations the mind can make, the single word clanged in my ears, tolling a warning to my passion-dulled brain. I was not his darling; Elizabeth, with her golden eyes and tawny skin, was the claimant to that title. I pulled free of his embrace.

"Christine?"

"I suppose that was to ensure I do as I'm told?" I gasped. "Make love to her and she'll drive Paul to town, hide in her hotel, and keep her mouth shut whenever Mavros comes calling?"

His cheeks flushed red and the pulse in his throat pounded fiercely. "Is that what you think this is about?"

"I don't know what this is about!" I cried. "I don't know if this is just a tactic, or if you mistakenly think you mean it, but I do know I'm not about to make the mistake of playing second fiddle when you're already in love with someone else!"

"I see," he said in a tightly controlled voice. "And precisely whom am I supposed to be in love with?"

"Elizabeth, of course."

"Of course! A woman who threw me over, married my brother, abandoned my son, and who, for years, I thought was dead."

"Yes, and look how you reacted when you found out she was alive!"

"I was pleased—for Michael's sake."

"Oh, I see. And yesterday at her hotel? The champagne and roses and your late night together? I suppose that was for Michael's sake, too?"

"Champagne and roses? What are you talking about?"

"Don't, Geoffrey! I was there. I know." My breath caught painfully in my chest, but the words tumbled out all too easily. "I wanted to find you, to tell you about Spiro's passport. When you weren't at your hotel, I thought you must still be with Elizabeth, so I went by her room at the Hilton. I went up to the door to knock.… I heard…voices inside the room, a man and a woman. I started to leave, but a room service waiter arrived with champagne and roses. Elizabeth came to the door in an apricot peignoir to collect it, and she called out to her companion—to you—that it had arrived. She called you 'darling.'"

He gazed at me for a moment in silence. "I drove Elizabeth back to her hotel yesterday," he said quietly, "because I wanted to tell her that Michael wasn't truly missing, but was actually safe with Paul. She did invite me up to her room, but I didn't stay long, and she was fully clothed the entire time I was there."

"But what about your 'late night'?" I said. "What about the note I slipped under your door yesterday afternoon? Why didn't you get it until this morning?"

"After I left the Hilton, I drove here to see for myself that Michael was safe, and once I'd arrived, I found it hard to leave him. As a result, I spent most of the night here. I didn't return to my hotel until early this morning, and it was then I found your note." He tipped my chin up so I had to meet his gaze. "Now then, my jealous darling, have I set your mind at ease?"

Slowly, I nodded, though a part of me was still filled with doubt. I couldn't help remembering Elizabeth's possessive grip on his arm in Lieutenant Mavros's office.

"Christine, I recognize that look. What's wrong? Don't you believe me?"

"I do," I said, trying to sound like I meant it. "But if you weren't the man in Elizabeth's hotel room, who was?"

"How the devil should I know?" he snapped irritably. Too irritably? Despite his protestations of indifference, was he jealous of Elizabeth's mysterious visitor? "What does it matter?" he said. "It's no business of ours."

"Perhaps not," I said, "but I keep wondering how Spiro found out where Michael was hidden."

"You said yourself someone rang up the University asking for Paul's address. Skouras must have discovered Paul's real identity and guessed, as you did, that he had a house here on the island."

"Maybe, but how did he know Michael was with Paul in the first place, unless somebody told him?"

"Somebody meaning Elizabeth. Dammit, Christine! Do you really believe she'd conspire against her own son?"

"She does stand to inherit millions," I retorted, irritated by his vehemence. I was tempted to say more, but common sense reasserted itself. "Look, I don't think she'd do anything to purposely hurt Michael. I just think she might have told Spiro about Paul, mistakenly thinking it was safe to do so."

"How would she know Skouras?" Geoffrey demanded.

"Judging from his passport," I said, "he travels a lot. He might have met her on one of his trips. Also, he was pretty late returning from town yesterday and something Demetra said might make sense if Spiro and Elizabeth were involved with each other."

Geoffrey's hands clenched into fists, and I felt another pang of uncertainty. Was he being honest with me about his feelings for Elizabeth? For that matter, was he being honest with himself?

I opened my mouth to ask him point-blank that very question, but I never got the chance. Michael came bursting out into the hallway, white-faced.

Geoffrey's own face paled. "What's the matter?" he demanded anxiously. "Are you hurt?"

Michael shook his head. "It's Paul. I think he's fainted."

Twenty-Seven

Paul's Fiat was not a powerful car, but I pushed it to the max and managed to get us back to Corfu Town slightly before five. Struggling to get tickets for the five-fifteen ferry, I was grateful for my Greek. With it, I was able to elbow my way through the chattering crowd of tourists and push my way to the front of the line like a native.

The next hurdle was getting the car onto the ferry. Paul waited on the upper deck while I backed the car up the gangplank. Three impatient sailors yelled and gestured conflicting instructions at me as I attempted to wedge the Fiat into a ridiculously narrow crevice between a large, canvas-covered truck and the bulwark. By the time I'd parked it to their satisfaction, I had only moments to squeeze out the door and scramble across the deck before the next car came roaring up the gangplank.

Peering down at me from above, Paul flipped his thumb up and grinned. "Not bad for a woman." I was too anxious about his pale face and listing posture to retort.

When I joined him on the upper deck he was still on his feet, but his grip on the railing was so fierce his knuckles had gone white. "Don't you think we should sit down somewhere?" I asked, motioning to the numerous benches still empty.

"Yes," he agreed, flashing me a mischievous look. "I suppose it might cause problems if I fainted again and fell over onto someone's automobile."

Despite the quip, he sank down onto the shaded bench I led him to with a grimace of relief, and murmuring that he would have to make his apologies to Geoffrey, soon closed his eyes and fell asleep with his head and good shoulder cradled in my lap.

The crossing from Corfu to Igoumenitsa took nearly two hours. I spent the time staring out at the rippling sea, my worried thoughts teetering between concern for Paul and anxiety that Spiro might even then be sneaking up on Geoffrey and Michael in a surprise attack. Despite the gentle rocking of the ship and the soothing touch of the breeze, by the time we reached Igoumenitsa's harbor I was glad for the excuse to rouse Paul and start making my way down to the car; if I'd been forced to remain still much longer with those thoughts, I think I would have screamed.

Strangely, once I was in the car again, I regained my equanimity. So much so, that when a policeman suddenly called out something and motioned for us to stop as we were leaving the docks headed for the Ioannina road, I was able to pull over and inquire calmly in Greek, "Yes, officer, is something wrong?"

The policeman gave me a long, appraising look and then shifted his attention to Paul. "Did you know your left front tire is almost flat?" Paul assured him we'd see to it right away, and declined the policeman's offer of an escort to the nearest garage.

It was nearly nine when we finally turned, new tire and all, down a quiet Ioannina street and pulled to a stop before a modern two-story building which contained the offices and home of Paul's cousin, who, according to Paul, also happened to be one of the best doctors in all Greece.

Paul managed the steps under his own power, but his pallor was worsening, and his skin was beginning to feel warm to the touch. Impatiently I jabbed the small, buzzer-like doorbell, only afterwards noticing the plaque that served as a sign for the doctor cousin's clinic.

"My God, Paul! *She's an obstetrician!* What in the world is she going to know about treating a bullet wound?"

The door opened as I said these last words. A pretty, dark-haired woman glanced quickly from me to my companion. "A bullet wound? Paul? What's going on?"

"Marina, excuse the late visit, but I have need of a doctor."

"You've been shot?"

He nodded. "My left shoulder. The bullet passed through, but I've lost some blood and I think I'm beginning to run a fever."

"Come inside." She took him by the hand, taking his pulse as she led the way to an examination room. "Can you help him up onto the table while I get some things I need?" she asked as she disappeared down the hall. "And please cover him with one of the blankets you'll find folded on the chair in the corner."

I did as I was told, and by the time she returned, Paul was stretched out and covered. Without a wasted motion, she crossed to him with a pair of round-edged scissors and cut away his shirt and the not-so-clean bandage underneath. "How long has the wound been like this?" she demanded in a fierce whisper.

I looked across at Paul, but his eyes were closed. "I'm not sure. Eight or nine hours I think."

She muttered something under her breath and gave him an injection of local anesthetic. Paul's eyes fluttered open. "You doctors and your needles!" he grumbled, but his eyes slowly closed again, and when Marina began cleaning the wound he didn't flinch.

"I presume he's had no other medical attention?" she asked.

"No, I'm afraid not," I said apologetically.

"I don't suppose you'd care to tell me why that is, or what it is my cousin has been doing to get himself shot?"

I shook my head. "I'm sorry. I'm afraid I can't."

She shrugged. "No matter. He'll be with us for a few days. I'll get it out of him eventually." She began suturing the wound closed. "In the meantime, thank you for taking care of him and bringing him here to me."

"It was the least I could do. But I'm afraid I have to ask a favor in return. I've no car of my own, and I need to get back to Igoumenitsa before ten so I can catch the ferry back to Corfu."

"I'm afraid my husband won't be back until late, but I can drive you, if you don't mind waiting a few minutes more. I want to give Paul an injection against the tetanus and some antibiotics before putting him to bed."

"Do you realize," she said some fifteen minutes later as we transferred my luggage from Paul's car to hers, "that I don't even know your name?"

"It's Christine, Christine Stewart."

"And I am Marina Iliadis." She held out her hand. "It is nice to meet you.

"Nice to meet you, too," I said, "though I'm sorry it isn't under better circumstances."

She smiled. "Me, too. But don't worry. I think that cousin of mine, despite his idiocy, will be fine."

Later on, as we were making our way out of town, she glanced over and caught me looking at my watch. "You do not need to worry," she assured me. "My husband scolds me that I still think I am in the war, because I drive so quickly." She pressed the accelerator and sent the car flying down the highway. "You see? We will arrive at the ferry on time."

"You were in a war?" I asked in surprise.

She shrugged. "In a manner of speaking. When I was younger I spent two years in Bosnia working with a group of doctors who treated wounded civilians and refugees. We were often close to battles, and we became accustomed to driving crazily to avoid snipers."

I stared at her calm profile in admiration. "No wonder Paul felt so confident you'd be able to handle a bullet wound!"

"Yes, I've treated more than a few of those I'm afraid." She fell silent, lost in far-away thoughts, and I tried hard not to think about one particular sniper who had already struck twice—and missed his target. I prayed there would be no third try.

We arrived at the ferry in time, though only just, and Marina and I said quick goodbyes as I scrambled aboard, suitcases in hand, only a moment before the ferry's muttering engine roared to life and the shore began to drift away into the darkening night.

I slept badly that night. I dreamt of careening cars and menacing snipers and Geoffrey standing alone in a square keening Michael's name. It was a relief when I finally woke to the ringing of the telephone and the comforting pink light of dawn. I reached over shakily and lifted the receiver.

"Hello?"

"I'm glad you finally answered. I was ready to ring off."

"I was asleep. Do you have any idea what time it is?"

"Five-thirty," Geoffrey replied promptly, "and lest you complain, let me say that I've had a devil of a time waiting even this long to assure myself you're still in one piece. When I phoned last night, you hadn't yet arrived."

"It took longer than expected to get Paul settled with his cousin, but I think he's going to be all right."

"And you?"

"I'm okay. I have to go see Lieutenant Mavros this morning to discuss my disappearing act yesterday, but what can he do besides throw me in jail?"

"Christine!"

"Just kidding. Though there are two policemen sitting outside my door who look like they mean business. They were waiting for me when I got back last night, along with a rather curt note from the lieutenant. I suspect they have orders not to let me out of their sight."

"As it may be a few days before I can keep an eye on you myself, I'm pleased to hear it."

"Easy for you!" I grumbled. Then I had a disquieting thought. "You don't think this phone is tapped, do you?"

He laughed, and the sound was warm and rich and reassuring. "Sweetheart, this isn't the States! I doubt Mavros can even get a wiretap, let alone have one installed on such short notice."

I sighed with relief. "In that case, have you found someplace safe to stay?"

"Yes," he replied quietly.

"Don't worry. I don't expect you to tell me where."

"I think you're safer not knowing," he said.

"What if I need to get in touch with you for some reason?"

"Leave a message with George at the 'Bella Roma.' I'll check in with him from time to time to see if you've called. Have you a pencil?" he asked. "I'll give you the number." I wrote it down. Sounding reluctant, he said, "I'm afraid I'd best be going now, Christine. I don't wish to leave Michael alone too long."

"Give him a hug from me."

"I will. Goodbye."

"Goodbye." I imagined him lowering the receiver back into the cradle. "Geoffrey!"

"Yes?"

"You will be careful, won't you?"

I thought I heard him smiling. "Don't worry, my dear, you won't be rid of me that easily."

Kyria Andriatsis bustled in a little after eight to bring me breakfast and indulge her curiosity about the two policemen stationed in the hallway. "There is some kind of trouble, *koritsi?*"

I told her briefly about the attacks on Michael, the shot fired at me, and Helen's murder. Her grandmotherly heart was outraged. "This is terrible! The boy, he is safe now?" Reluctantly, I said I didn't know. I described how Michael had disappeared from the hospital two days before.

Her eyes widened in alarm. "You do not know where he is?"

I shook my head, trying to be convincing. "No, I don't. I wish I did."

"*Panagia*! Perhaps he is in the hands of this pig, this murderer!"

"No!" I exclaimed without thinking. "I mean, it's possible he just ran away on his own because he was frightened."

She nodded. "I pray that it is so!" she said, crossing herself. "And you, you are still in danger?"

I shrugged. "I shouldn't be. I've got two guards out there keeping an eye me."

"Don't worry. Today I will go to St. Spiridon and light a candle for you. St. Spiridon, he will watch. He will keep you safe." And with that reassurance she reached up and patted my cheek, then turned and walked out the door.

An hour later, fortified by her cooking and wearing a dress which showed off my bandaged arm and made me look (I hoped) quite pathetic, I set out to see Lieutenant Mavros.

As I stepped out of the hotel, someone called my name, and I turned to see Robert Humphreys striding toward me. Before he could get too close, however, my two bodyguards stepped forward to block his way.

"What the devil—"

"It's all right," I called to the two men. "He's a friend." The burlier of the two policemen, Officer Pappas, cast a dubious look at the tall Englishman and reluctantly moved aside. His companion, whose name was Koulos, slowly followed suit.

"Christine, what is all this?"

"Don't worry, they're policemen. They've been assigned to protect me and make sure I don't stray too far."

He nodded. "I see. Well, I'm glad to see Mavros has some sense. I've been worried sick about you since I heard about Helen's murder and the shooting the other night. I hurried to Ithaki when I learned the news, but Skouras wouldn't tell me anything, and I didn't know where you were. It's a relief to see you safe and sound, though I wish I could say the same about Michael."

I reached out and squeezed his arm, frustrated I was not free to relieve his mind about Michael's safety. "Did you have any luck with the orderly?" I asked, trying to change the subject.

He shook his head. "No, I learned nothing new. How about you and your policeman?"

Feeling a wave of guilt, I lied, "He wasn't any help either."

Robert cast a look back at my two police guards. "Are you sure you ought to be going out? My confidence in the lieutenant's ability to deal with this situation diminishes by the hour, and if you're in danger, I don't think those two are going to offer much protection." He cast a disparaging look at the men, dismissing their wrinkled clothes and unkempt hair with a frown.

"Actually, I don't really have a choice. I'm on my way to see the lieutenant now—at his request."

"Then I think I'll accompany you, if you don't mind."

"No, that would be great," I said, relieved. "I need all the moral support I can get."

Lieutenant Mavros was not pleased to see Robert at my side as we entered his office. For a moment I thought he was going to insist on grilling me alone, but apparently he wasn't anxious to alienate the well-to-do lawyer. He merely said coldly, "I am relieved, Miss Stewart, to find that you are not lying dead in a ditch somewhere, as I had begun to believe after you gave my man the slip yesterday and disappeared."

"Lieutenant," I said, all injured innocence, "I'm sorry if I worried you, but surely you don't think I intentionally eluded one of your officers?"

The blue eyes flashed. "Did you or did you not slip out of the Museum of Oriental Art to avoid the man I'd assigned to keep watch on you?"

"I did slip out of the museum, but not to avoid your man. I didn't know your man was there. How could I? You never told me I was going to be followed."

"Why, then, did you leave?"

"I wasn't feeling well. The shock of Helen's death affected me more than I realized. I started feeling a little dizzy, so I went outside to get some air."

"And afterwards?" he demanded angrily.

"Afterwards?" I repeated vaguely. "I don't know. I guess I wandered around a bit."

"Until midnight?"

"I had a lot on my mind. A lot to think about."

"And during these long hours of aimless wanderings, you carried your luggage with you?"

I hesitated. "Actually, I-uh stashed it."

"Where?"

"In the garden in back of the museum. Behind some bushes."

"You really expect me to believe this preposterous story?"

Robert suddenly interrupted. "How much time do you intend to waste on this, Lieutenant? I think Miss Stewart has given you a perfectly credible account of yesterday's events. Let's move on. In case you've forgotten, there's still the boy's disappearance to be resolved."

"I have not forgotten, Mr. Humphreys. It is merely that I have other matters which also must be dealt with. A murder, for instance, and possibly another disappearance." He turned back to me. "You don't look surprised, Miss Stewart. Perhaps you were already aware that Geoffrey Redfield is missing?"

I didn't answer. Robert exclaimed sharply, "What do you mean missing? Has something happened to him?

Mavros shrugged. "Who can say? He did not return to his hotel last night, no one has heard from him, and he was last seen in the company of Miss Stewart before she herself disappeared for eleven hours." He turned to me, "Perhaps he confided to you where he was going, or what he planned to do after he left you?"

I shook my head. "No, but he was worried about Michael. Perhaps he's out searching the island for him."

"Or perhaps," replied the policeman, "he knows exactly where the boy is."

Robert's voice was coldly precise. "Am I to understand, Lieutenant, that you are accusing Geoffrey Redfield of abducting his own nephew?"

The lieutenant's gaze never moved from my face. "At the moment, Mr. Humphreys, I am merely discussing possibilities."

"What about Helen?" I asked, anxious to change the subject. "Is there any progress in your investigation of her murder?"

His eyebrows rose, mocking my transparent maneuver. "Some." Our eyes locked, and we gazed at each other in silence.

Robert exclaimed impatiently, "Well, man? What have you found out?"

The lieutenant shrugged and shifted his attention to the lawyer. "After she left Ithaki Wednesday morning, Helen went to stay with a sister who lives here in town. The sister says that when Helen arrived she was upset and talked of leaving the island. Later, Helen went for a walk, and when she returned she seemed in better spirits. That evening she told her sister she would be leaving the island, but she would be leaving it a rich woman. The sister tried to ask questions, but Helen wouldn't answer them. Both women went to bed, and by the time the sister woke in the morning Helen was gone."

"What do you make of all that?" I asked.

"It's suggestive of several things," the lieutenant said.

Robert commented, "It sounds to me as if she was planning to blackmail someone."

"Perhaps," Mavros replied.

"Maybe while she was on that walk she saw or heard something incriminating," I said.

Mavros nodded. "It is possible. However, we are still left with this question: why did she leave Ithaki in the first place?"

"From what her sister's told you," I said, "it sounds as if she was afraid of something."

"Perhaps the news that Michael had disappeared unnerved her," Robert suggested.

"Or perhaps," I said, "the news that someone else had reappeared did."

Suddenly I had both men's attention. Mavros said sharply, "Would you care to be more specific, Miss Stewart?"

I met his gaze squarely. "Have you forgotten, Lieutenant? Helen ran away from Ithaki the very same morning Spiro Skouras came back to it."

TWENTY-EIGHT

"There's something I've forgotten to tell you," I told Robert as we were leaving the police station some twenty minutes later.

"I'd say there were several things," he replied in a low voice, "but I think we ought to postpone discussing them until we're out of earshot of your two watchdogs."

"It's nothing like that—" I began.

"Wait until we're in the car," he said, taking my arm and steering me toward his rented grey sedan.

As he helped me into the passenger seat, the two policemen made as if to climb into the back, but Robert put out a hand to stop them. "I think you fellows can find your own ride." Shrugging, the two policemen retreated to an old beat-up Citroen. Robert climbed in next to me and started up the car.

We pulled out and the Citroen followed. We hadn't gone far when Robert said, a hint of reproof in his voice, "Why didn't you tell me Michael is with Geoffrey—and safe?"

I hesitated for a moment, hating to deceive him, but it wasn't my secret to share. "I'm sorry, Robert, you've got it wrong. I don't know where Michael is."

He turned his head to look at me. "I suppose he took him to protect him? Didn't he realize what a foolish thing that was to do?" He paused to hit the brakes as a small car darted in front of us.

"But Robert, Geoffrey was there with the rest of us in the lieutenant's office the morning after Michael disappeared," I reminded him. "If he was the one to take Michael, would he have left him alone somewhere unprotected?"

This time Robert kept his eyes on the road. "A good argument as far as it goes, Christine, but you've omitted one key point. Geoffrey has disappeared. He could well be with Michael now."

His expression grew grave. "Christine, even Mavros, inept as he is, can put two and two together to get four. Geoffrey has to bring Michael back, and he has to do it quickly. If the boy can be persuaded to hold his tongue, it's possible Mavros will accept the story that he simply ran away."

"But if Michael returns to Ithaki, he'll be in danger from Spiro."

"And if he doesn't return, Geoffrey's in danger of being charged with abduction, even murder, and you're in danger of being charged as his accomplice. The boy would be relatively safe. Skouras, or whoever is behind these attacks, wouldn't dare try anything now—with all the uproar over Helen's murder."

I shook my head, unconvinced.

"Please, Christine. Someone has to approach this rationally. Geoffrey's too caught up in emotion to think things through. As long as Mavros has an excuse to believe Geoffrey guilty, he'll ignore any evidence that points to anyone else's guilt. The danger to Michael will only grow, and when Geoffrey is arrested, what protection will Michael have then?"

I didn't answer. There was no answer.

We drove in silence the few remaining blocks. When we finally pulled up in front of the Hotel Kerkyra, Robert made no move to get out. Instead, he turned to me and, taking my hands in his, gave me a look that was at once stern and beseeching. "Christine, I'm glad Michael is safe for now, but I have the unnerving feeling this whole situation is careening toward disaster. If you don't think you can persuade Geoffrey to bring the boy back, then tell me where he is so I can try to make him see reason."

I was tempted. I was sorely tempted. But I'd made a promise to Geoffrey, and I had to hope that he knew what he was doing. I said in a tone of finality, "I'm sorry, Robert. You may be right, Michael may be with Geoffrey, but I have no idea where they are."

"Very well, Christine," he said wearily, running a hand through his hair in a gesture that reminded me painfully of

Geoffrey. "I believe you. I had hoped I was right, for then at least Michael would be safe, but I can't believe Geoffrey would take the boy without confiding in you." He gave me a rueful look, then shook himself and straightened in his seat. "I shall have to see what I can do. Mavros is hopeless. I have connections on the island. Perhaps I can get another officer assigned to the case—an officer who will take the search for Michael more seriously."

He came around and opened my door, but appeared distracted and made no move to accompany me upstairs. I thanked him and let him go, and it was only later, when I was ensconced in my room and my two police guards were installed outside the door, that I remembered I'd never gotten around to telling him what I'd meant to tell him outside the police station: that Mrs. Baxter was in the hospital with a bullet in her chest intended for me. Feeling a pang of guilt, I decided to go visit her myself that afternoon.

The peeling paint was depressingly familiar, and Mrs. Baxter, wan and fragile-looking, didn't open her eyes when I entered the room. "Despite appearances, she is doing very well," a deep voice murmured in my ear. I turned to find a short, heavy-set man with graying hair and large brown eyes regarding me with a tired smile.

"You're her doctor?"

He nodded and held out his hand. "Dr. Kedros. She is still sleepy from the medicine we have given her for the pain, but you need not worry about her. Despite her small size, she has the constitution of an ox, and—as I told her friend this morning—I have every confidence she will make a complete recovery."

"Her friend?"

"The English gentleman. What was his name? It is like the English nursery rhyme—Humpties, Dumpties, something like this."

"Robert Humphreys?"

The doctor nodded. He was here yesterday and again this

morning." He paused, regarding me inquiringly. "Excuse me, you are a relative? Perhaps the lady's daughter?"

I shook my head, realizing my guilt had been for nothing. Apparently Lieutenant Mavros had already told Robert about Mrs. Baxter and the shooting. "No, just another friend I'm afraid. I don't think she has any family here at the moment. She's on vacation, you see."

"Ah, yes, Kyria Redfield thought that might be the case. That is too bad."

"Kyria Redfield?" I repeated, startled. "Demetra Redfield was here?"

The doctor shrugged. "I do not know her first name, but a very thoughtful, kind woman." I blinked. He gestured over to a small table by the window. "She brought those flowers there.

She said she didn't know Mrs. Baxter, but the poor woman deserved to have someone remember her in her misfortune." The doctor sighed. "I had hoped—well, a woman Mrs. Baxter's age, I thought she would not be travelling alone. Still, by tomorrow she will be more alert and able to appreciate these visits by her friends. You will come back then?"

Distractedly, I told him I would.

"Good. Now I'm afraid you must excuse me, for I must see to my other patients."

The rest of the day dragged interminably. I wanted to be out doing something, helping somehow to bring this whole miserable business to an end. Instead I paced around my hotel room—avoiding the balcony at the request of my guards—and waited for the telephone to ring.

Around eight-thirty it did. Heart racing, I ran to pick it up, but it was only Robert calling to invite me out to dinner. Sick of being cooped up in that room with my thoughts whirling endlessly, I said yes.

He arrived promptly at nine and waited politely in the hall while I rushed to change into something more appropriate for dining with a man in an exquisitely tailored dinner jacket than jeans and a top. When I opened the door to let him know I was ready, he was standing with his back to me talking with the two policemen, and for a moment he looked so much like Geoffrey had the night we'd first had dinner together that my heart skipped a beat. Then he turned and faced me and the illusion was gone.

"Ready?" he asked with a smile.

"Yes," I said, trying not to let my disappointment show.

"It will do you good to have a decent meal, I think," he said as we started downstairs. "Though I hope you're not frightened about going out?"

"To be honest, I'm getting rather stir-crazy, and in any case, I think we're safe enough with them around." I glanced back at the two well-armed policeman trotting along behind us.

His lips tightened in a slight but eloquent expression of disdain, but all he said was, "How does perfectly-cooked Chateaubriand sound to you?"

"It sounds delicious, but where on earth—"

He held out his arm. "Why don't I show you?"

The restaurant was small and quiet and the food was sort of a Hellenized French—and delicious. Robert avoided all mention of Michael's whereabouts and gallantly carried the brunt of the mealtime conversation, keeping me entertained with stories of his childhood and growing up with the Redfields.

"Not that I knew Geoffrey all that well, then," he commented after dinner, as we sat sipping brandy and listening to the distant murmur of the sea. "He was simply the quiet little boy who always tried to tag along after William and me. He didn't succeed often, however; William rarely had patience to play nursemaid."

"I know he's dead and I'm sorry, but I don't think I would have liked William much. He never seems to have thought of anyone but himself."

His eyebrows rose slightly. "No, I suppose he didn't. But then, truly successful people rarely do, do they?"

I wanted to contradict him, but then I thought of my father, and my arguments stuck in my throat.

"Perhaps," he continued, "it comes of always having things go one's way, of accumulating more than one's fair share of good fortune. After all, there's little need to consider the wishes of others when you can obtain anything you need or want by yourself." His mouth twisted into a slightly bitter smile. "That was certainly true for William. As a boy, everything came easily to him; as a man, everything he touched turned to gold."

And you envied him for it, didn't you? I thought, surprised.

Robert lifted his glass and swirled the amber Metaxa around and around, then downed it in a single gulp and rose to his feet. "Excuse me, Christine, but I think I'd best go speak with the proprietor about our friends' bill. The prices here are a bit steep if you're on a policeman's wage." He disappeared toward the front of the restaurant, past the two policeman who sat at a far table consuming thick slices of roast lamb, and as I watched his receding back I was once again struck by the superficial resemblance to Geoffrey. For some reason it bothered me, but I couldn't think why.

Robert was gone for a surprisingly long time. When he reappeared he stopped by the policemen's table and murmured something which made the two men smile and nod their heads gratefully. Returning to our table he said, "That's taken care of. No, don't get up. There's no hurry to leave. You haven't yet had dessert; the specialty of the house is hazelnut torte."

Half-an-hour later, sated with torte and more Metaxa brandy than I had meant to drink, I sank back into the cool leather seat of the car and gazed up at the star-filled sky, feeling detached and vaguely melancholy. Robert briefly conferred with my two police guards and then slid into the seat beside me and started up the engine, smoothly slipping it into gear. The car glided out onto the highway. My glance drifted to the side mirror and I watched the slightly skewed headlight beams of the policemen's Citroen flash to life and swivel about to follow us.

The Metaxa had made me drowsy. The car's lulling vibrations and the velvety darkness of the night finished the job, and after a few miles I began to drift off to sleep.

A sudden sound jarred me awake. "What was that?" I squawked, disoriented.

Robert replied calmly, "What was what?"

"I don't know. Something—some sound—it scared me."

He glanced at me sideways. "I'm afraid I didn't hear anything. We hit a bit of a bump back there. Perhaps that was it?"

"I don't know. I don't think so." My gaze flicked to the side mirror and I let out a small gasp. There was nothing behind us but blackness. "The Citroen! It's gone!"

He glanced up at the rearview mirror. "It's probably just hidden from view by a curve." For a moment the blackness continued, then a pair of headlights swiveled around a bend in the road and dutifully fell into line behind us. I could sense him relax. "See? There it is."

I turned to look, and with a sinking feeling said, "That's not it."

"What do you mean? Of course it is."

"The headlights aren't the same," I said. "Didn't you notice? The headlights on the Citroen were crooked. One veered off to the right."

"I think you must be mistaken."

"No, I'm not. Look, Robert, I think we should go back. What if something's happened to them?"

His expression turned grim. "Then I'd better get you safely back to town."

"But—"

"If they've had some sort of mishap," he said, "a puncture or some sort of mechanical trouble, then they're perfectly capable of dealing with it on their own. If, on the other hand, something more sinister has occurred, then the last thing I should do is drive you back there into a possible trap."

"But we can't just leave them!" I exclaimed. "If they've had an accident, they may be hurt!"

"We'll telephone Lieutenant Mavros when we reach town and notify him of what's happened."

I didn't argue further. Instead, I considered his suggestion that the policemen's disappearance might be a trap. Was he right? Was Spiro lurking somewhere out in the darkness waiting for us? Waiting for me? Waiting to dispose of me as he had Helen?

I shivered. Poor Helen. Had she really been fool enough to think she could blackmail a murderer? I shook my head, trying to erase the image which my imagination seemed determined to create in vivid detail: Helen, walking quickly along the path toward the cliff, in a hurry to reach that last fateful rendezvous....

Rendezvous.

How had I forgotten? Helen on another rendezvous, a rendezvous in a church with a tall, light-haired man who from the back I'd assumed was Geoffrey. But what if it hadn't been Geoffrey at all?

What if it had been someone else?

I cast a covert glance at the man sitting next to me. His hands rested lightly on the wheel, but his face was set, determined. Fighting down a sense of panic, I stared ahead, wishing I could remember how far we were from the junction with the road north to Corfu Town.

The two policemen who were to guard me were gone. I was alone in a car with a man who—what? Had perhaps met in secret with a woman who was later murdered? That hardly made him a killer. Why was I letting myself get so worked up? I was in no danger. We would reach the junction, and we would turn north, and soon I would be safely back in my hotel room with the door locked and the bed covers pulled up to my chin.

But what if we turned south instead, or west? What if we didn't head back to town at all? Would anyone know where I'd been taken, or even by whom? There were no police behind us now, and all Robert had to do was claim he'd dropped me safely off at my hotel....

It was an alarmingly convincing scenario, but it suffered one serious flaw. I was wrong about there being no police behind us.

Eerie blue light swirled and eddied against the windows, the dashboard, our clothes. I twisted around to see a police car, lights flashing, bearing down on us. Robert turned off onto the shoulder of the road, shutting down the engine with a fierce twist of the key. As we waited for the policeman to approach, I tried to read his expression, but it was inscrutable, like a sphinx.

The policeman was young and appeared slightly wary as he gestured for Robert to roll down his window. "Excuse me, sir, but the lady with you, her name is Stewart? Miss Christine Stewart?"

"It is," Robert replied cautiously.

"Then I must ask her to return immediately with me to

town."

"May I ask why?"

"Lieutenant Mavros wishes to speak with her about an important matter."

"And that matter is?"

The policeman hesitated, then apparently gave in to the tone of authority in Robert's voice. "All I have been told is that an arrest has been made and the lieutenant wishes to ask Miss Stewart a few questions."

Robert swore under his breath, but I sat there mute, unable to accept the fact that Geoffrey had somehow allowed himself to be caught. "Am I being arrested, too, then?" I finally asked numbly.

The policeman regarded me with dark, apologetic eyes. "I'm sorry, miss. I do not know."

Robert said, "In that case, Officer, I believe I'll follow you, in case Miss Stewart finds herself in need of a lawyer."

Twenty-Nine

When I was finally ushered into the lieutenant's office, he was sitting at his desk poring over some papers. He didn't say anything, or lift his head to acknowledge my presence; he merely continued to read. I made my way to a chair and sat down. When he finally looked up, his expression was anything but welcoming.

"Miss Stewart."

"Lieutenant."

"I know the hour is late, but that cannot be helped. As you have probably already been informed, I've been forced to make an arrest, and there is little time left before the *British* police arrive to take custody of their prisoner."

"The British police? I don't understand. I know Michael's English, but he was taken from the hospital here on Corfu. Doesn't that make it your jurisdiction?"

"You are under a misapprehension. The charge is not kidnapping, but murder."

Suddenly my throat felt tight. "But that's ridiculous! Lieutenant, please! You can't really believe he threw Helen over that cliff?"

"You surprise me, Miss Stewart. I had not expected such a spirited defense from you, of all people. However, it is not Helen's murder that he has been arrested for, but that of William Redfield, in England, slightly over two months ago."

I stared at him, stunned. "But that's impossible—"

His voice grew hard, his blue eyes openly hostile. "Apparently someone provided the British police with new and incriminating evidence in the case. It seems Spiro lied about being in England on the day of Redfield's death, and new inquiries have led to a witness who identifies him as the cyclist who reported Redfield's car over the cliff."

A shaky feeling of relief washed over me. "Wait a minute, Lieutenant! Are you telling me it's *Spiro* you've arrested?"

"Not by choice! My hand was forced."

"You don't think he's guilty? How does he explain being at the scene of the crime?"

"He admits staging the accident," Mavros said heavily, "but he maintains that he did not kill Redfield, that Redfield was already dead."

"And you believe that?"

"It's no longer a matter of what I believe," he replied stiffly. He rose and crossed to the window and looked out. "I told him you would be of no help."

"You mean Spiro asked that I be brought here?"

He turned to face me. "For some reason he believes you may be able to prove his innocence. I told him that I thought it unlikely you would help, even if you could, but he insisted, and he is my friend. Of course, if you are unwilling to see him, I cannot force you. I do think, however, that the person who provided this new evidence to the British police has a responsibility to see that it is not used to convict an innocent man."

Our eyes met and locked.

"All right," I said reluctantly, "you win. I'll see him."

The room was small and bare, its only furniture a wooden table and two worn-looking chairs. Spiro was standing near the window, his face striped by the shadows of heavy metal bars, and when he turned I was shocked by the change in him. The cool charm and arrogant confidence were gone. He had the desperate, panicked air of a man being dragged toward the edge of an abyss.

"Christine, you must help me!"

"Spiro, I'm sorry. I don't think there's anything I can do."

"But there is! You must tell Ari where Redfield is hiding the boy. The boy knows the truth, Christine. He was there that day;

I think he must have seen the real killer. The British police will not listen to me—I am a Greek, a foreigner, but they will listen to the boy. He is my only hope."

His words startled me. How had he learned that Michael was home the day his father was murdered, and why did he believe Michael's testimony would help him? "What makes you think Michael is with Geoffrey?"

He flashed me an angry look. "Why do you protect him? Do you truly think he has taken the boy to keep him safe? Don't you realize he has kidnapped the boy to prevent Michael from telling the truth about his father's death?"

"Michael doesn't know the truth about his father's death!" I exclaimed. "He thinks his father had an accident on a foggy road—an accident you've as good as admitted you staged!"

"You don't understand!" he exclaimed. "Redfield was already dead when I pushed the car over the cliff!"

"So you say. But all that proves, even if it's true, is that you killed him somewhere else and then staged the accident to cover up the fact."

"*No*! He was already dead when I found him! He was lying face-down on the floor of his study with a small, bloody dent in the back of his head. Surely the boy must have seen or heard something?"

Slowly I shook my head. "Why didn't you call the police? Why did you trundle his dead body into a car, drive it forty miles away, and send it over a cliff to hide his murder and make his death look like an accident?"

"I had no choice! There had been arguments, violent arguments in the past about money. I was in charge of Redfield's holdings here in Greece. Just before his death there had been some large losses, checks paid out to companies that turned out not to exist. Redfield blamed me for the losses, accused me of embezzling the money. The charge was false, but until I found the true thief, I had no way to prove my innocence. I came to England because he threatened me with prosecution if the money was not returned. I arrived at his home to find him dead, murdered."

His eyes met mine. "What was I to do, Christine? Telephone the police to come and arrest me? Do you think for a moment they would have listened to my claims of innocence—a 'wog' embezzler who also happened to be the dead man's brother-in-law? No, they would have done as Geoffrey Redfield urged them to do and sent me, and possibly my sister, to jail."

"So the money you've been so desperate to get your hands on," I said, "was to pay back the money that was embezzled?"

His eyes widened in surprise and then he nodded wearily. "After the funeral, I was informed I would be allowed three months to pay back the missing money."

"And if you didn't pay?"

"Criminal charges would be filed against me here in Greece." His mouth twisted into a bitter smile. "Fate has played quite a joke upon me, don't you think, Christine? Two days ago I thought all my troubles ended because I had finally managed to obtain the money I needed to avoid going to jail for stealing. Now I am on my way to a British prison for murder."

"That's what your mysterious business on the mainland was?"

He nodded distractedly. "Actually, I never left the island."

"So how did you get the thirty thousand pounds?"

"A friend and I reached a mutually satisfying arrangement."

I suddenly thought of the admiring banker's wife. "Aspasia?"

"Yes," he admitted. "She made me a generous loan."

"And you were with her the afternoon Michael almost drowned?"

He nodded. "Yes."

I remembered what Geoffrey had said about Panos Sminiotiou's jealous temper. No wonder Aspasia had been unwilling to come forward to give Spiro an alibi. Not only had Spiro spent several days and nights in her arms, she'd offered him a loan of thirty-thousand pounds to get him there.

"And the morning Helen was killed? What were you doing up and about so early?"

"I heard a strange noise and went out to investigate."

"Did you see anything?"

"No."

"Hear anything out of the way?"

He replied impatiently, "I thought I heard a car, but it was probably Redfield. I found him hiding in the shadows when I returned to your room. Christine, there is no time for this. Will you tell Ari where the boy is?"

"No."

"Why not?" he demanded. "Don't you believe me?"

I shook my head. "The problem is that I do."

"Then why won't you help me? Why won't you help to bring the boy out of hiding?"

"Because I can't. Don't you see, Spiro? If you're innocent, then Michael is still very much in danger."

When I returned to Lieutenant Mavros's office, the door was closed, and I could hear angry voices inside arguing in Greek.

"What could I do?" demanded the lieutenant. "Grammos himself gave the orders." His voice dropped, deepened. "Demetra, my darling, please understand—I had no choice!"

A voice I recognized as Demetra's replied bitterly, "You could have warned him, Ari! You could have warned *me*!"

"What good would that have done? He cannot run from this!"

"At least he might have had a chance!" she cried. "What chance has he now?"

"I will prove him innocent, I promise you! Even the thick-headed British accept there can only be one person behind all these attacks. Once I find Helen's killer, I will have found the real murderer of your husband as well, and the British will be forced to set Spiro free."

"I've already told you the identity of your killer: my brother-in-law, Geoffrey! But without the boy, you'll never be able to prove it. Can't you make that Stewart woman tell you where he is?"

"I've tried, your brother is trying now, but I cannot force her to speak." His voice softened. "Please, my sweet dove, I know you are frightened, but I promise you, I will make all well for you in the end."

The voices grew quiet. I moved off down the hallway, in the direction of the stairs, but before I could make good my escape, Robert appeared from around a corner.

"Christine! Is it true? Have they arrested Skouras for

William's murder?"

I nodded and gave him a brief outline of what had happened, including Spiro's admission that he'd staged the accident. When I finished, Robert looked thoughtful. "Well, at least now Geoffrey can bring Michael out of hiding. You are planning to ring him up and give him the news, aren't you?"

"No."

"In heaven's name, why not?" he demanded.

"Don't you remember? I haven't the faintest idea where he is." I moved past him and started down the stairs.

"Wait, Christine! Let me drive you back to your hotel."

"No thanks," I said, hurrying down the steps. "My two watchdogs are waiting downstairs to give me a ride."

"No, they're not, Christine. The polite young fellow who drove you in told me that Pappas and Koulos might be delayed some time as a recovery van was being sent out for their car. It seems you were right about their having an accident; apparently one of their tires burst. Not surprising when you think what miserable care these Greeks take of their cars." He drew even with me, slid an arm through mine, and flashed me a faint smile. "Since your escorts aren't available, I think I'd best see you safely home myself."

"You don't have to bother, really."

"Oh, it's no bother at all, I assure you."

So arm-in-arm we descended the rest of the stairs and crossed through the lobby. We were almost out the door when a man's voice called out behind us, "Kyrios Humphreys!"

It was Takis. "I'm sorry, sir, but Lieutenant Mavros wishes to speak a few minutes with you before you leave."

"I was just on my way to drive Miss Stewart home," Robert snapped. "Surely it can wait until I return?"

Takis shook his head slowly; I wondered if it was still sore from the blow he'd taken from Helen's murderer. "I'm sorry, sir, but he is a very busy man tonight and later there are many things he must do."

"Don't worry, Robert. I'll be fine on my own." I slipped my arm from his and gave him a little push toward Takis. "I'm sure whatever the lieutenant needs to talk to you about is more important than seeing me home. I can catch a cab."

For a moment, his hazel eyes glittered in irritation, then a look of cool resignation settled across his aristocratic features. "All right, Sergeant, I'm coming." He turned briefly to me. "Goodbye for now, Christine. I'll be in touch."

I nodded and without another look slipped out the door into the cool night. Down the street, a taxi was dropping off a fare. I waved, and it slid toward me. Clambering inside, I slammed the door shut, and only then did I breathe a deep sigh of relief.

Safely back in my room, I locked the door and dragged a small bureau in front of it, wondering what I was going to do in the morning if my police guards didn't show up. With Spiro's arrest, and my refusal to provide any information about Geoffrey's whereabouts, it was quite possible Lieutenant Mavros would decide I no longer merited protection. Too bad I suspected I was now in greater need of it than I'd ever been before.

I was dead tired, but somehow a nightgown made me feel too vulnerable, so I changed back into jeans and a tee shirt before climbing into bed and pulling the covers up over me like a cocoon.

But sleep was elusive. Charged up with fear and adrenaline, I couldn't throttle my exhausted brain back down out of overdrive. It kept jamming facts together like incompatible pieces of a jigsaw puzzle it was desperate to make fit.

I didn't manage to drift off to sleep until nearly four, so when the phone rang at six I wasn't in the best of moods. "Hello?" I growled into the receiver, keeping my eyes grimly shut against the sunlight flooding the room.

"Good morning," replied Geoffrey cheerfully.

Reluctantly I opened my eyes part-way. "Is waking me up going to become a habit with you?"

"Perhaps. Would you like it to?"

I felt the corners of my mouth curl up into a smile. "Not if it's going to be by telephone."

"Most decidedly not by telephone!" he exclaimed, laughing. Then his voice sobered. "Christine, I have some important news."

Oh, no, here it comes, I thought. "What kind of news?"

"Good news I think, though you may not see it that way.

I've just spoken with Inspector Haggerty in London. They've found a witness who identifies Skouras as the cyclist who reported William's accident. That, along with information that Skouras embezzled money from my brother's company, has convinced the police to arrest him and charge him with William's murder. Haggerty and another officer are flying down today to escort him back to England."

He paused, waiting for my reaction. Reluctantly I took a deep breath and said, "I know."

"You what?"

"Mavros arrested Spiro last night. Spiro asked to speak with me, and Mavros had me brought in. I was down at the police station until nearly midnight."

"And when were you planning to tell me about all this?" he demanded tensely.

I chewed on my lip and remained silent.

"You weren't going to, were you?"

"No," I said.

There was an angry intake of breath. "May I ask why not?"

"I was afraid if I told you Spiro was in jail, you'd think the danger was over and bring Michael back out into the open."

"And why not? The sooner he returns, the easier it will be to come up with a plausible explanation for his absence. You were the one telling me I couldn't keep him on the run forever."

"I was wrong, and you were right. Michael's safer hidden away."

"If Skouras is in jail, Michael's in no danger."

"*Yes, he is!* Geoffrey, please, listen to me. You can't bring him back! There's still someone trying to kill him!"

"Don't be ridiculous! Do you actually think there are two killers out there?"

"No, just one. But Spiro isn't it."

"For heaven's sake, Christine! The police are about to arrest him for my brother's murder!"

"He staged the accident, yes, but he says your brother was already dead when he found him at the house, and I believe him."

"Of course you do!" The angry words shot down the wire like sparks. "He didn't kill my brother, and he didn't kill Helen, and he hasn't tried on at least four occasions to kill my son, or on at least two occasions to kill you!"

"I know you don't believe me, I don't have any proof to make you believe me, but please, I've got such a strong feeling about this—"

"I think it's rather obvious what you have a strong feeling about, Christine, or rather whom."

"Don't be ridiculous!" I snapped angrily. "It's not Spiro I'm in love with!" I glared at the receiver, my cheeks burning as I realized what I'd admitted.

There was a prolonged silence and then Geoffrey said quietly, "I suppose I can keep Michael tucked away a few more days if it will make you feel better."

"Thank you."

"And what exactly are you planning to do while I'm hidden away unable to keep an eye on you?"

"Pray for inspiration, I suppose, and try to figure out a motive. So far all I've got is a hunch that doesn't seem to make any sense."

"The real killer is Skouras," he insisted. "That's the only reason I'm agreeing to any of this."

"I almost wish you were right. It would make everything much simpler."

"Are those two policemen still keeping an eye on you?" he asked, his tone uneasy.

Were they? I didn't know, but I told him they were.

"Christine—"

"Don't worry," I said. "I have it on good authority that Saint Spiridon, himself, will be watching out for me."

"I don't suppose you could have picked a saint with a different name?"

"Tsk, tsk! If a Corfiote heard you say such a thing, he'd throw you into the sea. Anyway, Saint Spiridon's got a fair number of miracles under his belt; I think he can handle keeping one poor tourist safe."

"Christine! You almost have me changing my mind."

"No, please. I'll be fine."

"Well, if you need anything or have to get in touch with me, call George. You still have the number, don't you?"

I assured him I did, and we said our goodbyes. When I heard the receiver click and the line go dead, I sat there for a moment regretting the severed connection like a withdrawn touch. I felt, suddenly, very tired and alone.

Turning, I pressed my face against the cool softness of my pillow. Before I knew it, I'd fallen back to sleep.

THIRTY

It was an extremely vivid dream.

I was being chased by Mrs. Baxter through Corfu's twisting streets and alleyways. I fled because she had a gun, but she kept calling to me to come back because she had something important to tell me. I almost got away, but then a policeman stepped into my path and I tripped and fell.

"Why didn't you listen to me!" Mrs. Baxter cried out, as she tottered to a stop above me. "Didn't I tell you to stay away from married men?" She lifted her gun, pointed it down at me, and fired, but the bullet turned into a wedding ring which flew onto my finger.

"*Koritsi, koritsi*, wake up!"

I opened my eyes to find Kyria Andriatsis gazing down at me with a worried frown. "I am sorry to wake you like this, but I think you must come with me."

I gazed past her toward the door and the bureau, which had been pushed back into the room. "How did you get in?"

She shrugged impatiently. "My grandson, Yiannis, moved it out of the way. Please, I think you must come now."

"I don't understand. What's wrong?"

"The key, the master key for all the rooms, is missing. Someone has taken it." I looked up; her raisin eyes were grave. "Your policemen have gone, but the danger, it is not finished I think, eh?"

Slowly I shook my head. She nodded. "Then you must come with me downstairs. There is a room we keep only for the family. No one will know you are there."

With Yiannis's help, it didn't take long to move my things

downstairs, and after getting dressed I joined the large Andriatsis clan for morning coffee and toast made from sweet anise-flavored bread. They all seemed curious about me and the adventures that had landed me in their midst, but a single reprimand from *Yiayiá* was sufficient to silence their questions and limit their inquisitive looks to sidelong glances. Slowly they drifted out, and Kyria Andriatsis and I were left alone.

For a while we sipped our coffee in silence, then, as if reading my mind, she patted my hand and said calmly, "Don't fear, *koritsi*, Saint Spiridon will provide the answer."

I couldn't share her confidence that all would turn out well, but I smiled all the same. I was reminded of my own grandmother, who had always vowed any problem could be solved through prayer. My own faith in this maxim had fallen by the wayside during adolescence, when repeated requests for my father's return had gone unanswered, but I never quite lost my belief in my grandmother's powers to catch the Almighty's ear, in part because the answers she received in dreams, often proffered by some saint or other, always seemed to come true. I thought of my own dream about Mrs. Baxter, and couldn't help but grin imagining her as a bearer of divine inspiration.

Suddenly I spilled my coffee. Perhaps not a message from God, but from my own subconscious. "Kyria, may I use your telephone?"

She nodded. "Of course. Come this way."

It took a little time to find out the doctor's number, but once I'd dialed it, I was connected at once and put through to his office. He answered the phone impatiently, "*Embrós.*"

"Dr. Kedros, this is Christine Stewart. I met you yesterday when I came to visit a patient of yours, Mrs. Baxter."

"Ah, yes, I remember."

"How is she today?"

"Much better."

"Has she had any visitors today? Has anyone called up to ask how she is?"

"No visitors, but, yes, someone telephoned earlier to ask whether she was capable of speaking yet or not."

I gripped the receiver more tightly. "Doctor, I know you don't know me, and there's no time for me to explain, but I think it's possible that whoever shot Mrs. Baxter in the first place may try to finish the job. Would it be possible for you to have someone stay with her, or better yet, move her to another part of the hospital without anyone knowing?"

"I don't understand! I was informed by the police that Mrs. Baxter was injured by mistake, that her attacker was aiming at another woman."

"That's what we thought, but we were wrong. She was the real target all along, and she's still in danger."

"Why aren't you telling this to the police instead of to me?"

"I don't have any proof yet. I'm on my way to get some now, but it's going to take time, and I'm afraid there might not be much time left. Please, Doctor, what will it hurt to do as I say? If I'm wrong, no one's hurt, but if I'm right, you may be saving your patient's life!"

"I don't know...."

"Please!"

"Oh, all right, but I will expect you in my office this afternoon to explain all of this. Am I understood, young lady?"

"Yes, thank you, Dr. Kedros. Thank you very much!"

After hanging up with the doctor, I debated phoning Mavros, but decided that as long as Mrs. Baxter was safe, it would be better to approach the lieutenant when I actually had some facts to lay before him and not just a hunch based on a dream.

I told Kyria Andriatsis that I was going out, and she insisted that Yiannis drive me. I didn't complain. Since I no longer seemed to have my police guards, a young man built like an NFL linebacker might come in very handy.

It was early, and Kanoni was clogged with tour buses loading up passengers from various hotels for day tours of the island. Small, noisy mopeds darted between the diesel-belching behemoths, and cars like ours squeezed by on the narrow roads as best they could. In the distance, the roar of jets could be heard as they landed and took off from Corfu's airport, and nearby, the strains of a Greek rap song, saturated with Euro-pop bounciness and incongruously highlighted by electric bouzoukia, twittered through the air like the song of some strange bird.

When we turned up the Hilton's curved drive, however, everything suddenly seemed hushed. *It's just the trees,* I told myself, as a wave of uneasiness passed over me. They muffle sound. Nervously, I rubbed my arm. *We're on the other side of the peninsula from the airport, too, so of course it would seem less noisy.*

Apparently, I said this last out loud, for Yiannis smiled and said jokingly, "The rich can afford anything, even quiet."

The Hilton's lobby was full of people, and I scanned it nervously as we made our way to the elevators, but I saw no one I recognized. Of course, the real danger, if there was any, awaited me upstairs—in Room 512.

"Do you wish me to accompany you?" Yiannis asked as the elevator doors opened.

I shook my head. "No, I think I'm going to have to make this visit alone. But do you mind waiting for me here in the lobby? I shouldn't be too long."

"I'm in no hurry," he assured me.

She was fully dressed this time, in a rose-colored blouse and a short, cream skirt that showed off her tawny legs to perfection. She opened the door and stared at me blankly, apparently unaware she had ever seen me before. I introduced myself, and my name finally sent a flicker of recognition across her face.

Her golden eyes regarded me with hostility. "Ah, the little heroine who saved my son. To what do I owe the pleasure?"

"I thought it time you and I had a talk."

One carefully-shaped eyebrow rose in disdain. "I don't really see that there's much for us to discuss. If you expect me to fawn over you for your rescue of my son, you're in for a disappointment. I don't share Geoffrey's high opinion of you and your actions; as far as I'm concerned, my son nearly drowned because of your negligence."

"Actually," I said, "I'm here to talk about you, not me."

Thin, wary lines formed around her mouth. "I really have no desire to chat, so if you'll excuse me—"

I reached out and seized her left hand to prevent her from closing the door. "Sorry, afraid I can't. You see,"—I opened my hand and gently tapped her fourth finger—"I have a question to ask, and I'm going to insist on an answer."

She fell back a step, looking uneasy. "What question?"

I took a deep breath and stepped forward into the room. "Why have you been keeping your new marriage a secret, Mrs. Humphreys?"

She retreated back into the large suite, crossing to a table and picking up a slim, white cigarette and lighter. She lit the cigarette with hands that shook. "I suppose you've told Geoffrey?"

"No, not yet. I only figured it out myself this morning."

"And how did you do that, if I may ask?"

"It came to me in a dream."

"A *dream*?" she repeated scornfully. "Oh, that's right. I'd forgotten. You're from California, aren't you?"

I shrugged. "The subconscious is sometimes good at putting pieces together that don't at first fit. Like your knuckle."

"My knuckle?" she echoed disdainfully.

I nodded. "The knuckle on your finger—your left ring finger. I noticed it three days ago in Lieutenant Mavros's office. It was red and swollen. At first I thought maybe you'd been fighting."

Her mouth twisted at the suggestion.

"Then I remembered what a time my mother had taking off her wedding ring after she and my father divorced. She, like you, has a tendency toward large knuckles, and she really had to worry at the ring to get it off her finger. When she was done, her knuckle was red and swollen—just like yours looked the other day."

Elizabeth took several nervous drags on her cigarette. Was disdain beginning to erode into worry? "I assume there's more?" she said tensely.

I nodded. "It's been over three years since you and Jesse Conner divorced. You aren't the type of woman to keep wearing an ex-husband's ring, so I figured that meant you'd married again. But who? And why did you want to keep the marriage a secret?"

"Why don't you tell me?" she said.

"I briefly considered Spiro Skouras might be the lucky man, but Spiro doesn't seem the marrying type, and besides Greek brides wear their wedding bands on their right ring fingers, not their left.

"Then, thanks to Mrs. Baxter, it occurred to me that Robert might be a possibility." Elizabeth gazed at me blankly. "The lady who attached herself to you and Robert on your honeymoon," I prompted.

A flicker of recognition passed over her face, followed by a faint grimace of distaste.

"She's here on Corfu," I continued, "and through her I learned Robert recently married. I also learned Robert's honeymoon took place near Nice, which is close to Monaco, where you went to live after your divorce from Jesse Conner."

Elizabeth shrugged. "That's hardly proof. Besides, if I were married to Robert, why would I want to hide the fact?"

"I don't know," I admitted. "That's what I came here to find out. It could be that Geoffrey showed up on your doorstep and you didn't want him to know you weren't available.…" I paused, and our eyes met. She looked away. "Or it could be," I continued, "that you wanted to hide your connection to Robert, since you'll inherit the Redfield millions if Michael dies—"

A flicker of fear crossed her face. "Are you insinuating that I'm responsible for these attacks on my son?"

I shrugged. "Actually, it's your husband I suspect. He has almost as strong a motive as you do. Of course, the two of you could be in it together." Her fists clenched. I decided it was time for a provident lie. "By the way, I should warn you. I haven't told Geoffrey about this yet, but I have told the police."

Her face went white. "The police? But I don't know anything about these attacks on Michael! I'm as much a victim of all this as he is! Besides, he's safe enough! Geoffrey assured me that he was!" Her voice was climbing higher and higher. She stood there, poised on the edge of panic, then suddenly she pulled herself together. She drew herself up and her eyes narrowed belligerently.

"Of course," she said more slowly, "you have no real proof of any of this, do you? A few coincidences, perhaps, but nothing more. I'm sure if pressed I could come up with an equally compelling story for the police: the story of a jealous young woman willing to tell any lie in an attempt to win the man she's infatuated with from the woman he loves."

I regarded her steadily. "Geoffrey will believe me."

"Will he?" she countered. "I don't think so. He's still in love with me, you see, and is bound to take my word over yours." Her beautiful face assumed a look of smug calm. "In fact, after this mess is cleared up, I plan to obtain a very discreet divorce from Robert so Geoffrey and I can be married."

I stared at her, a sudden hollow feeling in my stomach. "What if he doesn't want to marry you?"

She flashed me a scornful look. "Don't overestimate your charms, my dear. Geoffrey and I have a history. In fact, I'm the mother of his son. Michael is his, you see, not William's."

I forced myself to look directly into those golden eyes. "I know."

She blinked in surprise, but continued on. "In any case, I don't need to wonder what Geoffrey will do. He's already asked me to marry him, and I've already agreed."

It was a knockout blow, but I was still standing, and I still had a warning to impart. "If something happens to Michael, you may not be around long enough to marry anyone."

She paled. "What are you talking about?"

"Hasn't it occurred to you that Robert may want more than half of Michael's inheritance?"

Her eyes widened. "Robert would never hurt me. Besides, nothing will happen to Michael. He's safe with Geoffrey's professor friend, Paul."

"Not anymore," I said.

"What do you mean?"

"Did you tell Robert who Michael was with?"

"What does it matter if I did?"

"Did you tell him Paul was a professor at Ionian University?"

"Why are you asking me these questions?" she demanded, her voice rising once more. "Has something happened? Tell me! I have a right to know."

"Someone drove out to Paul's house day before yesterday and took a shot at Michael through the window. Paul had a rifle within reach and fired back, and the attacker fled. Now whoever shot at them knew Michael was with Paul and knew Paul's real identity; he found the house by phoning the University. So let me repeat my question. Did you tell Robert who Paul really was?"

Her face was ashen. "What if I did? It wasn't Robert who fired that shot! It must have been that Greek they've arrested for William's murder!"

"Perhaps, but where was Robert the day before yesterday, say between twelve and three?"

Something flickered in her eyes and she ran her tongue nervously across her lips. Her answer, however, was interrupted by the telephone. Its loud, pealing ring startled us both. She crossed to the table to answer it.

"Hello? Oh, it's you." Her voice dropped and she turned her back to me. "We've got to talk. Can you come by? What? Yes, I know. She's here now. You have? I see. All right, I will."

She lowered the receiver and then turned to face me. "I don't care to continue this conversation. Please leave."

"Was that Robert? Did he tell you to get rid of me?"

"No more questions. I just want you to go. Now."

"Your ex-husband was murdered and your son may be next. Doesn't that matter to you?"

She replied tensely, "Do I have to send for someone from the hotel to escort you out?"

"No, I'm going." I crossed to the door and opened it, then turned. "You don't seem to care one way or the other, but Michael is okay. He wasn't hurt, though Paul took a bullet to the shoulder. And Mrs. Baxter is expected to pull through."

"Mrs. Baxter?" she exclaimed. "What happened to her?"

"Didn't you know? Someone took a shot at her Wednesday night and almost killed her."

The golden eyes widened.

"At first, there didn't seem to be a motive for the attack on her, but I can think of one now, can't you? She not only knows Robert is married, she can identify you as his wife."

Elizabeth shook her head, looking dazed. "It has to be a coincidence."

"Coincidence? She was shot the very day you arrived on Corfu."

She shook her head again and turned away. "Get out," she commanded hoarsely.

I did as she asked and headed downstairs to look for a phone. Fortunately, this was the Hilton, and finding one wasn't hard. Standing in front of the grey box, I dug out a piece of paper from my wallet and dialed the number scribbled on it, hoping desperately that Geoffrey himself might answer. But when the beeps stopped and a voice came on the line, it was only George.

"Christine?" His normally bouncy voice sounded anxious. "What's up?"

"Sorry to bother you, George, but Geoffrey told me that if I needed to get in touch with him, I should phone you."

"That's right. He's been checking in every hour. You in trouble?"

"No, but I need to talk to him as soon as possible."

"Sure thing. I'll tell him as soon as he calls. Does he know where to reach you?"

"He can call me at my hotel," I said.

"You want me to give him a message?"

I stared down at the phone grimly. "Sure. Tell him I know who's after Michael and why." I bit my lip and added, "Oh, and congratulate him on his engagement."

George whistled. "So that's the way the wind blows, eh? Well, I can't say I'm all that surprised." He chuckled. "I mean, it's pretty obvious he has it bad. Fact is, I haven't seen him mooning around like this since—"

I interrupted. "Sorry, George, but I've really got to go."

"Sure, don't worry. I'll give him your message."

"Thank you."

"Anytime."

I slammed down the receiver and stared at the grey phone, which had grown oddly blurry. I swiped at my eyes, angry that once again I'd played the fool. So much for Geoffrey's assurances. Even George had realized Geoffrey was still in love with Elizabeth. *It's pretty obvious he has it bad.*

I swiped at my eyes again, then put another coin in the telephone. Feeling sorry for myself would have to wait. It was time to lay my cards on the table for Lieutenant Mavros.

"Miss Stewart."

The voice startled me. I dropped the receiver back into the

cradle and spun round to find Demetra Redfield staring at me with angry, belligerent eyes. "What are you doing here?" I asked, more from curiosity than fear. After all, she wasn't the killer; Robert was.

"I followed you from your hotel."

Despite the ominous answer, I was too thickheaded to realize the danger. "But why?" I asked naively.

"My brother has been arrested for a murder he didn't commit."

"I know."

"And you will not tell the police where Geoffrey hides the boy."

"I can't," I told her. "I don't know."

Her small mouth tightened. "I think you do, but if you will not reveal the boy's whereabouts voluntarily, then I must force you." She pushed back a sweater draped over her right hand to reveal a small shiny revolver pointed directly at me. "Now, if you please, you will come with me." She shifted the sweater further back and pressed the gun against my side. "Do not cry out. I am experienced with guns and know very well how to use one. I will not hesitate to shoot you." She jabbed me once in the ribs for emphasis. "Now, we go—this way!"

I could see the back of Yiannis's head as he sat waiting for me at the far end of the lobby, but he might have been on the other side of Kanoni for all the good it did me. Demetra herded me in the opposite direction, and we turned down an almost deserted corridor and then ducked out a door marked "Fire Exit Only." Despite the sign, no alarm bell sounded, and as we emerged outside in back of the hotel, I had little hope anyone had noticed us.

"This isn't the way to help your brother," I said as she pushed me toward a small service parking lot where several cars were parked, including the Fiat. "How is kidnapping me going to help Spiro?"

Once again I received a jab in the ribs. "Keep going!"

"No."

"Do you wish me to shoot you?"

"I'm no use to you dead! Look, you say you want to help your brother; well, I want to help him, too, and unlike Michael

I actually can. I know who the real murderer is, and—"

"Quiet!" she commanded tensely. "You know nothing! You are a lovesick fool!"

Suddenly her gaze shifted from me to something behind me, but before I could turn to look, I was seized from behind and a cloth that smelled sickly-sweet was pressed against my nose and mouth.

A few moments later everything went black.

THIRTY-ONE

I woke in a darkened room feeling disoriented and sick.

The room seemed vaguely familiar. After a few minutes I realized why. It was Spiro's bedroom at Ithaki, and I was lying on his bed with my arms twisted up behind my back and my hands tied tightly together at the wrists. I kicked my legs weakly and discovered they, too, were tied together and useless for escape. Only my mouth was free, and for a moment I considered calling out for help, but before I could gather the strength, a wave of nausea overtook me and left me retching miserably into the covers.

The door opened and I heard the click-clack of high heels crossing the floor towards me. Eyes closed in misery, I finished what I was about and collapsed feebly back onto the unsoiled portion of the bed, barely noticing that the footsteps had stopped and that someone was swearing softly under her breath.

She retreated to the bathroom, and I heard her turn the tap on full force, then turn it abruptly off. Her heels click-clacked back across the room, and then I felt a cold, wet towel being wiped across my face, my mouth, my lips. It felt wonderful. I opened my eyes. Demetra was bent over me, looking down at me with a mixture of distaste and concern. "Is that better?" she asked.

I nodded.

Her mouth tightened. "Do you feel you will be sick again?"

"No," I said weakly, "I don't think so."

"Then I will help you to that chair so I may clean the bed."

It was easier said than done. Trussed-up like a chicken and weak from my bout of nausea, it required considerable hopping and wriggling on my part, and heaving and lifting on Demetra's, to get me settled into the blue armchair at the far end of the room. While Demetra went grimly about the task of stripping the bed, I struggled to get enough breath back to speak.

"I'll make you a deal," I finally said in a voice too drained to carry authority. "If you let me go now, I won't press charges."

Demetra looked up from tying the soiled sheets into a bundle. "You are in no position to bargain. Where is the boy?"

"I don't know."

"You're lying. I overheard you leave a message for Geoffrey with a man named George."

I swallowed hard. Why hadn't I been more careful? "You're right," I admitted, "but that just proves what I've been saying. I had to leave a message, because I have no idea where they are." Demetra didn't seem to be listening. "Look, Michael's not the answer to your problem, I am," I insisted. "I know who really killed your husband and why. I know the reason for Helen's murder, and for the attack on Mrs. Baxter, and why someone's been trying so hard to kill Michael. It's all about money, you see. Your husband's money and who inherits it if Michael dies."

She finally turned to look at me. "So, you admit it then? You admit it was Geoffrey who killed my husband?"

"No, not Geoffrey! Elizabeth is the one who would inherit if Michael dies."

"You expect me to believe that that *tsoula* murdered William?"

"Not her, her husband."

"Husband? She has no husband. She is a widow like me." There was a note of satisfaction in her voice as she said it.

"She recently remarried."

Demetra's eyes narrowed. "Who?"

I was about to answer, when the door opened and someone walked into the room. I turned my head to see who it was.

"Well, Christine, I see you've finally returned to the land of the living," said Robert Humphreys in a voice that set the hairs on the back of my neck on end.

"Demetra, why didn't you inform me our guest was awake?"

She regarded him with a frown and snapped, "She was sick all over the bed. I had to clean up the mess myself, since you made me send Maria and Aphrodite away. Anyway, I begin to think we have made a mistake. She claims the boy knows nothing. She says Geoffrey did not kill my husband, but that she knows who did and can prove my brother's innocence herself."

His gaze flicked sharply in my direction. "Does she? I can't say that I'm surprised. Poor girl. She's so besotted with Geoffrey she'll do anything to prevent his being brought to justice. But it's not just a matter of your brother's innocence, I'm afraid, but the boy's safety. Michael is the only one who can put the noose around Geoffrey's neck, and sooner or later he's going to succumb to the temptation to silence him forever."

"That's a lie!" I cried. "Geoffrey would never hurt Michael!"

He ignored me. "Demetra, we've gone over all this before. We have to get the boy back from Geoffrey, and trading the girl for him is the only chance we have."

"But what if she goes to the police? How will that help Spiro?"

"Go to the police? She's an accomplice to kidnapping. How can she go the police? No, this is the only way to ensure Michael's safety and see that justice is done. We must go forward with our plan. Unless, of course, you no longer care if your brother pays for Geoffrey's crime?"

She flushed angrily. "Of course I care! I will do anything to see that my brother goes free!"

"Good, then that's settled. Look, why don't you let me see to the girl and make her a bit more comfortable while you dispose of that lot. She and I can chat a bit, and perhaps I can persuade her to be a bit more cooperative."

She flashed him an anxious look. "You will not hurt her?"

The hazel eyes blinked in well-acted surprise. "Goodness, no. I'm merely going to use some lawyerly persuasion. After all, she may be infatuated with Geoffrey, but she does care for the boy as well. I think I can make her see reason."

Demetra nodded reluctantly and, gathering up the bundle of sheets, left the room. When Robert turned from watching her go, his mask of affability was gone. His expression as he crossed to stand over me was coldly furious.

"You! Again and again you get in my way, ruin my plans, and nose your way in where you're not wanted. Well, your run of luck has just ended. I've one last chance to make this whole thing come right, and *by God* this time you're not going to muck it up!"

The thundering anger in his voice made my heart race, but it was the coldly determined look in his eyes that caused my breath to catch in my throat.

"This isn't going to do you any good," I said. "I told the lieutenant everything. He knows about you and Elizabeth. If anything happens to me, it will be obvious who's responsible."

He smiled derisively. "Nice try, Christine, but it won't wash. I checked with the police. You haven't spoken to Mavros since last night, and in any case, the good lieutenant is no longer in a position to act. The hints I've dropped in a few high places have had their effect. He's been taken off the case."

I felt a sinking feeling in my stomach. "You're going to kill me, aren't you?"

"You're an intelligent girl. What do you think?"

"What about Demetra? She's hardly going to stand by and let you do me in."

"Demetra hasn't a clue as to what's really going on, and by the time she figures it out, your demise will be a *fait accompli*. Oh, and I wouldn't try to enlighten her if I were you. If she stops cooperating, I'll simply have to kill you both."

"Don't expect me to cooperate. I'm not going to help you get your hands on Michael."

"Actually, I don't need your help. I already have what I need. Demetra made a note of it while she was watching you in the Hilton lobby."

I suddenly felt cold. "George's number?"

He nodded. "She's already rung once. She left a message for Geoffrey suggesting an exchange: you for the boy."

"*No!*"

He ignored my protest. "We're scheduled to ring back—" he consulted his watch, "— five minutes from now."

"Geoffrey will never agree to turn Michael over to you."

"I think he will. After all, he's grown attached to you, and I don't think he'll relish the thought of you coming to harm."

"He doesn't care about me that much," I countered. "Certainly not enough to risk Michael's safety. As it turns out, the person he's in love with is your wife. Perhaps you should have kidnapped her."

He shrugged. "Whether he's in love with you or merely feels responsible for your well-being, I think I can count on him to do as we ask. After all, he won't think the boy's in any real danger. Demetra will insist—quite convincingly I assure you—that she only wishes Michael's return so she can prove Spiro innocent. Geoffrey won't have any reason to suspect I'm involved. No one will. Demetra's proven quite useful that way."

We heard her approaching down the hall. "Now remember," he said, "one false word, and I'll be forced to kill you both."

Demetra entered the room to find Robert removing the rope from my ankles. "I think we can trust her to be cooperative now," he said, rubbing my ankles and feet in an effort to restore circulation to them. I hated the feel of his hands on me, and desperately wanted to kick him away, but Demetra's life was at stake as well as my own, and in any case, my only hope of warning Geoffrey was to convince Robert he could trust me to behave. At last he finished, and as he stood up to help me to my feet our eyes met. I realized I'd made the right choice. He'd been testing me, and for the moment, anyway, I'd passed.

"Demetra, I believe it's time to make our call. Why don't you use the telephone in the study, and I'll help Christine over to your brother's desk and pick up the extension in here."

She nodded uneasily and started back toward the door.

Noting her reluctance, Robert said, "I presume there's no need to remind you that our only hope of persuading Geoffrey to give up the boy is to convince him you're serious about carrying out your threats if he doesn't comply with your demands."

"Don't worry. I understand what it is that I must do."

"Good."

After she'd gone, he said to me, "Geoffrey will probably insist on speaking with you. If he asks any questions, limit your responses to either 'yes' or 'no.' Do you understand?"

I didn't answer. He seized my still-tied arms and pushed them up toward the ceiling until they felt as if they were going to pop out of their sockets.

"Do…you…understand?"

"Yes," I gasped, "I understand."

"Good." He let my arms drop and, pulling me against him, led me over to Spiro's desk. "Demetra," he said, picking up the phone, "go ahead and dial the number now." Apparently she did so. Robert was holding me so tightly against him I could hear the phone ringing and hear George answer tensely, "*Embrós?*"

Demetra spoke in English, presumably for Robert's benefit. "This is the woman who called before. Is Geoffrey there?"

"He's here. Hang on."

There was a muffled sound of a receiver being passed from one person to another and then Geoffrey came on the line. "Is she all right?" he demanded hoarsely in a voice I barely recognized. "Damn it, if you've hurt her—"

"She is fine," Demetra interrupted. "And she will remain so as long as you do that which I say."

"*Demetra!* You're behind all this?"

She replied angrily, "I will not allow my brother to be punished for a crime he did not commit! The boy knows who really killed his father. Bring him back so that he can tell the police the truth, and Miss Stewart will be freed."

He said thickly, "And if I don't?"

Did she hesitate? "If you don't, then I will be forced to carry out my threat."

"No! What do you gain by her death?"

Her voice shook, but her tone was implacable. "I will do what I must to save my brother, Geoffrey. Bring the boy to Ithaki within the hour, or I will throw her from the cliff as you threw Helen, do not doubt it."

"Wait! How do I know you even have her? Let me talk to her!"

"Very well. For a moment only."

Robert held the receiver up to my mouth and ear, but his hazel eyes held a clear warning and infinite menace. "Geoffrey?" I said warily.

"Christine! Are you all right?"

"Yes."

"Don't worry. I'm going to get you out of this."

"You can't."

Robert wrenched my arms up behind me until I cried out in pain.

"*Christine.*"

This was probably the only chance I'd have to warn him. Reminding myself not to use names, I yelled loudly in Greek, "The lawyer's behind this! He's married to the boy's mother!"

Robert slammed the receiver down, and then slapped me so hard I toppled backwards onto the floor. "What the bloody hell did you say to him?" he demanded furiously.

I didn't answer. Instead I lay on the floor desperately wondering how I was going to warn Demetra not to translate what I'd said. If she did, we were both as good as dead.

He pulled me up to my feet and slapped me again, hard. "What did you tell him?"

"Nothing!"

He grabbed my jaw in an iron grip. "Do I have to break this to get the truth out of you?"

"I'm telling you! All I said was—"

Demetra suddenly appeared in the doorway. For a moment our eyes met, then she looked away. "What she said was that Geoffrey should not do as I say, because I am not to be trusted."

He gave my jaw a painful squeeze. "Stupid, my dear. Very stupid." His hand dropped away and he turned to Demetra. "I presume you managed to convince him he had no choice in the matter?"

"Her cries of pain convinced him more than any of my words could," she said heavily. "He is coming."

"Good."

I stared down at the floor in despair. My warning hadn't worked. Geoffrey was going to deliver Michael into Robert's trap, and there was nothing I could do to stop him.

I looked up to find Demetra staring at my face in dismay. "Was it really necessary to hurt her so?" she demanded.

He gave a slight shrug. "It proved persuasive, didn't it?"

She flashed him a look of disgust. "I do not wish to continue with this. This is not what I intended."

Robert reached into the pocket of his jacket and pulled out a glove which he slipped onto his right hand. "I'm afraid it's a bit late in the day for second thoughts. Either you continue with your role as planned, or I will be forced to shoot her here and now." From another pocket he drew out a revolver that looked like the one Demetra had threatened me with at the hotel, and pointed it directly at me. "Of course, that will leave you the interesting task of explaining to the police what Christine's body is doing in your house shot with your gun bearing your finger-prints."

Demetra's face went white. "The gun is not even loaded."

"It is now."

"All right," she said unsteadily, "I will do as you say."

"Excellent. Well then, now that we all understand each other, I think it's time to move this party up to the cliffs, where I can keep an eye on any unwelcome comings and goings. Demetra, if you'll assist our troublesome little friend here?"

Demetra took my arm.

Robert motioned with the gun. "You two lead the way."

It was not a pleasant feeling to be back up on the cliff where Helen had met her death, especially in the company of the man who'd sent her to it, and I was almost relieved when he jabbed the gun into my back and said, "No, not here. Further up. Along that track. I need to be able to see." My hands were still tied behind my back, so Demetra fell back behind me and helped steady me as I climbed up the steep and pebble-strewn path. When we finally reached the top, we were on a large out-cropping of rock, with a view of the entire area for a least a mile in each direction. Still carrying the gun in his right hand, Robert reached into his pocket with his left and pulled out an extremely compact and expensive-looking pair of binoculars.

"You do come prepared, don't you?" I said.

He flashed me a brief glance before lifting the binoculars to his eyes and surveying the area. "I find it pays to do so."

I saw Demetra eyeing the loosely held gun. Perhaps if I threw myself against him, she could wrestle it away without get-ting one of us shot? It wasn't much of a chance, but what else did we have? I readied myself to make a charge, but before I could begin, he lowered the binoculars and moved away.

"I want you to return down there and wait near the bottom of the drive," he told Demetra. "When Geoffrey arrives with the boy, lead them both up here for the exchange."

"Do I have a choice?" she replied bitterly.

"No. And lest you get any ideas about trying to warn Geoffrey or ring the police, I'll be watching you the entire time. If you take one false step or go within a hundred feet of the house, I'll be forced to toss our friend here off the edge of this very high rock and leave you to make the requisite explanations to Geoffrey and the authorities."

"Enough of your threats," she snapped. "I understand."

"Then you'd better get going."

She disappeared down the path, amidst the sound of crunching dirt and cascading pebbles, like a lifeline slipping just out of reach.

"Well, what now?" I said.

"Now?" he echoed. He crossed to me and suddenly, without warning, knocked my feet out from under me so that I fell face down into the dirt.

"Now," he said grimly, "we wait."

THIRTY-TWO

The next hour seemed interminable. Minutes crept by in slow motion, and imagined scenarios of what was to come kept running through my mind like replays of a nightmare. Finally, as Robert glanced impatiently down at his Rolex for the hundredth time, I broke the silence of our tense vigil.

"Look, I can't stand this anymore! My mouth is full of dirt, my arms and legs have gone to sleep, and any moment Geoffrey and Michael are going to come down that driveway and be lured up here so you can kill them. Why shouldn't I just roll myself over the edge now and be done with it?"

He heaved me up into a sitting position and said impatiently, "There! Stop your complaining."

"You haven't answered my question. You're going to kill me anyway, so presumably I have nothing to lose; why shouldn't I just go out with a bang now? At least then you can't use me as bait."

"You'll behave yourself, because while you live there's still the slim chance you may be able to save your friends."

He was right, of course. While there was life, there was hope, and I couldn't give up until all hope was gone. I bent down and rubbed my mouth against the side of my pants in an attempt to wipe some of the dirt away. Then I said, "It must have been hard growing up with him right next door."

Robert's eyes narrowed warily. "Who?"

"William, of course. The golden boy who went on to rule his own financial empire. He must have been a tough act to follow."

For a moment, Robert was silent. Then he said in a low,

thick voice, "To the contrary. He was nothing but a bourgeois upstart, a nouveau riche jackanapes with neither breeding nor culture, only the uncanny knack of making money grow."

"And I suppose it galled you to see him grow so rich," I said. "To have him throw his patronage to you like a bone. To be at his beck and call like any other employee."

His hands—the one still gloved, the other not—clenched and unclenched at his sides. "I was his best friend, and he treated me like a servant, like an errand boy subject to his slightest whim. Me! The son of an earl whose family traces its line back to the Conqueror himself!" His voice shook. "I didn't envy him—I hated him, and I dreamed of someday stripping him of his riches. Then one day the means fell right into my lap."

"Elizabeth?"

He nodded slowly. "I was vacationing in Monte Carlo and met her at a party. At first I was simply flabbergasted to learn she was alive, then I started thinking: if anything happened to William, Michael would inherit most of his fortune, but if anything then happened to Michael, this woman, this beautiful and desirable woman, would inherit all the money I wanted to be mine. And if I were her husband, half of it would be mine."

"So you planned to murder William even then?"

His eyebrows lifted a fraction. "It wasn't as definite as that. I merely played with the notion that he might encounter some unfortunate accident. But then Elizabeth responded favorably to my wooing and we married, and I began to imagine ways of hurrying William's bad fortune along."

"And Michael?"

"There was little hurry where he was concerned. Once he inherited from William, there was time to let nature take its course. After all, teenage boys are notoriously accident-prone, and there was no danger of Michael drawing up a will of his own until he turned eighteen."

"Then what changed your plan?" I asked.

His mouth tightened bitterly. "A damn test showing the little bastard wasn't William's son after all."

My breath caught. "Of course! William called your office that afternoon wanting to change his will. You claimed you never called him back, but you did, didn't you?"

Robert nodded. "He was enraged and impossible to reason with. He insisted I come at once to his house to draw up a new will disinheriting Michael and Geoffrey both."

"But you couldn't let him do that, could you?" I said. "If he disinherited Michael, you'd lose your chance to get your hands on his money. So you went to his house and bashed his head in."

His chin went up. "I didn't go there planning to kill him, but he wouldn't hear reason, so I grabbed what was nearest to hand and did what had to be done."

His matter-of-fact tone set my stomach churning. "I suppose you meant for Spiro to be blamed for his murder?"

"I knew William had summoned Skouras to discuss funds that had been embezzled from one of the Greek operations. I thought the police would find that an interesting motive."

"But Spiro threw you a loop, didn't he?" I said. "You must have been quite shaken to learn the man you'd left dead in his study had driven off a cliff."

Robert shrugged. "It worked out for the best in the end. There was still the problem of Michael to be dealt with. I had to get him away from Geoffrey, and quickly, before the fool made discovered that Michael was his son, not William's."

It was tempting to tell Robert that he was too late, that Geoffrey already knew, but I didn't want to give him a reason to add Geoffrey to his hit list. Instead, I said, "So you're the one who convinced Demetra to bring Michael to Corfu?"

"It wasn't difficult. I had only to point out how much she would lose financially if Geoffrey wrested custody from her and encourage her already strong belief that William would have wanted her, not Geoffrey, to raise the boy. I suggested it would be harder for him to gain custody of Michael if she and the boy left England for a while. I suspected she would opt for Greece. I had to arrange an accident for Michael, and I thought this an excellent venue in which to accomplish the task undetected."

He was like a general detailing a military campaign. "I suppose Helen was your source of information at the villa?"

He frowned. "Yes, she was useful for a time, but then she found out you'd seen us together at the church and panicked. I tried to buy her off cheaply, but she was a greedy woman, and when I mistakenly indicated an interest in an appointment card she'd found in one of Demetra's purses, she tried to blackmail an outrageous sum of money out of me for it."

"So that's what she came back to Ithaki for. Only you never intended to pay her, did you?"

"Do you take me for a fool?"

"You're certainly acting like one," I replied.

Barely-leashed anger roiled beneath the surface of his bland aristocratic face. He said through clenched teeth, "Would you care to explain that statement?"

"You've committed these murders, taken all these risks, yet you seem to have forgotten the most important element of your plan: Elizabeth. Without her, what have you got? Nothing. Even if you kill Michael, she'll inherit the money, not you. And I don't think she plans to stick around long enough to share it with you. She told me herself that as soon as this business with Michael is over, she plans to divorce you and marry Geoffrey."

For a moment he went very still, then suddenly he began to laugh. "That's really very funny, you know."

"Is it?" I said. "Personally, I don't see the humor."

"No, I suppose you wouldn't. Well, let me see if I can explain it to you. First, I don't plan for Geoffrey to live out the day, let alone long enough to steal my wife from me. And second, Elizabeth is going to have little time to enjoy her new-found wealth before a tragic boating accident off the coast of France leaves me a grieving but extremely wealthy widower."

"You'll never get away with it! Do you think so many unexplained deaths are going to go unnoticed, especially when they result in your becoming a very wealthy man?"

"What unexplained deaths?" he asked with a faint smile. "Spiro's already been arrested for William's murder. It can only be a matter of time before he's charged with Helen's as well. And Demetra, holding you and Geoffrey responsible for her brother's misfortune, will be blamed for killing you both, as well as the stepson she's already tried to kill several times before."

"The police will never buy it! Demetra will tell them what really happened!"

"No, sadly, she'll be overcome by guilt and will drown herself on that beach below."

"What about Elizabeth?" I said desperately. "I told her my suspicions of you! She's sure to figure out the truth!"

A muscle twitched along his temple. "Elizabeth will believe what I wish her to believe."

"Then Mrs. Baxter—"

He shook his head. "Mrs. Baxter was a danger only as long as she was in contact with you. Once I dispose of you, she ceases to be a threat."

I stared at him in mute despair. I was out of arguments and out of reasons to think he wasn't going to get away with it. All of it. There was nothing left to do but wait.

Not even that, apparently. Suddenly, out of the stillness, came the sound of a car's engine, and even from a distance I recognized the brown and battered Renault Geoffrey had brought from Italy turning down the drive.

THIRTY-THREE

"*Dammit, where's the boy?*" Robert demanded as he peered angrily through the small, black binoculars slung around his neck. "Geoffrey's getting out of the car, but there's no one with him!"

The words sent a spark of hope tingling through my chest. Perhaps Geoffrey had heeded my warning after all? I said lightly, "I told you he wouldn't risk Michael's safety."

Robert swore and seizing my arm, wrenched me to my feet. "Demetra's bringing him up. We'll see how he feels about seeing you splattered all over those rocks below." He dragged me toward the path leading down to the cliffs and shoved me forward so that I almost lost my footing and fell.

We reached the bottom of the path just as Demetra and Geoffrey emerged from the thicket of pines. Seeing us, Geoffrey started forward, but Robert pulled me against him and lifted the small revolver to my head.

"That's close enough, I think!" he yelled.

Geoffrey stopped dead. "Let her go, Robert! She's nothing to you. It's me you want—and Michael. There's nothing to be gained by hurting her."

"On the contrary, old chum, it would give me the greatest pleasure to hurt her! The little bitch has caused me a great deal of unnecessary trouble, and I'm sorely tempted to chuck her over the edge right now, as your arrival here without my dear ward has left me in a very foul mood indeed."

"If I turn Michael over to you, you'll let her go?"

"Yes," Robert replied. I started to protest, but he clamped an iron hand over my mouth. "One more peep from you," he whispered in my ear, "and I'll shoot him where he stands. Understood?" I nodded. Raising his voice, he called out, "You have my word, Geoffrey. Now where is he?"

"Behind you."

Robert spun round, and I with him, but the only thing behind us was a cliff. "I'm in no mood for games," he snarled.

"It's no game. Michael is behind you—down below, on the beach. If you look, you should be able to see him."

Dragging me with him, Robert moved to the edge of the cliff and looked over. A small figure gazed up at us and waved. I wanted to yell to him to run and hide, but Robert's hand was still clamped hard across my mouth.

"If this is some sort of trick—"

"No trick," Geoffrey said. "I simply had to make sure Christine was safe first."

"And how did he get down there?" Robert demanded.

"Swam, of course. He's a good little swimmer. He swam over from the neighboring cove."

"I see." Robert's lips curled into a rather nasty smile. "Well, since you've been so obliging as to bring the boy, I suppose it's time I kept my end of the bargain." He hurled me forwards with a force that sent me sprawling at Geoffrey's feet.

Geoffrey leaned down to help me up, keeping his eyes on Robert's face. "So she's free to go?"

Robert shook his head and pointed the gun at us. "I'm afraid she knows far too much for that. As do you."

Geoffrey pushed me behind him. Demetra called out in panic, "You cannot mean to kill them?"

"Why not? They're no longer of any use to me."

Geoffrey's voice lashed out like a whip, "There I beg to differ, *old chum*. You'll never get your hands on Michael without us, so if that matters to you, you'd better keep us very much alive."

Robert's eyes narrowed. "You must be joking! I'm perfectly capable of handling one small child on my own."

"Are you? Why don't you take another look?"

Scowling now, Robert turned to peer back down at the beach and without warning, Demetra launched herself at his gun hand. "What the devil—" Robert spun back around and slammed the gun savagely down on her head; she crumpled to the ground at his feet.

I started to run forward, but Geoffrey grabbed me and pulled me back. "No, Christine! There's nothing you can do."

Panting, Robert looked up from Demetra's still form. *"Where is he, Geoffrey?"*

"You're probably not aware of it, but at the end of the beach, right under these cliffs is the entrance to a cave that runs quite far back, all the way past the highway, in fact. Michael is in that cave, and your only hope of getting him out of it, without him disappearing out the other end, is for me to convince him that the danger's past, that Christine's safe, and that it's perfectly all right for him to come out."

Robert regarded him suspiciously. "And you'd be willing to do that?"

He replied coolly, "For a price."

"Geoffrey, no!"

Both men ignored me. "What price?"

"Christine and I walk away from this alive."

"Done."

"Geoffrey, you can't! You can't turn Michael over to him!"

"I'm sorry, Christine," Geoffrey said, "but it's our only chance."

"But he doesn't mean it!" I insisted. "He'll break his word like he did before!"

"The lady does have a point, Robert. I need some assurance of your good intentions."

Robert said warily, "What assurance?"

"Empty all the bullets out of your gun but one."

"You must be joking."

"Do it, or the deal's off. One bullet should be sufficient for you to maintain control, but this way, if you break your word, at least one of us will have a sporting chance to get away."

"Oh, very well." Robert stepped back warily, doubling the distance between himself and Geoffrey, then began quickly emptying bullets out of the chamber. He snapped it shut.

"Hold out the bullets so we can count them."

Robert held out his hand. There were five bullets in it. Geoffrey nodded. "All right, now toss them over the cliff."

Jaw clenched, Robert did as he was told. "All right, I've fulfilled my part of the bargain. Now fulfill yours."

Desperate, I grabbed Geoffrey's arm. "You can't do this! Michael's your son! You can't sacrifice him this way!"

"I'll do whatever I must to get us out of this alive," he replied coldly. Then he added under his breath, "Please, Christine, trust me."

"Geoffrey, I'm losing patience!" Robert called out.

"You'd best let me untie Christine's hands. Otherwise it might seem a bit suspicious when I tell Michael she's been freed."

"Oh, very well, get on with it."

Geoffrey's nimble fingers quickly managed to loosen the knots in the thin white rope which had bound me for so long, and soon I was rubbing at my sore and slightly bloodied wrists in relief. "Thank you," I murmured gratefully.

Something constricted in his face and briefly he lifted my wrists to his lips and kissed them. Then he turned abruptly and in a harsh voice said, "All right, Robert, we're ready. Let's get this bloody business over with."

We made our way down to the beach single file. Geoffrey led the way, with me following, and Robert bringing up the rear, his gun pressed firmly into my back. I found myself wondering about the gun, and about his surprising willingness to empty out its bullets. I knew he had no intention of leaving us alive, so why had he agreed to Geoffrey's stipulation? Unless.... A horrible suspicion filled my mind. What if the bullets he'd held out in his hand hadn't come from the gun at all, but from his pocket?

I stared at Geoffrey's tense back and wondered what to do. If I was right, I had to warn him; presumably whatever plan he had depended on there being only one bullet in Robert's gun. But what if I was wrong? In trying to warn Geoffrey, I might ruin our only chance for escape—and Michael's.

With a resigned sort of fatalism, I decided to wait and see. With luck, perhaps I'd be able to guess what Geoffrey's plan was before he put it into action.

The azure sea lapped lazily against the smooth, grey stones and from somewhere down the shore came the plaintive call of a sea bird. "All right, Geoffrey," Robert called, "which way?"

Geoffrey jerked his head to the left. "Down there."

I followed his gesture, searching for some sign of the cave. Near the end of the beach, where the cliffs jutted out and formed the mouth of the cove, I could make out a small, ragged shadow at their base. "There?"

Geoffrey's voice seemed stripped of all emotion. "Yes."

"Very well," Robert said. "We're almost in view then. We'd best begin our little pantomime. Geoffrey, you continue ahead. Christine, you're going to walk next to me and smile so we look like a couple of old friends." He pulled me close to him, and pressed the gun into my side.

"Actually," Geoffrey countered, "you'll need to send Christine up ahead to the cave. I told Michael not to come out unless she called to him, and he could see she wasn't being forced to do so." He fell back alongside us and pushed me up ahead. "Don't worry, Robert, I can serve as hostage as well as she can."

Robert wasn't pleased by the switch. He made a great show of jamming the gun into Geoffrey's side, and said angrily, "The little bitch had better do exactly as she's told, or I'm going to put a very large hole in you."

"Being rather dramatic, aren't we?" Geoffrey said drily. "Never fear, she'll do as you wish. Won't you, Christine?"

I nodded silently, disliking the switch almost as much as Robert had. With a gun pressed into my back, I hadn't had to make the hard choices; now I was faced with choosing between Michael's life or Geoffrey's.

How, in heaven's name, was I to choose?

We walked silently down the beach, and as we drew closer to the cliffs, the ragged shadow became larger and more clearly defined as the entrance to a cave. But it was too dark to see inside, and impossible to tell if a little boy was hiding there.

We stopped fifty feet away. Robert told me what he wanted me to say, and Geoffrey amended it slightly, using language Michael would be more likely to find reassuring. I listened to them both in numb disbelief. I wanted to cry out that I wouldn't do it, that I wasn't about to play Judas to a little boy I'd come to love, but the sight of that shiny gun pressed into the white folds of Geoffrey's shirt and Robert's finger shivering slightly on the trigger left me mute. I searched Geoffrey's face for a sign, for some unspoken message of reassurance, but his expression was stony and his eyes unreadable. I turned and started for the cave.

He had to have a plan. I knew it. I could feel it. But what could it possibly be? I thought again of his insistence that Robert be limited to a single bullet. He'd been equally insistent that I, not he, be the one to approach the cave, while he remained behind to serve as hostage....

I stumbled. A single bullet, and Geoffrey the only one close enough for it to be used upon. That was the plan. Sacrifice himself, so Michael and I could get away. The only problem was, I didn't want to get away if it was going to cost him his life.

Somewhere close by, the same bird gave another plaintive cry. If only I could get Robert to take a shot at me, then Geoffrey might be able to jump him. I started to turn....

Suddenly something small and hard crashed into me and knocked me to the ground. There was a shout, then the crack of gunfire and a cry that made my blood run cold. Struggling to throw off whatever was on top of me, I clambered to my feet and ran toward the place where both men lay in a terrifyingly still heap.

"Geoffrey!" I cried, dropping to my knees and rolling Robert's unconscious body off of him. Geoffrey's eyes were closed and his white shirt was soaked with blood. "Oh, God, no! Please! Don't you dare die on me!" I had to stop the bleeding. I fumbled with the buttons of his shirt, and then, in desperation, simply ripped it open. But where was the wound? In confusion, I ran my fingers across his chest and along his sides searching for it.

"I know you find it difficult to keep your hands off of me, my dear, but really—in front of the child?"

My eyes flew to his face. The emerald eyes were open and glittering with mischief. "The child?" I repeated stupidly.

"He means me," chimed a familiar voice behind me.

I turned. He stood there, clothes clinging to him damply, wet hair curling around his ears, looking like a dunked elf. I threw my arms around him. "Oh, Michael, you're safe!"

He regarded me apologetically. "I hope I didn't hurt you?"

"Hurt me?"

"When he knocked you to the ground like a bag of potatoes," remarked a third voice. I looked up to find Lieutenant Mavros, his hair and clothes similarly damp and a rifle slung over one shoulder, kneeling down beside Robert's inert body.

"It's called a tackle, Ari," Michael corrected, "and I don't think it's quite the thing to compare a lady to a sack of potatoes."

Geoffrey struggled to sit up, and I tried to stop him. "Don't! You're hurt! You shouldn't be moving."

"Nonsense. I'm all right," he insisted. "Just nicked in the leg, that's all."

"But your shirt, it's covered in blood."

"Not his blood," Mavros said, rising to his feet.

Geoffrey looked up at him questioningly. "Well?"

"He is dead."

"Dead?" I exclaimed in disbelief. "But how! I don't understand. What happened?"

But Mavros didn't answer. Instead he scanned the beach and demanded sharply, "Where is Demetra?"

"She's up on the cliff," I told him. "Robert hit her and knocked her out."

Mavros set off at a run. Geoffrey struggled to his feet as if to follow. "And where do you think you're going?" I growled, pointing to the jagged rip in his left pant leg that was slowly being stained with red. "Have you forgotten? You've been shot!"

He grimaced with pain and replied irritably, "I'm well aware of the fact, thank you. I simply thought I might be of use for a change, and go ring up the doctor."

I dispatched Michael up to the house to telephone Dr. Aristides and the police, then rounded on Geoffrey. "I suppose rescuing me from a murderer doesn't count as being of use?" In true heroine-style, I ripped off a piece of my blouse and pressed it against his leg to stop the bleeding.

He replied through clenched teeth, "I didn't rescue you from Robert; Mavros did."

"He was hiding in the cave with Michael?"

"Yes."

My gaze drifted unwillingly towards Robert's still form and I shivered. "Did he have to kill him?"

"If he hadn't," Geoffrey replied harshly, "it might very possibly be you lying there—or Michael. When Michael ran out of the cave and knocked you down so Mavros could get a clean shot, Robert came very close to shooting you both."

I said slowly, "But you wrestled him for the gun, didn't you? That's how you got shot in the leg."

He replied irritably, "I never managed to get the bloody thing away from him. If Mavros hadn't fired when he did, well, there were five more bullets in that gun...."

"Five!" I exclaimed. "So he did pull a switch!"

"Of course. He wasn't about to take a chance on either of us really getting away."

"And you knew that all the time? Why didn't you say something?"

"I wanted him to think he'd tricked us. Only if we believed we had a chance to escape, did our willingness to betray Michael make sense."

"What doesn't make sense to me is how you and the lieutenant came to plan this little rescue together in the first place. Last time I heard, he was threatening to arrest you for kidnapping."

"Let's just say he and I reached an agreement based on our intersecting interests: I wanted to save you from Robert; he wanted to save Demetra from becoming an accomplice to murder."

"She didn't really intend for me to get hurt, you know. She was just so desperate to help Spiro, she went along with whatever Robert suggested."

Jaw clenched, Geoffrey pushed back my hair to expose my bruised face. "You'll excuse me if I find it difficult to be so forgiving."

I looked up. Far above, I saw Mavros kneel down and then straighten up again with Demetra in his arms. "Well, in any case," I said, fighting the sudden ache in my chest, "it's over now. The danger's done with, Michael's safe, and you and Paul can go back to doing books instead of being partners in crime."

The emerald eyes regarded me intently. "And you? What about you? What are you going to do now?"

I tried to keep my voice steady. "I don't know. Go home, I guess."

THIRTY-FOUR

My suitcases were packed. My passport, airplane ticket, and farewell gift from Kyria Andriatsis, a brooch-sized icon of St. Spiridon, were all safely tucked away in my purse. I scanned the room to make sure I wasn't forgetting anything, then stepped out onto the balcony for one last look at Corfu before leaving.

There was a knock at the door, which I supposed was Yiannis come to drive me to the airport. "Come in!" I called out in Greek, wanting a little more time to drink in the view and commit it to memory. "The door's open!"

But it wasn't Yiannis who emerged from the room and joined me at the balcony's iron railing; it was Lieutenant Mavros, looking much too relaxed and happy to suit my mood. "I see now why Geoffrey despairs at your lack of caution," he chided. "What if I had been a burglar, or worse?"

Dark, lowering clouds gathered on the horizon signaling a storm on its way. "Sorry, but I'm in no mood for lectures."

"Forgive me, I did not intend one, especially as I am here to offer you my deepest thanks. Your statement to Colonel Grammos that Humphreys alone was responsible for your abduction, and that Demetra was merely a prisoner like yourself, has persuaded him not to charge her as an accessory to Humphreys's crimes."

"You don't have to thank me. What I told the Colonel was true in a way. Robert tricked her into doing what she did, and he would have killed her, just as he planned to kill me, if you and Geoffrey and Michael hadn't intervened."

"Still, it was generous of you; more generous than Demetra expected or feels she deserves. She is ashamed of what she did to you, and most anxious to ask your forgiveness, though she is not yet in a condition to do so in person."

"How is she?"

"She has a concussion, but the doctors do not think there will be any permanent effect. They say if she rests and takes care she will be fully recovered in a few weeks."

"And Spiro?"

"Who knows? It is possible that with Humphreys's confession to the murder and Geoffrey's request that the matter be allowed to drop for the boy's sake, the British may decide not to prosecute him at all." He smiled slightly and shrugged. "Spiro always manages to land on his feet. Even when we were boys, he had the devil's own luck."

"There's one thing I still don't understand. That night in the square when Mrs. Baxter was shot. I could have sworn I saw Demetra skulking around in the shadows. What was she doing there?"

Mavros flashed an indulgent smile. "She was following her brother. She suspected he had been with a woman when Michael was attacked, and she thought he was being gallant in withholding her name. She hoped to learn the woman's name herself and give it to me. She didn't realize her brother had a stronger reason for his silence than gallantry—thirty thousand pounds, to be precise."

The sea was darkening, turning from aqua to slate, and a brisk wind was beginning to blow. I looked down at my watch. "Well, Lieutenant, I'm afraid you're going to have to excuse me. It's getting late, and I'd better go downstairs and see what's happened to my ride to the airport."

He stared at me in surprise. "You are flying home?"

"Yes."

"And Geoffrey is not driving you to the airport himself?"

"No," I snapped, oddly irritated by the fact that he and Geoffrey now seemed to be on a first-name basis. "Why should he be?"

The perilously intelligent blue eyes regarded me steadily for some time. "He does not know you are leaving, does he?"

I turned away. "He does—in a general way."

"But that you are leaving now? Today?"

"No."

"May I ask why?"

"Why what?"

"Why you are slipping away like a thief in the night?"

I drew a deep, ragged breath and said, "Let's just say I hate goodbyes and leave it at that."

"I see. Well, I hope that will not prevent you from allowing me to drive you to the airport?"

"Thank you, but there's no need. I've already got—"

He held up a restraining hand. "No, it is the least I can do. After all, you have not only solved a most difficult case and saved my friend from being tried for murder, you have also protected the name and reputation of his dear sister—and my future wife."

It was my turn to stare. "You and Demetra are getting married?"

He nodded proudly. "When the proper period of mourning for her late husband has passed, yes."

"And Michael?"

"Demetra has already given custody of the boy to Geoffrey. She thinks it best, after everything that has happened, and in any case, when we marry she will be too busy with the children I plan to give her to have time for someone else's child."

So now there was nothing to keep Michael, Geoffrey, and Elizabeth from being one happy family. I forced myself to smile. "Well, congratulations to you both. I hope you'll be very happy."

"There is no doubt that I will be," he said with a grin. "I've loved Demetra since I was a boy. As for her, well, she was half in love with me before she met Redfield. I think in time I can persuade her to love the other half as well."

I should have smiled, but I just didn't have it in me. I glanced once more at my watch, grateful I was on my way home, where I wouldn't be surrounded by all this happiness. "Sorry, but I've really got to get going if I'm going to catch my flight."

"Yes, of course. Permit me to make one brief phone call and then I am at your disposal. What time does your flight depart?"

"Eleven."

"Oh. Then we have plenty of time."

Resigning myself, I showed him to the phone and then waited restively by the door, nervously fingering the soft leather of the purse Geoffrey had given me, while the policeman made his call.

He looked up from dialing the number. "This will not take long. I simply have to cancel an appointment—" Suddenly he shifted into Greek, "Hello? It's Ari. I just wanted to call you and let you know I won't be able to meet you this morning as planned. I have a friend from California who's going home today and I need to drive her to the airport to catch an eleven o'clock flight. Yes. See you then. *Adío.*" He hung up the phone and turned to me. "Shall we go?"

He was mercifully quiet as we loaded my suitcases into the car and started on our drive to the airport. However, when we turned down Dimokratias and drove past Geoffrey's hotel, he couldn't refrain from mentioning how surprised and disappointed he thought Geoffrey would be to find me gone.

"I think he has plenty of other things to keep him occupied at the moment," I murmured numbly. Like a son about to be reunited with his mother and a long-lost love who wanted him back.

The lieutenant shook his head, but didn't try to argue. I watched the Corfu Palace disappear in the sideview mirror and for a moment had to fight down the urge to ask him to stop and go back. We turned inland, threading our way through narrow, crowded streets until we emerged out onto a wide and relatively deserted highway. It stretched out straight and unbending amidst a dry and barren landscape that for one panicked moment seemed a perfect metaphor for the life I was returning to.

Soon we came to a blue sign, bearing the legend "*Aerodromio*" and featuring the white outline of a plane, which pointed toward a distant cluster of buildings. "We are almost there," he stated unnecessarily.

Despite our proximity, it was another twenty minutes before we actually walked through the sliding glass doors of the airport's terminal, because he insisted on driving round and round the parking lot searching for a space he considered sufficiently close. Once inside, he was equally slow to follow me to the Olympic Airlines counter. He had insisted on carrying my luggage, and I couldn't check in without it, but instead of heading toward the counter, he veered off toward a small souvenir kiosk proclaiming that he had to buy me something to take back to California. I should have protested—it was getting late, and I was in danger of missing my connection to Athens, but part of me was as reluctant to go as he seemed to be to have me leave.

I listlessly flicked through cheap strands of worry beads and glanced over small, plastic replicas of Greek sculpture. There was a head of Athena, a torso of Apollo, a well-endowed Priapus, a mischievous satyr chasing a nymph. I smiled at this last one. There was something about the satyr that reminded me of Spiro.

The man running the stand flashed me an encouraging grin. "Perhaps miss would like this," he pointed to a turquoise-colored paperweight with a black dot in the center, "to protect against the evil eye?"

"No, thank you."

"Then, perhaps, some beautiful postcards for your friends?"

I shook my head and turned away, colliding with someone to my right. "*Signómi*," I murmured in Greek without looking up.

"No," Geoffrey snapped back in English, "I will not excuse you. You truly meant to leave without a word, didn't you?"

I swiveled around in amazement. "Geoffrey! What are you doing here?"

He jerked his head impatiently towards the other end of the kiosk where Lieutenant Mavros had suddenly developed an intense interest in a rack of comic books. "Ari rang me up and told me he was driving you to the airport."

My gaze veered to the lieutenant's right, where a boy was intently perusing an Arabic newspaper he was holding upside down. "You brought Michael with you, too?"

"Why not? This involves him as well. You left without saying goodbye to either of us. Obviously you don't think I merit an explanation, but I think he does."

His anger, which seemed to vibrate in the air betwen us, was oddly comforting, but his accusation that I'd ill-treated Michael stung. "I'm sorry," I said stiffly. "I thought formal goodbyes would prove painful for all involved. I was just trying to do what was best."

"Were you?" he demanded. "Or were you just in such a hurry to leave you didn't care who you hurt?"

"That's not fair! I figured Michael would be too busy getting reacquainted with his mother to notice I'd gone."

Slowly Geoffrey shook his head and said quietly, "He'd have little chance for that. Elizabeth's left the island."

"*What*! Why?"

"It's possible she wanted to avoid awkward questions from the police, but personally I suspect she didn't care for the visit I paid her last night after I got out of hospital."

I stared at him in disbelief. He sounded so calm. "I suppose you were upset to find out about her marriage to Robert?"

He flashed me a curious look. "You could say that."

I took a deep breath and looked away. "If it makes any difference, you needn't be jealous. She wasn't in love with him."

He reached up and ran a warm hand along the side of my cheek. "You know, for such an intelligent woman, you can be a bloody fool sometimes. I don't care a pin whether Elizabeth loved him or not. I was furious with her for keeping her marriage a secret, because it prolonged this whole messy business and put you and Michael in danger."

"But I don't understand. What about your engagement?"

"What engagement?"

"Elizabeth said you'd proposed to her and she'd accepted. I thought you and she and Michael, well, that you were going to be a family at last...." My voice trailed away as I saw the truth in his face. "She lied?"

He nodded somberly. "After our discussion in Pagi I'm surprised you didn't realize that, but maybe Elizabeth's lie proved too convenient to dismiss?"

"What's that supposed to mean?"

"That I think you wanted an excuse to run away—from Michael and from me, and Elizabeth gave it to you."

I stared at him, at once both furious and unsure. "Why would I want to run away?"

"I don't know. Maybe because you're afraid?"

"You think I'm a coward?"

He took one of my hands and lifted it to reveal the darkened bruise on my wrist. He kissed it softly. "I think you are probably the bravest woman I know," he said in a low, emotion-filled voice that caused my throat to tighten, "but perhaps you aren't comfortable with the expectations you think I've developed during our…alliance." His voice turned rueful. "Still, I would like it if we could part friends."

I stared at him for a long moment in silence. Then I gathered up my courage and said, "You're right. I was running away."

He tensed, releasing my hand and taking a step back.

"But I wasn't running away because your expectations were too high. I was running away because…I love you. And I was afraid you might not love me back. I was scared to put it to the test."

For a long, heart-stopping moment he just stood there gazing down at me. Then he leaned the cane he was using for his injured leg against the shelf of plastic sculpture and drew me into his arms. He held me like that for some time before I murmured mischievously against his chest, "May I take this to mean you aren't still carrying a torch for Elizabeth?"

He pushed me away slightly so he could see my face. "I'm going to give you a chance to reconsider that question," he said sternly. Then he began to kiss me.

Considerable time passed. When we finally came up for air, he murmured against my hair, "Convinced?"

"Yes, though I'm tempted to say no and see what happens."

His green eyes gleamed. "Minx! Do you wish to see me arrested for indecent behavior by that surly airport policeman over there with the submachine gun slung round his neck?"

"No, I suppose not. Michael might not want a jailbird for a father."

"What about you?" he asked with deceptive lightness. "Would you care for one as a husband?"

"Are you asking me to marry you?"

"Yes."

"Why?" I demanded.

"What do you mean why?"

"The lieutenant said Demetra's given you custody of Michael. You aren't asking me to marry you simply because you're trying to round up a mother for him, are you?"

He said through gritted teeth, "This has nothing whatsoever to do with Michael."

"Then what *has* it to do with?"

"It has to do," he growled, "with the fact that I am enamored, besotted, charmed, fascinated, enchanted, infatuated, bewitched, and any other adjective you care to choose that describes a man stripped of all reason. In short, I'm in love with you and want to spend the rest of my life with you—if you'll have me."

I suddenly felt like a cat handed a bowl of cream. "All right," I purred.

"Is that a yes?"

There was one obvious way to allay his doubt, and I pursued it with a gusto that left us both breathless. Afterwards, however, I noticed he was frowning.

"Christine?"

"Yes?"

He took my hands in his. "This isn't too sudden for you, is it? I know I'm taking things a bit fast, but after coming so close to losing you—well, it's hard to be patient."

"Patience is an overrated virtue," I murmured, leaning forward to nuzzle his neck.

He chuckled and pushed me away so he could see my face. "What about Michael? Are you sure you don't mind marrying into a ready-made family? "

"I don't see why I should, since I love Michael almost as much as I love you."

His grin disappeared, replaced by an expression that turned my insides to jelly. He lifted my hands to his lips, kissing each palm. "I hope you're in the mood for an early and extensive honeymoon."

"I could be persuaded," I said with a grin, "but what about the surly policeman with the submachine gun? Perhaps we should wait until we get back to your hotel?"

"It's always something," he said in mock complaint. "Very well, I suppose we can wait. We'll have to send Michael off to do some sightseeing with Ari."

"There's always the Gorgon pediment at the Archaelogical Museum," I said with a chuckle. "It's not Monday, so the museum should be open."

Geoffrey regarded me quizzically.

"Sorry," I said. "Private joke. All this happiness is making me silly."

"So you *are* happy, Christine?"

"I'm going to give you a chance to reconsider that question," I said, trying to look stern, but merely managing to break into giggles, which Geoffrey found a very effective way of silencing.

"Mmmm," I murmured, as he finally set my mouth free. "I think, you'd better not do that anymore until we get back to the hotel, or I'll be the one getting arrested."

"Sorry," he said with an unrepentant grin. "I felt the need of a fortifying embrace to tide me over."

Suddenly, I noticed Michael edging hesitantly toward us. "I don't wish to interrupt—" he began.

Geoffrey held on to my hands, despite my attempts to pull them away, and said cheerfully, "You're not interrupting. As a matter of fact, we've something rather important to tell you. Christine has just agreed to be my wife."

Michael's owlish eyes opened wide and he let out a boyish whistle. "So that's it! Ari and I rather wondered what the two of you were, er, *discussing* for so long."

"Well," I said, suddenly nervous about what his reaction would be to the news, "what do you think?"

He regarded me solemnly. "I suppose this means you'll be staying here on Corfu for a few more days?"

I looked at Geoffrey, puzzled. He shook his head wordlessly and shrugged. "I suppose it does," I said, eyeing Michael warily.

"Then I think it's an excellent idea."

"You do?"

"Yes," said Michael with a broad grin. "You see, that jet taxiing down the runway happens to be your flight home."

Glossary of Greek Words

adio—goodbye
aerodromio—airport
argotera—later
bouzouki—Greek stringed instrument similar to a lute
deka-eksi—sixteen
den mylao Ellinika—I don't speak Greek
ella—come (as in "come here")
embros—come in; (on the telephone) hello
evharisto—thank you
fighasete—get out
kalimera—good morning or good day
kalinykta—good night
kalispera—good afternoon or good evening
kleftis—thief
koritsi—girl
kyria—ma'am, Mrs.
kyrie—sir
kyrios—Mr.
lepta—a Greek coin
logariasmos—bill or tab
loukomathes—Greek donuts rolled while hot in honey and ground nuts
malista—yes (formal or emphatic)
more—*idiot*
Paleon Frourion—The Old Fortress
Panagia—holy mother, the Virgin Mary

parakalo—please; (in response to a thank you) don't mention it

pastitsio—a Greek pasta dish reminiscent of lasagna

poulaki—little bird

signomi—excuse me; pardon me

sofrito—a Corfiote dish of veal cooked in a vinegar sauce

stavros—cross

ston kypo—in the garden

syrto—a Greek folk dance

thespinis—Miss

tsoula—a woman of loose moral character

tyropita—a small, cheese-filled pastry made with flaky filo dough

yiayia—grandmother

EKATERINE NIKAS learned early on that travel can lead to adventure when her first trip to Greece, at age six, coincided with a *coup d'etat*.

Journeys through the Swiss Alps, a job in a Danish nursery, and a freighter cruise to Brazil all provided their own adventures, but it was a honeymooon visit to the Greek island of Corfu that inspired *The Divded Child*.

She has received numerous awards for her writing, including the 1999 Karen Besecker Memorial Award for novice mystery writers by FUTURES magazine. Her short story "Fatal Tears" appears in the mystery anthology *A Deadly Dozen,* published by UglyTown.

When not writing, she keeps busy as a part-time multi=media programmer and full-time mom. She lives with her funny and talented husband and truly independent daughter in sunny California.

More romantic suspense from Avid Press...

Shadows in the Mist
by Maureen McMahon

When Suzanna Dirkston, daughter of wealthy shipping tycoon Leopald Dirkston, learns that her father is dead, she knows it was not an accident. Forced to return to the family homestead, Beacon, Suzanna is quick to sense the air of mystery and intrigue that hangs over the house and its inhabitants.

Her shock grows when she learns that her father—true to form—is still trying to manipulate her life even from the grave. His will stipulates that she must marry Grant Fenton, a man Leo rescued as a child from poverty and groomed to replace him at Dirkston Shipping. If she does not accede to the conditions of the will, she and her extended family will be left penniless.

As if this is not enough, she is plagued by strange dreams, mysterious apparitions and ghostly visitations—as well as an increasing attraction to the arrogant, brooding man she is to marry. Suzanna begins to fear not only for her sanity, but for her life as she unravels bit by bit the gruesome reality that lies hidden amid the

"**Countless readers who yearn for more of Mary Stewart's blend of romance with mystery, and for whom Barbara Michaels cannot alone fill the gap, should welcome Maureen McMahon's debut novel with open arms.**"
–Dianne Day, author of the Fremont Jones mysteries, including *Beacon Street Mourning*

Available now from Avid Press, Amazon.com, and wherever books are sold.

www.avidpress.com   or   1-888-AVIDBKS

Watch for Maureen McMahon's new release *Return of the Gulls*, coming soon from Avid Press.